MW01687536

MEXICAN FISH TALE

Christopher Heaps
and
Andrew N. Johnson

Voyageur Media
Portland, OR

Voyageur Media LLC
2224 N Willamette Blvd
Portland, OR 97217
www.mexicanfishtale.com
Printed in the United States of America

Mexican Fish Tale/ Christopher Heaps and Andrew N. Johnson. -- 1st ed.

ISBN 978-0-9982148-0-1 Print Edition
ISBN 978-0-9982148-1-8 Ebook Edition

For all the Davids out there, finding your way.

Enjoy the journey...

Day One

A horrendous pounding woke me. Lightning bolts flashed, herds of camels went stampeding through my head. I lifted my hands to my face to still the commotion, exhaled slowly, and felt my head throbbing. I turned on my side and pulled the pillow over my poor head, but even the rustle of the pillowcase caused untold agony.

Still the pounding continued. Someone was banging on my door. There could be no justification for such an intrusion at this hour. I cursed, got to my feet, put on my robe, and stomped through my single-wide trailer, there on the normally quiet outskirts of San Antonio, ten miles from anywhere. I reached the door and flung it open. I stood expectantly, shaggy brown hair nearing my shoulders, a full beard nearly six months old now, barefoot, with my hairy chest showing through my red robe.

Two earnest-faced white kids in black polyester suits stood on my porch, smiling at me weakly, looking like undertakers. The older one glanced sidelong at the deer skull on the porch railing. Some coyote had drug it into my back yard and left it over by the barbeque pit. I thought it a fine decoration and had arranged it to greet me whenever I came or went. The skull and its attached vertebrae were always a welcome sight, reminding me happily of my own mortality.

"*Yeah?*" I croaked.

The older one stepped forward nervously. He glanced over to the skull again, and back at me. "Ah, yes. Uh…we are…" He cleared his throat. "We would like to…" Suddenly he looked down and began fumbling around in a leather satchel he was carrying. He produced a large leather-bound book, held it up, and looked at me triumphantly, as though introducing a savage to the written word.

"The Bible! We would like to speak to you about the Bible, the divine Word of Jesus Christ. May we come in?"

I stared at him blankly. I turned and looked at the other one, but he just blinked and looked down at his shoes. I looked back to the one who had spoken. He smiled at me warmly.

Then I too looked quizzically at the deck. My head pounded, and my mind would not work properly at this unholy hour. I had no idea what the young man was saying, but I had seen that look before. I rubbed the sleep from my gummy eyes.

"What…who, *who?*"

"Jesus Christ? Our personal lord and…"

Suddenly it made sense.

"No … NOOOOOOOOOOO!"

I have a replica Norse battle axe that I keep above my door for emergency defensive purposes. I grabbed the axe and swung it overhead, my long hair flailing wildly about in a blur, my robe opening indiscreetly.

"SATAN IS *MY* LORD!!"

I brought the axe down with a smash, the blade biting deep into the wooden railing just behind the base of the deer skull. Vertebrae shot into the air, whizzing in various directions. One pinged off my bathroom window, another bounced down the wooden stairs. The overturned skull rolled off the rail and landed on the dirt below.

I looked up to see the pair sprinting down the driveway in their cheap plastic dress shoes. I was laughing so hard I momentarily forgot how horrible I felt. I laughed and laughed with glee as I danced around on my porch like a fiend. *I look like their lord, and they fear me as their lord!* Oh, it hurt to laugh, but I could not stop.

I pulled the axe from the railing and lamented the loss of my death muse, my tangible reminder of the nature of this life. Oh, but I was comforted by the image of Mormons at full clip. I had never seen Mormons run that fast. Come to think about it, I had never seen Mormons run at all. That ought to be enough to get me on the "do not visit" list.

I went back to bed, tried to calm down. I still had three hours to sleep. Oh, it hurt. My head, my nose … my stomach not quite right, either. I groaned as I lay down. The room lurched and spun about, and soon I realized my insides were spinning too, churning away.

My friend Mark Hanson found me hunched over the toilet bowl, spewing acidic bile. He patted me on the back, nearly knocking me over. "Hey, hey David? You okay?"

"What the fuck does it look like?" I spat wearily into the toilet. "How did you get in? … And, what the fuck are you doing here at nine o'clock anyway, ass?"

"Uh, well, the door was wide open, man. … Hey, who were those two guys in suits running down your driveway?"

"Mormons."

"Mormons?"

"Yeah, Mormons, man. … On a mission to piss me off."

"Well, Manfred called and said we have to get ready to go! Are you packed?"

"Of course I'm packed, man! What the fuck do you think?!"

"Alright, take it easy, man." He slapped me on the back again and chuckled. "I hear *The Dancing Bear* came out to play last night…"

"Shut the fuck up." I spat into the toilet again, looked up at him. "Go on, let me get ready! Can't you see I'm trying to get ready?"

"Uh, yeah, okay, I can see that. I'll be out there."

He retreated from the bowl-worshipping fiend into the living room. I kicked the bathroom door shut behind him. Noon, Manfred had said. And now he was changing the plan to nine o'clock, the bastard. I began searching through my bathroom cabinets for the beloved Excedrin.

* * * * *

As I showered and dressed, I thought of Mexico, that mysterious mountainous land to the south. I had been to the border area many times, but never to the interior. They are very different places, or so they said. It would be some trip, across the desert and through the mountains, deep into the heart of the country, all the way to the Pacific. I needed to get out of town for a while, clear my head, change my perspective a bit. The timing was right – my student loan check had just arrived.

Manfred had led the charge for the trip after befriending a few Mexican nationals living in San Antonio. He spoke solid Spanish thanks to his sharp mind and time spent overseeing construction projects. He was genuinely curious about what Mexico had to offer, and so was I. The Mexicans talked about a place that bore only a passing resemblance to the nation I had visited in places like Nuevo Laredo, Cuidad Juarez, and Tijuana. We thought it sounded worth exploring, and we thought it advisable to include Mark, both for his violence-deterring effect and for his knowledge of native Mexican cultures. And then there was an intangible element added to the proposed trip, a little *lagniappe*, as the Cajuns say, that made it practically irresistible.

I grabbed my two bags and went out to meet Mark. He is a hulking, misshapen, ogre of a man with baleful, pale blue eyes, a bulbous nose, and a twisted grin studded with brown, tobacco-stained teeth. His appearance, and at times his demeanor as well, are somewhat comical, and, frankly, he bears a passing resemblance to Shrek. He has what Southerners refer to as a "big personality." His sheer bulk makes him someone you do not want to fuck with. At most times he is a gentle giant. But he is slightly deranged. And he is as harsh toward enemies as he is gentle to friends. Fortunately, he has no trouble telling the difference between the two.

Mark likes to go to remote regions of the planet and dig up very old things. So, between extended periods of unemployment, he is a sometimes contract field archaeologist. His pale arms are covered with gruesome red scars. When I had first encountered him in his smoky lair, he had just returned from Belize, where he had spent several months in the jungle slowly uncovering and cataloguing ancient Mayan ruins. I had asked him about the open running sores covering his arms, then not yet scarred over. In his gravelly voice he answered, "Aww hell, that's just them insects, you know, get in 'ere and lay 'em eggs, you know what I mean?"

I grimaced. "Uh, yeah, bugs, so … uh, don't they have anything to keep the bugs off you, man? Out of your flesh? Some bug spray?"

He shrugged. "Yeah, but I ran outta money. It was bug spray or beer, you know?"

Indeed I do. And Mark is a man of clear priorities. The black-and-white world he inhabits is unclouded by the complexities that plague the rest of our grey-shaded lives. If you are his friend, he will give you the shirt off his back. If you are not his friend, woe-betide you. You always know where you stand with him. He tells it like he sees it and does what he wants. When they made him, *he* broke the mold.

And he's a good man in the pocket too. In fact, I owed him my life. He had saved me from certain doom, late one night. It had started innocently enough. We had a little business, me and Mark, meeting some guys in Houston who were coming in from New Orleans. We were at some shit-kicking honkey-tonk on the north side of town, waiting for our guys.

I had brought in a book, a textbook from an anthropology class I was taking, and not surprisingly I was the only one in the place reading. That caught the attention of our waitress, who just happened to be gorgeous *and* have an intellect. Well, we struck up a conversation, pleasantries were exchanged, and I invited her to join us after her shift. I would like to buy her a beer and talk with her some more, I told her. And our friends had arrived from New Awlins, so there was plenty to smoke as well.

She did just that at midnight, taking off her apron and sitting down across from me with a pretty smile. We were discussing *A People's History of the United States*, but after just a single beer she was lead away by the arm by a big, tough-looking redneck. His name was Travis and he didn't like some of the things I had to say. Then he had said both he and his lady-friend were leaving *right now, you fucking 'Merica-hatin' hippie*. But he hadn't actually left. He had waited for me in the parking lot with two other guys.

We closed the place down. Mark was headed for the head, and I went out to start the car. The parking lot was dark and deserted. Our friends were long gone. They came at me from the shadows, two more rednecks recruited by Travis together in front, and my nemesis trailing behind, holding a tire iron. The one on my left threw a haymaker at me, a big right hook. I blocked it with my left hand, as I had learned in my combat training. But the one on my right went low, punching me in the ribs. I never saw it coming and when I bent over in pain he shoved me to the ground. The guy on my left kicked me in the gut, ensuring that I stayed put. I was breathless, and Travis was approaching. I watched him raise the tire iron over his head.

Then I saw Mark Hanson emerge seemingly from nowhere. He grabbed Travis' upraised hand with one giant ogre-mitt and ripped the tire iron out of his hand with the other. He then began mercilessly whipping Travis about the head with it. Travis blocked a few blows with his hands, the steel rod thwacking dully against his knuckles and forearms. Then the blows began to rain down on his head. The second one hit him clean on the temple, and down he went.

The other two redneck dudes rushed Mark. He had just enough time to react, and did so adeptly. As they smacked into his torso on either side, he took a step backward and used one hand on each, pushing them downward as they hit him. One hit the ground with his full weight. The other staggered and then faced Mark. Before he could react, Mark stepped up and destroyed him with a full-force ogre-fist to the face. His nose exploded with blood and he went down too.

I looked over and the other guy was gone. Travis lay motionless with his eyes partly open. Streaks of blood ran across his face, dripping onto the dirt. Angry red welts swelled on his forearms. His right hand was mangled. I didn't know whether he was dead or alive. It is an image I will never forget.

We got the hell out of there as fast as we could. We never said a word about it, and we never heard a word about it. I had only confided the story to a few people, but some were skeptical when I told them I owed Mark Hanson my life, scoffing at the peril, at the unlikely story. But that was nonsense, I knew.

Now, I don't think that if you just put Mark Hanson in a room with three guys, one armed with a tire iron, that he's going to come out of it the champion every time, or even most of the time. He had the element of surprise in this encounter, and he – *we* – had the good fortune of him arriving at the instant when he could snatch the tire iron without being noticed by any of our three adversaries. So it was a unique situation.

But Mark rushed in regardless. I knew he would have rushed in regardless, whatever my tactical situation with respect to the redneck attackers. Even with zero odds, Mark Hanson would have fought for me, with me, to the death. And if he hadn't, they would have tried to kill me. Or tried to near-kill me, left me for dead or wishing I was dead. I owed the man my life, simple as that. You can't ask anything more from a man than what he did. It makes him your brother, forever. And forever, you will lay down your life for him as well. It's the bond of men, of honor. Platonic love.

The Klan-bush, we had come to call it. It had shaken me up a bit, more than I liked to admit. There was the hypervigilance, the constant situational awareness. And there were dreams, or nightmares, sleepless nights, re-living the whole evening while awake too, staring again into Travis' dull eyes, first in conversation and then on the ground, his head bashed in. The thoughts of the ambush came intrusively at all hours, the events unfolding automatically, over and over, interrupting all else.

Now I was a reluctantly-devolved pacifist. I would carry weapons with me wherever I went. When I went to a bar or anyplace new, I would carry my 9mm revolver in my pants, safety on. I completed my hidden defensive arsenal with various serrated tanto knives and military-grade pepper spray. I spent a great deal of time in the dojo, and most mornings I would run on the dirt roads in my rural neighborhood, getting experience using the pepper spray when the local dogs gave chase. Out at the single-wide, I would practice my draw and my shot, all the while hoping I would never have to do the unthinkable. Despite the fear, I always tried to see the positive in it. The whole thing had given me a lifelong friend, not to mention an always-needed reminder to be careful what I say.

On the face of it, Mark Hanson is a beer-swilling, whore-mongering, irreverent soul. One might be tempted to call him a redneck, except that he is educated and part of a family that lives in one of the wealthiest districts of San Antonio. So, we call him the Metroneck – when we're not calling him the Ogre. He lives with his seventy year-old father in their antebellum Alamo Heights estate. His older brothers have all moved out, moved into banking or the law or medicine, but Mark has stayed behind to tend to his elderly father's needs, running to Whataburger and mixing midnight martinis on request.

Sometimes I would go over to Mark's house with my friend Timmy for a final beer or three after the bars had closed. We would throw pebbles at Mark's window from the freshly manicured green lawn, waking him. He would appear at the window in his pajamas, sleepy and grumbling, but he would always dress and come on down. Then it was an all-night session drinking Lone Star beer and carrying on in the ever-smoky Dog House.

The Dog House is the former slave house behind the Big House, as we call the imposing white mansion still occupied by Mr. Hanson and his son. The Dog House *is* Mark Hanson. It reflects his very essence as a man, or rather, ogre. In the main hallway of the Big House, there hangs a portrait of a dour Southern Civil War officer to whom the Hansons are akin. By way of contrast, the Dog House has walls covered with African demon masks, old license plates, deer antlers, and the flags of the Welsh, Scots, Confederates, and of course the Jolly Roger.

And then there are the two antique wooden signs, both authentic. First, a 1929 city ordinance of Durant, Oklahoma, reading,

NO INDIANS ALLOWED LIQUOR AFTER SUNDOWN

Then, from some long-lost whorehouse:

LADIES, KINDLY DO YOUR SOLICITING
DISCRETELY

In the midst of such atavism – Mark Hanson is himself a living atavism – Timmy and Mark and I would drink Lone Star and sing the old songs, songs men can only properly sing after drinking a case or so of beer.

After my first night of carousing in the Dog House, I had passed out on the floor. It seemed like a good idea at the time. I awoke to a smell I could not identify, but which immediately made me think of the dump. Later that day, Mark told me story after story of all the various fluids that had graced the sickly grey-green mottled carpet over the years. I resolved never to sleep on that floor again, or even touch it with my unprotected skin.

* * * * *

Now, Mark was sprawled on my couch, the Ogre at rest. He eyed me as I set my bags down in the living room and replaced my battle axe above the door. "Hey, David. Hey, you don't have any guns or ammo on you, now do you?"

"No! No, man…"

"Did you check all the little pockets of your bags? Every zipper, you know? 'Cause even a bullet'll get you years in a Meskin prison. You know what I mean?"

"Yeah, yeah, I know. No ammo, man, no guns. I'm only bringing knives and the pepper spray."

We walked out to Mark's old truck, a battered burgundy Dodge Ram. He opened the door, reached behind the seat, and pulled out a machete. "This is all you need!" The blade, over two feet long, glinted in the sun. He smiled his crooked, brown smile. "In case we run into any dense foliage."

I blanched. "Uh, is that … ?"

"Oh, it's legal. All the peasants carry 'em down there. Just no firearms." He whipped the blade back and forth through the air, *whoop, whoop*. Shiner cans clanged out from behind the seat as he returned the knife-sword to its ready position in the truck. No one should enjoy a blade that much, I thought.

Mark Hanson was indeed our friend, but there was always a barely submerged air of sudden and inexplicable redneck violence attending him. I must admit he is not unique in that regard within our extended circle. I genuinely liked Mark, and I had grown to tolerate people with such tendencies, as one must when living among regular folks in the South. But the ways of the South had long since ceased to amuse me.

Our next stop was the household of Manfred Winkler, a West German beatnik turned entrepreneur. He had made his money in the former East Germany just after the Wall fell, selling Mercedes-Benz and BMW clunkers that no self-respecting Bavarian would be seen dead in to the unsuspecting aspiring capitalists of the newly-free East. Once, some vodka-soaked Russian soldiers had tried to trade him their T-72 tank for a finely aged BMW, but Manfred had wisely demurred.

With that small fortune, Manfred had emigrated to San Antonio, the promised-land of every Bavarian wanna-be cowboy. Now he owns a local contracting business and a few rental properties in the historic district of town. But he still rolls his own cigarettes, and still keeps his long hair back in a neat ponytail. He also wears a Stetson, blue jeans, and cowboy boots. And he drives a loud, diesel-powered silver F-350, often spending weekends a couple of hundred miles out west at his Hill Country trophy ranch. His affected Texas twang alternates with a guttural Bavarian accent. But after so many late-night conversations on philosophy, religion, politics, and life, I hardly heard the odd double accent anymore.

Yes, Manfred was living the German-American Dream. Just a week before this, our Mexican road-trip, he had roasted a whole pig in his backyard. Everyone we knew had come for the party. My friend Timmy had eaten one of the pig's eyes, much to Mark's disgust.

* * * * *

Mark's truck sputtered along the back roads from my Helotes single-wide trailer, through suburban San Antonio's sprawling loop-land, and we began to enter the yuppie holds inside the perimeter highway surrounding the city. Outside the ring-road were country folks on their ranches, either selling out to, or battling it out with, the developers' ever-encroaching new subdivisions and strip-malls. Inside the ring were long-established, solidly bourgeois, suburban communities, each cookie-cutter plasterboard house much like the last, each sanitized, road-centric neighborhood alternating with yet another needless shopping district. It was in this homogenized version of the Southwest that our Bavarian friend had found himself a comfortable living.

Mark drove over the knobby little mesquite-covered hills toward Manfred's house, surveying the increasingly crowded landscape as we went further into the polyglot American city. The San Antonio Hindu Center was next to a greasy Tex-Mex taco stand, and a few miles later we passed the First Chinese Baptist Church. Then we drove thirstily by a yuppie beer hall – sort of an upscale Hooters featuring over one hundred of the world's finest corporate beers, as well as cute, nineteen-year-old waitresses in plaid skirts – and finally pulled into Manfred's wooded neighborhood. A dirty, unused twin-hull catamaran sailboat languished in his driveway on a trailer.

And there was Manfred, leaning jauntily on his boat. He was ready to go, with his two bags in hand and a straw summer cowboy hat on his head. As we got out of Mark's truck, Manfred spaghetti-westerned, "Da da ding dang dang, da da ding dang dong. *Ja, ja*, howdy y'all!" We loaded his bags into the back of Mark's truck, and were off for the rental car.

"Sooo, David," Manfred said in his Bavarian accent, "you seem a little hung over. *Vat* did you get into last night?"

"Oh, ah, yeah. Somewhat, perhaps. I went out with Timmy and Richard and ... well, Ute was there, but she left. We went pub crawlin'."

Manfred was incredulous. "*You vent out partying* the night before a ten-day road-trip?"

"Well, it was a ... you know, an impromptu thing. Just a deal, you know?"

I had met up with Timmy, Richard, and Richard's wife Ute the night before to celebrate the end of our semester at the university. We went to a pub and had a few starter pints before Ute said she was heading home, leaving Richard there with us. That was when, on my way to the john, I was suddenly and unexpectedly overcome with nausea. I spewed my beer and nachos onto the floor, leaving a big chunky puddle there in the doorway of the pub's entrance. I looked around, but I don't think anyone saw me. Embarrassed, I immediately exited the front door and quickly walked around the entire block. When I re-entered, the wait staff was busy cleaning up the sloppy mess, still talking angrily about the phantom puker. I sat down with my friends, who were also ruminating upon that foul fiend. I decided it was probably time to leave, and that was when the party really started.

We went on to another bar, where Timmy had an encounter with an acquaintance of nefarious means. It was just a thing, an impromptu thing. A little deal. We needed to let off some steam. I had just gotten through a line when two muscular bouncers burst into the bathroom. Keyed up, I had quickly dashed past them, making a break for freedom with the incriminating little baggie palmed in my right hand. I power-walked straight out of the bar and, for the second time that night, I randomly circumnavigated an entire city block. I got back to the parking lot just as Timmy and Richard were pulling out.

We had a good laugh at the close call, and then moved on to another saloon, energized. It all came to an end a little after four, when we passed out in Richard's living room after taking a sixer back to his place. Needless to say, none of us had gotten much sleep. Sitting there in Mark's truck reminiscing on the previous evening, my nose was raw and burning, and the pain in my head was fierce and sharp, untouched by the overmatched Excedrin.

Manfred looked back at me owlishly, his green eyes big behind his wire-framed glasses. "You look rough. I guess you're not driving the first leg."

"Please, no." I rubbed my throbbing temples. "Hey, and what's up with fucking nine o'clock in the morning, man? Mark here came and woke me up! You said noon!"

"What about the Jesus-freaks?" Mark protested.

"What about them?" I asked, slow witted in my condition.

"They were there first!"

Damnit, Mark.

Manfred turned around again and looked back at me, his eyes earnest and wide. "You know vat, David? I was trying to go ahead and make a decent plan. If we leave at noon, this vill not give us adequate time for da trip down. Whereas a mid-morning departure would provide us ample time. And we need to make good time."

Ah, yes. How very German. "Okay, whatever. I just wish I had known, man. I'd have gotten in earlier last night. I only got four hours of sleep!"

Mark spoke up again. "Aww, quit yer damn whinin'. Aha ha ha ha ha!" The Ogre's signature hyena cackle flared, loud and raucous, like an air horn blown into a rumpled balloon.

No amount of preparation – none at all – could prepare one for hearing that inhuman outburst for the first time. It had a way of stopping conversations, provoking stares, and generally setting people aback. The sound bounced off the walls of the truck cab, piercing my skull.

"Jesus, Mark. Could you not..."

"What's that, David?" Mark hadn't heard me over the echoing sound of his own laughter.

I soon decided that the Excedrin was inadequate for its appointed task. I needed stronger medicine. "Mark, could you pull up at the store there? Thanks man. I'll be right back." I went into the icehouse, returning moments later. Manfred was holding a conversation with a homeless-looking fellow who stood beside the truck. As I got back in, Manfred passed some change out the window, and the man thanked him before walking away.

"What was all that about?"

"I vas performing our daily civic duty. We need only do it once per day; no more, *und* no less." Manfred eyed the bag in my hand. "Whatcha got there?"

"Oh, that's, uh...want a cold one?

"Beer? Drinking already!?"

I cracked open a can of Shiner Blonde and took a large gulp, my hand shaking. I polished off the first one quickly and the headache slacked. "Remind me, before we leave town. We really need some ice."

We pulled in at the auto rental house, over by the airport. Manfred glanced back at me, then my beer. "Maybe you should just wait here, dude." They went in to secure the ride while I sat in the stifling heat of the truck, sprawled across our bags in the back seat, pulling on my third of the ever-warming beers. We badly needed ice.

* * * * *

As I sat there sweating, my thoughts turned to Fiesta, the last time I had been this sweaty. Every spring, San Antonio erupts into a debauched, ten-day period of madness, celebrating the Texican's defeat of Santa Anna at San Jacinto in 1836. Even the town's Tejanos party unselfconsciously. Folks wander around with big plastic cups filled with beer and margaritas, wearing pins, medals, beads, and generally as little else as possible as they sweat away the hardened winter lard. Boisterous parades wind their way about the town, up and down the San Antonio River, and all around the twisting, paved cattle trails which are hereabouts called city streets. Fiesta royalty make their way around town in their bedecked staff cars, going to and from this and that event, courting the lowly and granting booty of medals and trinkets to the favored.

For ten days, it is permissible to drink to excess and to kiss other men's wives. I myself kissed one such wife, a fellow student of mine at the university, on the last night of Fiesta, scant weeks before our looming departure for Mexico. She had arrived at the event without her husband, joining our group at a table under a big old oak tree. We sat together drinking beer and talking intensely. Hours passed, and we grew drunker, pitcher after pitcher of lager coming to the table. Other friends came and went as our conversation deepened, spiraling on to a new level of familiarity.

We edged closer, and I could smell her sweet breath. Our legs touched. I looked at her beautiful lips. And I truly almost fell off the bench when she pulled me to her and kissed me. But I recovered well, and then we were kissing, sweating in the warm dusk, and we could not stop. As darkness fell, I invited her to join me back at the Dog House, where a house party would be underway. But when we arrived, the place was empty, and I remembered that Mark was still on his way back from a job somewhere. So I let myself in, put on some music, and plugged in the string lights. We smoked a joint, then made love slowly on the couch, which I had carefully covered.

I drove her home, happy and oblivious to the looming quagmire. She was a German woman from my English class, she was married to Javier, a Mexican national who taught engineering at another local university, and I was in love with the most stunning woman I had ever met. But it was Fiesta. It was just an impromptu thing, all for fun. It happens all the time. Yes, it had been a Fiesta to remember, a Fiesta to forget. Now I was caught, hopelessly in love with a woman with a husband. Now I was a low-down, wife-stealing philanderer. Morally bankrupt. Could love justify such conduct? True love? I had never felt more trapped, more miserable.

My phone rang. The screen read 'Regina.' I answered, "Hey!"

"Hel-low!"

"What are you doing?" I asked, not wanting a real answer.

"Hmmm. Well, just thinking of you. Of how much I already miss you."

"Yes, I was thinking of you, too. We must have read each other's minds."

"Some of that serendipity you were talking about?"

"Yes, maybe."

"So what's the schedule for y'all's trip?" Even though she was from Germany, she was quickly learning to speak Southern.

"Oh, uh, Manfred I think wants to push on to Monterrey or Saltillo by tonight. Then on past Mexico City the next day. Oaxaca after that. He wants to make good time."

"Of course. .... I thought you were leaving at noon."

"Manfred changed the plan. They're in the rental place getting the car now."

"Hmm."

"So what about *your* vacation?" I asked, now hoping for a detailed answer.

She sighed. "We're leaving tomorrow for Monterrey to pick up Javier's friends Cesar and Miguel, and then sometime after that we'll head down to Oaxaca; I'm not really sure I remember, exactly. ... Did you go out last night?"

"I went pub-crawlin' with Timmy and Richard...and Ute, for a while. Now I'm just sitting here sweating, practicing for Mexico."

"Ha, the sweaty bear! Sweating out the toxins?"

I took a pull on my beer. It was getting dangerously close to an undrinkable temperature. "Something like that. I wish I could kiss you right now."

Her response had the breathy tone I was hoping to elicit. "Oh, yes, me too! Maybe we'll see you down there in Oaxaca. I could kiss you there."

"I'll kiss you anywhere." I was unembarrassed by my own schmaltz.

"You're sweet. … But don't you think that would be… romantic? To run into each other like that? In Mexico?"

"Yeah, I do … As long as I don't run into Javier, too. How could we pull it off? Our cell phones won't work. I mean, the roaming charges…"

"No, not the phones. I mean, just happen to see each other somehow."

"Oh. Yes, that would be romantic. We'll just have to see. Regina," I pronounced her name the proper German way, with a hard 'g.' "I love you."

There was a slight pause. "I love you too," she said quietly. "I can't wait for this summer to be over. I won't be back until August! I won't see you for three months. … Unless I see you down there."

"…yes, unless that. I hope so."

"Well, hopeless, right?"

Reluctantly, I agreed. "Yes, hopeless. But I'll try. I'll e-mail you!"

"Yes, me too. When I can. … Well, I have to go. Javier will be back soon."

"Yeah. Well, okay. Good bye, *mein Schatz*. I'll miss you."

"*Ich dich auch.* Y'all have fun… Bye."

"Bye."

I sat there sweltering in the late-spring Texas heat, staring out the window. The beer was luke-warm now. We badly needed ice, but my attention turned back to her. My heart had become a painful lump of stone in my chest, weighing me down, ever down. I took no joy from my thoughts of our happy holiday road trip deep into Mexico. I would rather be with her, would rather spend the summer alone with her, off in some cave, away from the world, away from all of it.

I had been with her again for a few delicious moments at Manfred's pig-roast. She kept ferrying liquor to Javier, and as he became more and more drunk and unaware, our secretive trips to the bedroom would become longer and more frequent. Kissing her was the wildest ride ever, and like an addict, I needed more.

Javier had been part of the crowd in the backyard, watching Timmy eating the pig's eyes, but she and I were alone in one of the bedrooms, the entire world gone from us. Later, Javier passed out on the grass near the pig carcass, and she and I went out front to be alone without fear of interruption. Exactly when he awoke we could not later say for certain, nor could we be sure of just what he had seen, but he definitely saw us talking, saw us and just sat inside by the big front window, saying nothing, doing nothing, just watching us sit on the catamaran as we talked. I suppose that is all he saw.

She had been mine that evening, for a time. Perhaps her husband had seen it, or had found out about it. But it did not matter now, because she would be with him all summer. Always with her husband, and not with me.

In a moment of weakness, I had confided my love for her to my sister, confessing that I had continued my pursuit even after learning about her marital status. She told me that I was destined to fail however it all turned out, and that a philanderer well deserves his share of the hell he helps to create. I could see the look of disgust and disappointment in her face, dear sweet Kate, who had always cared for me so. I supposed that she was right, and that took me even lower.

* * * * *

I took a final slug of warm Shiner, grimaced, and put my empty back into the bag. Movement drew my eye, pulling me out of my morose reverie; a large, pearly-white Buick LeSabre pulled up behind Mark's truck, and out hopped my boys. "Hey, we got a free up-grade," Mark said, grinning.

"*Ja*, it was this or a Chevy Impala, and *zha*t is a piece of shit," said Manfred, walking around the front of the sedan. "With this, ve can tour Mexico in style."

"Wel-done, boys." I said, grabbing our bags and tossing them in the trunk of the Buick. Mark took off for his house in his truck, Manfred and I following in the shiny new Buick. But Mark missed the exit, heading off in the wrong direction entirely. I sighed. "Just go the right way. We'll wait for him at his place. He *always* does this – takes the wrong turn. We'll have to do all the navigating down there."

"He really doesn't know the way to his own house? In his own town? Didn't he grow up here?"

"He's not the world's best driver. But he means well. He's a good man."

"*Ja ja*, he's that, no doubt." But Manfred scowled next to me, mildly disgusted with Mark's navigatory blunder and the resulting delay.

If Mark Hanson was an ogre, then Manfred Winkler could be fairly characterized as elfin. With his slightly receding hair drawn back into a ponytail, and his pleasant and friendly manner, yet still palpably controlling condensation, he resembled no one so much as Tolkien's elf-lord Elrond. Manfred was always polite and considerate, yet still somehow faintly superior in his knowledge, and especially in his precisely logical decision-making processes.

As he spoke with you casually about ordering a beer in a bar or what time to go see the Spurs play, his German intellect was always almost visibly working, analyzing the situation. "You know vat, why don't we head on down to the game a little bit early. That way we can get ready, and get a good parking spot." And you could easily imagine him using the same tone with his subcontractors and clients. "*Ja ja, diese hier* tile is good for da kitchen, but in the bathroom...why don't we go ahead and examine this tile over here? I believe that it is a much more effective anti-mold material."

After each statement he would look at you with his round, earnest green eyes, blinking, calmly challenging you to contradict his inexorable logic. And with the basketball game and the bathroom tile alike, it was the same tone, the same logic. No demarcation existed for him between work and play. With Manfred, everything was well-ordered and in its proper place, be it a work-day or a holiday. There was a reason for everything. Everything had to be planned out for maximum efficiency, whether it was his road-trip or your home renovation.

He carefully parceled out his perfunctory moments of pleasure in a strict, miserly fashion, taking his vacations only when he could work no more. And his emotions were always completely subsumed beneath the controlling intellect. For that reason, I always valued his opinion highly, untainted as it was by irrelevant concerns. He was my closest advisor, my *Mister Spock*. But just once, I wanted to see him lose control for a little while, to let the feelings have a go at making a decision.

In many ways he was the exact opposite of the Ogre. I had spent time with them both together, but only within the well-regulated confines of San Antonio. Now I was headed with the unusual pair one thousand miles south, into the unknown. For the sake of the group, I hoped we would effectively counter-balance each other, somehow maintaining a stable mixture of egos.

Like it or not, I would be the group axis, as I so often was. *The Dancing Bear*, they had come to call me, performing passionately for the amusement of others, playfully holding things together, stoking the group harmony. At least that's the way I looked from the outside, shaggy and outgoing, the life of the party. I had taken the nickname with good grace, as a man does, wearing the mask no matter what was churning inside.

* * * * *

We pulled up at the Hanson's residence, to the Big House, there in the fashionable Alamo Heights district of San Antonio. We sat on the back porch next to the Buick, waiting for Mark to return from his erroneous excursion. The Dog House and its well-used barbeque pit sat further back on the property. Manfred leaned against the car, rolling a cigarette, when the back door opened behind us.

"Well, hello theah, boys." It was the venerable Mr. Hanson himself, coming out to see us off. He turned his wry, old-school wit on me, as he so often did. "Well, David. It's so verruh reassurin' to see you'll be goin' on this trip." Manfred barely suppressed a chuckle, and I put my beer down for the obligatory handshake.

"Hello, sir. I believe we've met once before. I'm Manfred Winkler, you may remember."

"Oh, Ah remembah. How do you do?"

"Very well, sir, thank you."

"Are you boys ready? All packed?"

"Yessir, we're all ready. We just have to get Mark's bags and we're off. We got a free up-grade." I pointed to our grand Buick, shining in the sun. "We're waiting on Mark. He took a wrong turn."

Mr. Hanson smiled at this. "You boys have an enjoyable Fiesta?"

"Yessir. Went to most all the things. Had a good time. Got a lot of medals."

He nodded. "Mighty fine, mighty fine."

Just then, the Hansons' African-American maid emerged from the Big House with Mark's gear. Manfred and I took it from her and loaded it in the trunk.

"Well, you boys be careful down theah," Mr. Hanson said. "Don't y'all end up in a Meskin prison, y' heah?" He chuckled. We nodded our assent, and the elderly Southern gentleman stepped back inside as Mark pulled up the long drive.

"Hey, sorry guys, I took a wrong turn. You know?"

"We know. We already loaded your gear. Let's go."

After a quick stop for ice, more beer, a bottle of rum, a six-pack of Coke, some limes, and a jalapeño, we headed out on the interstate. There we were: the wild ogre, the logical elf, and the passionate dancing bear, drifting down the freeway in our great American land yacht. South we went on I-35, south across the rolling plains of southern Texas, baking in the sun. Prickly-pear cacti competed with gnarled mesquite trees and chaparral scrub-brush for what little water flowed over the land. Ranch after gigantic, cattle-stocked ranch passed by out the window, everywhere looking dry as a bone. Up front, the boys were holding a council of war.

"Alright, we vant to get ready and go right across the border, stopping only for da necessary papers. Ve vill need visas and automobile registration. Ve can make Monterrey or Saltillo by nightfall."

Mark would have none of it. "Whores! We have to go to Boy's Town on the way, get some whores!"

"Vell, Mark, don't you think they haf these whores down in Saltillo?"

"No! I tell you what, the ones in Boy's Town are the best, you know?"

I came in on Mark's side, just for the sake of letting him get out unwanted demons, the kind that are no good for long-distance travel. "Well, Manfred, if you think about it, we'll not finish getting our papers in Nuevo Laredo until mid-afternoon, and if we just check into a hotel right away, we'll have time for lunch. Then we could head down to Boy's Town. Get there early, *ahem*, *finish* early, and get an early start in the morning. We'll be well past Saltillo by noon tomorrow. Whereas if we try to push on to Saltillo tonight, well, Mark here won't finish his business until late… we'll probably be only *leaving* Saltillo by noon, with that plan, and a lot more hassle for everybody. So that's one idea, anyway."

Mark liked the proposal. "Hey, he's right. It's a quick cab ride to Boy's Town, you know? What d'ya think, Manfred?"

"I vas only trying to think of the larger trip. There are whores all over Mexico. We have to make good time. Ve haf a schedule to keep! I thought we vere in agreement to go ahead and push down to the coast as quickly as possible, *und den* take our time coming back north. That way ve haf optimum time to enjoy ourselves on the beach."

"Manfred, man, quit being so precise, so…so German! We're on vacation, man! We'll still make Oaxaca City in three days driving with either plan. Let's let Mark have his whores. It'll be better for everyone that way." I tried to catch Manfred's eye, give him a subtle look, some sort of signal…

"Yeah! I'm for that plan!"

Manfred glanced at me in the rear-view mirror, his face taking on a thoughtful cast. "You know what, perhaps you are right. I think ve should stay the night in Nuevo Laredo. We vill go to Boy's Town." Mark cheered. I opened another beer and sat back, surveying the increasingly deserted landscape.

We finished our visa and automobile paperwork by two o'clock, having crossed the border from Laredo an hour earlier. We checked into Mark's old haunt, the Hotel La Reforma. The clerk at the desk greeted him by name. "*Buenas tardes, Señor* Hanson. It has been far too long since your last stay with us. And these are your guests?" We finished checking in, then I went up to our three-man room for a very necessary siesta, and the boys went for some tacos.

* * * * *

That evening, much refreshed, we walked through the gritty border town of Nuevo Laredo. Parts of the city looked like a war zone, because they were – the frontline of the *Norte Americanos*' War on Drugs. One block featured a row of abandoned storefront buildings where people were squatting, another a two-story pile of garbage in a vacant lot, and a third a colony of crippled beggars living together in an alley. As we walked, urchins approached, hopefully offering their array of services for *los gringos*. "Dok-tor? You wan' scripts?" "Viagra?" "Shoe-shine?" "Xanax?"

The contrast was as stark as night and day between the relative wealth of Laredo, just across the Rio Grande, and this impoverished border city founded by Laredo's loyal Mexican citizens fleeing the advancing US Army in 1846. How ironic that civilized, urbane Mexicans had founded Nuevo Laredo after fleeing the invading Gringo Hordes. And now, Nuevo Laredo was wrecked, the enduring victim of the Drug War. But it was the border, not the interior. Things would be different in the interior, I thought.

We hailed a cab, headed for the surreal scene at Boy's Town. A peculiar meeting place of sorts between first and third worlds, Boy's Town was many things to many people. To the pimps and whores, it was food on the table. To the hustlers, it was the Main Chance. And to the johns, it was a variably good piece of ass. But to Mark Hanson, it was heaven on earth, a veritable ogre's paradise.

Located just upriver on the outskirts of Nuevo Laredo, Boy's Town is not just a whorehouse – like, say, the world-renowned Bunny Ranch – but rather a walled compound, the inside of which is filled with a complex of buildings, with many houses catering to different clientele, all haphazardly placed around a disorderly central plaza of packed dirt.

The taxi pulled in through the gate, past the concrete walls enclosing the compound. The driver let us out not far from the tiny police hut near the front entrance. Whores, pimps, hustlers, and johns all milled about in a drunken, carnival-like atmosphere. In the waning light, Mark pointed to a dilapidated, unlikely looking structure called Papa Gallos. "Hey guys, let's go in that one there. What d'ya think, David?"

I shrugged. "Alright by me, as long as the beer's cold."

Mark turned his pumpkin-sized ogre-head the other way. "What about you, Manfred?"

"Mark, I say we go in that one, there." Manfred pointed to the building Mark had selected, then looked at me deadpan, blinking.

Inside, the lights were dim, presumably to enhance the mood, or maybe to hide the actual quality of the goods. A server approached directly, queried us in rapid Spanish.

"*Sí, muchas gracias. Tres cervezas* Sol *con limón, por favór*," Manfred replied smoothly.

"Nice, man. I'll get my Spanish back as I go, but it'll take a few days. In the meantime, it's good to have you along, if only for that reason."

"At least I'm good for something," he said, smiling.

The place was nearly deserted, but shortly a woman sidled up to us. Her dark hair was pulled back from her low forehead, which shined with a sheen of grease. Her face displayed harsh acne scars. She was at least forty, and had the look of a woman who had seen too much for too long. "You wanna girlfrien'?" she said in a deep voice.

"Uh, no grassy-ass," Mark rasped. But the woman did not retreat. "No grassy-ass. *No quiero*!" Still she persisted, running a hand over Mark's mottled arm. He pretended she wasn't there, looking down at his *cerveza* Sol, playing with the lime, until she finally departed.

"Mark, man, what was wrong with her?" I asked. "She was ready to go!"

"Aw, it's still early. Slim pickens and all. You know? The good ones'll come out in a little while. You know what I mean?" Manfred and I nodded our understanding.

We went around to several buildings in the next few hours, drinking and talking to the rickety women. Each building featured a different theme. One was tropical, with turtles and birds in cages. Another was Asian-themed and featured fish swimming around in a stagnant, scum-covered pool in the courtyard. Finally we wound up back at Papa Gallos, but the place had transformed.

"See what I mean, guys? Now it's good pickens!" Mark was beside himself with excitement. And he was right. Before, only one or two tired old women had stood watch. Now, a couple of hours later, the place was swarming with Salma Hayek look-alikes.

I discretely turned away a solicitor. Before I could turn back to him, Mark had disappeared with a group of women. Manfred watched him go. "Da da ding, da da ding dang dong. So. Why don't you go back with one?"

"Well, you see, it's like ol' Timmy told me. He was down here once, paid his forty dollars, and went in the back room with one of the girls. And right in the middle of the act, she brought her arm around, looked at her watch, and told him, 'You have fifteen minutes.' Of course, I think she'd already been with the Ogre first," I smiled. "But really, these girls just don't do it for me, Manfred. I like a woman to *actually be into* the sex act. You know, a little emotion? *Real* passion? Not these cold-hearted mannequins. When you really think about it, making sex into a business transaction kinda ruins it."

I gave Manfred a satisfied look and took a long swig from my beer. "Say, I don't see you back there...what's your story? Some kind of ethical problem? You know, you're just supporting the local economy."

"Well David. You know I have a girlfriend. So I don't believe in da two-timing. I stay true to her." He paused, took a drink. "Are you sure that's not the reason for your abstinence? Staying true to someone?"

"Aw, man, you know I'm single. I just don't dig the whore scene. Who would I have to be faithful to, anyway?"

"*Ach*, well, you've been spending a lot of time around Regina lately. Like at Fiesta. *Ja, ja, und* at all your keg parties at the single-wide. No?"

"Oh, her? No man, we're just friends, you know? Good friends. She's married." I focused very closely on my bottle of beer, suddenly not wanting to look him in the eye.

"Yes, David – of course I know she's married. But if you are just friends, then why were you two making out at my pig-roast?"

Now I looked him in the eye. "You saw that? I mean... did anyone else see that?"

"I don't think so. So vat's going on?"

"Ah, well ... You see..." My hands clasped, unclasped. "I mean, you know, we do...talk and stuff." I signaled the boy for another beer.

"And stuff?"

"Yeah, you know. We're friends! Look, she's married. Sure, but she may not be forever."

Manfred's eyebrows rose slightly, "Is that your hope, David?"

The boy came with my beer. "So what if it is," I said, gritting my teeth.

Manfred frowned. "So. How exactly did you get into this mess? Vat are you doing falling in love with a married German woman?" Manfred sat back in his chair, watching me intently. "Would you like a shot of tequila?"

"Sure man."

Manfred flagged down the boy. "*Dos mas cerveza* Sol *con limón, y queremos dos tequilas de* Herradura Reposada, *por favór*." Then, turning to me, "So?"

"Man, I ... I would never have gotten involved ... you know, even talked with her, but she, uh, she told me when we met that she 'had a boyfriend'. And it didn't seem so serious."

"So she lied to you."

"Yeah, well, but she didn't plan it, it just happened when she met me, you know, an impromptu comment. I guess she really liked me, and didn't want to scare me off by saying she was hitched. But she didn't even have a ring on. It looked like a green light, right? So when I finally found out she was actually married, I *did* back off, sure I did! … At least until the pig-roast."

"Hmm."

"Look, it's … we only flirt a bit, so … I'm not too worried about it, you know? It'll work itself out."

The tequila arrived, with more beers. Manfred said, "*Salúd*. To good travels with good friends!" We clicked glasses, threw back the shots, and chased them with a long swallow of Sol. I sat there looking at the sultry women, wishing I were somewhere else. Manfred stared at me like a cat from across the table. "So David. Vat are you going to do now?"

"*Vat* do you mean, *do*?" I mimicked him. "I'll do nothing. I mean, there isn't anything to be done." I shrugged, smiling. "But don't you think we're perfect for each other? She, the unfaithful wife, and me, the bride-thieving home-wrecker? Isn't that a perfect match!?" Like Kate had said. I looked at him expectantly.

Manfred let out a dry chuckle. "I guess you know Javier told me at the pig-roast that he and Regina are coming down to Oaxaca in a few days?"

"Uh, yeah, she said something about that, I think. Sometime next week, I guess. I'm not really sure I remember, exactly. They're supposed to go all the way to Panama. Back to Texas in six weeks or so. Then they're off to Germany for a month. So it's all hopeless anyway!" I squeezed lime into my beer and looked up to see Manfred staring back, inscrutable.

"David. You know what. I really like Javier. He's a good man. You shouldn't mess with his wife."

"Yeah, I know. … I'm not *messing* with her, man! Don't worry about it, alright? I won't even see her until the fall semester, and I'm sure it will have all cooled off by then. Okay? It's nothing. Let's just enjoy our vacation."

I sat there toying with the tequila glass, looking at the salty mess on the table. "And, you know, if their marriage *is* dead, it won't be my fault. I mean, it's the natural order of things, right? Me taking his wife. You know, since I'm Texan and he's Mexican." I smiled up at Manfred, immediately regretting my poor attempt at humor. His polite chuckle was slight and anemic, disturbed as he was at the tear in the social fabric.

We sat there at the little round table in Papa Gallos, watching the ladies do their thing as we drank our tequila and beer. My mind wandered, as it had done so often lately, and ended up right back at her. She was one of the most intelligent women I had ever met. She had the most alluring energy, something I could not quite put my finger on, but something that nonetheless made her a creature beyond mere appeal for me. Her sense of humor was well-developed, running along similar lines as mine. It was as if she was on the inside made to match me perfectly.

Physically, she was exquisitely beautiful, with a tall, slender figure, her fair hair framing a face sculpted by the gods themselves. She was without blemish in every respect, but her most striking feature was her bold, confident eyes. They were practically startling. In conversation, her eyes somehow drew you out, charmed you, made you feel alive. I saw her do it to many men. She saw into me, and held my gaze warmly, engagingly. Whenever we would embrace, I would immediately become maddened by her lovely natural scent, clearly genetically engineered to drive me absolutely insane, which I was suspecting myself of being lately, very much so.

I remembered that day she had sauntered into class late, the first time I had laid eyes on her. How I had even then adored her from sight alone, knowing nothing of her heart. And just as soon as I had actually met her, I was immediately and forever snared like a wretched bear in an excruciating trap. And I do believe that she knew it, right away.

I remembered too when Mark had first met Regina, earlier that spring. We had been in the Dog House, drinking the Lone Star. With Mark's consent, I had invited the German girl and her Mexican 'boyfriend' over one Friday evening for a few local Texan beers and a healthy dose of Texan culture via Mark Hanson and the Dog House itself. At the time, I was still thinking of her as a woman I would simply have to wean away from a mere boyfriend, a woman who would make the correct choice soon, easily, when the right opportunity presented itself. There was no ring on her finger, and that was enough for me to make a play. I had no idea that I was setting myself up for philandering.

Mark let the two in, handed them each a cold beer.

"*Gracias*," said Javier.

Regina glided gracefully across the smelly, testosterone-oozing Dog House as if she were at a masked ball. The entire smoke-filled room took on a numinous glow as her slender body alighted on the edge of Mark's filthy couch. Javier, mouth set in a straight line, accepted his Lone Star stoically and took the place next to her. I saw him eyeing the Confederate flag in front of him on the tar-stained wall. It was my first time meeting the boyfriend of the woman I wanted so badly.

"Sorry it's not a Tecate," I said, grinning.

"No, that is all right," he replied in his thick Spanish accent. "I guess Regina told you Tecate is my favorite beer, but I also like the Lone Star."

Regina made a quick little glance and smirk at that patent lie, but Mark interrupted. "So, yeah! You teach at, uh, Incarnate Word University?" Mark knew of my affection for Regina, and thus the hidden purpose for the night's gathering, and – while not at all in favor of white German women dating brown Mexican nationals – he seemed to me to be nervous, clearly uncomfortable with the chancy encounter I had arranged on his turf for the evening.

"Yes," said Javier stiffly. He looked like it would have killed him to smile. "I teach engineering to the undergrads. It is so heartless. I *hate* it."

Regina rolled her eyes.

"Oh?" I said.

"Yes."

"And so, uh, what Meskin city you from, man?" Mark asked awkwardly.

"I am from Monterrey." He looked back at me. "Regina tells me you are a writer?"

"I am."

Javier nodded thoughtfully. "I have always wanted to write."

"Do you write now?"

"No. But it is a thing I would like to do."

"Well. You just have to do it. Every day. You've got to stick to it with the energy of a benny addict. Talking about it never helps."

I was happy to show him up a bit, but had I crossed a line with that? We all sat there for a long moment in the Dog House, drinking the Lone Star beer.

To me Regina said, "That book you gave me to read? The one by Carl Jung?"

"Yeah?"

"Well, I don't agree with any of it."

"No?"

"No."

"And why not?" I shrugged. "He's *your* people."

"No, he's Swiss! And I just don't. His concepts of *anima* and *animus*, I can't accept that. And especially this *shadow* thing. Because if it's true, then so many things that I believe in must be false."

"Well, isn't that how we learn new things, by giving up old ones?"

Javier and Mark were talking amongst themselves about something having to do with Mark's wall-mounted Mayan artifacts. But I could tell that Javier was actually listening intently to me talking to his girlfriend.

"Jung paints this false picture of people striving toward some inherent wholeness. I just don't buy that."

"That people strive, or that there is an inherent wholeness?"

"Both! I think people are basically selfish and lazy, and that there is no so-called wholeness."

"So you think people are inherently trick-ass?" I smiled at her.

She laughed. "Yes, I do. People are always trying to acquire power over others, just study history. And look at what they do with it." She shook her head. "Just look at what they do with it!"

"No, it's not that simple. It's a process. People can care for others with their power, and sometimes they do. And anyway, there is no inherent wholeness, not until people create that wholeness themselves. It's not inherent at all. And all Jung says is that such an image of psychological health exists as a template, a universal image, what he calls an *archetype*, within all of us."

She shook her head. "No, that doesn't make any sense."

"Aww, y'all quit that Joseph Campbell hippie-talkin' over there! Aha ha ha ha ha!" Mark handed out a new round of beers for all, hoping to move the conversation, but we were undeterred.

"Why doesn't it make sense?"

"How could people know what something is before it even exists? That's teleology!"

"And that's pseudo-logical. An artist can have a conception of a completed work before it's finished, or even begun. Like the universal mandala. And so, Q.E.D., there you go."

We stared admiringly at each other for a long moment, a moment that was not at all lost on Mark and Javier. I didn't care. It was just her boyfriend – and what's a boyfriend? I was clearly filling a conversational void, if not a more profound one, within her. Let him watch, and perhaps he would come to understand that I was the better match for her.

We all drank a few more beers, chatting more or less amicably about Jung, Mayan artifacts, engineering, and writing, and then the two visitors bade a friendly goodbye. I hugged Regina as she left, and then Javier came up and gave me his own friendly bear-hug. Keep your friends close and your enemies closer, I guess.

It didn't help that Javier was basically an intelligent, likable guy. He was admittedly a bit odd, seeming weak and torn, but there was nothing particularly odious about him. I wished that there were. That would have made things easier for me. But he merely seemed to me to be rather indecisive, such as with his ineffectual desire to write. So he had an unpleasant job; don't we all? Regardless of the situation, he seemed detached, brooding, depressed even, as if he were in mourning for some reason, as if something important in his life were not quite right, or was missing, but he could never face up to it. His laughter, when it came, always seemed artificial and forced. He seemed like a man beaten down by reality, paralyzed by something on some deep, inner level, afraid to draw his sword and have at life, to make some opportunities for himself. I could understand why Regina would grow tired of that.

Javier did not command much respect from me, it is true, but *that* was the reason, his apparent surrender to life. Not because I felt I had some superior might or some superior claim to Regina. The strongest emotion I found within me for him was only a sort of half-hearted pity. In any case, I wanted his girlfriend, and really didn't enjoy thinking much about the man with whom she ran for now. If only he wasn't such a relatively nice guy. That would have made everything so much easier. Perhaps easier for Regina as well. Or at least I had convinced myself.

And I could never understand why the two of them were together in the first place. She was so charming and charismatic, but he was like a half-dead fish, a low-level technocrat, forgettable. There was no imagination in his engineer's mind. No joy in his soul. No extra zeros in his bank account. He wasn't even very handsome, with a long, drawn horse-face, a sallow, washed-out complexion, and sadly drooping eyes. Next to him, she was incandescent, a glowing star. What did she see in him? My fiery passion was a far better match for her sensual energy than his lackluster countenance. Regina and I made a beautiful blazing fire together. What did they have that could match that, besides inertia, a half-forgotten fling year ago, now become a yoke? Nothing, it seemed to me.

Less than a week after our Dog House rendezvous, I discovered from some mutual friends that Javier was actually

Regina's husband. And I was confronted with the fact that she had lied to me. I also then realized that Javier had no idea I had been thinking the entire time that he was a mere boyfriend. She had of course withheld that lie from him, brazenly risking having her lies exposed when we met. I was impressed with her daring, but for days after the discovery my heart had smoldered with the bitter fires of betrayal.

She had made me into an unwitting accomplice with her deceit. Normally a woman capable of such actions should be gently unhooked and thrown back into the stormy seas. There are plenty of other, more trustworthy fish out there. Ah, but that fire … and something about her drew me to her and kept me there. *I* was the one who was hooked.

I did confront her on campus that next week, sitting with her by the brimming fountain in the student plaza. She had not been the least bit remorseful, and we then pleasantly agreed to just be friends. But sitting there looking into her magnetic grey-blue eyes, eyes that seemed to pierce right down, deep into my innermost heart, I found that I was not so angry with her after all. How could I be, when she looked at me like that?

Afterward we continued to share a class together, sometimes exchanging meaningfully long glances. Then, a month later, came Fiesta, and then the pig-roast. I savored the memory of our encounter in Manfred's dimly-lit guest room, the rest of the world melting away.

* * * * *

The sound of Manfred's voice broke me from my reminiscing. He was ordering another round from the boy. I said, "I wonder how Mark's doing. How many do you think he's up to, huh?" Manfred shrugged, frowning, and was about to respond when Mark came up, four sweaty, tired Mexican women surrounding him.

"Hey guys, I'm back." His broad grin stretched from ear to ear, a horrific sight for the uninitiated.

I handed him a fresh beer. "Oh, yeah, how'd it go?"

"Went fine. Had four of 'em." He swilled his beer, spilling a good ounce or two down his chin, and slammed the bottle down on the table. Half of the remaining contents turned immediately to foam, which ran onto the table. He belched broadly. "Yeah, I had four."

Manfred leaned forward, his eyes wide. "Four – in succession? Or at one time?"

Mark shrugged nonchalantly. "At once. All at once." Just then one of the four crept up, grabbed Mark by the arm. "You give tip? *¿Por favór?*"

Mark shook off her hand, his large ham-finger wagging in her face. "No! You've already *been* paid!" Then, "Hey, you guys hungry? Let's go get some fajitas, what d'ya think?"

Outside, we did just that. We found a stand in the dirt plaza and dined like starving kings on grilled strips of fajita meat wrapped in fresh corn tortillas. No *cervezas* Sol, but we settled for a round of Coronas without complaint. Several sauces were on the table, all spicy, all good. I ate two fajitas, Manfred four, and Mark seven, replenishing his spent vigor. Two old men came up with guitars and played for us for a few dollars. The evening was quite relaxing. Life was good. I even managed to not think about Regina for a little while.

But Mark had not had enough. “Hey, hey guys! Hey, let’s go see the Donkey Show, what d’ya think?”

Manfred and I looked at one another. “Donkey Show?” I asked, afraid of the answer.

“Yeah, David, the Donkey Show, you know? It’s got a real live donkey!”

Manfred said, “Well, with that name, I should hope so.”

“Aww, come on, let’s go.” We walked further into the compound, passing pimps and underage girls standing in doorways set into a whitewashed concrete wall. We walked past a long lineup to a brown brick structure surrounded by palm trees. A lit neon sign above the door read:

THE DONKEY SHOW

Mark brayed, “H E E – H A W! Aha ha ha ha ha! Let’s go in!” Several boys in white jackets let us in the door.

Inside it was dark, very dark. Aside from a pale light behind the bar, the room was lit only by strung Christmas lights. We sat down in front of a semi-circular raised platform, on which a woman danced. Beverages were bought and consumed. Working girls came and sat on our laps, soliciting discreetly. At twice the normal price, drinks were bought for them as well. I pulled out what I thought was a twenty dollar bill and handed it to the boy. I received a one-dollar bill in return. It was dark, and I doubted myself.

What did I give him? Only a five? I think not ... I looked after the boy, but he was gone. I looked at Mark. Having just paid another boy, he sat there looking puzzled, the woman on his lap stroking his shoulder distractingly.

"Mark, did you..."

"Yeah! Hey, I didn't..."

Manfred was arguing with his boy about the same thing. He became quite agitated, getting up suddenly and spilling his young lady roughly onto the floor. He came over to me. "David, dey haf been ripping us off! I gave da waiter a hundred dollar bill, and he gives me back change *für* only da twenty!" His finger waggled angrily in the air as he ranted.

Just then a black soldier down on leave who had been sitting next to us spoke up. "Yo man, where mah cell phone at? It *wa' righ' heah unda mah chaih*!"

Manfred said, "*Deise hier ist Scheisse.* Follow me." All four of us walked out, the waiters protesting. Manfred told them firmly in Spanish that we were heading to the little police station at the entrance to the Boy's Town compound. We walked away, leaving the white-jacketed boys all clustered up, chattering away in protest.

The black soldier blanched. "Sheeit, Ah ain't messin' wi' no Meskin po-po! Ain't goin' ta no Meskin prison, *ee-duh*!"

"What about your cell phone?" I asked.

"Fuck it, it wa' free!" He turned away.

We walked down through the plaza and entered the small police station. Several Mexican cops sat around drinking coffee, clearly bored with the night's lack of action. Manfred said, "*Buenas noches, Señores.*" Still in Spanish he continued,

"We have been robbed. The waiters of the Donkey Show," he pointed up the way, "have taken our money. They have taken over eighty dollars US from me, and from David..."

I said, "It was almost twenty dollars, man. *Viente dólores*."

Mark said, "Yeah, me too! Uh, *y mi* tam-bee-ann."

The cops conferred briefly, then set out with us to the Donkey Show. When we returned, only the woman behind the bar and the boy who had served Manfred were still there. All the customers had left. Even the whores were gone. The police questioned the boy sharply, but he vehemently denied everything. The police refused to accept his explanation, making clear he was not believed, and eventually he sheepishly pulled Manfred's eighty-something dollars from his pocket. The police handcuffed him and led him away, the woman behind the bar stammering apologies all the while. It felt like contrived theater.

"What about *my* money?" I protested.

Mark joined in, "Yeah, what about me?"

But there was no help for it. The other culprits had left the scene, and the bar had left only the one boy to take the fall, the sacrificial lamb. The routine was well rehearsed. Back at the police station, we filled out paperwork and the boy sat in a cell glumly. I heard the police say the Donkey Show bar would have to pay five hundred pesos to get him out, which was only about fifty dollars US. Our paperwork consisted only of our names and US addresses. The police, taking our word for it, did not even ask to see proper identification.

As we walked back out to the Boy's Town plaza, I said, "I bet they threw our paperwork in the garbage as soon as we left."

"*Ja, ja*,"

"And we didn't even get to see any donkeys!" I intoned.

"You know vat, David? We *vere* da donkeys."

"Aha ha ha ha!"

Having been bitten by this scam, it would have been a good time to concede defeat for the night, but Mark would have none of it. The Ogre would have more whores. We followed him deeper into the Boy's Town compound, now filling with off-duty Mexican and *norteamericano* truck drivers, as well as sailors and soldiers on liberty. The atmosphere in the compound took on a frenetic energy. We walked up the way and entered a darkened structure.

Inside, the workers were not soliciting discretely, not at all. Except for them, the place was deserted. The bones of their grossly over-painted faces were too prominent, too jutting. They sat forcefully upon our laps, their hands taking great and immediate liberties. Mine tried to kiss me on the lips, mouth open. I pushed her away and off of my lap. Something was wrong. Mark sprang to his feet suddenly and yelled, "Aw hell, these uns here are guys!" We scrambled back out on to the dirt plaza, shuddering. "Let's just keep this between us, okay y'all?"

"Of course."

Manfred was scowling darkly. He did not say a word.

Not willing to retire in such an inglorious manner, we went back down to Papa Gallos, now clearly one of the more popular mainstream houses, and one which we hoped would neither feature she-males nor make asses out of us. Inside, Mark immediately went to the back with one of the ladies. Within minutes he returned. "David!" He handed me a plastic bank card. "Hey, hey David! Can you go down to the ATM? It's right outside the gate. Go ahead and get me another two hundred dollars, you know?" He stage-whispered the code to me.

I sighed and nodded my agreement. On my way down the plaza, near the gate and the cash machine, a group of four policemen stopped me, shining flashlights in my face, blinding me. They were the cops from the police station at the gate.

"*Buenas noches, Señor*. We are going to now search you for illegal weapons.

I only had a little pocket blade on me, so I shrugged, "*Todo bien, Señor*." As soon as they found the blade they grabbed my arm.

"*Señor*, we are now arresting you for the having of an illegal weapon."

"Hey, it's just a pocket knife!" I hollered. "That's not illegal in Mexico!"

"*No Señor*, but a knife is illegal in the Boy's Town. The sign at the entrance says this."

"I didn't see any sign! The taxi must have just blazed by it!"

They shrugged, uncaring. "*Es la ley*. Ignorance of the law is no excuse, *Señor*." They led me down to the police station and locked me in a cell. The thieving wait-staff boy was gone, but a grizzled, middle-aged white man was in there, pacing and grumbling in his cell.

I gave him the question one typically asks in situations such as these. "What are you in here for, man?"

He hocked and spat. "A damn weapons violation! I've been comin' here for eight years, and this here is bullshit! Fuckin' Meskins."

"Yeah, me too. What kind of weapon?"

"Fuckin' Swiss Army knife." I looked through the bars into the office of the one-room station. The police were clustered around their little desk in their rumpled off-blue uniforms, laughing and smoking, comparing confiscated blades. Mine was a nasty affair, glazed black, part of the blade serrated. It was still supposed to be legal. The Swiss Army knife was a miniature, a tiny knife with not even all the options. I sighed. I began pacing with the old man.

A half-hour later another fellow came for my grizzled cellmate. They were gringo truck drivers from New Mexico on their way to Corpus, stopping off for some action. The new fellow said to his colleague, "How much money you got with you, Frank? They said five hundred, but I got 'em down to two-fifty." Frank had the money on him, just enough. They paid the "fine," and the police politely released Frank, not bothering with a shred of paperwork. They hadn't even taken his name.

Now I was alone in the small, ten-square-foot cell. A tiny, doorless alcove off to the side held a shit-filled toilet with no seat and no toilet paper. When I pissed in it, flies buzzed about angrily. I paced about angrily myself, enraged at the ongoing shakedown. Where the hell was Mark?

A cop came by, smirking. "Just calm down, *Señor*. The judge will see you in the morning." Pacing all the while, I glared back at him. I passed very close by the bars where he stood, getting ever more impatient, my anger boiling, barely contained. The bars were good, I thought, preventing me from doing something eminently stupid to the little Mexican pig. Finally I saw Manfred and Mark come up. They were frantic. Manfred spoke with the police, but they just shrugged and said in English, "Five hundred dollars US, *Señor*, we can no accept less. It is for the judge."

The police let Mark come in, and I passed him back his card. "Get the money, man! Get me out of here!"

Mark left for the cash machine. Then Manfred came over. "David, try to remain calm. Ve are doing our best to get you out. I haf no more cash on me, *und* my cards are back in the safe at da hotel. Mark vill get the cash." That calmed me a bit.

Then the cop said for Manfred quit talking to the criminal, to get away from the cell. Again, I was alone in the stinking hole, my only company the rats squeaking from the dark corners. Just that morning I had been sleeping soundly in my own bed, disturbed only by roving bands of Mormons. I did not have enough cash on me either, and, unlike most gringo college students, I had no credit cards. I paced and paced.

Mark came back. He and Manfred spoke together outside, discussing something heatedly. Why didn't he just pay them? Manfred came back over and spoke to the cops, and they let him come over to me. I stopped pacing.

"David, Mark has no more money for his legal limit."

"What the fuck are you talking about!?"

"He cannot pull any more cash out of da machine today. Too many whores. Ve must wait until morning."

"Morning? Jesus, that's when I see the judge, man!"

"I seriously doubt there is any judge. These police here only vant da money. It is a shakedown."

"I'm going to be stuck here in this Meskin prison!"

"Vell, I think it is more of a jail than a prison."

I would have tried to throttle him through the bars, but I noticed action outside. A woman in an old green Dodge minivan – the national car of Mexican-Americans, I thought to myself – had pulled up and was talking with Mark. Soon she emerged from the car and came inside the station, began speaking with the police in rapid-fire Spanish, every now and then pointing over at me. Mark came over to me, his thick cigarette-breath adding to the stench in the cell.

"Hey David," he said breathlessly, "that's that whore I was with earlier."

"Which one?" I smiled up at him.

He ignored the comment. "She's gonna vouch for you."

"She's *what*?"

"Vouch for you, man. She's telling the cops we're cool guys, you know, that we're her friends. You know what I mean?"

"Uh, ok then." I was bewildered. Would this help?

Indeed, the woman was gesturing toward me, speaking earnestly. The police listened and began to look slightly disappointed. I looked on, astonished, growing cautiously hopeful.

Evidently the woman had some pull here. A *whore* with the power to get foreigners out of prison ...? Or jail, anyway. Now that was a woman with *real* power. Power over herself and others. That had to be an uncommon thing in a place such as this. A *Madame-Don.* Or *Don Whore?* More like *WTF* for this gringo.

A cop came over to the cell and lectured me on the importance of obeying the law. He told me I was a guest in his country, and that I had no right to come down here and take the women for myself and not obey the law. *Es la ley*, he said. He told me that in his country they know how to deal with breakers of the law.

He spoke to me in Spanish for fifteen minutes, with me nodding solemnly at times when I thought it appropriate despite my limited comprehension. Then he unlocked the cell and I walked free. As I left the jail I saw one of the cops leaning back in a chair, his feet up on the desk, cleaning his fingernails contentedly with my serrated blade. Goodbye, old friend, I thought.

* * * * *

His demons spent, Mark Hanson had finally had enough whores. The exorcism was complete. We thanked the Dodge-driving woman profusely, and she offered us a joint.

We filled the minivan with smoke, Scooby Doo style, as she drove us back to the Hotel La Reforma.

As we readied for bed, Mark raised a stink. "Aww, why do you have to sleep naked, Manfred? Can't you just wear pajamas like a normal person?" He was lying on his back on his single bed in our three-man room, his large ogre-bulk covered by his very own baby-blue pajamas. Manfred was on the other side of me in his own bed, lying on his back under the covers.

"Vell, Mark, vere you born *mit* da pajamas? Vat makes *dat* zo normal?" Manfred's accent had become thicker in his tired and inebriated condition.

"Yeah, Mark. What the fuck are you talking about? Quit being such a damn puritan!"

Manfred warmed to the theme. "*Ja*, I haf noticed dat Americans tend to haf a very varped morality."

Mark would have none of it. "Aw, I don't want to hear any of that sing-a-long new-age bullshit! You guys are nothin' but a bunch of hippie queers! You didn't even get any whores!"

"Hey, just 'cause we're long-hairs doesn't make us queers. And we didn't get any whores 'cause *we don't have to pay for it*! Ha ha ha ha ha."

"*Ja*, Mark, *und* ve don't haf to wear da pajamas, either," Manfred chortled.

"Least ways I didn't get locked up."

"I was getting *your* money, ass!"

"H E E – H A W!"

Hoping to get Mark on his side so he might not snore so much, I stripped off my boxers below the sheets and gleefully threw them high into the air. They arched overhead, landing on the foot of Mark's bed.

"Ugh!" He kicked the underwear onto the floor disgustedly. "Buncha hippie queers!" Just as planned, he rolled over on his side, turning away from us. Finally we found sleep, Mark's ogre-snores drifting with great volume into the hot Mexican night.

Day Two

I awoke to a strange noise, something weird and unidentifiable. It was a wet, gurgling sound, nearby, something dripping, something draining ... I sat up, looked around alertly. Manfred was sleeping peacefully, his back toward me. On the other side I saw Mark, and the mystery resolved itself. His sinuses, or bronchial ... something in there. I really didn't want to know.

Mark smoked about two packs a day, sometimes more, and he was not a healthy man. At times of rest, his charcoal deposits would come loose from their respiratory moorings and start moving around in there. This, in addition to the snoring, caused a great upheaval lasting several minutes, with several different phases of hacking, coughing, snorting, and spitting.

I took the first shower. When I emerged, Manfred was lying awake in bed, watching the Box in Spanish. Mark was out in the hallway, alternating between deep drags on a cigarette, hits on his albuterol inhaler, and wet, wracking coughs. Soon he came in, still in his PJs. "It's your turn in the shower," I said. "Are you okay?"

"Oh, yeah. I just have, uh, a little cold …" He pressed one finger along the side of his nose and noisily blew a stream of snot out the other nostril, onto the carpet in front of the door. I quickly danced aside, saving my bare feet from the spray. It was like the Dog House, but then, that was why we always wore shoes in there. Manfred and I both protested loudly.

"*Nein! Dass ist Sheisse!*"

"That's sick, man. Do it over there, in the corner, or in the sink or something. Not in the middle of the floor. Jesus."

Mark shrugged and retreated into the bathroom, suppressing more hacking coughs.

From his bed, Manfred said, "Is he really okay?"

I shrugged. "Probably not. I don't know. He does this every morning, coughs up a lung. And the snot-rockets."

"*Sheisse*," he muttered.

I dressed and went down for breakfast.

The Hotel La Reforma is known for its twenty-four hour-a-day restaurant and bar. The staff will send up beer at four in the morning, no questions asked. The bar was even willing to flag down street-walking hookers for its patrons. With an impulsive early-morning phone call down to the bar, and the right phrasing, up would come an impromptu whore with your beer. That level of service is difficult to find in American hotels.

The restaurant, however, is not known for its food. I was working on my second sour, watery coffee when Manfred and Mark arrived. Mark's coughing had subsided, he having applied the proper amount of soothing tar to his scarred and battered lungs. We ordered *huevos rancheros*. The eggs were runny. Instead of proper orange juice, we received sickly-sweet yellow sugar-water, Sunny D or whatever, in small five-ounce glasses.

Mark attempted to order bacon. "Do you … uh, *quiero la tocina*, uh, uh … *crispy*?" He spread his fingers out hopefully, from a central position to either side, in what he hoped would suffice as the international sign for "crispy." None of us knew the Spanish word. When the bacon came, it was only half-cooked, and Mark would have none of it. The bill came to over two hundred and fifty pesos. Manfred was forced into duty explaining the Ogre's dissatisfaction with *la tocino*, and politely requesting a discount on the egregious bill.

My hands had begun to tremble slightly. I looked over at Mark. "I'm gonna go outside and have a toke. My bag's already packed. Just bring it down when you're done packing and I'll meet y'all outside, ok?"

Mark was distracted, trying to follow Manfred's negotiations in Spanish, and didn't bother even looking at me. "Sure, David." I donned my sunglasses and floppy fishing hat before stepping out onto the bright sidewalk. There, I lit the roach from the evening before and puffed on it as I strolled down to the sunny plaza. I wanted something strong, but the tavern was not open. It was after eleven now, but the damn place was still closed. I walked on through the Sunday morning crowds, trying several more restaurants, but all they had was Carta Blanca and Negro Modelo and Bohemia and Tecate … fucking sangria, no real liquor at all. I asked around at some shops, and was told of a place up the way that served liquor on Sundays. It was evidently not the custom in Nuevo Laredo to serve liquor on Sundays.

I sat down inside the restaurant. Mexican families were everywhere enjoying their after-Mass meal, their happy children swarming all around unattended, running freely about in the manner of children everywhere, the way American children used to. Everyone was so fucking happy, together with their families. I sat alone at my table, there in Nuevo Laredo, still wearing my protective headgear, gritting my teeth with the angst. My waiter approached, and I ordered a whiskey and a *cerveza* Sol, just to avoid any possible withdrawal symptoms. The waiter's eyebrows rose slightly at my order, but he left without comment. He returned with a big tray, which he sat down on a stand. Then he put my whiskey and *cerveza* Sol before me, along with a full plate of guacamole, chips, and two kinds of salsa.

"Oh, no *Señor*, I don't want any food, man. Just the drinks."

"*¿Cómo?*"

"*No quiero la comida, por favór, amigo.*"

"Ah. *Pero es la ley, Señor.*"

"Huh?"

"*Es la ley.*"

"Ahh. Okay. *Todo bien.*"

It's the law. Yessir, and we must respect the law. Cannot come down here and break the laws, take the women for myself, disrespect the land and the people. In this land, they know how to deal with law-breakers. I sat alone at my table nibbling absently on my legal meal as I slurped down my beverages. I ordered a few more. After a while, Mark came in.

"Dammit, David, Manfred's pissed! We've been waitin' on you for an hour! What are you doin'?"

"Just having some lunch, man. Sit down, have a beer with me. How'd you find me here?"

"Only place in Nuevo Laredo that sells liquor on Sunday. I had to ask around, but I knew your habits. Aha ha ha ha ha! Come on, Manfred's waiting at the hotel."

"Oh, ah, alright, okay." I shot my third Wild Turkey and gulped down the rest of my *cerveza* Sol.

* * * * *

As we reached the car, a beggar approached, hobbling up on legs twisted and bent. "Daily civic duty?" I asked.

Manfred smiled. "Only once per day; no more, *und* no less."

I gave the man five pesos. Manfred turned back to me, pointing toward my wallet. "Und five more for making us wait an extra hour today."

Sheepishly, I handed the man another five-peso note. "That some kind of Buddhist thing?"

"No, dude, dat is known as 'sing-a-long new-age bullshit.'"

Mark groaned, and we resumed our long, thousand-mile trek deep into the heart of Mexico. Our road trip was on! I hoped it would not be at all like the first day. But then, we were going into the interior, and Nuevo Laredo is not the interior. We were set to not cease our travels for this day until we had passed by Mexico City and gone nearly one hundred kilometers onward to Puebla. That was our plan.

Sitting there in the back, next to the ice-chest with the beer, I opened a Modelo, grabbed the bottle of rum, and began cutting up a lime with one of my spare knives I had wisely left in reserve at the Hotel La Reforma. "Do you want a beer, Mark?"

"May I make a suggestion?" Manfred interjected. "Why don't we go ahead and do the drinking in rotation. The person in the back – that's currently you, David – he may drink his fill. Meanwhile, the person in the front passenger seat can get ready and sober up from his turn at drinking in the back. The driver will drive. He will not drink. When the driver gets tired of the foolishness of the drunk in the back – or if he gets thirsty, whichever comes first – the driver may then retire to the drinking position in the back, next to the ice chest. *Ja*, with da beer. The drunk guy then moves forward to the passenger side to begin sobering up, and the passenger – now relatively sober – may then go ahead and take his turn at driving. Make sense?"

How very German. "Sounds like you've got it all planned out, Manfred," I said, taking a long pull on my beer. I wiped my knife clean on my shorts and replaced it in my pocket. "So what you're really saying is, you'd like to be the next drunk guy in the back, with the beer." Manfred smiled.

"Hey Manfred. Why do you have to plan everything out, you know?" Mark loudly scratched his scar-covered arm as he talked, and I began to wonder where this comment would take us.

"I do not have to plan everything, Mark," Manfred said in a calm, reasonable tone, his green eyes earnestly wide. "I vas merely making a suggestion for the benefit of the group. Do you have another suggestion?"

"Well, no. I guess not." He sighed loudly. "Yeah, okay. You're right."

I shook my head. The road trip was really on now.

"Damn," I said, sprawled out across the back seat, "can't these people ever finish a building?" We were passing another series of one-story concrete structures standing alone in the bleak desert, mere shells with iron rebar sticking out all around like twisted antennae. Ever-present signs for the two main political parties in Mexico loudly battled it out on the walls of the buildings, the slogans and party initials sloppily painted on each neighboring incomplete structure:

PAN PAN PAN

PRI PRI PRI

"This place looks like Sarajevo," I said. "Do people really live in there?"

Manfred turned to me, "You know why most of the buildings are unfinished in Mexico? Because the tax cannot be collected on a property while construction is still ongoing."

"Oh, so you mean …"

"That's right. Except for exempt organizations – churches, government buildings, the like – and rich folk, of course – no one finishes their building. And when the tax man comes around, they say 'Sorry! We're still working on the place.' And they pay no tax."

"It sure looks ugly."

"No time for aesthetics when your concern is food on the table."

"No, I guess not."

We moved swiftly through the brush-country, making good time. The vista stretched far and away to distant brown mountains, which rose up to a dry blue sky, itself filled only with thin wisps of useless clouds and a brutal solar orb burning away unremittingly. Back on the sun-seared earth, giant cacti were in abundance, randomly dotting the broad, dusty landscape. Sometimes peasants loped by on foot or pedaled the occasional bicycle, but always well off to the side. We were on one of the new Mexican toll roads – called *cuotas* – which were just as good as most interstate highways stateside. We only had to watch for *federales* lying in wait for speeders. When we passed one, though, they never seemed very concerned with our excessive speed, and just watched us stream by.

On the old roads throughout the Mexican interior, travel was far slower. Livestock and peasants would often crowd the road unexpectedly, and huge, erratically-placed speed-bumps called *topes* would suddenly rise up out of the pavement to destroy one's undercarriage. But not so on these new NAFTA-procured toll roads. We sailed along the *cuota* in our big pearl-white Buick LeSabre, drinking *cerveza* Modelo, riding through the desert like sheiks in the cool air-conditioning. Mark lit another cigarette, his fourth in the last hour.

"Are you smoking again, Mark?" Manfred asked.

"Isn't this a non-smoking rental?" I asked.

"Aww, hell guys, I'm not smokin' that much." He coughed loudly, only somewhat blocking the spray from his mouth with his closed ham-fist.

We passed the exits for Monterrey, the largest industrial center in northern Mexico, bustling, crowded and smoggy, and for Saltillo, a sleepy little frontier town by comparison, filled with peaceful, tree-lined plazas and towering statues of Mexican priests and generals. And then we moved further south, into the big mountains. Up we drove, the road bending sharply with the landscape. Manfred handled the unwieldy Buick like a professional, keeping his speed around the curves. Mark chain-smoked nervously in his seat, his knuckles white with fear.

Soon the mountains leveled off before us, the landscape turning to pure sandy desert, harsh and unforgiving. I could see for many miles into the hazy wasteland, surveying the mirages shimmering up like half-forgotten dreams, and gnarly brush of a type not found in Texas. Up ahead on the opposite side of the divided *cuota* we saw several military vehicles, Humvees and larger troop trucks, and many soldiers armed with rifles, staggered about. The olive-clad soldiers were all small and very dark-skinned. They appeared to be stopping and inspecting north-bound traffic.

"A military checkpoint, manned by the Mexican army," said Manfred. "Ve shouldn't hit many going south, but on our way back ... They don't much care about contraband coming in from the States. It's the people going back to the north which are the concern of the Mexican government."

"You mean the concern of *our* government?"

"*Ja genau*, who do you think is funding all these checkpoints? It's *our* Drug War which spawns all this," he said, waving his hand at the receding checkpoint. "Are you getting hungry?"

"Uh yeah, hey! Let's stop and get some food. Maybe give the car a break. Get some gas, you know?" Mark was firm and adamant.

"Vell, Mark, we don't yet need gas, and the car's fine. But we could stop for some lunch."

"Yes," I said from the back. "I could eat."

So we pulled off at a roadside *comida*, little more than a shanty truck-stop in the empty desert. Lining the entire exterior of the building were thin sheet-metal panels imprinted with the red-lettered Tecate beer logo all around, the Mexican *aquila* emblazoned boldly in black above the words:

TECATE TECATE TECATE TECATE

The scrappy-looking advertising was apparently doing double duty as construction material. Old tires were piled up all around the place. I stayed in the Buick for a moment to finish my Modelo, staring at a rusty Tecate logo as I slurped down the last of the beer. Seeing the beer logo brought unpleasant memories to my mind. Tecate was really not my favorite beer.

Outside, the still desert air was hot and dry. I sat down at our table, looking at Manfred. "Did you already order? What are we having?"

"That guy said he would take care of us," he said, pointing to a bent-over old man behind the counter. Long strips of flypaper hung from the ceiling all around, completely covered with dead insects. Other patrons, mostly truck drivers, ate at the tables. The old man hobbled over, smiling, and we ordered two Cokes and an orange Fanta for Mark. I bummed one of Mark's cigarettes.

The food came, a large oval plate of steaming fajita meat, fresh corn tortillas, goat cheese, and several sauces. We were pleased. It was delicious. We ate most of it, but could not finish. As I chewed on the tender meats, my mind wandered. I began again to think thoughts better left submerged. The old man hobbled over once more, smiling with our bill, which came to three hundred and seventy pesos.

"What?" I snapped. "That's like, almost forty bucks, man! This meal wouldn't have cost but half that in the States!"

"*Vell*, it vas a learning experience. I guess the old man really did 'take care of us.'"

"Hey, at least the food was good. You know? What d'ya think, David?"

"I'm sick of these trick-ass scams, man!" I snarled, smacking down my share of the pesos, and stalked out to the Buick.

It was locked. I sat out in the desert, sweating in the scorching sun. The sweat dried almost as soon as it had formed on my skin. I sat there morosely watching the heat radiate off the hot rubber tires scattered about the sandy parking lot. Every now and then I would grudgingly glance at a Tecate sign. Finally, Manfred and Mark came out from the roadhouse. Without a word, we took our seats and sped off down the *cuota*.

I was angry, gritting my teeth in the backseat. My irrational outburst had been set off by the overpriced meal, but of course that was not the actual problem. I tried to relax, breathe deep, give a moment's thought as to what was really bothering me. The madness of the night before should be cause enough, but I knew that was not it. I had been lucky there, and I knew it. But in another regard I was not lucky, and I knew that as well.

I still had this albatross around my neck, this married woman conundrum. I knew that she had lied, that this affair was ill-advised, but I could not so easily change my heart. I was not merely trying to dally with another man's wife. I loved her, I knew, and I wanted to make her mine.

She would be in Oaxaca. She would e-mail me. We could do this. I had to believe. I had to try. I had to try to see her.

It would be an omen if we could pull it off. An omen is what we needed. How else to make the hopeless thing work?

* * * * *

As the Buick continued through the arid lands of central Mexico, I sat in the back seat, by the ice-chest with the beer, gritting my teeth with the angst. I looked at my friends up front, excited with the journey. I sighed softly, shook my head, and took another beer from the ice-chest. I breathed in, out, deeply, relaxing, resolving to think no more of it, to simply enjoy my vacation, to enjoy my time with my boys.

Up front, Mark was pointing with his sausage-finger. "See, there it is, Manfred, the Tropic of Cancer. Everything south of here is officially Central America." We had just passed under a bright green sign proclaiming the boundary.

"Vell, I did not know that, Mr. Hanson. I always thought it began in Guatemala."

"No, right here!" He turned around and fixed me with an Ogre-grin. "Hey David, you're in Central America!"

Indeed, we were entering the verdant interior of Mexico. Soon the land began to rise, up into the central highlands, the desert heat dropping off as we gained elevation. Manfred pulled off for another Pemex, and to let Mark take his turn at the wheel.

"Are all the gas stations in Mexico Pemex?"

"*Ja*, most of them. State-owned industry."

In the manner of men, Manfred and Mark pretended I had not snapped at them for no reason whatsoever and then silently ignored them from the back seat, apparently in a funk for several hours. We were all good friends. All was back to normal. Then Mark took the wheel.

The road was not particularly curvy, nor the traffic especially heavy, but Mark drove the Buick as if he were Jeff Gordon on bad crack. He was only going eighty kilometers-per-hour or so. Manfred had at times gone nearly twice that speed and the ride had been mellow, as smooth as a baby's crib-swing. Now, both Manfred and I began to sweat in the air-conditioning, our fists clenched.

"Jesus! What are you doing to the brakes, Mark?"

"Sorry, David! I just hit them! There's a truck up there!"

"I see the fucking truck, man! It's like, a hundred meters or whatever. And don't *hit* the brakes, just push into the pedal slowly and gently. This is a GM car, after all. How long have you had your driving license?"

"Hey, sorry, man! I'm doing the best I can here," he said as he swerved sickeningly to one side and then the other, passing a Volkswagen bus with manic, jerking motions. The maneuver should have been routine.

Manfred and I put up with the automotive madness for a long, grim, silent hour, our nausea building. The brakes squeaked with every sudden, needless deceleration. I had visions of the Buick rolling, side over side, down the *cuota*, for no good reason at all. We weren't even making good time. Finally, I spotted a gas station. "Hey, hey Mark, pull over up here, at the Pemex, man. Yeah. That's it, easy does it. We need ice. We're almost out, right Manfred?"

"*Ja ja*, the ice is really running low!"

I went in the station, paid for a bag of ice, came out and handed it to Mark, who was smoking next to the car. "Could you put that in the chest, man? And, ah, could I have a turn at driving? It's been two days and I haven't had a turn yet. Mark handed me the keys and then dealt with the ice, spilling a good portion of it onto the pavement.

Back on the road, Manfred looked at me, smiling. "Decided to haf a go at it, *nicht*?"

I smiled back, nodded. Mark sat behind us, oblivious. He opened a beer, relaxing. Higher into the mountains we went.

I am not normally a vindictive person. This time, though, I decided to enjoy myself and have a little fun with Mark at the same time. Each turn was sharper than the last, and the slope grew steeper with every mile. Deep canyons and sheer cliffs beckoned far below. I took every turn at the highest possible speed, seeking out that edge I knew so well.

"This boat of a Buick sure handles sluggishly, huh Manfred?" I could barely keep a straight face. The tires squealed ever-so-slightly as I pushed the tired American sedan around another fishhook turn. I chuckled under my breath and slammed down the gas pedal on the straightaway, passing a chicken-bus like it was standing still.

"*Ja ja*, she handles like a slow boat, alright."

"Hey! Hey guys … Could you please …" Manfred and I were quietly cracking up, giggling, faces turned away from Mark. "Hey! Could you please slow it down a little fucking bit?" We could hear his breathing, fast and labored, coming in great hyperventilating gasps.

Manfred said, "Oh! You want us to slow it down? But we're making such good time!"

"Yeah, Mark. We have to keep to schedule. What exactly is the problem?"

"The problem is … when the tires squeal like that, it means you're going too fast, is the problem!"

Manfred turned his calm gaze back toward Mark. "Mark, the reason those tires are squealing is because they are a low grade of tire on a low-grade American car. If we were in a Mercedes, there would be no squealing."

"What kind of tires are they, Manfred?" I asked, jerking the car to the left around another hairpin. Mark lit another cigarette.

"Well, David. *Diese hier* are *dose dier* Firestone tires."

We could hold it in no longer. We burst out laughing. Mark just continued smoking in the back.

I continued driving like a New Yorker for several more hours, making good time. The desert had completely given way to the rich highland landscape of central Mexico. Although the land was still relatively arid, the ranches were getting closer together, and the land began to host an increasing number of farms and villages, all seemingly thriving in the Mediterranean climate of the rugged hills. An old Indian farmer drove his burro along the side of the *cuota*. He waved at us as we passed. The sky was sharp and clear, pale blue against the rich greens and browns of the hills and higher mountains before us. "These places sort of remind me of parts of Spain," said Manfred.

"Yeah," I agreed. "Or maybe Tuscany, thereabouts."

"Oh? When were you there?"

"After high school I went around southern Europe for a few months."

We continued admiring the increasingly fertile landscape for a while. Mark remained silent, chain smoking behind me. After a while longer I became aware of a crick in my back. I looked around, shifting in my seat, realizing the chair was somehow askew. Mark had his knees pressed tensely against my back. "Mark, what did you … You, you *broke the seat*, man! *How in the hell …?*"

"No!" he roared. "What are you…I didn't…how would I have broken the seat, David?"

"Exactly the question! How did your ogre-ass do it, exactly? Manfred, how was the seat when you last drove?"

"The seat was fine."

"See! *You*, Mark! *You* broke the seat, ass!"

Mark Hanson truly was an ogre. As I sat there in front of him, I wondered about the next nine days. I wondered at the wisdom of egging him on so. Prior to the trip, the longest I had spent with him was only a day or two at a time. He was normally a fairly cool character, but he had been known to suddenly snap, usually with the massive application of alcohol or other substances, conditions I fully expected on this road-trip. I had heard vague reports of strange incidents from those who had traveled far with him in times past … aberrant, near-medieval on-the-road behavior … the consideration of which was not at all to mention his normal San Antonio antics.

Once, a big group of us had been out at the single-wide, drinking my home-brewed beer. Mark had brought his own bottle of Wild Turkey. As the party spun further out of control, we had all noticed his absence. How and when he slipped away, no one could say. Later, around two in the morning, we heard the loud motor of my chainsaw crank up and begin to buzz away. Out the door we scrambled, and there he was, the Ogre, but somehow different, somehow *changed*, chainsaw in hand, "Aha ha ha ha ha!" came the cackle, the chain biting ever-deeper into an old dead pecan tree in my front yard, wood chips flying like shrapnel.

Fortunately, my few rural neighbors were used to unannounced bursts of controlled gunfire from the woods behind my trailer, as well as loud, drunken yelling in the wee hours of the morning, but still, this was a bit much. After the tree was sundered twain, falling with a branch-breaking crash, the chainsaw mercifully sputtered to silence, and the Ogre lumbered back across the yard to the single-wide as if nothing were untoward. He put the chainsaw down next to my deer skull, swiped some sawdust off his mottled forearms, came through the door, and said, "Hey! Hey, David! Enough of that damn whiskey. Can I, uh, get one of your home-brews?" Silently, I handed him a beer.

Then there was the time he and our big African-American friend H-Bomb had gotten into a game of fisticuffs outside the Dog House. Some little argument flaring out of control, Mark Hanson and the Hube, our big black friend, the Black Ogre. They were riled up, and out came the maddened ham-fists, their huge bodies flying around, the krakens unleashed. The rest of us were all ducking and rolling aside, trying to get out of the way, no one daring to try to break up the fight; that would have been suicide. No, we let them fight that one out. Most fights actually only last a handful of seconds, but this went on for several minutes – minutes of punishment for both ogres. But they both took it. They gave and gave, and they took it. Finally, they were just too tired, too thirsty. Someone handed each of the bloodied pair a fresh Lone Star, and the fight was officially over. Afterward, I walked around and replaced a dozen or so divots on the Hansons' lawn.

Yes, Mark Hanson was an ogre. But he sometimes morphed into something else. There were times when the Ogre lost all control, becoming transmogrified into a terrible were-beast, something out of the very old, grimly-told tales of the darkest myths. The phenomenon rarely occurred, but when it did, you knew it. You knew it, and you never forgot afterward. Sitting there in front of Mark, driving the Buick LeSabre through the green mountains of central Mexico, I did not forget it.

* * * * *

Later that afternoon, I pulled off at another Pemex about a hundred kilometers north of the Distrito Federál – the administrative district around Mexico City, the largest city in the world. We were deep into the interior now. The further south we traveled, the more surreal my surroundings seemed to become, ever more disconnected from any memory of that foggy existence way back in Texas.

"Manfred, you want to drive the last couple of hours? We only have a couple of hundred kilometers to go until Puebla. These mountains can wear a man out."

"Sure David. I don't mind driving the last shift." I sat in my old place by the ice-chest with the beer, letting Mark move up into the passenger seat. He was happy to stretch his legs. Manfred passed back an atlas, two maps, and a guidebook we had brought. "David, would you care to navigate our way around the city while I drive? And Mr. Hanson here can relax."

"Yeah! Jesus, you drive like a maniac, David!"

"Just relax, man. ... I think we should avoid driving through the heart of the city. We should be able to find a loop around it. This atlas shows one coming up."

"*Ja*, sounds *gut*. Just tell me when we get to the exit."

But we never did. Traffic became thicker as we moved closer to the DF, the road becoming clogged with multicolored VW Beetles and huge trucks belching great streams of black fumes into the sky. The road signs were not in normal Spanish, but in some strange Aztecan Nahuatl dialect I could barely decipher.

We were starting-and-stopping, moving along at a fair crawl of fifteen kilometers-per-hour or so in the traffic. The air had grown feted, dark and heavy with foul pollution. Large hills rose to all sides, covered with strange lean-to contraptions thrown together from a marvelously wide array of colorful materials. Corrugated aluminum siding, wood scraps, cardboard, irregular concrete pieces, brightly colored cloth - anything and everything was utilized to create shelter in these sprawling shanty-towns. Not a single tree or a blade of grass remained. Just miles and miles of hills covered with destitute human beings trying to get as close as possible to the heart of the action.

I looked around at the traffic. Many of the cars were new, most late model Volkswagens. To my left, an attractive, made-up woman in a shiny Jetta chatted on her cell phone, looking like any first-world urbanite inanely conversing with a piece of black plastic.

To the right I saw … "Ah, Jesus. Look at that!" A huge mound of murky refuse had grown up there next to the highway, hundreds of feet high, as high as any of its neighboring hills. Scores of people swarmed about it, climbing up, bending over, pulling things out, looking like ants in the distance. "*What are they doing*?"

"Scavengers," Manfred replied. "Looking for food, or building materials. Anything." We were silent for a while after that, shocked by such profound poverty. As we moved further into the northern areas of the city, Wal-Marts and McDonalds and other solid emblems of global capital came into view. I turned in my seat, looking back once more at the gargantuan trash mound with people buzzing atop it like flies. I shook my head in dread. We were not in Texas anymore.

As we moved further down into the gigantic fishbowl Valley of Mexico, surrounded by hulking purple volcanoes, the air grew ever more foul, stinking with industrial pollution and the emissions of millions of automobiles creeping all around the city. The air was thick, visible now, a yellow-brown color. It was difficult to breathe, to get a proper lungful. My eyes began to burn.

The city itself seemed alive, enveloping us. We became totally swamped in the traffic of the DF, and I became frantic, looking for information on the various maps at my disposal. But they were almost all pre-NAFTA, and hopelessly out of date; only the guidebook recently purchased by Manfred was at all useful. The only problem with it was that its maps still didn't accurately reflect the spreading, twisted morass of clogged motorways encircling the mega-city.

"This map doesn't even show a loop!" I exclaimed in frustration.

"Well, David, I don't see any loop yet."

"Maybe they tore it down. Or built over it, or whatever. Anyway, if we just stay on the *cuota*, we should be fine, according to this ..."

I gave the guidebook a closer inspection. I flipped through it, looking up the section about Oaxaca, our eventual destination. I read, began chuckling. "Listen to this: 'Some find the Oaxacan specialties shocking at first – spicy fried grasshoppers, called *chapulines*.' Hmm. And, 'Zipolite still has a reputation as the place to zone out on various illegal substances,' as it is 'where hippie holdovers once spent weeks and months camping on the sand.' That sounds good, right? We should go there."

"Yeah, David, I told ya you aint nothin' but a damn dirty hippie. Aha ha ha ha ha!"

"Mark, you know, you're right … but at least now I've found me a damn hippie guide book!"

Manfred intervened. "David, the amusement is all well and fine, but we are now in da city. Could you please tend to the navigation? And please don't talk about da food."

"Man, Manfred, that's what I was doing. I was just familiarizing myself with the text! And that's not food. Those were grasshoppers, man."

"Okay, *gut*, David. Now could you find out in that there Hippie Book where to go now that we are in the city?"

It was our first taste of the madness of the Mexican megalopolis. We drove around in that smoggy, overcrowded chaos for nearly three hours, dodging the swarms of Volkswagens, searching for a *cuota* through or around the city, bewildered if not entirely lost. Usually we were headed in the proper direction, but moving much too slowly. We were no longer making good time. The Hippie Book was little help, stating only that in Mexico City one should avoid being kidnapped or robbed or worse, as many of the locals prey on relatively wealthy gringo tourists. Great. Yeah, we'll try to avoid getting killed while we slowly suffocate. My eyes burned still.

We finally found that there was no *cuota* loop, no freeway, just millions of drivers attempting to navigate an overgrown morass of surface streets, an urban automotive nightmare. It was the five-hour-long rush hour. Everything moved along with a jerking, start-and-stop rhythm, going nowhere fast, honking VWs all around. Even Los Angeles had better traffic.

* * * * *

Just when we thought the city endless, we saw greenspace. As we approached, it became clear that it was a huge park filled with trees and grassy fields, an urban oasis. A stately stone building rose majestically from a hilltop at the center of the green island.

"Look at that," I said, pointing to the large, light-colored castle looming above us. "Let's stop for a minute. Stretch our legs. Maybe have a little puff? … And perhaps we can get our bearings from the top of that hill."

Manfred pulled the Buick to the side of the road. "*Ja*, a break vouldn't hurt at dis point."

I consulted the inadequate maps and the Hippie Book to triangulate our location. "That building is Chapultepec Castle, and the park is also called Chapultepec."

"Cha-pult-e-pec." Mark repeated slowly to no one in particular.

We locked the Buick and walked through the trees for a moment before finding a spot in the shade of large tree. A few people strolled by on the path about fifty yards away, but the place was otherwise quite secluded, the sounds of the city only a faint hum. We stood under the tree, breathing deeply and stretching. I fashioned a clip from a twig and lit the dwindling roach, passing it to Mark after a couple of quick hits.

Mark lifted his head and slowly released a billowing mushroom cloud into the air above us, the smoke mingling with the leaves. "Cha-pult-e-pec," he said again, staring absently at the castle.

"Like the jazz club in Denver!" he exclaimed.

"Well, no … what?"

"Yeah, there's a place in Denver called *El Chapultepec*, the grasshopper. Like *chapulines*, I guess. It's famous. It's the only Meskin jazz club I ever heard of. I used to go there a bunch when I was working that roughneck job."

Manfred and I exchanged glances. Now Manfred exhaled slowly. "I thought you didn't like jazz, Mark."

"I don't, but it was close to the place I was renting, and they had the cheapest drinks in town. Plus, there were always girls in there even though it wasn't, you know, fancy. 'Cause they always had live music."

"So jazz and Mexican food, huh? I can dig it."

"Yeah, David. I told you about this place before. This is the place where the owner told me that Jack Kerouac used to get high in the parking lot and then spend the evening listening to jazz in the club. They let him drink for free. You know, back in the day."

"Oh yeah. Cool."

"Ja. So David, this is why you are a writer, no? Because if you ever write something worth reading, you will get to drink for free."

"Aha ha ha ha ha!"

"And listen to jazz?"

Manfred handed me the roach. "De perks of being a writer. *Und* I know how much you like jazz. Da first uniquely American art form, as you always say."

I took the last hit. Manfred produced a small plastic bag holding two small green buds.

"Where'd you get that?!"

"I brought it across the border from home."

"What?!"

"Aha ha ha ha ha!"

"That's pretty risky, man. Surprisingly risky *for you*, don't you think?"

"Vell, David, not in this instance. In this instance, I have eliminated the risk."

"*Eliminated* it? Pray tell, how does one eliminate the risk of getting caught bringing contraband across an international border?"

"Well, I know that we are far less likely to get searched going south, so that lowers the risk. Then I apply a method for transporting the smoke that both conceals it very well and ensures I can dispose of it during a search before anyone can find it."

"Awww, man, that's sick!"

"Was … was that smoke *in your ass*, man?"

"No. Of course not, David. … Did you notice that I was eating sunflower seeds when we crossed da border?"

"Yeah, I did."

Manfred removed one of the buds from the baggie and began breaking it up. "I put these buds in my mouth, in my cheeks, with the seeds. If Mister Border Inspector notices a bulge in my cheeks, it is obviously attributable to the seeds. And there is no smell because the buds are all wet with saliva. But if any sort of trouble arises, if necessary I can make a show of spitting out the seeds in my mouth – thus rendering my mouth empty from the inspector's perspective – while I swallow the buds. And I have thereby eliminated any real risk of being caught."

Mark and I looked at each other with pure wonder. "And then you just dry out the buds, after?"

"Exactly. The saliva does not break down the buds if they are only in the mouth for a little while. And the cannabis is not water-soluble, so no potency is lost. You just have to let the bud dry off for an hour or so."

"You're a fucking genius, man. A certifiable weed genius."

"Thank you, David. Of course the method is limited in the amount one can carry, but it should be a sufficient supply to hold us over until we get further south." Manfred finished rolling the fresh joint and put it back in the sack with the other bud. "Let's save this one for after we get out of da city."

"It's like my boy Bill Hicks says, 'There's a war against people on drugs, and the people on drugs are winning.'"

"Aha ha ha ha ha!"

"Well, a few of us are," Manfred said with a wink.

I looked around, noticing the trees closely for the first time, the mottled patterns on the rough bark, the flashing of the sunlight off the leaves quivering in the breeze, a green blur above us. I was surrounded by woody green life, and I felt my consciousness merging with the forest, my breathing becoming part of the slowly vibrating pattern of the living Earth.

Mark brought me back to the present. "Hey, let's go check out the castle real quick!"

We walked up the hill to a grand, triple-arched entrance made of huge stone slabs, with a large glittering crystal chandelier in the foyer. I was captivated by the light playing off the many cuts in the stones, flashing like a classical disco ball. *Chapultepec* did indeed mean grasshopper in the Nahuatl language of the Aztecs, and the castle was now the National History Museum. It was built in the late 1700s by the Spanish Viceroy of New Spain, as his official residence. From there, the Viceroy had ruled over Mexico, Central America, most of the Caribbean, and all of the United States west of the Mississippi except for the Oregon Territory – a fittingly large empire for such a beautiful palace. The site was sacred to the conquered Aztecs and was chosen for its expansive views of the Valley of Mexico.

Later, Emperor Maximilian the First ruled the Second Mexican Empire from the castle. That was after the end of Spanish rule and after the Americans had reduced Mexico's size by more than half, surging across the continent and seizing everything in the north from Texas to California. Maximilian himself was a Vienna-born Hapsburg, installed as the puppet of Napoleon, who was eager to re-assert French influence in North America and gain access to Mexico's vast silver and gold resources to fuel his European war machine. Maximilian's imperial rule was supported by the *hacendados*, Mexico's European land-owning elite, and was marked by constant civil war. Maximilian I was a classically wicked ruler, issuing the *Black Decree*, which condemned more than 11 thousand resistance fighters to death without trial and fanned the flames of hatred and war.

But, once again, the United States stepped in and altered Mexican history, turning its attention southward after the end of its own civil war. President Lincoln had been unable to help, lamenting the European powers' domination of Mexico helplessly as he sent his armies to subdue the South. But after that national disaster, President Buchanan seized the peacetime opportunity to implement the Monroe Doctrine for the first time, lending support to the Republican forces of President Benito Juárez, and ordering Napoleon to remove all French forces from Mexico in accordance with America's own imperial decree proclaiming dominion over the entire Western Hemisphere.

In classical French fashion, Napoleon promptly abandoned Mexico in the face of the American threat. The Republican forces laid siege to Mexico City after a string of victories throughout the east. Maximilian fled to Quértaro, where he was again surrounded. He attempted to escape through enemy lines, but was caught and summarily executed with a handful of his top generals, decisively ending the monarchy and direct European influence in Mexico. That was the last time Chapultepec Castle was used as the residence of a ruler, the only royal palace in North America ever to be used as the actual home of a sovereign.

The building itself was a neo-gothic marvel, looking every bit like a modern imperial palace, from the classic courtyard garden and fountain to the circular turret atop the building flying the *tricolor*. Much of the main floor was open-air in the Roman style, with a patio that stretched the entire length of the palace and looked out over the city's downtown area, the glass-and-steel skyscrapers contrasting sharply with the surrounding old stone buildings, all standing above the tree-tops of Chapultepec Park in the foreground, the jagged mountains in the background. The view was magnificent.

The floors were covered with large marble tiles set in a black-and-white checkered pattern, still in perfect condition. The rooms were dominated by large marble pillars supporting high gilded ceilings and grandly arched doorways. I could not have imagined a better setting for the many exhibits on Mexican history, from the time of the ancients all the way up to World War II. The boys had to practically drag me out of the place, as I had lost all track of time and become engrossed in the exhibits as the afternoon wore on.

* * * * *

We returned to the road and to the now-familiar gridlock and heavy air. We continued our slow crawl through the city, growing weary and hungry, and before long we were like three old menopausal women snapping at each other bitterly with every mile. It was well into the night now, and we were all exhausted, nerves raw. "Okay, man," I said after we had finally fought our way to the eastern edge of the DF, "Just pull over up there, here! Look, a taco place, a *comida*! Just pull off here, to the right. Plus, we could all use a few beers. And the *baños*."

"I don't know," said Manfred. "I do not trust the sanitary condition of most of these roadside *comidas*."

"No! I'm hungry now!" Mark said. The Ogre needed to feed. Indeed, we were all hungry, hungry and tired. We pulled off onto the service road and parked in front of the open-faced *comida*. We got out, and Manfred left the car running. "Just in case we need to make a quick getaway," he said as he locked the doors with the key-remote. It was not a nice part of town, but then, aside from the park, we had not seen any nice parts. We went in to find three lean young men sitting about in tattered jeans and grimy white tank tops, lazily nursing beers. Manfred began negotiations in Spanish with the old woman who ran the place, Mark by his side. I went for the toilets, in the back.

When I emerged a minute later, Manfred and Mark were holding three *cervezas* Indio. Mark was handing the woman some pesos.

"Hey, man. Where you from?" The question was more of an accusation, coming from a Mexican man sitting next to me. His eyelids were heavy across his closed, hostile face, his black hair was long and thick, bound behind his head.

"Uh…" I knew the Buick's plates had already given us away. "Texas. We're from Texas."

He looked over at another fellow sitting slouched in a wooden chair. They exchanged glances. I saw them both sit up a little straighter. I also noticed that the number of lean, hungry young men in the place had suddenly doubled, with newcomers arriving off the dingy sidewalk, also wearing dirty wife-beaters and chain wallets. All the men were muttering, eyeing us darkly and with purposeful intent.

Moving smoothly but quickly, I strode up to Manfred and grabbed an Indio. "These paid for?" I asked.

"Yes, but I don't think I vant to eat here. The sanitary…"

"Good, let's go. We're getting cased. Mark! Eyes up." We moved quickly to the waiting car with many eyes following us. The young bucks were all moving toward us now in a murmuring mob. Manfred unlocked the doors with the remote just as we arrived. I monitored the approach of the malevolent posse while the boys got in, then slammed my door shut behind me. I heard the locks click as we sped off, our tires spinning in the dirt.

Mark turned around. "What the hell…"

"Here." I passed up one of my knives, clutching another and the pepper-spray as well. "We shouldn't leave that machete in the trunk!"

"Dude, *dat vas close!* Maybe we should wait to eat until ve are out of *diese hier* damn city."

"Yeah, I think you're right." I opened the Hippie Book, its vague warning prescient. "Alright. Just keep going this way – it's east – and eventually we'll get out of the city. We'll find a way to Puebla from there. And some food!"

An hour and many ragged kilometers later we finally found the *cuota* for Puebla. We were exhausted, hungry, and thirsty again. We had slammed our beers quickly, trying to soften the adrenaline shot with the alcohol.

Finally, well out of town and into the mountains east of the DF, we saw a truck-stop. They only had white-bread sandwiches packed in cellophane, which proved to be soggy and tasteless, but by that time we were hungry enough to eat a sandwich from a gas station. Fortunately, we were able to wash them down with a six-pack of *cerveza* Modelo.

I took the wheel, as Manfred was far too weary to drive.

"The woman at the truck-stop said ve should stop ahead, little place called San Martín. Good lodging there, no crime. A quiet little place."

We soon found the exit. I drove through the city streets, bottoming out on *tope* after *tope*, ignoring the disparaging comments from Manfred and Mark, at last finding the recommended hotel, the San Miguél. We paid for the rooms, sticking Mark in his own so he could snore and hack and wheeze and smoke in contented ogre-peace. That day we had driven almost seven hundred miles; over one thousand kilometers. I was asleep just as my head hit the pillow.

Day Three

Sunlight streamed in brightly through the open window, filling the room and waking me. Manfred lay in the other bed, snoring softly. A light breeze blew in sweet, cool mountain air, and birds chirped from the trees outside. I took my time showering.

"Good morning, David," Manfred said when I emerged from the *baño*, toweling off. "How did you sleep?"

"I'm not really sure I remember, exactly."

"Sounds like you slept well, then."

"Yes, I think that's a safe assumption." I dressed and packed my bags, leaving them on the unmade bed. "Your turn in the shower, man. I'm going to see about some chow, and, uh, check on Mark."

Manfred grinned. "Yes, I'll see you out there." I went out into the hall, passing Mark's room. Loud coughing could be heard inside. I let him be, walking on, shaking my head. Down at the end of the hall by the stairs was a little *comida*, a smiling young lady busy inside. I sat at one of the tables, the only patron.

"*Buenas dias. ¿Quieres café?*"

"*Sí, muchas gracias, con leche, por favór.*" The *comidarilla* poured the coffee with a pretty smile. It was local blend, quite flavorful. The juice I requested was squeezed before my eyes, and poured into a tall glass. It was pulpy and fresh, surely full of needed vitamins. I ordered from the menu, not sure what was coming but not at all worried either. Soon the food arrived and I dug in to my plate of eggs with cheese and peppers, crispy bacon on the side. Everything was well-prepared and of the highest quality.

Mark bounced in. "Hey David! How's it goin'?"

"Good, man. This food is damn good – the best meal I've had down here yet!" I talked with my mouth full, washing it down with the orange juice. "And get some of this juice. It's the real thing – not that Sunny D crap or whatever."

Mark looked over at the *comidarilla* washing dishes mere yards from us. "Uh, yeah, hey! Hey!" She looked over at Mark. "Yeah, hey! Could I, uh … *quiero,* uh … pancakes? *Stacks*?" He held his hands horizontally, one hovering over the other. "Yeah, and … uh, *tocino* … crispy *tocino*?" Mark signed with his fingers again, squinting up at the woman. "And, uh, orange juice, uh, *de naranja?*" Somehow the women understood, even though I had already deduced her lack of English. She retreated to the kitchen, clearly relieved at the end of the loud Spanglish hand-waving routine.

"Man, Mark," I said through a mouthful of crispy bacon, "We are now there, if you know what I mean. We are *there, man*. You know?"

"No, what do you mean, David?"

"I mean, look around you! We're done with that hole of a place, Mexico City, or *day-effay*, or however you say it. We're in southern Mexico! The interior, man! The people are nice, the air is clean." I took another bite, finishing up. "Food's good!" I grabbed my coffee cup, pointed at Mark with it. "This trip has shifted into another gear." I threw back the rest of my coffee, my *real* coffee.

"Yeah, this is a pretty nice place." The young lady brought Mark his juice and poured me a fresh cup with a smile. "Uh, grassy-ass. ... So, David, when do you think we'll make it to Oaxaca City?"

"Oh, I guess a few hours, I don't know. I need to see the map. I was just trying to get us out of the damn Distrito Federál yesterday."

"Yeah, hey, you did a good job, you know? We almost got rolled in that *comida* place. I would have taken out a few of those little dudes, but I couldn't hold 'em all off, you know?"

"Yeah." I shuddered at the thought of what would have gone down if we hadn't gotten out of there when we did.

"I think Manfred deserves a lot of credit as well, for doing all the driving through that shite."

"Yeah, well, I just was a little, you know, not, uh ... I didn't really like Mexico City."

"That's all right, man. I didn't either."

Manfred strode up, smiling. "Man, this place is nice!"

"You should try the food," I said, pushing my clean plate away.

"And the juice," Mark said.

"And the coffee," I said, waving at the lady again with an upraised hand, smiling. She smiled back, approaching the table, refilling my cup with steaming *café*. Manfred ordered breakfast, then turned back to us and began rolling a cigarette. "You guys ready to head to Oaxaca City after this? I think we can make it in about four hours. We should have no traffic or crime problems on the way according to the maps, which I have been examining."

Mark lit up a cigarette of his own. "Yeah, hey, Manfred, we were just talking about that." He began coughing, and a nearly thirty-second hacking fit ensued. I sipped my coffee and tried not to look at Manfred. "Uh, sorry. Uh, we were just wondering, how long do you think it will take us to get to Oaxaca City?" He looked at Manfred, waiting expectantly for the answer.

Manfred and I did now look at each other, our brows furrowed. I looked away before I cracked.

"You know what, Mark, I think it vill take about four hours."

I had to say something. "Mark, what the fuck? Were you listening to Manfred's story? He just said 'four hours' already! What the fuck are you talking about?"

"Hey, sorry! I just didn't hear him! Jesus!" Just then the bacon came with Mark's stacks. He drenched the pancakes in half a bottle of syrup, but the bacon lacked the charred character he required. He would have none of it, and a second round of loud, slow Spanglish and ham-hand-waving ensued. This time the lady fixed him good, taking the plate back and returning with several pieces of soot-black bacon-charcoal. The Ogre crunched away nonetheless.

* * * * *

"Are you smoking again?" Manfred asked. I had just relieved Mark from his always-terrifying hour at the wheel, and was now making good time southeast through the lush mountains of Oaxaca.

"Yeah, Mark. How many you up to in the last hour?"

"Aww, hell, y'all quit givin' me such a hard time!"

"Ve are just concerned about your health," Manfred said in his most earnest voice.

Mark groaned. "Do we have to go through this again?"

"No, man. I'm sorry. I'll just concentrate on the road," I said, pulling a sharp turn around a slow-moving truck, our tires squealing.

"Yeah, concentrate!" Mark yelled from the back.

The landscape was interminably beautiful, completely unspoiled by development. Once we had passed Puebla it had been smooth sailing all the way through the sparsely settled *Estado de Oaxaca*. We passed several tollbooths on our *cuota* through the mountains, but little else of note except a series of outstanding panorama. Occasionally we stopped for photos, and mid-morning we stood over a lovely vista and passed around Manfred's joint, which we had neglected to smoke in yesterday evening's frantic scramble out of Mexico City. The surreal madness of the previous two days had already receded into the depths of my memory, my mind engrossed with the beautiful country passing by. In a strange way, I felt welcomed, like I belonged there in Oaxaca.

We drove into Oaxaca City early that afternoon. I was tired from driving the *cuota*, but we hadn't wanted Mark to do it, and Manfred had needed a break from pulling heavy duty through Mexico City. The capital city of Oaxaca State strongly resembled many an old world *ciudad,* with its churches, cathedrals, plazas, and sixteenth century Moorish-influenced Spanish architecture. It was set in a broad, winding valley, twin meandering ridges framing it to either side. The conquistadors had found a beautiful land indeed, and they sited their city well. The air was fresh and crisp at that elevation, and everything looked clean and well-tended. The drivers were all polite and quite responsible, handling our large Buick with smiles all around. "These Mexicans don't drive like our Mexicans in San Antonio," I mused. "Or the ones in DF."

"Different tribe," said Manfred.

"So what's the plan, man? Do we eat, then find a hotel? I'm starving!"

"Vell David, don't you think it would be better to go ahead and find ze rooms? That way we can get ready, and enjoy the rest of the day. Have some beers, some tequila ... relax by the pool..."

Mark perked up in back. "The hotel has a pool?"

"Vell, Mark, we just don't know! Okay, okay, let's just park here, it looks like the city center, and we'll walk around to some of the hotels. What does the Hippie Book say?"

The Hippie Book did have a few suggestions, but we ended up – through Manfred's strong haggling skills and his passable Spanish – getting a fair deal at an outstanding location not on the Book's list of recommendations. Moorish-inspired architecture, wrought-iron trellises, arches atop columns – and yes, a pool – left us all pleased at our fortune.

The blue pool shimmered invitingly from the center of the ornate courtyard. The hotel rose up four stories above the courtyard, which was well-stocked with all manner of colorful tropical flowers in wall-mounted brass sconces. I tapped on a wall. It was solid rock, not built-over plaster façade as one would so often find stateside. It was the type of place that in a first-world country would have been exorbitantly costly, but here in the Mexican interior was quite reasonable. The proprietor explained that it had once been the private residence of a wealthy *peninsulare*, but had been recently converted for its current use as a hotel. Indeed, I could well imagine the pampered life of the nobleman there in the opulent setting.

"Mark," intoned Manfred, "I think it would be better if…"

"Yeah, I know. Just give me the single-man room. *'Cause I snore*." He lit up a cigarette. We signed for the rooms and walked back to the car.

"*Und* ve can park the car in an enclosed garage overnight. They said it has a guard," Manfred said, getting behind the wheel.

"Not bad for under a hundred dollars a night."

"Yes, and that's for both rooms." Manfred found the car-lot in an open-air courtyard nearly empty of other cars, just a few blocks from our hotel, although I had not yet found my bearings in the strange but beautiful new city. We walked back with our bags, dropped them off, and went out into the city to find a restaurant.

It was getting on toward late afternoon when we finally settled on a suitable place featuring local cuisine, the exquisite Restaurant Terranova. We ordered *cervezas* Sol all around, with matching tequilas. Mark had some chicken, Manfred the lamb, and I somehow ended up with some type of meat loaf, which did not disappoint. We dined *al fresco*, at a table on the central plaza of the city. While we ate, vendors came at us from all sides, hawking wares of varying quality. We sent them away after a polite inspection, not yet interested in shopping. Then a beggar came. Manfred gave him ten pesos. "Once per day; no more..."

"Yeah, and no less. Daily *fuckin'* civic duty. Aha ha ha ha ha!" Mark cackled, red in the face. He ordered another tequila from the serving boy. "Hey Manfred, what d'ya think about a swim after this? Coupla more beers, then a swim ... you know? That pool looked good. I think there's a bar over there, too. You know what I mean?"

"Yes, Mark; I saw the wet bar. Sounds *gut*. What do you think, David?" Manfred was focused on building consensus within the group, as usual.

"Ahh, well ... I'm just going to go find, ah ... I just want to take a look around, you know. I'll meet you back there in a short while."

"Going to find an Internet café?" Manfred stared at me, his voice trailing upward in a tone clearly intended as condescending.

I glared back. "*Yes*. So fucking what? I just want to check my e-mail, is that alright with you?"

Mark ordered another round of beers from the boy. It began to rain. I glanced at my watch: Five o'clock. Mark broke the silence again. "Hey, guys, let's not brawl, you know? Let's just have a good time. You know what I mean?"

Just then the headwaiter came into view. "You want I can move your table out of the rain, *Señors?* So's yous not get wet? *Bueno*." We all helped him move our drinks and what was left of the food to a nearby table under an awning. At the table next to us sat a young woman reading a book. She was pretty, with olive skin, long black hair, and large almond eyes. She saw us sit down and smiled, showing a set of perfect white teeth, and went back to her book.

Just then another vendor crept up, speaking fast Spanish. Manfred said, "He wants to sell us these things to eat. They are the grasshoppers we read about in the Hippie Book, da *chapulines*. A local delicacy. We should try them." He spoke for a moment more with the peasant vendor. "Plain or spicy?"

Mark would have none of it. "Hell, you guys are crazy! I ain't eatin' no damn crickets!"

"I'll try some of the spicy," I said.

Manfred selected a handful, placing them on the table between us. He paid the vendor. We tried some; they were good, and spicy-hot, a little crunchy.

"*Man*. Oh." Mark looked green, swallowed. "Oh. *Uhh*. You guys are foul!"

"No, you should try them, they're really good," came a feminine voice in an English accent. We all turned our attention to the woman. "I've been down here for days eating them. They're very nutritious."

"Oh?" Manfred asked. "Are you traveling from England?"

The woman smiled. "Yes, London. I'm going all over. I've been in Guatemala, Costa Rica, and South America before that. I'm on a bit of a walkabout. Next is Mexico City."

"*Nein*!"

"Hell no!"

"You don't want to go there!" We protested vigorously in unison.

"And why not?" she asked, surprised.

Manfred began, "It is crowded, and very polluted, and difficult to drive in da city. In addition, we were almost rolled at a roadside *comida*."

"Rolled? What do you mean?"

"Mugged," I said. "I think the technical term would be, 'assaulted and robbed'. You have to be careful there. It's dangerous and some of the locals prey on tourists. It even says so in here." I held the Hippie Book up in the air like a bible.

"Oh, it can't be so bad as all that, now can it?" She was beginning to look worried.

Mark jumped in. "Yeah, it's *real* bad. I wouldn't go there again." He pointed to the large, tattered, aluminum-frame backpack leaning against the wall next to her. "And with that pack, you'll be marked from the start."

"Oh dear," she said in an endearingly English tone, clearly concerned now.

"Do you know anyone there?" Manfred asked.

"Yes, I was going to have some friends I know meet me there at the bus station. The bus leaves here in a couple of hours; I was just waiting."

I thought for a moment. "When does the bus arrive in Mexico City?

She shook her head. "Not until two or three in the morning."

Manfred frowned. "That's not good. You know vat, you should at least try to get there during the daylight hours. That would be much safer."

She looked unhappy. "I didn't want to stay here another night. I've been in this city nearly a week already!"

"You don't like it?" Mark rasped.

"No, it's lovely, but … I'm going around the world for a year, you know. I'm from Cyprus, but I've been working in London, saving up. I've been planning this trip for years!"

"Vell, if your friends are going to pick you up, you should be fine."

"I'm not sure they are. I just e-mailed them, but I haven't got back any reply, not yet."

We watched her quietly ponder her dilemma as we snacked on grasshoppers.

"I'm still not eatin' those crickets!" Mark bellowed.

Manfred said, "Mark, these are grasshoppers, not crickets, and you should really try one, they are very good. Don't you want some of the local cuisine?"

"Just try one, Mark. They're not so bad. All you ever eat is chicken and hamburgers." I looked at the young lady. "Would you like a cricket? I mean, a grasshopper? I mean … please excuse us; I'm David Jackson, he's Manfred Winkler, and this here is Mark Hanson." Everyone nodded.

"Nice to meet you, I'm Farina Mavrikios," she said. "Where are you from?"

"Ve are from Texas."

Farina furrowed her brow, then smiled. "You don't sound like you're from Texas. Well," she pointed to Mark, "*he* does!"

We laughed. "*Ja*, I am from Germany. These two from Texas, but we all live there now." Just then the boy came around. We ordered more beers and tequilas for ourselves and for Farina as well. We shared tales of our travels, but then she had to go.

"I've got to catch that bus. It was so nice to meet you." We exchanged e-mail addresses and she went to find her bus.

"I hope that girl is okay in da city," Manfred said.

"Yeah, but she's been all over. She'll be alright." It had stopped raining. I finished my beer. "I'm going to go for a walk. I'll see you guys back at the pool." I threw my share of the pesos down on the table, now littered with beer bottles. Mark was moving the grasshoppers around, gingerly poking one of them with his fat finger, his face aghast.

"David, are you sure you can find your way back to da hotel?" Manfred looked at me, swaying slightly in his chair.

"Uh … uh, which way…" I looked around, unsure.

Manfred pointed back over his shoulder, along the side of the plaza. A cathedral loomed to his left. I looked at his finger, the plaza, the cathedral, down the road, presumably toward our hotel…

"Okay. I got it. See y'all in an hour or so." I waved, left them sitting there finishing their latest round of tequilas and *cervezas* Sol.

* * * * *

I had seen several Internet cafés near the main plaza where we had eaten. I quickly came across one, dodging the Indians on the sidewalk. Some sort of peasant protest was underway – Mixtecos eternally unhappy with the exploitative policies of the government in the DF. *Los Indios* were being pushed off of their land, land their families had farmed for centuries, squeezed out and strongly encouraged to move to the northern cities and work in new *maquiladoras* built by western transnational corporations. It was all a part of the NAFTA deal, but to these folk it seemed to be a raw deal indeed.

The Indians were sprawled all around the sidewalks on the plaza. They were eating, sleeping, talking, and basically just living there in the town square. I had to duck under or hop over the countless ropes supporting their protective tents and awnings to avoid being garroted or tripped. Their protest signs and banners screamed out defiance from every corner of the plaza. I entered the café, paid the attendant the ten pesos for one hour, and sat at the terminal.

I was immediately confused. The keyboard was arranged in a different manner from those stateside, with all the keys in different places, some keys missing, and some new additions entirely. "Great, a Meskin computer," I grumbled under my breath. "Different tribe..."

Finally I figured out the system and found my e-mail provider. I had a few messages – one of which, I saw, was from Regina. My pulse quickened. I hit the little envelope symbol for the message. It read:

Hello!

We are now in Monterrey. I am so bored here! I'm so tired of dealing with Javier's annoying family. It's always gossip about this person, gossip about that person. So petty. And he's no help, all the time with Cesar and Miguel and the rest of the men. So I have to babysit the women. It's sooo old fashioned. But, that's a Mexican family!

I miss you. I don't think I'll run into you on this fucking trip... I don't know what I was thinking. I really don't want to get my hopes up. Or yours! We'll be leaving here tomorrow, anyway, heading to Oaxaca City. I don't know when we'll get there, or how long we'll stay... And there's no way to find you without cell phones! So we'd better just forget it. I'll see you back in San Antonio. Ich vermisse dich! I can't write anymore, I'm tying up the phone line, Javier's out, but back soon, and so I have to go.

Love, Regina

Well, that was that. She was right; it was hopeless. Hopeless and pointless. I let out a long sigh, feeling all the joy of the day evaporate into a dead ache, a black hole in my heart. The whole thing was ill-conceived and hopeless. But I could only bite deeper. If I let her go now, I would never know if it could have worked. I wrote back:

Regina,

We are herre! Here in Oaxaaca Citty, and it is so beautifulll. Ssssorry abouut my horrible typping, it's not me—or the teqquila—it's the ttrick-ass Mexicann computtters! Really, the keyboard's all different, but I'll get used to it. This city is beautiful.

I know it's hopeless. I still want to see you. I've been thinking about you ever since we left, since I saw you last at the pig-roast. I know we can't expect anything, but that doesn't mean we can't try. I will attempt to delay our departure for the coast for as long as I can. Or maybe we could come back here after a few days at the beach.

As for meeting, I'll try to be in the main plaza of the city (where we had the best meal today – the food is sehr lecker!) at 10pm every night we are here. Just look for me – it might work.

I love you!

David

I reset the trick-ass computer and went back out into the cool evening, now getting dark. I felt low, low as the Indians I stepped over and around. Angrily painted signs adorned their shanty protest stations. Some slept, some ate, some chattered away in Spanish or their native Mixtec tongue. Rifle-toting *federale* soldiers stood silent watch over them. I walked through them all, my mind worlds away.

Never fall in love, I thought numbly. And if you do, never fall in love with a married woman! Surely I deserved the emotional thrashing that I got. I walked on, passing cafés and restaurants and *las farmacias* and finally a mezcál store. I realized I had been walking through the city streets for quite a while. I went into the store. Dozens of different bottles of mezcál lined the walls.

After a short conversation in mangled Spanish, I walked out with a full bottle of mezcál in a brown paper sack. I sat there on the sidewalk and unscrewed the cap. People swarmed about, as if in some sort of festival, *la fiesta*. I watched them all go by as I poured the golden liquid down my throat and felt the burn in my belly. I took another long swig and looked around.

The city resembled any one of several dozen I had seen throughout the Mediterranean world, sporting many plazas, cathedrals, smaller churches, and cobble-stoned streets all laid out in a grid-like pattern. If one was not familiar with the locale, each block much resembled the last. I started back the way I had come. Soon I found the plaza where we had eaten the grasshoppers with the comely Greek Cypriot traveling around the world out of London. I found our restaurant, looked up the street Manfred had indicated, past the cathedral – paused for another significant gulp of the formidable mezcál – and began up the way.

An hour or so later, a systematic search of several nearby streets had not yielded our hotel. But I had found several different plazas. In one was a folk festival, peopled by many families with happy little children in abundance. A clown on stilts juggled pins in the center of the crowd, and a mime's comic antics brought much applause, and even tears of laughter from one woman. Beggars sat outside the entrances to the cathedrals and churches, gratefully accepting donations from entering pilgrims and tourists. I would have entered the cathedral and said a forlorn prayer myself but for the encumbering bottle of mezcál.

I was growing foot-sore wandering around. The mezcál bottle was nearly a third empty now. I saw some benches up ahead and wearily sank into one. I swigged from the bottle, then sucked on some of the salty mixture enclosed in the little bag tied around the bottle's neck. I spent long minutes examining the strange little worm floating within the bottle. I felt broken, like a bum. My head was spinning a bit, but at least the painful thoughts were banished.

After a time, a middle-aged Indian woman sat next to me on the bench. "Want some mezcál? Uh..." I had to think for a second. "*¿Quieres la mezcál?*" She regarded me strangely for a moment, then quickly took the bottle and turned it up. She smacked her lips noisily and nodded in thanks as she passed it back.

As I took my own pull, a fellow about my age sat down on the ground in front of the woman. They spoke for a while. Then she said something and looked at me. I spoke to him, "*¿Quieres mezcál?*" He grinned and took the bottle.

His name was Tomás, hers Isobél. We sat there for a while, drinking the harsh cactus-juice. I felt like a local. They were local artists – not bums, like me – and invited me to their friend's café for breakfast, just up the street. I promised to come.

"And what you are doing here?" Tomás said in his best English.

"I'm an artist, too. A writer. My friends and I are here traveling on vacation."

"Just here? Where else you go?"

"Oh, down to Puerto Escondido. We're looking for mushrooms there. Do you know if they have any?"

He smiled. "No, you will no find mushrooms on the beach. But if you come to the café, I will show you." He took another long swig from the bottle.

"Uh, *show* me? Oh, ok. Good, good," I hit the mezcál again. "I, uh … I kind of lost my hotel. It has arches, and, uh … and a pool … and it's *real* niiiice." I was drunk enough that my old Southern drawl was creeping in. I hoped they wouldn't notice. "It's down there pretty close to that plaza," I pointed. "Do you have any idea which street, uh, *que calle?*"

He shook his head. "What is the name of your hotel?"

I shrugged. "I don't really remember it, exactly. I just know it has a pool. And arches."

"*Hombre*, if you knew the name, then I could then help you. But now…" He smiled again, shrugging.

I thanked them, said I'd surely find it, and I'd see them at their friend's café some morning soon. They each took a farewell pull on the fast-emptying bottle, and I headed back in the direction of the plaza.

I staggered along for a while, not lost exactly, but quite bewildered, and more than a bit drunk. I tried to rack my sodden brain, to remember some distinguishing nearby feature, but it all looked the same. I leaned against the wall, dropping my head. I thought about the hotel's façade. I thought about the street. I thought about Regina, and realized I had thought enough. I turned around and looked at the open doorway nearby. Inside I heard splashing, laughing. Suddenly I understood I had been leaning up against my very hotel for the last several minutes. I sighed and went inside with the much-diminished bottle of mezcál.

As I entered the courtyard, I lurched unsteadily toward the pool. Manfred was laying on a towel, a woman nearby on another. Mark splashed about, a water-ogre. "Hey, hey David! What happened?"

I shrugged. "I took a walk. Want some mezcál? There's still the worm." I passed him the bottle and shambled over toward Manfred.

"David, are you fucking this up?" He grinned up at me from his towel. I tried to focus, squinting at the figure next to him.

It was the lass from Cyprus. "Farina!" I hiccupped, embarrassingly. "I thought you had to catch the bus!" I hiccupped again.

"I missed it, so I found your friends here. I decided to take your advice and leave in the morning. I e-mailed my friends the change of plans." She looked me up and down, unsure what to make of the shaggy drunken bear. "What happened to you? We wondered about you."

"Oh, I was, uh … Just went for a walk. You mean, you found this place? How'd you know where it was? Did you know the name of the hotel?"

"This place? It was easy to find. Everyone in town knows this place."

"Ah." I sank down next to them.

"Hey David! Get in! The water's great." Mark took another hit from the bottle of mezcál.

I sat there beside the pool. Arches and people and columns whirled about. Nothing would stay still, not even the ground.

From the pool, Mark said. "Hey, David. You alright?"

Manfred put a steadying hand on my shoulder. "*Ja*, dude, you look green. Do you vant a beer or something? Did you drink all that mezcál by yourself?"

"I … No. My friends did, too. Tomás…" I got to my feet and tottered, nearly falling into the pool. I recovered and stood up straight, attempting to regain some measure of dignity. Then I turned around and puked into a potted plant.

"Oh, David. Oh, man. Aha ha ha ha ha!" Mark splashed around the pool with glee. "This is good mezcál. Do you have any more?" My only answer was my continued retching. Mark kept on, "Hey, it's how you began this trip, and it's probably how you'll end it."

"*Ja*, he is consistent, right?"

"Aha ha ha ha ha ha!"

After I had finished my business with the plant, I felt much better. I wiped my mouth on my sleeve, dropped my wallet by the soiled plant, and jumped into the pool right next to Mark, cannonball style, drenching Manfred and Farina. I really felt much better.

"See that, Farina? We grow them tough in Texas!" Manfred was showing off the dancing bear to his guest, enjoying the evening's entertainment despite the soaking.

"Should he be swimming? After that?"

"Aww, it's probably what's best for him. He does it all the time. Think he has an ulcer or something." Mark nodded solemnly.

Farina grimaced. "Oh."

Mark and I began dunking each other, he getting the better of me with his ogre-bulk. I got out and toweled off, overhearing Manfred and Farina's conversation, and sat down on the other side of Farina from Manfred.

"…*ja, aber* it substantially raises their standard of living."

"But it forces them against their will!" she said.

"What's that?" I asked.

"Ve are debating the relative merits of NAFTA, vis-à-vis the peasant protest ve saw today in da plaza."

"These *peasants*," Farina said, looking sidelong at Manfred, "have just as much of a right to choose their fate as you and I."

I said, "Yeah, but, they get jobs, you know. Money for their families."

"Yes, and at the end of the day," said Farina, "their traditions are destroyed, the people are uprooted from their land, and they work in factories making a fraction of what a typical western worker receives."

I shook my head. "I suppose you can't halt globalization."

"No one is talking about halting globalisation," she replied. "You're right; it can't be halted. What we're talking about is a fair deal."

Mark put down the wormless, empty bottle of cactus-madness, its power spent. "What are you, Franklin Delano Roosevelt? Aha ha ha ha ha!"

"That's *TR*, ass!"

Farina resumed, "I mean, these people should have a say in what happens. It's their lives were talking about here. For the global managers, it is merely profit. But they put that ahead of life."

Manfred frowned. "I don't know. Do people always choose what's best for them when given a chance?"

"Definitely not. If anything, that's democracy's weakness. But if people are disenfranchised, as with NAFTA, the WTO, the World Bank, and an imperialist American foreign policy, a government agenda serving only the interests of a tiny transnational elite, you get a lot of frustration in the world. People feel like they have no say in things, like they're just cogs in the machine."

"No," Manfred said, pointing, "that there is conspiracy theory. We vote in the West. You are saying a small cabal runs things like in the old Eastern Bloc."

"Yah, spot on, mate, you know they do! And it's no conspiracy, just people acting in their own class interests. The

West *is* entirely democratic on the surface, but underneath it's something else entirely. The real power is hidden."

Mark splashed us all from his watery lair. "Buncha communist hippies!"

I shook the water off my face like a wet bear. "I think people just don't like change, no matter what form it comes in."

Farina shook her head. "It's not change which is the problem. It's having it rammed down your throat."

Manfred said, "So you think that these *Volk* would be happier back on da farm."

"Yes!" Farina said.

I smiled. "We could always go down to the plaza and ask them."

She looked at me. "Do you speak Zapotec?"

"Mixtec!" Mark yelled from the pool.

Farina looked at him, then back at me.

I shrugged, "He's probably right. He is an archaeologist, after all." I noticed Farina looking steadily at me. Her long hair framed her face attractively, her skin was soft, caramel and clear, her lips full. She smiled at me.

I stood up. "I'm going to find that beer." I grabbed my wallet and walked toward the bar, ordering a Modelo Especiál. "*¿Con limón? Gracias.*" The bartender nodded toward me. I sat at the bar. It was easy in front of friends to throw on a cheery conversational façade over my morose heart. But after a while it took a lot of energy. The bartender brought my drink, sat it down on a napkin before me. He could see just how happy I really was, and it was the same for him. I didn't have to act around him. So what use are friends around whom I must act?

The bartender passed a delicious-looking piña colada to a woman behind me. A bit sloshed over the rim onto my knee.

"*Lo siento mucho*." He looked at me. "*¿Todo bien?*"

"*Todo bien, amigo*. Maybe I'll get it by osmosis." He smiled, but I could see he did not understand. I sighed, feeling very alone in the world. I got up, intending to retire to my room for the night.

"Hey David! Hey, wait up!" Mark came running up with the empty bottle of mezcál in one hand and a half-full Modelo in the other. "Hey, Manfred and that hippie chick are slugs, you know, they don't want to go out to a bar. Manfred says he's tired, and Farina says she has to catch the bus early. They just wanna talk red politics. You feel like going out?"

"Oh, man, not really. I..." I thought for a second. Going out with Mark Hanson certainly beat crying myself to sleep, my head buried ungloriously in my sodden pillow. This was a damn *vacation*, after all. "Uh, okay, yeah man. Let's go party. You ready?"

Mark stretched his visage into a broad ogre-grin. "You know it! Just let me get my money, you know?"

"I know man. I'm just going to throw on some dry clothes."

Then we headed out, ready to take on the town. There by the front desk we ran into some men whom we had met earlier in the lobby, down from Puebla with their families.

They knew a happening spot up the way, so we tagged along, tromping up the cobble-stoned streets behind them.

"Mark, now pay attention to where we're headed. We don't want to forget the way back to the hotel, get lost, or anything."

"It's right up here," the guy said. "We won't get lost."

"Yes we could! I was, uh..."

Mark stopped, looking at me. "David. You weren't *lost* that whole time, were you?"

I stopped with him, leaning on a nearby building for support. "No man! I wasn't *lost*, I was ... just a little preoccupied for about three hours. I met some friends. I know a cool place to have some breakfast."

"The hotel serves breakfast."

"We don't have to eat there every morning, do we?"

"Well, no, but..."

"We'll just play it by ear."

"Right." We were walking again, our nightclub up ahead, the party just getting started. "Hey David. Manfred said something today. He said, when you were going to the, uh, computer place or wherever..."

"You mean the Internet café?"

"Yeah. Whatever. He said you were probably going to e-mail that German chick, that Regina girl. You're not hung up on *her*, man? Are you? Man, she's not worth a ... Don't you know she's just using you!? She's married!"

"Yeah, no fucking shit, she's married. I'm not ... Look man, don't believe everything Manfred says, okay? And I don't really want to talk about it."

"Fine. I'm just … Hey, you know I'm just concerned about *you*, right? Don't want to see you hurt. And her husband is a Meskin. Be careful. You're on his turf, you know."

I wheeled around, poked my finger in Mark's face. "I said I don't want to talk about it!" I turned and kept walking, several paces ahead of him. *Just using you*. The phrase reverberated in my head. I couldn't believe she was inherently trick-ass.

We entered the club in silence. The place was filled with well-dressed Latinos, chatting and dancing. A band jammed in the corner. We moved around and through the people, ordered rum over ice at the bar. I sipped my rum and stepped out on a balcony, trying to relax. Mark was probably right, I knew. Married women having an affair are *always* using the other guy – to hurt the husband, to get what she wasn't getting at home, or whatever. I *knew* that. It didn't change a thing. Besides, this was different. She was different.

I walked further out onto the balcony and looked around the city. I had a great view. I could see several of the areas I had wandered earlier … there was a plaza, there another … there a familiar cathedral, and another … but that one…

I tapped the arm of the fellow next to me and pointed toward an unfamiliar cathedral to the north. It had twin blue-and-white-checkered gilded domes, quite distinctive. "Uh, *que es el nombre de la*, uh, *este?*"

"*Es el* Templo de Santo Domingo de Guzmán."

"*Muchas gracias, señor.*" I stood there for a while, staring at the twin domes and savoring my rum. I had a plan.

We could meet there. Too damn many plazas, but only one building like that. She couldn't miss it.

After several more hours, and some more drinks, Mark and I sopped up a last double rum, then stumbled down the street. We had bid the club and all of our new-found friends farewell.

"Now don' forge' uh way t'shu hotel."

"I know, it's right up here," Mark mumbled. We staggered around for another ten minutes, but had no luck.

"Oh no, not again!" I bellowed in drunken despair. "We're fucked!

I attempted to sit down on the sidewalk, but my momentum kept taking me down and I ended up lying on my side, pinned to the ground by the unusually strong gravity. I was content to remain there with my cheek pressed against the cool sidewalk. "Jus' leave meh here, I canno' take an more-a thi-shit. I can' go on. Somebod gon hafta come up in here an' git me!" The city spun overhead, I laughed heartily. "Weeeeeeee."

"Man, David! You gotta get up! This is Mexico!" Mark was trying to pull my dead weight off the ground. "We gotta to find the hotel!"

I sat up sluggishly, sullenly. "We *can't* find the damn hotel, I already tried that. Sonofabitch is gone again! Whash a-name ah-da plash? *Hotel de plastered-o?* Ha ha ha ha ha!"

Mark shrugged, "I don't know, dude." He bent down and looked at me closely. I stared vacantly at his bulbous nose and pale eyes. "But we can't sleep here, you know? You don't want to end up in a Meskin prison. You know what I mean?" He shoved his scarred, tree-trunk arms under my shoulders, embraced me in a smothering bear hug, and hauled me to my feet. I staggered, thanking him.

"If you don't know the fucking name, how'd you find it before?" he said.

The world was dim with drink, but I made out a taxi up ahead. We stumbled up to it. "*¿Hab-ala Ingláisss?*" I hissed, swaying and gripping the door of the cab for stability. "*Bueno.*" I stepped back and swept my arm toward Mark. "Ah, we seem to have misplaced our hotel." I laughed. "Can you help usss fin' it?"

"What's the name?" said the cab driver.

For the second time that night, I vaguely described what little I could articulate about the hotel. "Uh, well, I dunno … but I know it's got a pool! Yeah, it's got a pool, and some arshessss, columns, columns, big fucking columns…" I gestured, lifting my hands over my head and attempting to touch them together before tottering. "And it's real, real, *niiice*. Not far from here. Prob'ly a coupla blocks or so…?" I waived my hand around, indicating that it could be in any direction.

The cab driver looked us over, sighed, and muttered something under his breath. Mark and I looked at each other. Then he said, "Get in, get in."

After we had closed the door, the cab driver put the Volkswagen Beetle into gear and drove up the street exactly one block. "This it? *¿Todo bein?*" Mark and I looked at each other again and shook our heads.

"We can't tell Manfred about this," Mark said.

I pulled some pesos from my wallet without even looking at the amount and thrust the bills clumsily at the driver. "Thisssiss fer you."

He stared at the money only a few inches from his face. "*No, no necesito, no gracias. Buenas noche!*" He sped off, laughing.

"Oh shit, we're locked out!" Mark started banging his ogre-fist on the large wooden door to the hotel, which had been open when we left. "We're fucked!" The sharp clapping sound echoed down the street and no doubt through the courtyard inside as well.

"Calm down man, you'll wake everyone!" As I advanced toward the door, it opened and the proprietor lunged out, shaking his finger in Mark's face, barking at him in Spanish. "*Lo sssiento, lo siento musho, musho,*" I said as we pushed past him, heading for our rooms. "Mark, you can't freak out like that," I whispered loudly. "You'll wake up the whole damn place, man! You'll get us booted!"

"All I know is I'm ready to sleep in my bed," Mark declared very loudly, passing by the empty, darkened pool. He went to the door of his room, opened it with his key, and stepped inside. I heard a woman shriek, then yelling. I rushed to the door. Inside on the bed was a blurry indiscriminate mass of shifting motion under the sheets.

"Goddam it, that's my room! They're in my bed!" He said, stomping out of the room and slamming the door behind him.

"What?"

"Manfred's with that hippie chick in my bed!"

"But … So what exactly is the problem?"

"The problem … he said for *you two* to sleep in the double room. I want my room!"

"Well, what is the difference, man?"

"I want my room!" he bellowed.

"Sssshhhhhh!"

Mark grumbled at the closed door, "Why don't you fuck on your own goddamn rack," and stalked off toward the other room. I followed wearily along behind. But my door was locked, and I had not the key.

"Wait here, man, I have to get the key from Manfred." I left before he began grumbling again. I went back to the single room and knocked softly. Manfred cracked the door.

"Sorry man. I need the key to the other room."

"Man, *vat the fuck* got into him?" Manfred asked blearily as he handed me the key. Farina was huddled under the covers, lying there still looking startled. She gave me a sleepy little wave.

"Just some rum, I guess. And that worm. Sorry. He gets like this sometimes. Forget about it. I'll go try to calm him down. Get some resht, or, uh … whathaveyou," I waved my hand in Farina's direction, grinning at him dumbly. Manfred nodded sleepily, oblivious, and went back into the room and closed the door. I went back to Mark, now pacing outside the closed door of the other room.

"What the hell, right!" he yelled. "What the fuck does he think he's doing? That was *my* room!"

I was tired of it all. "Who gives a fuck! Will you just take it easy?" I opened the door and immediately got into one of the beds.

"I can't believe they were in *my* bed!"

"Mark, who gives a shit! You have a fucking bed right there!"

"Yeah, but I wanted *my*..."

"Mark, will you shut the fuck up! You're not four! Just go to sleep!"

"I'm *going* to sleep, dude. I was just saying..."

"Mark! Enough! Just calm down. Here, smoke a damn cigarette!" I threw my pack at his chest.

As I passed out, I could hear the ogre still muttering.

Day Four

Before I knew I was awake and moving, I had responded to the loud knocking and opened the door. Manfred stalked into the room, lightning coming out of his head, his eyes bright with flame. "So, Mr. Hanson! You seemed a bit upset last night! *Vere you not*?

My head felt like lightning had struck it alright.

Mark groaned from his bed. "Yeah, I just don't understand why you…" He broke into heaving, wracking coughs, frothy spittle flying from his mouth. I turned away in disgust, my head pounding. I rubbed my throbbing temples.

"Where's Farina?" Mark wheezed.

Manfred leveled his stare at him. "She left to catch her bus, frightened out of her mind, early this morning. In da taxi."

"Did she sleep much, after…"

He shook his head. "Not at all. Thanks to you. … She vas our guest!"

Mark hit his albuterol inhaler a few times, lit a cigarette, and hit the inhaler once more. The cigarette smoke was nauseating. He gave a last ineffectual cough and attempted to clear his tar-filled throat. "Hey, man, look. I just didn't understand why y'all had to sleep in my bed, that's all! You wanted me to have my own room, then you went and took it! What the hell?" He took a deep drag on his cigarette.

Manfred's affect changed, taking on a more earnest, reasonable cast. "I vas trying to be considerate of the entire group. The girl needed a place to stay the night. We had convinced her it would be safer to do so. So we had to put her up. You guys vere out drinking, and I figured she *und* I could just crash in that room together. It seemed the more convenient plan for you two. I didn't expect there would be any problems." He paused, looked at me. "Did you have a good time?"

I kept rubbing my temples, lightning still flashing before my eyes. "Yeah, man. We went to the club, and then we … uh, took a cab ride. There was no problem." I saw Mark look over at me, but I ignored him. "Until we got here. Now where's those Excedrin? … Hey, where's my bag?" I started in on the bottled water beside my bed, slurping down huge gulps.

"Remember, David, we threw all the bags in the other room when we checked in. It's in there."

"Thanks, Manfred. Now if you don't mind, uh…" I glanced at the door to the bathroom, trying to give him a meaningful look. "I'd love to keep chatting, but…" I felt distinctly ill.

He nodded. "I'll see you out there for breakfast. Then we're going to Monte Albán!"

"Great." I groaned. "I'm never drinking that foul mezcál again." Mark was blowing snot out of a nostril onto the middle of the carpet again. I looked away and quickly ducked into the bathroom, shutting the door behind me.

* * * * *

Breakfast was a horribly bright affair in the hotel's patio restaurant. I wore my sunglasses at the table. I suspected the waiter of being purposefully and unnecessarily loud, repaying us for our boisterous early-morning entry to the hotel. I endured the meal in grim silence and without complaint, hardly tasting the food.

But not Mark. He raised a stink. "Aww, man, this damn bacon … It's only half-cooked! Look at that fat! These Meskins don't know a damn thing about bacon!"

"Perhaps you would prefer da chicken."

"You're damn right! I tell you what, I'm never eatin' bacon in Mexico again!"

That settled, we finished the meal and walked toward our car, there in the enclosed lot. On the way, we passed the magnificent temple I had seen the night before, the bright blue and white domes shining in the morning sun. Despite my equally magnificent hangover, I felt a sudden surge of energy. "Hey, guys! Let's take a quick look at this place. It's called El Templo de Santo Domingo de Guzmán." They were agreeable, since it was on our way. We walked across the stone-paved court, past a man-made pool filled with flowers and lily-pads. Up close, the ornate cathedral was much more impressive than from afar. A ceremony was taking place inside, so we were only able to view the narthex. Gold was everywhere, paneling the walls and bordering the doors. Like a crew of Vikings in search of booty, we were enthralled by the ecclesiastical display of precious metals.

This is it, I thought. The perfect place to arrange to meet her. As romantic as she could ever desire, at least on such short notice. At least now I knew the name of the place. She would be able to find it.

We continued on to the car-lot. It was locked, with no attendant in view.

"At the front desk they said the person should be here. He must be taking a shit or something. We vill wait." With no other option, we sat down, settled in to wait for the boy.

Mark raised a stink again. "Hell with that. I'm gonna go find a store, get some cigarettes. You know? Y'all can wait for him. You know what I mean?"

My head was pounding. "Yeah, we *know*, man. Get me a pack, too, will you? And a bottled water, please. A large." Mark nodded and loped off down the street.

When he was gone, Manfred said, "You know what, dude, he smokes a *lot*. He smoked three packs yesterday!"

"Four. He had another pack at the club, plus whatever was left in mine, uh, in our room. The doctor said he only had five years to live."

"Really?"

"That's what he told me once."

"Do you think he was joking?"

I shrugged. "You've traveled with him now for four days. Do *you* think he's joking?"

"I ... I guess not. Man, vat got into him last night? He really was an ogre!"

"No," I shook my head. "He's always an ogre. What you saw last night was Minotaur-mode."

"Mino-*vat*?"

"Oh, I don't know how to say in German. Minotaur ... it's from Greek myth. You know ... Knossos? Crete? A bull-man, devours all the virgins?"

"Ah. *Minotauros*. Yes, he was that, right? ... You know vat, I think he doesn't respond too well to our teasing. Calling him an ogre, giving him hell about his smoking. I don't know about you, but we've still got a week left on this trip. Why don't we go ahead and handle him with a little more care. For the benefit of the group. What do you think?"

I smiled. "The care and feeding of the Ogre?"

"We don't need any more incidents like last night."

"Well, true, but ... it's just so much fun!"

"Now David..."

"Okay, yeah, okay ... you're right. We'll give him a break. For the benefit of the group!" Just then the boy arrived and let us into the lot. We tipped him a peso.

But I wasn't about to let Manfred off so easily. As we got into the Buick I said to him, "So man. How was she?"

Manfred stared back at me with an innocent, blank expression. "Vat do you mean, David?"

"Oh come on. *Farina*. How was it?"

"David, you know I haf a girlfriend. I was simply trying to produce properly convenient sleeping arrangements for the benefit of the group." He blinked, earnestly.

"Sure man." I nodded. I was entirely sure that was not all he had been trying to produce, but I let it lie. We were just driving out onto the street when Mark came chugging up, out of breath.

"Hey, hey! Y'all just gonna leave me?!" he said in a panicked voice. We stopped, let him in. "Hey, guys, check it out. I bought two packs, and I got the third one for free!" Mark was pleased.

I started to respond, then Manfred caught my eye. "Oh, yeah, man, that's pretty cool. Good deal. Hey, where's my water?"

"Oh yeah, the water. Sorry, I forgot."

* * * * *

Our first sight-seeing stop was not Monte Albán, but a massive tree outside of town. It was over two thousand years old, a young sapling in the time of Julius Caesar, so said the sign. Twenty lanky men holding hands could not have circled its girth. Tourists milled about, and vendors lined the way with carts of food and trinkets. We stayed for an hour, taking pictures and walking in circles around the huge *d'Arbla*. "How'd they know how old it is?" I asked.

"They have ways of dating it, dude," Mark said with certainty.

"You mean, like when you cut it down and count the rings?"

"No! It's science, man. I know all about scientific dating."

"Oh, yeah, because of your archaeology training, right?"

"That's right. It's all calibrated very precisely, and then published in peer-reviewed journals."

Manfred asked, "Is dating your archaeological specialty, Mark?"

"No, I'm a metallurgist."

"Well, the tree's wood," I said. "How do they date that?"

"I don't know! Goddam! That's not my specialty!" We went back to the car, drove up the winding mountain road to Monte Albán. In fine ecumenical spirit, we allowed Mark to operate the Buick-boat, which he advanced up the mountainside very cautiously.

Monte Albán is a huge complex of pre-Columbian buildings covering an entire mountaintop overlooking the Valley of Oaxaca, which contains the modern Oaxaca City. Meticulously terraced hills surrounded the site, once irrigated and farmed by native slaves. Giant stone pyramids stood among the sparse vegetation in various states of decay and destruction. For nearly a thousand years, an ancient city stood here, one of the first cities in Mesoamerica, its name now forgotten. It was the former capital of the Zapotec Empire, a great mountain-fortress-city, where warrior-kings ruled an empire that spread over the entire valley and surrounding mountains, down to the Pacific Coast. "Be'ena' Za'a" they called themselves, "The Cloud People."

We parked and walked up the dirt path to the visitor's center. I could see the verdant Oaxaca valley spreading out below us, the once-domain of the ancient sky-emperors. Near the center sat our temporary home, Oaxaca City. It looked strangely archaic and small compared to a sprawling, metallic American city, but vastly more beautiful, more natural.

We passed a vendor selling grilled meats. I paused, feeling a rumble in my belly, but Manfred said, "No dude, think of the sanitary condition. Ve are on top of a mountain. Where do they get their water?"

I sighed, "Yeah, I guess you're right."

Mark said, "Hey, let's get some pizza at the hotel after this. I saw it on the menu. What d'ya think?"

"Can we get bacon on it?" I asked.

"Fuck you! Aha ha ha ha ha ha!"

We paid the fee and entered the compound. Inside, old, ruined stone buildings sat atop terraced earthen mounds. Strange symbols were carved on the stone-work. Grass-covered stairs led up to the top of many mounds, which were often several hundred feet high. We began climbing one, but Manfred and I quickly left Mark behind. We waited at the top for him.

"Uhh, ho. Ahh!" he heaved, plopping down next to us. He lit a cigarette.

"You okay, man?"

"Oh, yeah. Ho. … Just gotta rest a second, you know?" He inhaled loudly. "You guys go on ahead. I'll catch up."

"No, Mark. We vill wait for you. Enjoy the view; we are on schedule." Manfred looked around. Seeing no one nearby, he produced the second bud and began rolling another joint, perhaps our last for a while. I would have to inquire of Tomás. We passed the joint around, high on the mountaintop. Mark alternated between hits on the joint and his cigarette.

I looked around. I could now see the entire valley for miles around, and the tops of the surrounding mountains beyond, like the view from an airplane window. I looked back to the site's complex of mounds and stone structures. "Hey Mark. See that central field, between all the mounds and stone buildings? Looks like a longish football field? What was that for?"

"Oh, yeah. Uh, that's … that's a central plaza, where all the people would, you know, conduct their business."

Manfred said, "No, I think that is where they landed the spaceships."

Mark groaned, "Oh, come on."

"*Ja, und* see that building up there? That was the control tower."

"Oh man, you're not one of those, are you?"

"One of what? No, really; you can see there, in the field – it's not really a field – see how long it is? That is so the spaceships could make their landing."

"Oh, Jesus. Come on, Manfred. You know that's bullshit." Mark protested, oblivious.

"No, I'm serious. I read about it in a scientific journal."

I asked, "Was it a peer-reviewed journal?"

"Yeah, was it peer-reviewed, Manfred?"

"Vell, I'm sure it was all proper and academic, *ja, ja*."

I walked over to a stone wall covered with carvings. I surveyed them, pointed to one. "Look here, Mark. This looks like a spaceship. These are all representative symbols, right? It looks like a spaceship to me."

Mark heaved himself up slowly, walked over to the wall. "Man, David, that's *an eagle*, not a fucking spaceship."

Manfred came over. "Are you sure, Mark? It looks like a spaceship to me. *Und* this one looks like a guy in a spacesuit."

"No, goddamit! That's a *jaguar god*! Man, don't you guys know anything? These things are *peer-reviewed*, they're specialists, man, fuck! They spend their whole careers studying this stuff! It's very scientific, Jesus!"

"This is stone," I said. "I thought your specialty was metallurgy."

"Oh, fuck it. I'm goin' over there." He walked off in a huff toward another mound as we laughed.

"Man, Manfred, I thought you said we weren't going to fuck with him anymore. You started that one!"

"*Ja*, I know, but … It's just so much fun!" He laughed, but sobered quickly. "No, you're right; we need to be nicer to him. From now on, okay?"

"Yeah," I grinned, "from now on."

We rejoined Mark down in the central plaza. "Hey, man, we were just joking around. I believe in aliens, but I don't think they're here yet!" I chuckled, smiling at him. He nodded. "Hey, this stuff is cool. Tell us about it." I pointed to the walls covered with strange hieroglyphs. Upon further inspection, a pattern emerged. Each section featured a single head with elaborate headdress.

Through the interpretive signs, and with some help from Mark, I was able to deduce that the practice of the rulers of the burgeoning imperial city was to send their "extra" people out into the countryside, as "colonists," to live in neighboring towns and villages, operating businesses on behalf of the cloud-emperors. If the colonists were not accepted by their new community, they were sent back to their destination a second time with a military escort. The heads on the stones were believed to represent the rulers of lands conquered by the empire, their kingdoms provincialized. The upside-down heads depicted the rulers of the lands that were taken by force. But this was all an educated guess – much of the hieroglyphic writing remained undeciphered, a language lost to the ages, like the name of the place.

What *was* known was that the people had emerged from the earth, transforming from jaguars and trees into men and women. The rulers had descended from supernatural beings that lived among the clouds, visitors from another world, perhaps. They were looked after by two main gods. Cocijo was the rain-god, though his name literally meant "lightning." He was depicted as a fork-tongued jaguar, and he had created the entire world just by breathing out. Coquihani was the second god, the god of light. It all seemed very reasonable to me, at least as reasonable as the Christian myths.

The gods received many sacrifices, both human and animal. As the empire grew, the Cloud People had butted up against the Aztec Empire. King Cosijoeza, upon learning that the strange metal-wearing invaders from beyond the seas had defeated the mighty Aztecs, ordered his forces not to attack the Spaniards. But eventually *Los Conquistadores* had turned their attention to the Zapotec, destroying the empire in the 1500s in a series of military campaigns into the mountains, the foreigners aided greatly by the superior lethality of their steel and their European germs.

After another two hours of an actually rather outstanding tour of the archaeological site given by Maestro Mark – punctuated by intermittent smoke-breaks – we headed back toward the Buick. As we approached the boundary between the archaeological complex and the gravel parking lot, we saw a swinging metal gate before us, its two halves chained together in the middle. I judged its height at a meter, and knew I could take it. Manfred and Mark were going around the gate to either side along with the other tourists.

I put one hand on the gate and swung my legs up. The chain was looser than I had realized, the play on the gate-arm too free, and it suddenly moved forward under my weight. My shin came down directly on the heavy metal, my entire weight bearing down on it. The pain flashed through me, a lightning bolt hurled by the jaguar-god. Somehow I managed to land on both feet, stumbling somewhat, but I did not go down. Manfred and Mark chuckled behind me. I smiled ruefully. "Kinda clumsy today. Tad under the weather, I guess."

My leg ached as I hobbled to the car. I took my place in the back seat and examined the source of the pain. The skin was scraped, but not broken. I had two kneecaps on the left leg, however; one just under the main one. The mashed spot was reddening angrily, swelling rapidly. It could have been a clean break, I thought. My luck could have been worse.

* * * * *

Back down the mountain from Monte Albán, we settled in at the hotel for a late lunch at a sun-lit table by the pool. My hangover was stronger than ever, suggesting to me I had still been somewhat drunk that morning. I looked across the table. The menu shook in Mark's hands. I ordered a *cerveza* Carta Blanca. "*¿Con limón, comprende*?"

Mark looked over at me, "Hey David. You don't have to order limes down here every time you get a beer. The limes come with the beer, you know? It's automatic, you know what I mean?"

"Yeah, man, I know. I just want to make sure, okay?" The boy came with my beer, putting a plate full of sliced lime down in front of me. He did not look at me, and walked away without a further word. "See? You're just pissing them off!"

I squeezed one of the lime wedges into my beer and stared at Mark. "Or maybe they're pissed because of our grand entrance last night. We've got to be a little more discreet, you know, Mark? We don't want to end up in a Mexican prison!"

"*Ja*, dude. We don't want to make a bad name for ourselves."

Just then the men down from Puebla sat with their families at a table next to ours. We waved, but they just looked away, ignoring us.

"It may be a little late to salvage our reputation," I said sadly.

The boy returned and we ordered pizza, *sin tocina*. "*¿Quiero un tequila blanco? Bueno.*" The boy left with our orders. The bottle trembled slightly in my hand. Shortly the food arrived.

Around a mouthful of pizza, Manfred said, "So, I haf been examining the maps. Tomorrow we shall leave for Puerto Escondido. The clerk at the front desk said we should make it in about six hours." He glanced significantly at Mark. "*Ja*, that's *six hours.* Und he has shown me the most direct route." He took a drink from his bottled water. "Ve are on schedule."

I shot my tequila, waved at the boy for another. "*¿Y un cerveza* Carta Blanca, *por favór?*"

The boy stopped and looked at me. "*¿Con limón?*"

"Uh, *sí, sí. Gracias.* I drank deeply of my beer. "So, Manfred. What's on the schedule after Puerto Escondido?"

Manfred looked across the table at me, his expression blank. "Well, David. I don't know. Hang out on the beach a while, then head back north. … *Not* through Mexico City."

The boy came with my beer. I ordered another couple of tequilas. "Well, yeah, that's … I agree. Not through the DF. But…well, I was thinking…" I paused for effect, slammed a shot of fiery-smooth tequila *blanco*, and chased it with a long swig of Carta Blanca. "Why don't we come back up through Oaxaca City? I mean, this place is still unexplored. It's a, you know, a big city, and there's still so much to see … and from here we could leave north by a different route, *not* through Mexico City."

Manfred frowned, shook his head. "No dude, that would fuck up the plan. We are here southeast of Mexico City. If we came back here after the beach, it would cause us many extra hours of driving. Ve would mess up da schedule." He looked at me thoughtfully. "Why do you want to come back here?"

"Yeah, David! Why do you want to come back here, you know? I tell you what, I'm ready for that beach! You know what I mean?" Mark started in on his second *cerveza* Modelo.

I took another shot of tequila, sucked on a lime wedge, and cleared my throat. "I just said why I want to come back here. We've barely seen this place! Just a few bewildering blocks, a big tree, and some crumbling ruins on top of an old mountain. There's museums, shops, good food, uh … some cathedrals…" Manfred and Mark were looking at each other, confused. "I mean, there's still so much to see! Don't you think?"

Manfred was quiet for a long moment. Now he and Mark exchanged a pregnant glance. "David." He sounded calm, reasoned, slightly disappointed. "We don't need to come back to this place. Why would you want to do that?

The whole idea was to see as much as possible in ten days. That vas always da plan."

"Yes, as much as possible! And there's so much here to see!" Sweat broke out on my brow. My beer was shaking in my hand. I put it down. "Okay. If we can't come back here, let's just stay one extra day. That's fair, right?" I looked at each of them in turn. They were ill at ease.

Manfred said quietly, "What do you want to do while you are here, David?"

"Well, there's … ah, you know, museums, and … *art*. I met these two artists yesterday, we could go see their gallery! They have a breakfast café! There are cathedrals…"

"And Internet cafés," said Manfred. I looked at him across the table. Mark was silent, looking off at the pool.

"What do you mean?" I asked innocently.

"You know vat, David? We are down on this trip all together. It is not fair to us to fuck up our vacation just so you can meet with your lover."

Well, that was direct. I sank down in my seat, deflated. Manfred stared at me, and Mark looked over, shaking his head. "Yeah," he rasped, "you don't need to see that kraut girl, anyway. She's nothin' but trouble, you know?"

"What the fuck are y'all talking about!? I just want to see the sights…"

"Yes, yes, da sights!"

"Aha ha ha ha ha!"

"Fuck! Okay, look, this is important to me! It won't fuck up the goddamn plan, Manfred! We're on the fucking schedule, okay? It's just one thing I ask, one thing, and I haven't asked for a damn thing on this trip. You've got your plan, and Mark, uh ... you've had several whores! You guys have gotten everything you've wanted on this trip. I'm just asking y'all to consider coming back through here after the coast." I looked at each of them in turn. "That's all. *Okay*?"

Manfred pushed his chair back. "I must find ze toilets." He walked off.

Mark was slowly shaking his ogre-head. "David, I have to tell you. I'm disappointed in you. You know?"

"Listen, Mark. You know how stubborn Manfred can be. He's *German*, right? This is no big deal, really. Just go along with me on this, and ... and I'll support you in any side trips you want to take. Like..."

"Like Taxco?"

"Yeah, alright! We'll go there on our way back. I promise it won't fuck up the plan. Just back me up, okay?"

He looked uneasy. "I don't know..."

"C'mon, Mark! Just back me up, okay? ... Mark?" I looked at him hard. "Just back me up, here. We don't have to do just what Manfred wants."

"I don't know ... I don't like this Regina business."

"Don't worry about that. That's *my* problem. And it's no problem! Everything's cool, man. Trust me."

Mark was still shaking his head when Manfred returned from the toilets.

"So what do you think, Manfred? Are we gonna work together on this?"

Manfred looked at me silently for a moment. "David, I just don't like how you are being so selfish. I understand what you want to do. Frankly, I don't vant to be involved in any way. This simply does not benefit the group." He blinked and stared at me, green eyes wide.

I saw then that they were both immovable. "Ah, well … Fuck it." I tossed a spent lime onto my plate.

We sat around the wrought-iron table in silence for a while, soaking up the hot Mexican sun.

"I think it vill be better for us all this way, David. Really."

"Thanks," I said, "I sure do appreciate that. As long as it benefits the goddam group, right?"

"Aww hell, dude, don't be bitter." Mark grinned his grotesque ogre-grin at me. "So, hey, David. What's Javier's wife like in bed, huh?"

"Fuck you!" I got up suddenly, meaning to lunge forward across the table, but then almost fell over as my stiff, swollen leg failed to bear my weight. The leg throbbed magnificently. The boys laughed as I stumbled, my hair falling down over my face.

I stood there, gripping the back of my chair tightly with both hands clenched, glaring back at them sitting there at the table littered with pizza crusts and empty bottles. I pushed my hair back. "I am not a dancing bear…" I hissed slowly through my teeth, "…here for your amusement!" I began to limp away.

Mark said, "Hey David! You want to go for a swim when you get back?"

I paused, staring back at him. "Uh, sure thing, Mark. I'll be looking forward to it. Go ahead and start without me. I'll just be a fucking minute."

It began to rain. I looked at my watch: Five o'clock. With a vague sense of déjà vu, I was determined not to repeat my mistake. "What's the name of this damn hotel?" Manfred pulled a card out of his wallet, handed it to me. "Hotel Gala de Oaxaca. Great." I left them there and hobbled out into the city, the monsoonal winds blowing about great sheets of water.

* * * * *

My in-box was empty. I sat there in the café, dripping, staring at the screen for several long minutes. Then I wrote:

Regina,

Well, so much for that. I tried to convince the guys to stay here a little longer, or to come back through here from the coast. No go. In fact, I think they're on to me. I had to back off. It was just not to be.

We're leaving for Puerto Escondido tomorrow morning. I couldn't change the group's plans. I was all set to meet you here, at the Templo de Santo Domingo de Guzmán. It would have worked! Anyway, I'll still drop by the Templo tonight at 10. Just in case…

I'm sorry! I tried. Just have a good time and be careful down here. I'll be in Texas when you get back. I miss you.

Love,

David

I hit 'send' and slowly got up. My lame leg did not support my full weight. I limped out of the café, out into the city. I felt dizzy. I walked – hobbled – for a while in some random direction, the rain washing away salty tears. Finally the external deluge stopped, and I choked down the inner. I was numb, empty. It was all pointless. I did not care about anything.

After stopping for a spicy street-side chicken fajita, I walked aimlessly along the cobble-stoned streets, one *calle* after another. I found myself back in the plaza clotted with angry Indians, still watched over by armed soldiers. The Indians were all chanting in Mixtec, rhythmically, monotonously, their fists pumping in the air in time. The police just stood there, silently watching, ready. Their faces were hard behind the face-shields of their riot helmets. I turned around, leaving the disturbing scene.

I walked a few blocks and came upon the place where Tomás had said the breakfast café would be. I went inside and walked through a big open room containing a half-dozen tables and brilliant modern folk art hanging on the walls. At the back was a tiny kitchen, with a girl chopping vegetables.

"*¿Donde está* Tomás?"

She said something I did not understand, then disappeared. Soon she came back, trailed by my new friend.

"*Buenas tardes, amigo*! You come to the café, as you promise! Come on, come upstairs. We are watching the *fútbol* game." He led me up a spiral iron staircase, hardly more than a ladder. I followed as best I could, favoring my stiff, throbbing leg. "What happened to your leg?" he asked.

"Oh, yeah. I smashed it up at Monte Albán. I must have insulted one of the old gods. My luck's not so good today." We came to the top. In the loft, two young men with long, thick black hair and strong Indian features sat on a couch, regulation shot glasses and an open bottle of mezcál on the table before them. A *fútbol* match blared forth from the Box in the corner. Tomás and I sat with them. I sighed as my body's weight left the troubled leg. "Where's Isobél?"

"For the game? No, *hombre* ... no women, now. Only the men now!" He began pouring shots of mezcál for all. "Funny you say such a thing, though, *amigo*. The jaguar god is known for its power to bring the person bad luck."

I looked sharply at him. "*Jaguar* god? How did you know that?"

He looked up at me blankly. "What you mean? I know nothing. Is only an old Zapotecan legend. Here, have some mezcál." He handed me a full glass.

"Great. Now I'm cursed," I said, putting back the shot. It was a superior grade of mescal – something after the previous night I had not thought possible. "Man, this stuff is pretty good. It's even ... well, *spiced*, right?"

Tomás said, "What you mean, *cursed*?" He rapped his knuckles on the wooden table as he eyed me with eyebrows raised.

"Uh, hey man, it's nothing! I've probably used up all the bad luck anyway. And who cares? We all create our own luck. Right?" I knocked my fingers on the table as well, just in case.

Tomás just shook his head and looked away, no longer interested in discussing local customs and taboos with a loco *yanqui*. We watched the constant action of the *fútbol* match, our attention distracted only for occasional mezcál pours. I tried, with some success, to chat with the two Indians, but they seemed to speak no English. Often they spoke to one another in an Indian tongue. Tomás and I quipped amicably about nothing in particular, men together watching the Universal Game. "*Gooaal*!" and "*Olé*!" punctuated the room from time to time.

At half-time, Tomás got up and went downstairs. He returned carrying a small brown paper bag, which he handed to me as he sat down. I unrolled the crumpled bag and looked inside. I could see several dark brown sticks, about two inches long, with reddish-brown bulbs at one end. I pulled one out and inspected it. *Psilocybe Mexicana*, the "Mexican Liberty Cap," a mushroom common to the highlands of Mexico. The Aztecs called it *teonanácatl*, the "god mushroom." It was, and remains, an entheogen in many native Mexican cultures, a substance used to draw out the divine within, to connect to the universal spirit, to transform oneself and one's relationship with the world. *The divine trip.* That was my intended use for these particular specimens, *to get a few things straight with the Lord*, as they say down South.

It was this species, *p. mexicana*, that Dr. Albert Hoffman, the German-Swiss chemist, first used to isolate and describe the psycho-transformational compounds *psilocybin* and *psilocin*. Hoffman had experimented on himself, consuming 32 of the mushrooms one day. He wrote:

As I was perfectly aware that my knowledge of the Mexican origin of the mushrooms would lead me to imagine only Mexican scenery, I tried deliberately to look on my environment as I knew it normally. But all voluntary efforts to look at things in their customary forms and colours proved ineffective. Whether my eyes were closed or open, I saw only Mexican motifs and colours. When the doctor supervising the experiment bent over me to check my blood pressure, he was transformed into an Aztec priest, and I would not have been astonished if he had drawn an obsidian knife. In spite of the seriousness of the situation, it amused me to see how the Germanic face of my colleague had acquired a purely Indian expression. At the peak of the intoxication, about one and one-half hours after ingestion of the mushrooms, the rush of interior pictures, mostly changing in shape and colour, reached such an alarming degree that I feared I would be torn into this whirlpool of form and colour and would dissolve. After about six hours, the dream came to an end. Subjectively, I had no idea how long this condition had lasted. I felt my return to everyday reality to be a happy return from a strange, fantastic but quite really experienced world into an old and familiar home.

The end of the match brought my attention back to my immediate surroundings. I handed Tomás the two hundred pesos that he had requested in exchange for the blessed sacrament he had provided for my journey. I held up one final drink and noticed with satisfaction that the shot-glass held steady in my hand. I toasted my friends – "*Salúd*!" – and put it back. Then it was a promise to return the next day for art and breakfast, and a final *adios*. I let myself down the stairs, two arms and one leg picking up the slack from my lower left limb. I was sweating profusely. My face felt hot, heat radiating off my head in pulsing waves. I felt feverish and began to wonder about the full extent of my accursed bad luck.

I walked up the hill toward our grand cathedral, the designated meeting place. Sweat poured off my face, though the night was cool. I was practically dragging my gimpy leg behind me. I thought of the old Viking saying: a man should not limp with both legs the same length. I felt high, high and dizzy.

I made it to the Templo de Santo Domingo de Guzmán just before ten o'clock. I waited one full hour for her, damp and disoriented, but only lovers and little urchins passed through the stone-paved court. I sat alone on a low wall as the pond gurgled softly off to the side, watching the happy couples in their bliss. I took a couple of quick puffs on the roach I had stashed in my shirt pocket. I felt as though I was descended from the clouds, alien to the earth-borne and their earthly love.

A small one approached, begging pesos, but I just got up, ignoring my civic duty, and left him there with hands outstretched. I limped back down toward the hotel like a bastard. I heard a nearby emergency siren and saw flashing red lights up the way. A roar like the wild ocean came upon me, and when I looked over I saw the Indians, screaming and yelling, heading my way down a side street. The military police were just behind them, driving them on like maddened stampeding cattle.

I overrode the pain in my leg and hoofed it fast, darting around a corner, down an alley, back against another corner, up the other way … I stopped, breathing heavily. The leg throbbed with renewed vigor. The street fighting had passed me by.

As I began running, I had seen one of the cops smash his club down on a fleeing Indian's head, another lightning bolt thrown by the jaguar-god. The Indian had crumpled and was immediately trampled by his fellow protesters. I leaned against the wall, trying to get the image out of my head. But I kept seeing the ghastly vision, hearing the dull crack of bone, even over the roar of the riot. I guess the Interior has its own curses, I thought.

I wasted no time in finding my hotel. I was numb, disconnected from what I was doing. Mark was still in the pool, nursing a beer.

"I tell you whut, David! The water's great! Hey, why are you all wet already?"

I could barely focus on the objects in front of me. I could not think properly. Something was wrong. I mumbled something incoherent to Mark, gave a tired wave in the direction of the pool. I found my room, let myself in. Manfred was in bed, watching the Box in Spanish.

"Hello there, dude. How was your walk?"

"Yeah, uh … alright. I think I'm going to bed now." I collapsed on the bed, the room spinning. Something was wrong.

"Damn, David – vere you *playing* in a *fussball* match? You are all sweaty! You're soaked!"

I groaned and passed out, my mind entering strange places.

Day Five

There were many levels, but it was okay, you could float up and down to them. I floated up to the next one. It was dark, dark as night, but we could all see. Everyone was there, and I knew them, but could not name them. They were just the people in this place. The war was on, and if He died, it would all be over. All would be lost. We hid Him, and had a Trusted One watching over, protecting Him. We even changed His form. We could all do that, change our forms. It was what one could do in this place. Something was wrong.

Regina floated up to me in the murky dark. "You can sit between my parents. But they're really weird!"

"That's okay," I said. I floated between them. They were indeed her parents, as I had seen them in the photos she had shown me. But something was wrong with them. Something to do with this place. The father leered at me, showing sharp, blackened teeth. His black eyes gleamed, blind, blind. I retreated, floated over toward the mother. It was meal-time. She cackled and tried to mouth my hand, which I had extended in

greeting. She gummed it, drooling dark saliva down my wrist. Everyone at the circular table laughed at me.

I was then on a long staircase, miles long. I was near the top, and had a great view in the blackness. Soldiers were above and below on the staircase, at the top and the bottom, and to either side on floating platforms. They were in ancient garb, looking as eagle warriors in grass kilts, their thick black hair bound behind their head-gear. Someone was with me, in some form I did not know. The soldiers would kill us if we were seen, and there was no cover. My companion said not to worry, but we were spotted, and the soldiers charged from all directions, obsidian-edged blades raised. We were doomed.

Then I was in the small, hidden room, with Him. He was fat, in a sweat-soaked brown t-shirt, His natty beard swarming down His neck, over His chest. I was a third person observer, a silent, helpless witness. The Trusted One was there to the right, guarding Him. But something was wrong. Something to do with the guard, the Trusted One. The guard changed his shape. Briefly the guard was Regina, for a flicker of an instant. But then the Trusted Guard became a third form. I then saw two of Him, doppelgangers, staring at each other, identical. Something was wrong. The trusted guard on the right – as Him –pulled out his pistol and unceremoniously put five slugs into His chest.

He fell, ichor-dark blood flowing freely. In death, He changed his shape, His form. It was me. The guard laughed, rotten teeth showing black with blood, dark cat-eyes flashing red. The eyes flowed with His blood, and it was the same. The guard laughed again, standing over His still, bloody form, and looking right at me for the first time, said in a rough voice, "You should never have let me watch over Him."

The guard changed one last time, and in her own sensuous voice Regina said, "You should never have trusted me with Him." Something was wrong, Regina laughed, and all was lost. She had unmasked. That was how it was in that place.

I awoke thrashing, awash in sweat and sodden bedsheets. My leg pulsed painfully, a dull ache intermittent with a sharp, piercing throb. I had not broken it. Sometimes a clean break is better. I reeled. My head felt as though it had been stuffed with giant wads of narcotic cotton. I seemed to *float* curiously above my soggy bed, a disquieting sensation. For a long moment I knew not where I was.

The Box blared on the wooden armoire, a satellite-casted European *fútbol* match in play. I watched it dreamily. Manfred opened the bathroom door, steam billowing out behind him. "Good morning, David. Did you sleep well?" He began dressing.

"Huh? Oh … what? What was the question?" I looked around the room, dizzy and suddenly sick. My stomach rumbled ominously "I, uh…" I lurched out of bed, headed for the toilet, but went to ground immediately as my leg gave out.

"Dude, are you okay?" Manfred looked down at me. I pulled myself up slowly, using the bed for support. I limped into the bathroom and shut the door. I made it to the toilet just in time, heaving black bile onto the back of the bowl.

"I'll be fine, man," I said through the door, sweat forming anew, a huge bead dangling from the end of my nose. Strangely detached, I watched it drop to the floor. Time stretched out before me.

Then, slowly and carefully, I limped back to the sick-bed. "I think I lost weight."

"You don't look so good, David." Manfred turned off the Box.

"Uhh, I don't feel so good, man. I think I have a fever. And my stomach … ohh. *Sheisse*. This isn't good."

Manfred laid a hand across my sweat-soaked brow. "*Sheisse* is right, dude. You're burning up!"

Just then Mark burst into the room like a wild Kramer-ogre. "Hey guys! Ready for breakfast? I want some chicken breakfast tacos!" I gagged at the thought of food. Mark looked me over. "What the hell's wrong with you?"

"He has the Revenge."

Mark groaned. "Oh no! David, you're not supposed to drink the water, you know? You'll be like this for at least … uh, when did this start?"

I opened a fresh bottled water and drank deep, wetting my parched throat. My head was spinning as fast as it ever had. "Oh, uh … I guess last night. Yesterday evening. Uh-huh." I floated yet above the bed, my stomach turning over and over, gurgling and growling.

"Man! Are you stupid? You're not supposed to drink the water, you know?" He shook his head.

I tried to sit up in the sick-bed. "Mark, I … I only drank a bottled water. And, of course, there was the mezcál."

Manfred looked disgusted. "Mezcál again, David? … And now look at you! You're not worth a wet sack of shit!"

"Aha ha ha ha ha!"

"No! No, man, I'm just … I didn't have any water, man! And that mezcál's *good for you*, you know? Fights infections and whatnot. All I had was…" I thought back. It was all murky, but… "I did have some street chicken. From a vendor. It was pretty good. Damn spicy, though." I clutched my stomach. "Uhh … oh. Shit. Do we have to talk about food?"

"David, I haf told you about the sanitary condition of most of those street-side vendors. You have gone and caught yourself da Revenge."

I groaned. "Yeah, I know. I've got the Revenge all right. I was cursed, too."

"Yeah, sure enough. I tell you what, David, you've got the Revenge! Aha ha ha ha ha!"

I got to my feet gingerly and again hobbled slowly but urgently to the toilet.

* * * * *

Later, I sat outside the front of the hotel with the bags, on the sidewalk. I sweated heavily, leaning up against the building. I had bought another bottled water at the bar, where the bartender had eyed me wearily as he poured the water into a large styrofoam cup for me. Now I drank from it, setting it on the ground beside me, the bags several yards away on my other side. Pedestrians passed by, stepping around me as if I were a protesting Indian. I watched their feet go by and heard a *pla-ploop* as several coins splashed into my water. "Daily civic duty..." I mumbled weakly, smiling for some reason I could not fully fathom. Soon the Buick pulled up.

"Dude, you vant to sit in the front?" Manfred held the door open for me as Mark heaved the bags in the trunk. "That way you can stretch out."

I pulled myself up the side of the building weakly. "Yeah, okay. That'll be better for my stomach." I limped to the waiting car.

"Now vhere is that damn breakfast café you are always blathering about?"

"Oh, yeah. Breakfast café. Right. Uh, it's, uh … go up three … no, four blocks, take a right, and park there. It's not far."

Mark spoke up from the back. "I hope they have some chicken, you know?"

"No. I hope they have some fruits and grains. I am tired of these greasy, unhealthy Mexican breakfasts. I vant a proper German breakfast!"

I moaned, feeling my stomach churn. "I don't think I want any breakfast. But let's go on in."

Inside, we sat at a table. As we waited on the girl from the kitchen, we surveyed the art. Many of the paintings were of morbid, bloody-looking skeleton- and skull-shapes, and others depicted gory battle scenes. Every table hosted twisted and grotesque sculptures. "Man, this place is cool! Look at this stuff!" Mark Hanson was in his element.

I shook my head, took in a painting hanging on a wall behind Mark's head. It was of a man, a fierce man in a grass-woven kilt, naked above the waist. His oiled skin glistened darkly over tight muscles. In his hand he hefted an obsidian-edged long blade. His thick, straight black hair was pulled back behind his strong-featured, bronzed face. The expression on the warrior's face was closed, hard and hostile, staring out at me without pity or remorse, as if such emotions were unthinkable, unknown to his world. I shuddered, felt a strange dread, some odd disquieting feeling of doomful *déjà vu*, but could not quite place it. I looked away from the fell figure.

The girl came to collect our orders. She seemed quiet and unnaturally subdued. Manfred happily ordered a fruit bowl, with oat-bran and milk, and Mark grumbled when he discovered no *pollo* on the menu, but settled on some ham and eggs. I ordered coffee and a water, feeling bold.

"¿Tomás *está aquí?*" I asked, intending to introduce my friends old and new.

The girl's eyes welled with tears. She said, "*¿Mi* poor *hermano?* You don't know? He is in the hospital. He heard the noise, the fighting on the street … *la policia* hit him … he should have stayed inside." She choked, her eyes watering. "*Mi familia* is there now. His head is broken … but I must run the café." She dabbed at her eyes with a tissue pulled from her pocket. "The doctor says he will make it." She made the sign of the cross and wandered off distractedly toward the kitchen.

Stunned, I sat there silently through the breakfast, thinking about luck, both good and bad. Except for politeness' sake, I ignored Manfred and Mark. My coffee reacted poorly with my stomach, and I spent half the time in the *baños*.

As we drove out of town, I noticed the Indians and their tented encampments were all gone from the plaza. The police were still there, grimly stomping around on smashed protest signs. When Manfred and Mark asked what had happened, all I had the strength to say was that the protest was over. We departed Oaxaca City, and with it was forever gone, I knew, all hope of encountering Regina. I hoped I had left my accursed bad luck behind as well, there with poor Tomás.

The Revenge, however, remained with me. I sat in the front, clammy, stretching out my leg. I loosened my belt, giving my churning guts ample room. Cold sweat constantly beaded on my brow, which I periodically mopped with a hand towel I had taken from the hotel. I thought about poor Tomás, surely still worse off than me in some Mexican hospital. Different tribes … Bad luck, bad luck … Revenge indeed! … never mess with a Mexican's wife, never on his own turf, protected by savage jaguar-gods … horrible bad luck, slopping all around on innocent souls…

I tried to get a grip on myself, refusing to prolong the futile train of thought which led only to bitter despair. It was only self-torture to think about her. All for nothing. *Todo para nada*. My numbed, delirious mind and battered, fever-wracked body were the just fruits of my ill-favored, accursed, philandering arrogance.

Stuck down by the lightning bolt of justice. I pulled myself together somewhat more, tried to fight the fog, to maintain a focus on the group's meandering conversations and the ever-changing view out the windows of the Buick.

Mark spoke up in back. "Manfred, now, don't go crazy up there! I know you're a good driver, a German and all, but just, you know … take it easy."

"Mark, I am sorry if you haf a problem with the driving. I will drive safely but swiftly. There will be no problems." We moved at high speed through the mountains south of Oaxaca City, headed for the Pacific coast and the small, sleepy fishing village of Puerto Escondido. The mountains would rise up, gaining elevation for several hours; then we would plunge down from the high range, down to the foggy coast. So said the map in the Hippie Book. Hilly green pastures passed by out my window, each farmer's land demarcated from his neighbor's by long, low stone walls, the old grey stones piled one atop another to create durable, lasting boundaries, the way they did in the old country.

I sat up front, sweating, drinking water to re-hydrate, and taking in the scenery. The verdant fields were smooth and rolling in contrast to the bumpy, poorly paved road we were driving on. The fields came right up to the road without the inevitable barbed-wire fence that separate the two in the States. "This sure ain't a *cuota*, is it, Manfred?"

"No, dude, this is a regular Mexican highway." He slowed as we went over another irregular *tope*. Off to the right, a peasant led a yoked team of oxen through a field.

"You sure don't see this kind of thing very often stateside," I said.

"Yeah, where's his tractor? Aha ha ha ha!"

"You know vat? That there is one fairly wealthy peasant. He has two oxen! Doing fairly well, I think."

"Yeah," I agreed. "I bet he's got a huge family. Not just two-point-three children, like some yuppie breeder. He must have a dozen kids!"

Mark rasped, "Yeah, some of 'em daughters. A cute little Injun girl. I wanna get me a squaw! Aha ha ha ha ha!"

"Mister Hanson, you are a sick man."

"Yeah Manfred, I know. The doctor only gave me ten years to live."

I looked back at him. "I thought you only had five years!"

"Well, he said I'm doing better. Gave me a few more years." He lit up a cigarette.

We slowed to a stop as a donkey ambled lazily across the road. The lack of fencing insured a steady stream of intrusive livestock over the road. Next the chickens delayed our journey, following along one behind the other like a poorly disciplined troop of ducks. Then more irregular *topes*, built to no uniform standard, each one different than the last, all placed in front of whatever small village we happened to be passing through.

In each village, the structures had a shanty look to them, cobbled together from whatever floated down the river or fell off the back of the truck. Only the outhouses were made of decent wood, but the ubiquitous cross-topped churches were of course made with proper brick and mortar.

More sullen, machete-toting peasants walked by the roadside, as much a native part of the scenic landscape as the randomly wandering livestock. Mark said, "Hey Manfred, I don't see any of that NAFTA money down here, you know? This place might as well be stuck in the sixteenth century!"

"You know vat, Mark? The *maquiladoras* up by the border are the main recipients of such funding. That, and special projects like building *cuotas* and military checkpoints and lining the pockets of key magistrates with some nice pesos, and other well thought-out investments in infrastructure. All they vant down here is to take da resources."

My feverish mind replayed the image of the policeman's truncheon smacking down on the Indian protester's head. "If this is how poor these poor bastards live, I guess I can't blame them for protesting a bit," I mumbled weakly.

"*Nein*, David, dey should be happy with the jobs the companies offer them."

I shook my head. "I'm not so sure."

Manfred looked at me. "You've been talking to Farina too much."

"Well. … When you think about it, these folks *have* been oppressed for ages. First by the Spaniards, then by the Mexican upper classes, the church and all, and now by the transnational corporations. That's not democratic. It's five hundred years of imperialist domination. Maybe Farina was right."

"Man, David, you sound like a goddam communist!"

"Mark, I am not a communist, I'm just not a dip-shit redneck reactionary! You know, if we're gonna call names.

And anyway, I don't understand why you would support the current administration unless you own an oil company or United Fruit or whatever."

"How can you talk that way? Our president won fair and square, and you shouldn't bad-mouth him like that! Especially now that we're at war."

"This *war* will never end, for one thing, and for another the president *stole* the damn election, just like they do down here in Mexico!" I turned to Mark. "Have you been watching Fox News again?"

"Aww hell, y'all are nothin' but a bunch of damn bleedin'-heart liberals!"

Manfred would not stand for being found guilty by association. "I am a German intellectual, Mark, not a bleeding-heart liberal. And you know what, maybe David has a point. Besides, you know better than that." He looked over at me. "He is not a liberal. He is a freethinking anarchist philanderer!"

"Aha ha ha ha ha!"

Scowling, I shook my head and looked back out the window.

* * * * *

We went higher into the coastal range, the Sierra Madre Sur. Villages were fewer here, the land less suitable for agriculture, and with them went the obstructing peasants and livestock and countless *topes*. Manfred began once again to demonstrate his skill at mountain driving.

"Oh shit. Is it gonna be like this the whole way?" Mark was chain-smoking in the back, only letting go of the handle above his head to light another cigarette. The driving was somewhat dizzying in my delicate condition, but we were making good time. We had a few hairy moments as we passed slow-moving trucks and buses, barely able to see the road beyond. The Buick's engine whined as our Bavarian chauffer pushed the car to its limits, up and around sharp, rocky curves beneath steep peaks.

"You're pretty good at this, Manfred."

"We are making good time. I am ready to be on the beach!"

"So am I!" said Mark. "But what's the hurry? Goddam!" His face was nearly as sweaty as mine.

"Don't forget," I said dreamily. "We have those mushrooms."

"David, you couldn't even eat breakfast, much less da mushrooms. Do you really think you need those things in your condition?"

"No, I don't *need* 'em, man. ... Or, maybe I do," I said, wiping my brow with my towel, "but let's stop there for lunch anyway. I could eat them later on the beach. I won't be like this forever."

Mark said, "Lunch, yeah! I'm gonna eat one of those chickens!"

"Yes, *und* find yourself a nice squaw."

Manfred passed several villages, slowing over the *topes*, but none seemed to have any *comidas* or restaurants of any sort. All the mountain villages looked much the same, anyway, with no commercial signs advertising food or fungus for sale.

Then, down in some valley by a sluggishly flowing brown river, we found a shanty *comida* serving chicken. The people were all barefoot and dark brown, full Indian. Tomorrow's *pollo* raced over the dirt, squawking about our feet, oblivious to their impending doom. Mark ordered grilled chicken marinated with red *achiote* paste, as did Manfred. A round of beers followed. I stuck with the *caldo pollo* and a water, nursing my weak belly.

"What's so good about the sanitary condition here, Manfred?" I asked, eyeing the river flowing by slowly like a fat, dirty snake.

"Well. They have water. It should be fine."

"Yeah, look at the water. Very sanitary." A chicken pecked at my foot, squawking loudly as I booted him away. Manfred finished his meal and enjoyed a cigarette. We took our places in the boat and got back on the road.

Dropping down from the summit of the high coastal ridge, we dove into the belt of tropical jungle lining the Pacific coastline. Peasants with machetes continually appeared by the side of the road. The narrow, winding road had us stuck behind a slow-moving old pickup truck, the back filled with sullen Indians holding machétes. A blue plastic tarp covered a rusty aluminum frame, keeping the truckload of men dry. They watched us from the back with hard, cold faces. They just stared at us, never breaking their gaze. I wondered where they we all going in the middle of the day like that. At last we passed them, and I felt a psychic weight lifting.

Then the Buick's brakes were taking the heat, squealing frequently as we careened madly downslope for the next hour. My feverish condition, coupled with the lurching of the car, made me dizzy again. My stomach wrestled with the chicken soup. I told Manfred to pull off to the side so that I might be ill. Mark added, "Yeah, give the brakes a rest!"

The boys joined me, seeing to their own calls of nature. Big, colorful birds flew overhead, their strange cries muffled in the thick, humid air. The dense jungle came right up to the road, untold mysteries hidden within. Some unknown animal howled in joy, or rage, nearby. Bemused, we walked slowly back to the Buick. This was definitely the Interior.

As we moved further south, down the mountains, the jungle quickly became thinner, with massive stretches burnt out, cleared in the classic slash-and-burn style. Some of the fields were still smoking ominously.

"I guess this is some of that burning rainforest we're always hearing about," I said.

"Burn, baby, burn!" Mark rasped.

"Aw, come on. First-generation jungle doesn't just grow back overnight, you know, man. But it's all in the name of Progress!" I waved my hand at the still-smoking fields out the window, machete-wielding Indians staring at me with the characteristic unselfconsciousness of rural folk everywhere.

"I still say you sound like a commie."

"Mark, I'm not a fucking commie, I just think there's a better way to do things! Democracy in action. I think the transnational corporations have a slightly more powerful voice than these poor folks, who really, at the end of the day, don't even get a vote."

"Whatever, Farina," Mark said, opening himself a beer from the cooler. "It's always easy to criticize the way things are, but what's your alternative? You just gonna throw rocks all day or do you have any better ideas?"

"Well, that's a good point. Uh ... well, to start with, maybe these peasants ... who owns this land? Maybe these peasants should have some say in what happens here. I mean, they live here, right? Some sort of co-operative deal where they own shares in the corporation they work for..."

"The ... peasants? The workers, you mean? Owning the land collectively? That's called communism!"

"Man, what are you, Joe fucking McCarthy? If it's anything, it's a bit socialistic, I admit, but how else are you going to cure runaway capitalism without a measured tonic of judicious socialism?"

Manfred joined in, "*Ja*, it's done pretty well in Europe. A good mixture of capitalism and socialism."

"Well, that's not the way we do things in America!" Mark said triumphantly.

"Mark, you know man, *this isn't America*. And I would probably agree with you if my name were Rockefeller or Cheney or if I were a goddam captain of industry or whatever. Why do you rednecks always vote against your class interests?"

"You're the one who lives in a single-wide."

"I just moved there because it's quiet enough to write and it's near campus, ass!"

"And anyway, I vote for white people's interests!"

Manfred looked at Mark in the rear-view mirror. "Mark, are you a racist?"

"I ain't racist, I just hate them damn niggers."

I shook my head. Sometimes there were no words for the ingrained, hateful stupidity of American racists. I glanced over at Manfred. "Yeah, he's a racist. But like any good cracker he doesn't mind a nice squaw every now and then."

"SQUAWS! … Hey, hey! You know what you call a nigger from Plano, Texas?"

I winced, sighed, and gave in to the inevitable. "What, man?"

He shrugged. "Just a Plano nigger."

"Uh, yeah. I get it." He really meant no harm long as you meant none, and the black and white he saw did not apply to skin so much as to character. Or so I told myself.

Calmly, Manfred said, "Mark, you know what. I would appreciate it if you would please use the term 'African-American.' That would be more pleasant for everybody.

"Aww, hell, it ain't like we got any damn niggers in the car!"

"No, Mark," I said, "that's where you're wrong. Haven't you heard? We're *all* niggers now! Unless you own that oil company. Real wages haven't increased in over *twenty years* in the US." I shook my head. "Jesus, Mark, don't you have any PC in you? You can't *talk* like that these days! It's just simple respect, courtesy to everyone."

"David, the first PC word I say'll be my last, so help me God! Aha ha ha ha!"

The originally promising conversation having degenerated thusly, we thankfully began to see some renewed signs of civilization: an erstwhile *comida*, the occasional fellow vehicle, and – unfortunately for the struggling Buick – more *topes*. A thick fog settled in and surrounded us.

"That fog is coming off da Pacific. We are getting close," Manfred said. "Soon we will be on da beach!" And then, after nearly six hours of feverish, nauseating lurching about in the Buick, ahead we saw the soft, hazy glint of blue water. The fog gave way before a salty breeze. One thousand miles south from San Antonio we had traveled, through desert and mountains and city and village and jungle and slowly burning fields, constantly bedeviled by oxen and donkeys and chickens and peasants and *topes* and Volkswagens, not to mention the Revenge. And now, the majestic Pacific Ocean, the beach – the end of the road. Paradise lay there before us. Oh, the joy!

"Ding a ding, da da ding dang ding! David, see if you can find us a nice hotel in that there Hippie Book." Manfred was pulling off the paved highway onto the dirt tracks of Puerto Escondido.

"I'm sure there'll be something good. This is Hippie Country, after all." And it was. Tanned gringos and latinos toted around brightly colored surfboards, smiling and laughing. Everyone had a beer or a surfboard in their hands, and sometimes both. Even the little brown kids were more sun-baked than usual, their hair carelessly wind-blown, their faces cheerful. The usual Volkswagen Beetles were souped-up, painted in garish hues and gay patterns, often with boards strapped on top. Snorkeling couples walked to or from whatever cove or inlet they were exploring, hand in hand, their masks and air-tubes dangling from their tanned necks as they talked, laughed, and kissed. An old El Camino rumbled by before us, a small fishing boat on the trailer towed behind. I felt the last thousand miles of journey and stress and mashed leg and Revenge-ravaged intestines and heart-sickness fall away like a greasy old wrapping off of a fat tamale, unwanted and useless. In fact, looking around me I no longer felt so poorly at all.

I looked in the Hippie Book, found the proper section. "Well. There's a few good ones to choose from. Do we want 'Moderate' or 'Inexpensive?' Those are the only two choices here."

"Let's try the 'Moderate' section first, no?"

"Okay. ... Hey! Listen: She writes, 'My favorite budget hotel in all of Mexico is the Flor de Alejandra' ... on 'Entrada Playa Marinero between Carretera Costera and the beach. Now owned by a Czech and Italian/Canadian couple, the hotel continues the tradition of Lino and Alejandra Francato, who created the intimate inn. Small but pretty and clean rooms are decorated with bright wall paintings. On the roof are two larger apartments as well as a recently retiled swimming pool and bar, with hammocks hanging in the shade.' Well, shit, man, that sounds good, right!?"

Mark rasped, "Hell yeah! Let's check that one out! I tell you what, I'm ready for that beach! And, to get out of this goddam car. Okay?"

"Mark, ve are almost there. You've done very well on the trip down, which I know was unpleasant for you. But look, we are here, on da Pacific!"

As we pulled up adjacent to the pastel-toned hotel, I looked down the alleyway into which we had turned. Down the sandy path, past a few *comidas* and houses and other indeterminate structures, I could see the sparkling waves of the high surf, merely a couple of hundred short yards away. Palm trees swayed softly in the sea breeze. Street dogs ran about foraging for food, and little brown children sprinted across the sand. Two muscular fellows with surfboards passed us on foot, headed, no doubt, for the Mexican Pipeline.

We got out of the Buick, stretching our legs. The humidity attacked me, enveloping my body like a warm, wet glove. As if back in the womb, I was suddenly so damp it no longer mattered if I sweated. My left leg still throbbed, but seemed the better for the time I had spent off it in the car. We locked the Buick and went up the stone steps, through an iron portcullis, and into the three-story hotel.

Inside were placed large, leafy plants in sculpted clay pots every few yards. Rooms alternated with small alcoves all around the perimeter of the interior, with stairs in the corners to the upper levels. The floor was patterned with an attractive white tile with interwoven mosaics. The center of the hotel was marked off by a wooden rail, painted a bright, azure blue. Inside the square rail was a high shower faucet, set within a flourishing indoor garden. The open courtyard continued upward to a skylight, from which golden sunshine streamed down into the hotel's interior like a gift from the sun-god. It was glorious.

Manfred whistled softly, "Man. Looks pretty good. Let's find the guy."

We turned to the left, and there, inconspicuously placed, was the lobby – just a counter, chair, and an empty birdcage set in an alcove. Several keys hung on a lacquered board behind the counter, which had maps and restaurant brochures casually strewn about it.

Beside the counter a door opened, and out came a small, dapper man in a Hawaiian shirt, with a brightly colored bird on his shoulder. The bird's head bobbed and jerked about, curiously taking in the newcomers. "Hi there. I'm Paul," the man said slowly and precisely, without hurry. He smiled softly, his face tranquil.

"Yes, hello. I am Manfred, *und* this is Mark and David." We smiled, nodded. "Ve are looking for two rooms. A two-man and a one-man, if possible."

Paul shook his head slowly, "I don't have any one-man rooms, but … well, this *is* still the off-season. I could give you a cut rate on two two-man rooms." He had a slight lisp overlain with a gentle eastern-European accent. His green and blue bird chirped, moving around on his shoulder to get a better view of us.

Manfred looked over at Mark and me. We smiled, shrugged, nodded assent. "Yes, that sounds *gut*. May we have a look around?"

"Certainly." We followed him up the closest set of stairs to the second level, walking past the rooms to our left and the blue rail to our right. He opened a door with a key.

Manfred said, "What do you think?" I looked in the room. Two made-up double beds sat opposite an armoire. A fan circled lazily overhead. Between the beds was a mural; dark-green jungle leaves contrasted with a black jaguar's sharp, bright yellow eyes. They seemed to follow me about the room.

I said, "Uh, yeah. It's nice. You wanna take this one, Mark?"

"Sure, this one's fine, yeah."

Paul led us further down the way to a room set in the corner and let us in. That room was like the first, but featured two windows. I could see the beach in the distance, and sunlight flashed off the water into my eyes. The mural displayed a large complex of ancient Indian temples, much like Monte Albán. Sacrificial smoke rose from the top of one of the larger temples. Tiny Indians in grass kilts were going about their daily business beneath the temple.

I sighed. "Alright, I guess this is fine."

Manfred said, "You don't like it?"

"No, no, it's fine."

Paul said, "I have other rooms if you'd…"

"No, it's really nice. This one's fine."

"Why don't I show you the rest of the building." Paul led us up the stairs again. We followed sedately, matching his leisurely pace. The third floor was actually a terrace. It was humid and warm out, but the softly whistling sea breeze cooled our sweaty skin. Paul walked by an unused wet bar, to a corner where two hammocks hung from wooden poles supporting a palm-thatched roof. It was all constructed of natural, hand-crafted materials. It was a welcome image, tropical and rustic to my American mind, conditioned as it was in a steel-based, factory-wrought civilization. A pool sat shimmering in the center of the sunny southern end of the terrace, ringed with blue and orange tiles. The pool looked cool and inviting, and if it were not for the pending business I would have gone straight over and gotten in.

Large tropical plants grew in painted clay planters all about the terrace, some of the plants drooping and brown for lack of water. Paul saw me eyeing the dry foliage. "Yes, we're just finishing our dry season. The rains should begin any day now. In a few months, all these plants will be happily blooming again." Paul waved his arm about and his bird chirped agreement, head bobbing.

Paul pointed seaward toward the clouded sky, which was a moving mass of angry purple and black. As if on cue, a slight rumble vibrated through the air. He shrugged. "It does that every afternoon, but not any real rain yet, sometimes just a sprinkle or two. … So, what do you think?"

Manfred smiled. "We'll take it." We went back down to the tiny lobby and concluded the paperwork.

"How long will you be staying with us?" Paul asked as he got two sets of keys down off the lacquered board.

"Vell, we haven't really any set plan..." Manfred looked at me. I looked away, ignoring the blatant irony, suppressing the urge for a cheap shot. "Why don't we just go ahead and let you know a day in advance when we plan to check out?"

Paul nodded at Manfred. "Yes, that's fine, just fine. You're most welcome to stay as long as you'd like. If you are still around this Sunday evening, we have the distinct honor of hosting Puerto Escondido's Masked Ball, which will be held on our rooftop terrace. The event is held annually, and inaugurates the tourist season." Paul's bird nodded along. "Where are you coming from?"

"Texas. We drove down last Sunday, through Mexico City..."

"Oh, really? You drove the whole way?"

"Yes, and then we visited Oaxaca City. Oh, by the way, vat are your provisions for parking? We have our car right out front, just to the right of the entrance."

Paul moved into the alcove, maneuvering around the birdcage to a small window. He peered out. "Oh, that's fine. You might want to move back up the alley just a bit; I usually park my Jeep there. Joanna's out now..."

"No problem. But on the street is fine? Safe?"

Paul smiled, soft wrinkles in his tan skin formed around the corners of his eyes and mouth. "Yes, yes, it's very safe. No problems around here. No excitement. Just lazy days in the sun and the surf."

Manfred smiled broadly. "That's why we're here!"

We thanked our host, went out to unload the Buick. Manfred backed it up the alley a car-length, and we carried our bags up to the rooms.

I said, "That ball sounds like a good idea, right y'all? If we're still here."

"Aww, I don't know about that Mardi Graw crap. Hey! Y'all ready? Let's go to the beach!"

"Yes, right away!" I agreed. "Let me change into some clean clothes, and we'll head on down there." Manfred and I quickly threw on Hawaiian shirts – the uniform of the day – and met Mark, who was pacing impatiently in the lobby. We walked down the dirt alley and out onto the beach, where we saw two thatched-roof beach cabanas setting on the white sand. The one to the right of the alley was deserted, unused. The cabana to the left was manned by a tanned, scrawny little guy wearing only shorts, his dark brown hair sweaty and matted atop his narrow head. He looked tired, like he didn't quite eat enough. We strode up to the cabana, which contained an oval bar surrounded by wooden stools, with a table in the middle holding a wide array of bottled liquor. White plastic banners sporting the Corona logo hung from some of the supporting poles, flapping slightly in the breeze. We were the only customers, and we seated ourselves.

The man spoke English with a singsong cadence and a strange blend of Spanish and southern-European accents. "Hey there! Well, I've got me some new customers! Come on, come on, sit down, just relax, let Dimitri take care of you! Just relax, yes, that's right, relax, sit down there, that's it, okay! Alright, what can I get you? You name it, I've got it. I've got Carta Blanca, the *grande*, you know, the large liters, and Coronas, and Negro Modelo, and Pacifico, and a full bar here, you know, a full bar, totally complete, I can make just about anything, and if not, I'll go send my boy to get it, whatever you need, just tell me, don't hesitate to ask. I have Coronas..." His voice raised on the last sentence, going for a quick sale of what was no doubt the most popular item with *los gringos*.

Dimitri moved about the cabana's interior as he talked, in constant motion, cutting limes, opening coolers, and grabbing beers for our perusal, never stopping. I watched him, bemused. He never finished any one task in a single action, but seemed to move randomly from one thing to another. He began cutting up a lime on the table, stopping with it only partially cut. Leaving the knife protruding from the green fruit, he stepped to his left, opened a cooler, and waved a Corona about. Then, back to finish the first slice on the lime before grabbing a bottle of rum, swinging it near our faces. He ducked beneath the bar for a moment, popping back up with frosted beer steins, chattering away the whole time. He was quite good entertainment for such a relaxed place.

Manfred said, "Vell guys, what do you think?"

Mark had not sat on a stool with us, but in one of several white plastic chairs scattered about the immediate area. He slouched deep in his chair, the Ogre at rest. "I tell you what. I want a piña colada!" Manfred and I ordered the same.

"Piña coladas! Yes, yes! *Bueno*, piña coladas! Dimitri's bar is the place! Coming right up! Okay, here they go!" Dimitri set to work with a will. It was truly a spectacle to behold. He would fill one glass with ice, grab another from an overhead shelf, place it down on the bar, grab the rum, pour a shot, move back to the second glass and fill it with ice, then pour the rum into the first, and so on, never ceasing in his motion or in his happy, inane narrative monologue.

There seemed to be neither rhyme nor reason to his bartending method, other than to never cease moving. Sometimes he seemed to forget exactly what he was doing, but he would always somehow reorient himself. I became slightly dizzy watching him work, but in short order, before us were placed three blessed piña coladas, creamy, frothy, and slightly pink. The drinks got made, properly and quickly, and that was all that mattered, however odd the method.

We moved down to the plastic chairs with Mark, bringing him his beverage. We toasted and sank into our chairs. We sat within a circle of logs, lain end to end around the entire cabana area. I supposed they were effective at keeping out the sand crabs and their ilk. To our right, the sun began setting behind the low green coastal hills, the light softening. The surf rumbled on, growing quieter as the wind slacked. We sat silently, enjoying the moment and the fruits of our labors, looking south-west out toward the grand Pacific, the setting sun alighting the water in magnificent hues of burnt amber and golden bronze. Seagulls scrambled their sorties overhead, and three slightly underfed dogs trotted up to inspect us.

Dimitri spoke up from the cabana behind us. "Hey *mis amigos*, those there are my dogs, they are good guys, they keep a good watch on the place you know. Just don't you mind them a bit."

"Oh, no man, they're fine. Just fine." I petted one, scratching him behind his ear. His tail wagged in appreciation. He gave me a thorough sniffing and then sprawled out on the sand beside my chair. His ribs showed through his wiry fur. As with Dimitri, I wondered at his diet.

I breathed in deeply, taking in my environment, savoring several long pulls off my piña colada. I thought about just how fine everything was. My leg was improving, my stomach now seemed to be cast out of iron, and here we were, in Paradise. I sighed, a long exhale, and hit the piña again. It really was all very fine. No worries, at last. I looked over at Manfred, who was feeling the same vibe. Mark had wandered out to play in the surf, a sea-ogre.

I yawned and stretched, scratching my hairy chest showing through my open shirt. "You know what, Manfred? We are *there*, man. You know what I mean? We have *arrived*."

"*Ja*, David. I think you're right." Manfred spoke softly. He was as relaxed as I had ever seen him. He slouched comfortably in his chair, his own new best friend panting in the sand beside him.

"Man, I don't care what happens after this," I declared. "If we just stay here the rest of the trip, that would suit me. I mean, we've *earned* this. Don't you think?"

"*Ja ja*, we've come a long way."

"One thousand miles!"

"One thousand miles, *genau*."

"I don't know what Mark thinks, but I could just sit here on the beach until we have to head back to Texas. Just enjoy ourselves. Do some snorkeling, some swimming."

Manfred was only half-listening, which was very fine. "Dude, you know vat, that sounds *gut*! We can even attend that Masked Ball."

"Yes." I looked over to my left, eyeing an old catamaran up on the beach. "We could even get a sail in."

Manfred sat up a bit in his chair, looked over at the sailboat. He adjusted his straw cowboy hat idly. "Da de ding dang ding. *Ja ja*, dot's a good *eye-dear*, too."

"Why don't we see what Mark thinks about staying here the next few days. We won't have to worry about driving for a while – I know he'll like that – and we can just relax. Not worry about plans, or any of that mess. Just be beach bums for a while. Honestly, I'm sick of traveling. I just want to chill."

"That sounds fine to me." Manfred finished his drink. "You vant another piña, David?"

I finished mine, smiled. I hadn't felt so fine the entire trip. "Yes. Yes I do!"

* * * * *

Later that evening, freshly showered, we took Paul's suggestion and walked up the beach to town for dinner. We passed the end of our final joint back and forth as we strolled along. "Danny's Terrace," said Manfred as we walked northwest, the surf to our left. "The best seafood in town, according to Mr. Paul there."

Mark would have none of it. "Naw, I don't eat things that live in the ocean. Bottom feeders! Ugg! Aha ha ha ha! I think I'll get me a steak!"

"Don't you vant some of the local cuisine, Mark? Ve are on da coast, you know."

"*Hell* no! Damn fish, swimmin' around down there … you don't know where they been!"

"The ocean?" I said. "Come on, Mark. Don't you want some calamari? I hear it's good and fresh."

"Hey, guys, why don't I just get a steak, you know?"

"*Sehr gut*, Mr. Hanson. You go ahead and get yourself a steak." We walked past wooden fishing boats pulled up on the sand for the night, nets neatly stowed within the open cockpits. Soon we neared the little town. There were eight or ten restaurants beachside. Narrow, cobble-stoned streets, lined with tourist shops, led back from the beach to the town's *el centro*, a short block away. We entered Danny's Terrace.

Inside, we were seated with an enticing view of the main beach. The dinner was excellent. Manfred and I enjoyed shrimp hors d'oeuvres and *pescado de ajo* entrees, each fish lightly coated with a superb sauce. We shared a bottle of good dry white wine. Mark had Wild Turkey with his thin Mexican steak. I said, "Man, Mark, you don't know what you're missing. You're a saucier, right? You should try this garlic sauce!"

"I already told you, my sauces are for steaks!" Mark bellowed. "Hey, hey!" he hollered at the boy. "Another whiskey! *Por* fa-*vor*. ... ha *ha*!"

"A good steak doesn't need a sauce," I said. "Besides, you're from Texas. Steak Country. Why do you go to the Pacific coast of Mexico and get a thin, shoe-leather Mexican steak?"

"No!" He pounded his ham-fist down on the table for emphasis. The cutlery bounced, and a few heads turned. "Hell, it would be good with one of my sauces on it!"

"I'm sure it would be. But the point is..."

"Man, David, you wouldn't know a good steak if it bit you. H E E – H A W! Aha ha ha ha ha!" He was at full bellow now.

The boy came with Mark's whiskey, setting it on the table quickly and beating a hasty retreat. Manfred looked around, said, "Guys, why don't we do this. Go ahead and just keep our voices down just a little bit. Ve are in a fine-dining establishment, *und* ve don't want to make a bad name for ourselves." That was more for Mark's benefit than mine, but I nodded assent anyway. But not Mark. He raised a stink.

"Aww, Manfred, you're *always* tryin' to ... you know? ... Uh, I mean, can't we just relax? We're on vacation! *Damn*!" He bashed his fist on the table again, knocking over his water glass. Oblivious, he shot his whiskey and waved at the boy for another. "You know what I mean?"

"You know what, Mark? I vas only trying to keep us out of trouble. You go ahead *und* be as loud as you want, okay?"

It was my turn at calming the beast. "Mark! Hey, man. Manfred and I were talking earlier, on the beach. We thought, well, why don't we stay down here for a while? You know, until it's time to go back. Have a good vacation … it's pretty nice down here, and we can all just relax for a few days, not have any worries, just hang out on the beach with our good pal Dimitri. Go swimming, snorkeling … uh," I waved my hand around, "…uh, there's *boats*…"

"Yeah, sounds good, as long as we don't have to *plan* every-damn-thing!" He smacked down on the table again.

I spoke again before Manfred could respond. "Yeah, that's the idea, see? Just chill down here, no worries, man, no big plans, just be beach bums for a while. What do you think?"

"As long as I can hit Taxco on the way back. The silver capital of the world!" He finished his latest whiskey and waved at the boy for another, on a roll now.

Looking down at the wet table, Manfred sighed wearily and said, "I don't see why not. Ve can make it there from here, and Saltillo from there. Texas the next day after that."

Mark put his whiskey down. "Hey, guys." He leaned over, looked around suspiciously, and lowered his voice to a comically loud whisper. "Why don't we try to get some more smoke while we're down here. You know? Little bit o' the ol' bud-a-roos … Aha ha ha ha!" He breathed his whiskey-breath on us and cackled ogre-style.

"Actually, I *haf* already taken care of that. When we get back to the hotel."

"Paul?" I asked.

"No, it was ... you know, there on the beach. At the cabana."

"Ah, Dimitri!" I affected an exaggerated Romanian accent, based primarily on my many years of listening to the Count on Sesame Street. "*Di-mi-tri* vill take *care* ov you, eh! Aa Aa Aa!" Manfred glared at me, blinking. "Ah, well, that's good, man. Good! How much?"

"Oh, he said he'd let us know when he got it, shouldn't be too much."

"What are y'all talkin' about over there?"

"Mark, I was saying ve should have some smoke there at da hotel when we finish our dinner. Why don't we get ready and pay the bill, and go see?"

Dimitri was at the bar when we reached the cabana. He shook his head, said to come back in an hour. As we walked up the alley, Manfred said, "Let's go get that ice-chest out of the car. Ve should fill it up with some more ice *und* beer, maybe get a bottle of tequila. That way we can save some pesos while we are down here. I mean, I like Dimitri and all, but it's cheaper to have our own booze. *Und* ve can take it up to da roof."

We took the ice-chest back into the town. A few tourists and locals and off-duty surfers strolled about; the little beach town was tranquil and personal during the off-season. We mixed right in. We found a little kiosk liquor store with everything we needed and headed back down the beach. I carried one side of the ice-chest, Mark the other. As we walked, he frantically leapt away from a tiny scurrying sand crab, dropping his end. The swinging ice-chest slammed into my left leg, just below the knee. I yelped in pain, dropped the chest and hopped around for a moment, suppressing a scream.

"Hey, David, let's go … get the … what the hell's wrong with you?"

"Shut the fuck up!" I stopped hopping, grabbed both handles of the fully packed cooler and power-walked the last hundred yards to the cabana, my friends trailing along. Behind me I heard Manfred, "Dude, you don't have to do that!" I just walked faster, gritting my teeth. The exertion took my mind off the intense, renewed pain from my leg. Dimitri was behind the bar as usual.

I thrust the heavy chest into the sand, collapsed into a chair, my leg throbbing once again. As I caught my breath, Dimitri smiled and winked at me. I caught the signal and hobbled over to him. "Hey *amigo*, your friend wanted me to … oh, there he is." Manfred and Mark walked up.

"Hello Dimitri!" Manfred stepped up beside me. Mark helped himself to the ice-chest. I joined him, leaving the other two to their business.

Mark handed me a beer, saying, "Hey, sorry about that, man. You know? That lobster or whatever just got under my foot, you know? And I tripped, just dropped the other end … you know what I mean?"

"Lobster? … Ah, yeah, it's alright. I got a bit angry when it smashed my leg again. I'm sorry, too."

"Hey, you know, I'm about tired of Manfred and his goddam planning. He's really getting on my nerves. Telling me to quiet down. You know? We're on vacation!"

I sighed, began cutting into a lime for my Modelo. "Yeah, I know, man. He means well, though. And we *were* a bit loud. Let's just try to have a good time. Okay?"

"Hey, how's your Revenge? You still sick?"

"Oh, no, I'm feeling much better. Ever since we got down here everything's just sort of..." Manfred came over, sat down on the other side of me.

"Well fellas, we got the smoke."

"Oh yeah? How much was it?" I asked.

"Four hundred pesos."

"So, like..."

"About forty bucks."

"Ah. If it's good, that will be a good price.

"Do we have any papers?"

"*Ja*, we can use the papers from my tobacco pouch."

"Well that's handy. Is that why you roll your own?"

He smiled. "No dude, I just think they taste better than the commercial brands."

Mark came in, clueless again. "So, guys. What's the score on the smoke?"

"Well, Mr. Hanson, we got da smoke. But I want to go ahead and wait until we are on the terrace of our hotel until we try it."

"Naw, it looks like it's cool here. Dimitri won't mind, you know? Let's go ahead and blaze it up, you know? What d'ya..."

Just then we heard the sounds of motors coming up the darkened beach. From the brightly-lit cabana-bar behind us Dimitri hissed, "*Policía*! Da pigs, man!" I saw Manfred moving his bare foot around in the sand, digging around with tiny, barely noticeable movements. Three red, four-wheeled ATVs roared up in unison out of the darkness, all from different directions. The policemen dismounted and walked over to Dimitri at the bar. We just sat there, trying to still our hearts. One cop talked to Dimitri in Spanish, every now and then looking over at us, while the others just sat there on stools, surveying the scene without a word. I got up, stretched, walked over to the cooler and helped myself to another Modelo.

"Want one, Manfred? Mark?"

"About six or seven, actually. No, one will do, thank you." Mark just sat in his seat, smoking his cigarette, looking straight ahead at the moonlit ocean. I walked back with the beers.

The police all wore matching beach uniforms: black tactical high-tops, black socks, black BDU shorts, black weapon belts, and black short-sleeved jerseys with a big white "POLICE" in English on the back, just in case the tourists didn't know the Spanish word. Unlike *norteamericano* cops, they were all in good shape. No donut bellies. They looked like they meant business.

Dimitri and the police talked for a good ten minutes. The black-shirted cops seemed in no hurry to leave for anything. Occasionally their hand radios would squawk in excited, unprofessional-sounding Spanish, but this never elicited any response from the staid officers. Finally they sauntered back to their ATVs and roared off into the dim night.

Mark let out a big WHOOSH of air from his lungs, then a belated cough. I said, "Why don't we, uh, head on back to the hotel. Ready?"

"Just a minute." Manfred was bent over, digging around in the sand.

"What the fuck are you doing?"

"I am trying to … retrieve … this bag … of smoke!" Manfred extracted the plastic bag, shook off some sand, and quickly pocketed it.

"Oh, so that's what you were rooting around for there. Pretty slick. I thought you were digging to China or something, trying to get away."

"We don't vant to end up in a Mexican prison." It had become our mantra.

"No, that we don't."

As we lugged the ice-chest past the bar, Dimitri said, "Well, these cops, it's their regular beat, so, they just, always, yeah, comin' around here askin' questions, but they never … oh no, not me, not Dimitri!" He held his hands up, palms forward. Then went back to work at his bar, agitated, roving, looking for something to do, some drink to make.

Some things are the same everywhere. "No problem. We'll see you tomorrow, man. What time you open?"

"Seven."

"Seven?"

"Seven."

"Uh, okay. You mean, in the evening?"

"Morning." He sagged, stood still. He had run completely out of steam.

"Well, right. Okay. See you tomorrow morning, then."

We carried the ice-chest up the beach, up the alley, past the hotel's night porter, and up the stairs, up to the moon-lit terrace. I went back to my room for some privacy, rolled a joint from the bag. Manfred's thin, narrow cigarette papers were sadly inadequate for the task, but somehow I managed despite the harsh field conditions. When I returned to the roof, two interlopers were sitting with Manfred and Mark around a table by the pool.

"Hello! Who's this?"

Manfred waved his hands at the newbies. "These are our new friends, Jill and Mike."

Mark said, "Yeah, hey, David! Hey, hey, they're Scottish! Like you, David, you know?"

"Oh, well, I'm not really Scottish, just some of the blood…"

"Oh really? Ya ha' Scottish blood?" said Jill.

"Well, some. And German and English, some Irish, and Welsh. And I'm sure there's a Viking or two in the woodpile. Just a regular American mutt."

Mike was not impressed. "Oh, for fuck sake, you rootless Americans ha' nothin' better to do than go over yer bloody genealogies." He held one of our Modelos in his hand, I noticed.

"Ah, dinna mind 'im. He's right pissed, 'e is," said Jill.

"So are we," I said. I walked up to Mike, looked him right in the eye, and throwing on my deepest Southern accent, said, "And e'erythin' yawll say 'bout us 'mericans miiiight be true. But at least we weren't conquered by a bunch-a effete wankers!"

"Ha *ha*!"

"Yes!" Mike and I slapped hands, new-found mates.

"Least ways you're not after quoting that shite *Braveheart*. Next American I see spouting off about how bloody good that movie was … how *historically accurate*! … and *Trainspotting*, now *there* was a canny film, right!" He swilled his beer down to empty, crushed the can, smacked it down to the table with pure Scot gusto. He was one of us.

"You ready for another?"

Manfred said, "David, do you have the, uh, thing? Da smoke?"

"Just a minute, let me get us beer." I grabbed Mike and myself two from the cooler. "Anyone else thirsty?"

Jill said, "Yah, cheers mate." I got her one as well.

"Uh," I looked at Manfred, "is it cool?" I glanced over at the Scots.

Manfred smiled. "All *gut*, dude."

I pulled out the joint, lit it with Mark's lighter.

Mark rasped, "*And* he wears a kilt!"

Mike was incredulous again. "No, who? *This* one?"

"Yeah, Clan Mackintosh. Traced matrilinealy, the way the Picts used to."

Jill said, "So you're a Mackintosh on your mother's side?"

"Well, yes; way, way back."

"How far back?"

"Like three or four hundred years."

"Oh."

I paused to take a toke. Passing the spliff to my left, I said, "Enough about me and my damn pedigree or whatever. I'm fallen gentry, and that's all y'all need to know." I exhaled a great billowing cloud of smoke, savoring the taste, that familiar deeply relaxed feeling creeping in. "Now what are y'all doing down in these here wild lands?"

Mike said, "We're down on holiday, same as you. We were down the coast in Huatulco, but that was shite, expensive and crowded, so we took the bus up here yesterday. Glad we did, aren't we love?"

"Oh, yah, it's righ' lovely here!"

"So ver are you from in Scotland?"

"Glasgow," Mike said, taking the joint from Jill. Manfred went over to the cooler and pulled out the bottle of Herradura Reposada. We passed it around behind the joint.

Mark said, "Yeah, I've been there."

Mike exhaled. "Oh, Glasgow? 'Tha' righ'?"

"Yeah. Been all through the Isles."

"Mark here's an archaeologist," I said. "A metallurgist."

"Oh, grand!" Jill said.

"Yeah, every coupla years I go over there. Field expedition, you know? I always find some time to just tour the castles, in Wales, Scotland … you know? I've been there a few times." He took the joint, puffed, coughed, then chased his hit with a golden wash of the smooth tequila.

Mike's attitude had softened now. "Hey, you mates are alrigh'. We ran into too many Americans of the yuppie type down in Huatulco. You're no' like the others."

"Aha ha ha ha ha!"

I said, "Of course Manfred here is a German."

"David, I am an American citizen. I received my papers this spring."

"Oh yeah, your pig-roast was the party, right? We celebrated."

"*Ja ja*, we did."

"That was a fine party."

Manfred looked at me. I could see him smiling in the dim light. I looked away before he said anything more.

"Mike, have you been to the Western Hemisphere before?" I asked.

"Yah, we've been to New York, last year for business. We got stuck there after September Eleventh."

"Oh! That must've sucked."

"Sure an' they were doin' me bleedin' head in, they were. My co-worker over with us was Pakistani. He got the grilling, sure he did. Took hours. I thought they'd never let 'im go."

"He was from Pakistan?"

"No! His parents were born in London. He's never even been to the homeland. Doesn't speak the language. Isn't even Islamic!"

Mark was confused. "What is he then?"

"Anglican. Bloody English. Just dark-skinned."

"Hell yeah! It's still a white man's world!"

"Oh Jesus." I shook my head, looked down at the tiles between my feet.

Jill looked at me, concerned. "Wha's tha' supposed to mean?"

"It's nothing," I said. "Just a little redneck philosophy." Christ, was I really apologizing for this? The debt…

I got up and jumped in the pool, swimming around in the moonlight, ever so high. I could make out little of the conversation at the table, just low murmured voices, with an occasional "Bloody hell!" punctuated by an "Aha ha ha ha ha!" I smiled, floating. After a while Jill and Mike bid their goodbyes, waved at me and headed off to their room. I got out, toweled off. "I think I'm for the rack. Y'all coming?"

Manfred said, "Oh, in a little bit. I think I'll swing a while in the hammock." Mark was silent, intent on the tequila bottle.

"Well, see you in the morning."

"*Ja, gute Nacht*." I left them there, went down to the room. It was warm, so I lay in my boxer shorts, uncovered on the bed. The fan made its slow circles overhead. I could hear the curling, crashing surf through the open window. I thought of Jill and Mike, the happy couple. So lucky. I thought of Regina. I lay there for some time, thinking how much different my night would have been if she were with me, lying there next to me, in my arms. How different my life would be if we were together. I willed it to be. I thought if I had any power in my being, in my willing, let it be. Let it be. I tried to focus all my heart into her, wherever she was. And if not, damn it. Damn it all. I lay awake like that for some time, alone in the darkness, thinking pointless, futile thoughts.

Day Six

I turned over in my bed. Across the room, Manfred laid still, a white sheet twisted all around him. I looked down toward my feet. In the armoire's mirror, I could see the smoking temple painted above my head. *Sacrifice.* The word came unbidden to my head in the thoughtless vacuum of my morning mind. *Sacrifice.* There is always a sacrifice, a price to be paid.

I looked away from the mirror, got up, quietly put on some shorts. I walked over to the window and looked down at the beach. A few surfers were out there, catching the morning waves at the high tide. Down below the window I saw the wall that surrounded the hotel's perimeter. Broken brown, green, and clear glass had been set in the top of the concrete wall as it had dried, jagged ends all sticking up, a crude but effective deterrent to unwanted interlopers. Surely illegal in the States, I thought. An invitation for a lawsuit. Here they know how to deal with law-breakers. With a final glance at the smoking temple, I silently let myself out of the room.

Upstairs on the terrace, I surveyed the damage. Beer cans and spent limes covered the table where we had sat the night before. Fortunately, except for a few errant seeds and stems, someone had collected the cannabis. Our ice-chest was there on the blue tiles. The tequila bottle still held over three-fourths of its contents. Not wanting to make a bad impression on whatever cleaning staff lurked about, I tidied up a bit. There appeared to be no trashcan, so I made a big mound of cans and lime rinds on the table. The seeds I threw into a potted plant, hoping for some joyful happenstance germination, Johnny Appleseed-style.

I sat down and had a cold beer for breakfast. Manfred found me swinging in one of the hammocks, out of the morning sun. "Good morning, David."

"*Ja, guten morgen*, Manfred."

"Practicing your German, *nicht*?"

"Yeah, why not."

Manfred chuckled, sat down at the table. "You cleaned up?"

"A little. I didn't hear you come in last night."

"No, you were dead."

"Yes. I slept well."

"Good, good." We sat silently for a while, enjoying the still-cool tropical morning. Everything around me was eminently beautiful. Manfred pulled out a sandwich bag filled with a fat wad of pungent, sticky smoke. "You want to do the honors again?"

I badly botched the roll. Pot poked through the paper in various places and the gum wasn't sticking properly. It came apart as I tried to light it.

"You did a better job last night!" Manfred said. He undid my work, took out another paper, and produced a very Germanic joint, a perfect white cylinder, the ends pinched.

We sat enjoying the morning, listening to the foreign birds and the dull roar of the surf. Everything was calm, soft. After a while, we wondered where the time had gone. I stashed the roach in the same potted plant that had received the seeds. Manfred's voice seemed to come through a tunnel. "You vant to get ready and see about some breakfast?" He eyed my beer. "Something a bit more substantial?"

"Sure."

We went down to the main floor. As I took the stairs I noted the much-improved condition of my sore leg. To the left of the entrance was a *comida*. A group of chubby Mexican women chatted at a table, but sprang to action as we arrived, their first customers.

Mark joined us as we were stirring *leche* into our coffee. "Mornin' guys."

"Good morning Mr. Hanson. How did you sleep?"

"Oh, yeah, pretty good. Hey! Y'all wanna go snorkelin' after breakfast? Mike said there's a good place, up the beach past town. Next bay over. Think it's Manzanillo Beach or somethin'. Suppos'd to have lotsa cool fish!"

"I thought you didn't like fish," I said, glancing at Manfred.

"Man, David, I don't like to *eat* 'em … you know? I like to see 'em swim. You know what I mean?"

"That sounds like a good idea," said Manfred. "Vat do you think about some snorkeling, David?"

"No, I'm just going to park myself right down there on that beach all day. I really don't want to hike to the other side of town. My leg, you know."

"Are you sure?"

"Yeah. I'll probably go tomorrow or the next day. I just want to relax today, take it easy. Do absolutely nothing, just for one day." They shrugged, and out came our food. After breakfast and showers, we went down to the beach cabana-bar, where Dimitri was on duty.

"There they are! *Buenas días*!" He held up his hands. "My friends, you know, what can I do? What can I make up for you? Coronas?"

"Do you have a *cerveza* Sol?"

He must have opened every cooler twice, but came up finally and said, "No, no Sol, but there's Pacifico, Corona, the *grande* Carta Blanca…" He began opening all the coolers again. "Negro…"

"Just a Pacifico, then, please. With a lime."

"*Of course* the lime, Dimitri knows!"

"Want a beer, Manfred? Mark?"

"No dude, I think I'll wait for lunch."

Mark came up to the bar. "Sure, yeah, I'll have a large Carta Blanca." Dimitri put one of the liter bottles down in front of Mark.

Manfred and I went for a quick swim in the light morning surf. Mark was still sitting at the bar when we emerged dripping from the salty spray, invigorated. Manfred paced impatiently around in the sand for a few moments, then said, "Mark, will you be ready to go after you finish that? We'll grab some lunch in town on the way."

"Yeah, after I drink this we'll leave. I want some chicken for lunch!" Mark was already over halfway done with his liter of beer. He belched loudly.

Manfred and I sat in some chairs away from the cabana, drying off in the sun. Manfred looked around at the sandy beach, his eyes coming to rest on the catamaran down the way. The rigging looked old and tattered, the hulls were scraped and poorly painted in an unsightly shade of yellow. The canvas trampoline stretched between the two parallel hulls had seen better days.

"David? You know I have one of those things sitting in my driveway on a trailer?"

"Yeah, I've seen it."

"You know how to do any sailing?"

"Some, sure. Not those things much, but it's not too hard."

"Why don't we go ahead and see if we can charter a sail on that there boat, and then maybe ve can take mine to the lake sometime."

"And not look like total idiots out there?" I chuckled.

"Precisely. Get a little experience, right?"

"Sure. That'd be fun. Maybe Dimitri knows who to talk to; I'll bet he does. I'll check it out."

"I vould appreciate it. Und I will do some investigation of the local conditions, prevailing winds, local hazards, best routes, that kind of thing. … And when we come back later maybe I can meet you for a pint of Guinness at the Irish pub in town, just off the square there."

"An Irish pub, here?"

"*Ja*, the Irish are everywhere, David. Like leprechauns. … *Und da* Mexicans, no?" He smiled.

"Yeah, and the Mormons too." He laughed and went walking up the beach with Mark, headed toward town. I sat at the bar with Dimitri. He was full of nervous energy, and he took it all out on his poor bar, cleaning everything two or three times with an off-colored rag as he chattered. I looked in my wallet, counting the few remaining pesos.

"Where you from, Dimitri?"

"I'm Greek-Mexican. Family's from Mexico City." He spied me frowning dubiously into my wallet. "Man, you have good credit here, you fellas do. Your friend Manfred, he's alright, yes, and you have full credit here. Just pay when you head out."

I closed my wallet. "Thanks, Dimitri. We're good for it. I was just thinking I might have to start mooching off my friends. The pesos are starting to run a little low."

"What you do up in the States?"

"I'm a writer."

"Make any money off that?"

"*Some*," I lied. "I tend bar a little on the side, for some extra cash while I'm in school."

"*Si si*, I know all about that!" He never stopped moving, not even for a moment. Where did all his energy come from?

I finished my beer. "Could I get one of those piña coladas when you get a chance?"

"Sure, dude. Dimitri can make anything you want. Anything you need, Dimitri can get, okay?" Then it was another confusing episode of drink-making Dimitri-style. But somehow, the drink was ready in short order. He was a manic spectacle, ever agitated. I had never seen anything like it before, in any bar in any of my travels around the world.

"Dimitri, you see that catamaran?" I pointed. "Manfred and I were wandering if you knew who to talk to for a charter, for a sail."

"Oh, yeah, sure, that's old Adolfo's. He'll be 'round here in just a minute, I'll introduce you."

"Thanks, man."

Soon, a raggedy man with ill-kempt, longish hair came down the alley, across the beach, and shambled up to the bar. His clothes looked slept-in, as did his hair. Dimitri handed him a Corona. "Hey Tom."

"Hey Dimi."

"This is … what did you say your name was, dude?"

"David." We shook hands.

Tom said, "Well, I just thought I'd come by, see what's goin' on, eh?" He spoke slowly and lazily, as if the effort tired him.

"Where are you from, Tom?"

He turned his droopy, half-lidded eyes to me and said, "Oh, I'm from Vancouver. I just come down here for six months every year. Got half a month to go. I'm waiting for my check to come in, but, it hasn't, uh...." Tom tipped back his Corona, and the conversation sort of trailed off after that as he focused on his morning beer.

After a while I said, "I'm from Texas. Down here on holiday."

"Oh. Really? ... oh." We sat there for a while, Dimitri cleaning the bar for the fifth time. The day was getting hotter as we sat drinking. I look down the beach, waves of solar heat rose off the bleached sand. Dimitri stopped wiping the bar, slowing down, clearly running out of his miraculous steam. He sagged, standing as still as a statue for a minute. Tom and I watched him quietly. Then he crept over to Tom slowly, muttering something. He pointed toward a row of thatched huts just off the sand surrounded by palm trees. Tom nodded.

Dimitri turned to me. "Dude, I hate to ask you this, but ... you wanna watch the bar for a minute? Tom and I, we just gotta go ... you know." He winked. "Just gotta go up to my place, take a quick break, back in a minute. I *beeen* here since seven!" He came out from behind the bar, bending under the folding section as he went through the open space underneath. "Just serve anyone who comes, take their money ... you were a bartender beeefore?"

"Before?"

"Beeefore you was a writer? Just help yourself to anything. We'll just be right back!"

"Oh, well, sure, man! I'll keep 'em happy!" The two trudged slowly across the hot, shimmering sand, up toward the row of huts, Dimitri's dogs loping along behind. I opened myself a fresh beer as part of my wages.

They were gone for much longer than a minute. An older man approached up the beach, from town. He wore off-white linen slacks, a patterned Oxford shirt, and a tan Panama hat over his white hair. He came up to the bar, placing a fat black-leather fanny pack heavily on the varnished surface. He looked around, his eyes finally coming to rest upon me. "Where's Dimitri?"

"He's, uh … he just went home for a minute. You want something to drink?"

"Dimitri hired you?"

"Yes. … Well, just temporary help." I extended my hand. "I'm David."

"Hmm. Well, I'm Adolfo," he shook my hand, "and I'll have a Corona."

"Groovy." I slid under the bar, found him his beer. "Hey, Adolfo! Yeah! Dimitri said that you own that catamaran, don't you?"

"Sure do."

I handed him a cut lime wedge. "A friend and I were wondering if we could charter the thing, take it out for a spin."

He thought for a second. "Sure, I could let you take it out."

"Okay, how much? What's your rate?"

He drank from his beer. "It's... two hundred and fifty pesos for the day."

I came out from behind the bar, re-taking my former seat. "Tell you what. My friend Manfred is the one with the cash, and he has some questions about the local conditions. He went out for the day, but could you meet with him sometime? Discuss things with him?"

"Oh, sure," he nodded. "I'll be back here at eight."

"Eight tonight?"

"Yes."

"Well, good. I'll tell him to meet you here." I sipped my beer. "So, what's your story? You live down here?"

"I do. I own several local businesses."

"You speak English very well."

"I travel extensively in the States."

"Oh? And what kind of businesses do you have?"

He looked up and down the beach, then at me, sizing me up. He took in my shoulder-length hair, casual tourist attire, angular *norteño* face … then nodded in apparent satisfaction. "Well, I provide services for the tourists down here. You know, yachting, deep-sea fishing, water taxis, bungee jumping. We can even tow you behind a boat on a hang-glider!" He laughed. "And, of course … we like to keep our clientele happy, so..." He opened his fanny pack and pulled out a large, bulging bag of green and purple smoke. I could immediately smell its strong piney-skunky fragrance from where I sat. "You're a friend of Dimitri's, so I know you're cool." He extracted a big bud from the bag. I noticed the crystals gleaming in the sun as he rotated the cola between his fingers. "Here, go ahead and take this, as a sampler. Just let me know if you need any more, okay?"

I took the big bud gingerly, looking around for any more of those ATV-mounted cops. The beach looked clear, for now. "Uh, thanks, man ... thanks a lot! That's really cool!"

"Don't mention it. Just let me know if you need ... *anything*." He sniffed significantly.

I chose to ignore the sniff. "Sure, man. I'll pass this, and your offer of, uh, boating services, on to my friends." I was starting to sound a little drunk. I finished my beer and grabbed another from behind the bar.

Dimitri and Tom came back then, hopping quickly on their bare feet across the baking sand. "Oh, David! No! You didn't serve *him*, did you? *This* riff-raff? Not allowed! Not allowed here, not at Dimitri's bar! Ha!"

Adolfo raised his voice. "Stow it. *Who* keeps you in business? Who keeps you happy?"

"Aww, you know Dimitri's playin'... just horsin' around ... that beer's on me!"

"Better!"

The two were smiling. Dimitri looked around, surveying the beach. He moved closer to Adolfo as they discussed some transaction. When Adolfo went back up the beach to town a few minutes later, the weight of his fanny pack had been considerably reduced, but now it was lined with pesos.

"Hey Dimitri," I said. "Something I don't understand. What happens if those cops, the ones on the ATVs, what happens if they stop ol' boy there and ask him to see inside his pack?"

Dimitri's strange energy had fully returned since his break. He hopped around the bar, a manic blur of motion. Tom's leg jerked up and down on his bar stool beside me. Both of their eyes were wide and red.

"He has to pay the guy."

"Just pay him?"

"He has to pay the guy."

"That's it?"

"That's it. He just has to pay the fine. It's, uh, like, two thousand pesos for something like that. He just has to pay the fine, that's all."

"I like the justice system down here," I said, finishing my neglected piña colada with a slurp.

"Oh, no, it gets expensive."

"I'm sure it does." But I bet it beats 38 months in a federal penitentiary, I thought. Yet all systems have their drawbacks, and pretty soon I saw what he meant. As I worked on another beer, two police roared up on ATVs. They came over and sat on the other side of Tom, across the bar from me. Tom and I just drank in silence while Dimitri and one of the police spoke rapidly together in Spanish. Dimitri fished around in his pockets, then around the bar, eventually collecting a big wad of pesos which he handed to the cop. After a further brief conversation, the officers left, riding off to collect more tribute.

We sat for a while, drinking and watching the few tourists walk by. Tom and Dimitri were full of idle, pointless chatter. Dimitri produced a toothpick of a joint, too thin, like its creator. We passed it around, always on the watch for the Beach Patrol, and then I announced I was going into town. The joint had somewhat quieted down my jerky barmates. Their eyes were now grossly bloodshot. You guys make it pretty easy for *la policia*, I thought.

I walked up the beach, feeling the sun's intense heat bouncing back up off the sand. Huge white waves curled and broke to my left, crashing down and running up the beach, moving up the soft, gently sloped surface right to my feet. Further on I walked, dodging tiny scurrying sand crabs and beached jellyfish. Fat, pregnant coconuts hung from the trees lining the beach, and lush green hills framed the horizon beyond. I came to a few fishermen gathered near the surf in a loose knot. They were barefoot, their wide, tough feet scarred and calloused and very brown. They all wore t-shirts and loose-fitting dungarees of varying hues. One sported a faded, tattered white t-shirt featuring Michael Jordan and the Chicago Bulls. As I walked up one of the men looked at me.

"You help us, *Señor*? With the boat?" he said in Spanish.

I looked out to sea. A dory boat was just then chugging in, its bow jerking up and down violently as it passed through the surf line.

"*Claro que sí.*" I joined them.

The skiff approached, its engine straining as it caught in the trough of each wave. We formed two staggered lines on either side of its path. Then the boat hit the shallows, picking up speed in the smoother waters. The flat, angled hull grounded on the sand below the bow, the friction immediately slowing the skiff. We charged in toward the slowing skiff, grabbing on and pushing as we ran with it. I found a place aft, putting my weight into the stern, Michael Jordan and Scotty Pippen next to me. The helmsman pulled up and cut the outboard engine, our human labor now sufficing. We pushed it into line with a dozen-odd other skiffs, ours fitting snugly into its predetermined beach-slip. We let go and commenced to back-slapping. Noticing some renewed throbbing in my leg, I bid my new fisher-mates farewell with handshakes all around and slowly moved on up the beach into the town.

I walked past Danny's Terrace, where the lunch crowd now congregated. An alley lined with shops turned north into town past the restaurant, and I followed it to the tourist district in the town's *el centro*. There on the east-west running, exclusively pedestrian Zona Peatonal, was the main tourist drag, the Adoquinado. I walked slowly past Indians on brightly colored blankets, their native wares of gourds and beaded trinkets displayed on them. I browsed through quaint shops with Oaxacan and Guatemalan crafts, and boutiques featuring garish, overpriced sportswear and other souvenirs and inessentials. A young woman sitting in the shade by a money exchange smiled up at me, showing several gaps where teeth should have been. It was a cheerful smile, and I returned it. I saw a few open-faced taco stands, a pharmacy, a *zapataría*, and a few darkened, deserted discothèques. A broom-wielding boy mucked out the trash in the street from the previous night's fiesta. I went into a nearly empty Internet café.

My in-box held one message from Regina. It read:

Hello!

We are in Oaxaca city! We finally made it, hooray!! I can't believe we've made it this far, this fast. I have been such a slave driver, Javier and Miguel and Cesar must really hate me. We are all already so tired of traveling together, I don't know how the rest of the trip is going to work. I really hoped you would be here. I knew you were already gone but I went last night to the cathedral you mentioned anyway. It was really beautiful. Javier wondered why I wanted to go out alone, and we had a big fight. I'm so sick of him. I just really want to see you. I miss you! Oh well, enough of that. I'll just try to forget about it. I hope you guys are having a fun trip. Say hi to Manfred and Mark for me.

Deine, Regina

I sat there for a minute, re-reading her letter a few times, thinking. Then I wrote:

My Love,

I think I'm in heaven. This place is just perfect. The fishermen and the surfers and even the few tourists are servants of the God of Light, and I am finally ascended to their heavenly cloud-home. Puerto Escondido is the name of this earthly manifestation, and we are staying for four more nights on the beach and at the roof-terrace pool of the lovely Hotel Flor de Alejandra, and all the worries of our mad trip are now gone from us, for we are surrounded by Paradise. We will snorkel and swim and sail and eat and drink to our hearts' content, and never mind tomorrow, for today is most blessed indeed.

Yours always,
David

I hit "send," stood up and stretched contentedly, moved back out into the Zona Peatonal. Locals and a few sparsely scattered *norteamericano* tourists ambled lazily about in the noonday sun, in no particular rush about anything at all. I joined them, walking back down the Adoquinado. I went into a *comida* and sat down. I ordered a *cerveza* Sol and two fish tacos, eating the homemade food slowly and with great delight. When I finished I licked my fingers clean, enjoying the strong flavors of the sea. I washed it all down with a second Sol, then ambled back through the now *siesta*-quieted town to the beach. A few folks lay on towels, or played in the surf. The fishermen not out on the water were napping in the sun-shaded lee of their skiffs, there on the cool sand. I went on down the sparkling beach past them all, feeling hopeful and relaxed. My day's work was done.

* * * * *

I received no sleep though, no rest at all, for my *siesta*, thanks to Dimitri's impromptu gift. I paced around the hotel's pool, gritting my teeth, eyes wide, nose burning. I was now as manic as that crazy barkeep whose energy-secret I now fully understood. I drank the last of the beers in our cooler, washing the foul chalky taste out of my mouth and futilely trying to regain some sort of internal chemical homeostasis. Every so often I would bolt for the bathroom to tend to my runny nose. The sound of voices startled me, and I looked up to see my Scottish friends walk up, carrying two six-packs of Modelo and a bag of ice.

"Cheers mate! Sure an' you can cease yer whingin', we've brought some re-supply." Mike re-filled the ice-chest.

"Yeah! Hey, that's alright!" I stood there, staring at them with wide, red eyes.

Jill looked at me for a moment. "You're lookin' right sprightly today."

I suppressed a damning sniffle. "Yeah, uh, well … It's a beautiful day, isn't it?"

Was that a little too cheery?

Jill regarded me. "Yah, just lovely. A bit hot, though."

I staggered a bit over toward the pool. Mike said, "What happened to your dodgy leg?"

"Oh, ah, that's nothing, doesn't even hurt, man." I held his gaze as I took my wallet and keys from my shorts, pulled my shirt over my head, and tossed them onto a poolside chair. "But I could do with a little cool-off." I pantomimed a backward fall into the pool, the cool water engulfing me, sloshing over the sides and onto the tiles. I surfaced slowly, blowing out spray as I exhaled, like a whale.

"Where're yer mates?" Mike asked.

"Oh, they, uh, went up to Manzanillo Beach or somewheres to go snorkeling."

"You dinna wanna go wi' 'em?"

"Oh no, I had some business in town."

"Yah?"

"I had to check my e-mail."

Mike smiled. "Girlfriend?"

"Uh, something like that."

Mike took off his shirt and joined me in the pool. He handed me a fresh beer. I cut up a lime for us on the concrete sill of the pool. Jill situated herself in a shaded hammock and began reading a novel.

"So, you're not married?"

"No. *I'm* not."

"Oh. You mean … yer friends are?"

"No, they're not either. I mean … oh, you know, it doesn't matter. Never mind." I sniffed, wiping my nose with my wet wrist.

"Mate, wha'? Y' alrigh'?"

Sniff! "Yeah, uh … just some allergies," I mumbled. I excused myself, headed for the bathroom and the blessed toilet paper.

Mike was swimming around in the pool. "So wha' d'ya think o' tha' fuckin' cowboy eejit in the White House, spreadin' his shite all over the planet?"

I was charged up, chock full of conversational energy. "Well, that sounds about right. Of course, *I* didn't vote for him."

"Is tha' right? So you voted for Gore?"

"No, Ralph Nader."

"Bloody hell, mate, tha's like votin' for Bush!"

"No, man, I refuse to be chastised for my vote! We've got to get the Green Party going strong. Bush might be a warmonger and worse than Gore would have been, there's no doubt there. But that's far from saying Gore's any good. The Democrats are a bunch of pussies, unable or afraid to enact any *real* change even when they have the opportunity, the necessary political power. They're bought and sold too." I was growing louder, more animated. "We waste billions on a totally failed Drug War – you know the last time drug use went down in the United States? – throw millions of people in jail for nothing, give billions in so-called *aid* to dictators, and neglect our own education, health care, and infrastructure. It's a disgrace! A national disgrace." I looked at them, wild-eyed, my arms in the air. They were staring at me intently. " We need *real progress* in America!"

"Aye, that you do!" Mike said smiling, favorably impressed. Jill nodded. "Maybe you should be runnin, ay? They exchanged glances, surprised at the forcefulness of my oratory.

"Y' alrigh', mate?"

I was choking, could not speak properly; the numbing chemical drainage was seeping down the back of my throat and gagging me. "Ak ..." I coughed, trying not to hurl.

"Why ya whingin'?"

"It's ... just, draining..."

Mike's eyes widened with understanding. "Ah. Alrigh' then. Slag it off there, mate."

I went back to the bathroom to collect myself. A few deep breaths, get a grip ... better now, much better after the hurl ... the nauseous feeling passing ... might as well blow the damn nose again ... damn Dimitri anyway.

I arrived back on the terrace and immediately began sprinting toward the pool. At the edge, I leaped and assumed the familiar cannonball position. I smacked down hard, sending a powerful wave onto the tiles and giving Mike and Jill a good shower. I emerged with my arms in the air, victorious, and Mike and Jill cheered, laughing at me. "Tha's good crack, tha' is!" Mike handed me a new beer. "You really *aren't* like the others, eh?"

We splashed around for another hour or so before enjoying a smoke from an impromptu pipe I had constructed from a stray apple. But then the intense afternoon sun visited its tropical lethargy on the Scots. As they began to doze, the conversation faltered, ceased. I was winding down myself, but knew if I went to sleep right then I might not reawaken for many hours. My burning nose had finally settled down, the foul drainage gone. I was once again reminded of that shite drug's unpleasant aftereffects.

* * * * *

I walked quickly into town, still jacked up, testing the limits of my improving leg. I found the Irish pub, went in, and ordered a full-sized, Imperial pint of Guinness. The way it was meant to be. After all that watery Mexican beer, drowned in sour lime juice, a thick, hearty pint of Guinness sounded just fine to me. The bartender – an actual Irishman named Flynn – placed my pint before me. I examined the slowly blossoming head of my Guinness with lustful glee. The bubbles drew gently downward toward the bottom of the glass in calmly rippling waves of pure nitrogen bliss. Like a graven sacrament, a well-wrought shamrock graced the creamy head. After a short time the head settled, the soft line of creamy-white bubbles becoming clearly demarcated from the rich onyx depths below. I licked my lips, then upset the lovely tableau with thirsty gusto. Every time I tilted the glass back and slapped it back down on the dark-brown bar, the bubbles would begin their entrancing downward spiral anew. I watched them with fascination, admiration. The pint of Guinness was a trustworthy thing, sitting there in front of me. It had no trick-ass shadow. I could put my faith in it.

Flynn brought me another Guinness after a while. Flynn was a good man, he was. I enjoyed a few pints of delicious Guinness there in Flynn's Irish Pub, I did. Sometimes the pint of Guinness would go blurry before me, go blurry and become hard to see, but if I gnashed my teeth hard enough and assumed my customary bear-mask, the image cleared up soon enough. It was good to be a dancing bear, it was. After a while a woman came by, sat down next to me. I had had a few Guinnesses already, I don't know how many. The woman was nice to me. She asked why did I look so down, why the long face, laddie. She spoke with the most charming Irish accent, she did. She was middle-aged, like Flynn the bartender, but she was so nice to me, asking after me and all, and I enjoyed her honest, open attention, her compassion, I did. The woman was not like the others, no she wasn't.

But after a while Flynn became agitated and aggressive, and the woman left, moving away down the bar, and as he sternly brought me another pint, he waved his fist in the air and said, "Hea' now, don' ya be after flirtin' wi' me ol' lady, now, do ya unnerstan'?" I mumbled, "Sorrr, mate," wondering where I had gone so wrong in life to come to this point of moral foulness.

Manfred came in. "Da da ding, da da dang dang dong. Hello dude … vat's wrong with you?"

"Jaysus, sure an' nothin's wrong wi' your thirsty man, if he'll only be no' placin' his hands all over another fellow's wife!"

"Yes … *Yes*!" agreed Manfred. My head sunk lower in shame.

Manfred looked at me. "Bad day, dude?"

I drank deep of my Guinness. It was good to drink real beer for a change. "Naw, man … I'm jusss thinkin, 's all."

"Still thinking about Regina, you mean?"

I was far too drunk to deny it. "Yeah, well. I thought I might see her down here, in Oaxaca, you know. But it wasn't to be. I just wanted to talk to her, you know, get some resolution, some clarity." I looked at him, bleary, tottering on my stool. "Well, at the end of the day, I couldn't *not* do it, you know?"

Flynn placed a pint in front of Manfred. He smiled. "*Ja*, dude, but that there is a double negative." He looked at me hunched over the bar. I finished another pint, and Manfred his first. Manfred chatted with Flynn for a while.

"She's got a bit of Loki in her though, sure enough. So, what did she say?"

I looked up at him in some surprise. "Huh … What'sss the question?"

He grimaced. "I said, what did she say?"

"I'm not … sure … I don' 'member essactly." I drank the rest of my pint. "But iss all fer the besss, y'know'ahmsayin?" Ya know wha' th' Buddhists say about desire and th' heart, ri'?"

"What?"

"Uh, you can't, uh … don't let it, you know … ah, it's not…"

He shook his head, got up off his barstool. "Come on, David, let's go." He got out his wallet and, while fishing around for some pesos, pulled out a crisp US twenty. The bar's dim lighting briefly illuminated it, mixing with the Guinness in my head, and it flashed with a green glow, then returned to normal, the effect short-lived. Just a trick of the lighting perhaps, or trick-ass leprechauns. Then I thought that there are no real green lights. They are really all red. Manfred led me away gently.

* * * * *

After a sobering shower and a bite to eat, I went down to the beach again. Manfred was sitting in one of the plastic chairs near the cabana. I saw Mark at the bar, Dimitri moving around in his usual blur of crazy motion. Several tourists were sitting there, nursing drinks. Reggae music blared from a portable cassette player on the bar. I sat next to Manfred.

"Hey there. Y'all have fun snorkeling?"

"Oh, howdy dude. Yeah, it was really nice. The water was very clear, *und* you could see all kinds of coral and fish."

"Wow, sounds neat."

"*Ja*, it was. Da da ding dang dong…"

"Oh, hey! I found out about that catamaran. The guy will meet you right here at eight tonight."

"Which guy?"

"Uh, the owner. He said we could take it out for a sail. You want to go in the morning?"

"*Ja*, sure. What's his rate?"

"Two hundred fifty pesos for the day."

"Gut, I will talk to him." Manfred looked at his watch. "He should be here soon."

"Well, I'll leave you to it," I said, yawning. "I'll be ready to go. See you in the morning."

Day Seven

I awoke staring up at the smoking temple overhead. Manfred was gone. I showered and avoided looking at the temple as I dressed. I went downstairs for some breakfast and came around the corner to find Manfred and Mark drinking coffee, huddled at a table near the kitchen. "... and then he is in a terrible mood, sulking for the rest of the ...," Manfred was saying.

"What's that?" I said, surprising them. Manfred looked at me, expressionless.

"David, how are you this morning?"

I sat down and focused on Manfred. "Oh, I'm fine. What was that you were just saying? Something about sulking?"

"It's nothing, David. Are we ready to order some breakfast?"

"If you have something to say about me, I'd appreciate it if you'd say it to my face."

"Very well, David. I was just trying not to hurt your feelings. It's just that you seem to be letting this Regina business affect your mood a little too much, and affect your vacation, in a way that's not so good."

"Yeah David, you're supposed to be forgettin' about all that crap while we're down here. Remember?" Mark slugged me on the shoulder.

I looked at him. "You're absolutely right, man. And I *had* forgotten all about it..." I turned back to Manfred, "until Manfred brought it up again."

"David, you were very bummed out about it yesterday at the pub."

"Was I?" My memory was fuzzy, only the trick-ass green light coming to mind. "No, I was just drunk, man. One too many Guinnesses, you know? And the business with the, ah ... that was just a little misunderstanding, no big deal."

"Aww, hell. Just quit bein' a damn pussy, is all. Aha ha ha ha ha. We're here to have a good time."

I ordered a coffee and changed the subject. "Uh, hey! Did you meet that guy last night?"

"Adolfo? *Ja*, we had a fine evening. Ve had a few drinks there with Dimitri."

"So are we going sailing?"

"Later this morning."

"Ah, good."

* * * * *

After breakfast, I went back up to the room, donned my floppy fishing hat and my sunglasses, and then rubbed a little sunscreen into my nose, neck, and arms. Down at the beach, Manfred was unlocking a cable holding the catamaran in place with a small key. He removed the cable from the hull, fastened it back again, and put the key in his pocket. He was shirtless, wearing only his Stetson and shorts.

We pushed the cat down the sand and into the water. We waded out until the water reached mid-thigh and then gave one final shove before hopping on. We sat side-by-side on the canvas, our feet dangling in the water, looking southward over the surf, to the open ocean, the breeze blowing gently in our face. The cat bobbed in the waves, the sea a deep green-blue color. "So, what's the plan?" I asked.

"Well, the hardest thing to do in sailing is to work windward, moving at a very close angle to the wind. We have a wind coming out of the east now, so we can tack back and forth to go eastward, past Zicatela," he pointed to the port side, at the low green point of land at the end of the beach, "And then we can run with the wind back here. Should be a couple of hours in this wind." The wind blew stiffly and steadily out of the east, at least 10 knots sustained.

"Great. So, an out and back. Let's aim for the point and go from there."

"Excellent."

We moved the sail into place at what we thought was a 45-degree angle to the wind, taking us south-southeast. We moved mostly southward over the next half-hour or so, making little progress toward the east. "Let's reverse the tack," I said. Get on a northeasterly course. That's the shortest route to the point now."

"*Ja*, but we are facing south now. We can't turn the boat into the wind, so we will have to jib – turn around all the way – before we can get back to northeast." I was confused. I thought about it, and he was right, at least in principle. We caught the wind and were able to turn due westward, our speed building with the wind behind us. The twin hulls were cutting through whitecaps now, in the opposite direction we wanted to go, pushing ahead quickly in the stiff wind. We were moving away from the land quickly, now a couple of miles offshore.

"We need to turn back toward land now." I shouted over the waves. "Get back north, and go from there." Manfred agreed, and we moved the sail farther out on the port side. We got around to a west-northwest heading, but we could go no further in the northerly direction. We were still moving fast, and the land wasn't getting any closer. We tried for another 20 minutes or so to bring the cat around, without success.

"Cut the sail," I said. We brought the sail down and slowed considerably. We sat on the cat looking at each other in the stiff wind, Marcus holding his hat to his head, as he had being doing for the last hour or so. I turned and pissed over the port side. I was worried, and Marcus looked worried too. "We have to figure out how to turn northward. Unless we can start moving northward, we can't get any closer to land."

"Ja, we only seem to be able to go west, or south. And now the wind is out of the northeast."

"Then we should be able to get in irons and go almost due north."

"Okay, let's try again." For the first time, I was beginning to wonder what I had gotten myself into. I knew the basics of sailing, but I was overmatched here. And it seemed as though Manfred was as well. The day was growing hot, and the sun reflected brightly off the water. I was getting thirsty, sweating. We were now almost three miles offshore, by my estimation. And as we drifted with our sail slack, I could tell that the current was taking us westward. We put up the sail again, and again we were only able to achieve a northwestward course. We were unable to move the cat any closer to shore, that much was clear now. And the current and the wind were combining to take us out into the open Pacific. This is how we are going to die, I thought.

Manfred pulled the sail slack again. "Ve are not making *any* progress," he said, clearly frustrated now. He looked at me, and I could see a veiled panic beneath the surface of his cool exterior.

"Yeah. But we have to keep trying. Or try something else. Can you think of another way to change the heading northward?"

He was quiet for a long minute. I could tell he too was staring intently at the place on the horizon where the land was still visible, judging the distance. It seemed to be shrinking by the minute. "No," he said finally, looking northward.

The whine of a motorboat sounded in the distance, the third or fourth one we'd seen so far that morning. It was a big, 40-foot powerboat, and it was growing closer. Soon it was within 50 yards, bouncing along at 30 knots or so, white spray arching away from its shiny bow as it headed out to sea. Without saying a word, we both got to our feet and started yelling, waving our arms above our heads. The boat cut power, the bow falling back toward the surface. The people on board began waving back. The boat turned course and chugged closer, and someone onboard turned down the blaring Mexican polka music. The crew consisted of seven young Mexicans, all holding beers, the men shirtless and the women in bikinis. As they came alongside, one of the men shouted cheerily, "You wanna *cerveza*?"

"Si!" we yelled in unison. He reached into a cooler and stumbled forward, tossing a beer can high into the air, headed a few feet to my right, destined for the water. I leaned over, balanced precariously on the edge of the hull, and snagged the can out of the air with my outstretched right hand. The group cheered. They were partying hard, all seemingly pretty drunk. I passed the beer to Manfred and the man tossed a second can, which was much closer to the target. We popped our beers and toasted.

"Thank you for stopping," I said. "We've been having some trouble getting back that way." I pointed toward the land. "Could you give us a tow? We would really appreciate it." The men looked at each other. They were obviously headed in the other direction. I was just about ready to say, *Please tow us, or we are probably going to die at sea.* The man behind the wheel said, "Where?"

"Well, we came out of Puerto Escondido, but if you could just take us a little bit back that direction, closer to shore, that would be enough."

The men looked at each other, finally seeming to understand that something was not quite right with us. The man behind the wheel nodded, and circled the boat around to our north. The third man threw a rope out of the back, and Manfred lashed it to a cleat on the hull. The boat slowly stirred to life again, smoke and spray rising from the motor, and we managed to keep the cat facing straight behind it in the churning water. Before long, we were up to around 10 knots, bouncing in the wake of the powerful engine, like we were waterskiing. We had halved the distance to shore when the man cut the engine again. "Thees far enough, *señor*?" They clearly wanted the answer to be yes, but I feared we were still in the offshore current and still unlikely to make significant progress back northward.

"Just a little further, please. *Por favor.*"

They turned around and pushed the throttle forward, and we began chugging along again. Soon we were able to make out the beach west of town, and the man cut the engine. "Throw over the rope," he said simply, clearly done with his charitable work for the day and ready to return to the *señoritas*. We were around a mile offshore, and there would not be another chance to get closer. We would have to do the rest ourselves, if we could.

"Thank you! *Muchas gracias!*" We yelled, waved, and began trying to get the sail right again. By now it was afternoon and the sun beat down on us, blazing directly overhead, seeming very close indeed. Beads of sweat ran down my neck. I took off my hat, soaked with sweat, and wiped my brow. The single beer had only sharpened my thirst. Manfred's shoulders looked quite red. Again, we were not able to make any real progress toward the shore. We were clearly both in over our heads, our meager sailing skills inadequate for the one-two punch of stiff wind and strong current carrying us westward into the open ocean. We cut the sail again, our frustration palpable.

"David, what are we going to do?"

I stood up and looked at Manfred blinking on the edge of the cat, his back red, his eyes downcast. It was the first time I had ever seen him without a plan, at least when one was clearly in order. "Well, we can't keep drifting out to sea, that's for sure. This is as close as we're going to get to the shore, obviously, and we can't let ourselves get that far out again. I don't think we can make it to shore from there. But we can make it if we go now. I think we have to abandon ship, swim for shore."

"But we will lose the catamaran. We will have to pay for it." It was said not as an objection really, more of an observation of fact.

I looked him in the eye. "Would you rather pay for it with your life?"

"David, I'm afraid you are right. I wish it hadn't come to this, but it has. We have to face the facts. We can't make it back to shore. We are going to die unless we do this."

"Yes." We held each other's stare for a moment. Whatever the actual distance to the shore, it was deceptively close. It would be a long, tough swim. I nodded. "Okay, let's do it." I looked down, remembering the length of rope coiled on the hull. "We can try pulling the cat with us. Maybe if we take turns we can get it to shore." I tied a big loop in the end of the rope and jumped into the water. It was cool and refreshing. I had to resist the urge to drink it. I put the rope over my head and around my waist and began swimming for shore. Progress was slow, but I was moving in the right direction for the first time all day, digging hard with my arms and kicking with my feet, over and over, falling into a rhythm. Manfred was moving much faster, but turned around when he saw I was tiring. "Let me take it," he said.

We switched off like that a half-dozen times, moving painfully slowly toward shore, swimming and pulling for over two hours, sweat pouring off of our heads. As soon as my feet could touch the sea floor, I began walking the cat in slowly, pushing instead of pulling for a change. We reached the beach around mid-afternoon and collapsed on the boiling sand, exhausted, like castaways from a shipwreck. We each sported red welts on our chest where we had strained against the rope, our ribs sore. Manfred's entire upper body was bright red. We sat on the beach quietly, breathing deeply, thankful to be back on the land where we belonged, thinking about our brush with death.

We walked eastward down the beach for a few minutes before realizing that we were apparently not on Manzanillo Beach west of town, which meant that we were not even close to Puerto Escondido, but at least four or five kilometers to the west, probably more. We were the unwitting victims of a vicious rip current that had pulled us away from shore, even against our sail, and deposited us in the major near-shore ocean current, the westward-flowing North Equatorial Current. It had nearly killed us, the novice gringo sailors from Texas. Embarrassed at my own near-fatal incompetence, I shook my head silently.

Manfred looked badly sunburned, dehydrated, and dispirited. I had never seen him like this. I too was badly dehydrated, having foolishly compounded the situation with the *cerveza*. At that point, it had appeared that we were saved. But what kind of idiot goes on a three-hour tour in the tropics with no water? What kind indeed. I flushed with silent humiliation and continued trudging along, looking at my feet. And it was far from over still. I suppose it wasn't out of the question that one of us would now collapse of heat exhaustion before we made it back to town, perhaps dying in the process, our cells starved of precious water for too long.

We moved gingerly across the hot beach, our feet burning with every step. We found shade under some large palms and sat glumly looking at the surf. The beach stretched to the horizon in either direction, with no town in sight. A hike down the open beach, even four or five clicks, was probably far too long for us to attempt now, in the heat of the afternoon, in our debilitated condition. With no on around on the beach, we decided to rest a while and then walk inland, find the coast road. We would flag down someone there on the road, and try to get a ride into town.

We found a dirt road headed north and followed it for what seemed like forever through the thick green canopy. It was probably not quite a mile, but here the road was farther inland than I had expected. Perhaps that explained the lack of folks on the beach. At last, the track intersected with the coast road at a small village. There was no store or gas station, but on the other side of the road an older man sat on his porch in a big chair, dozing in the afternoon shade. He awakened as we stepped onto the porch. Manfred humbly explained our predicament in Spanish and then said he would be eternally grateful if we could use his phone to call our hotel and have our friend come and pick us up.

The man graciously invited us in, and on the wall in the small kitchen hung a large, plumb-colored rotary phone from the late 1970s. I sat down at the kitchen table and leafed through encyclopedia-sized phone book, reading out the number for Manfred. The phone whirred at the point of Manfred's finger, and then he explained our predicament again for Paul. Manfred held the line for several minutes, but Paul was unable to locate Mark. He promised to deliver the message to Mark when he returned, and offered to arrange for a taxi to pick us up instead.

We decided to spend the money required for a taxi, since there was no telling when the Ogre would return from whatever he had gotten himself into. Hell, maybe he had already found his way into a Mexican prison. The man took a large drinking glass out of the cabinet next to the sink, turned on the cold faucet, and filled the glass. He held it out toward me. Politely, but reluctantly, I declined. It took all the strength I had to refuse his offer. We thanked the man for his help and sat in the shade of his front yard waiting for the taxi, watching VWs whiz by on the narrow road cut into the coastal jungle. Manfred's skin was as red as a Maine lobster. Blisters were beginning to bubble up on his shoulders.

"*Scheisse*," he said, noticing them and patting them gingerly. Every inch of his upper body was angry and reddened, the heat still emanating from the boiling skin cells. Only his shoulders had received enough radiation to blister, it appeared. Still, this would be a setback for him. Uncharacteristically, he had been unprepared, and now he would pay the price. A sacrifice. But a small price, perhaps, in the context of the sacrifice we had almost made, almost having paid the ultimate price. We had nimbly dodged a lightning bolt sent by the jaguar god. We were lucky, but not unscathed. Was the punishment of the gods now sloshing over onto Manfred? I certainly felt responsible, as I had been totally unprepared myself, at least with regard to sailing competency.

He sighed and leaned forward, painfully. He was sober, more calm than ever, seemingly withdrawn. "David, we would be dead if it weren't for those drunk Mexican kids."

"Yeah, man. I feel … grateful, I guess. And very lucky. And very stupid." I looked at him and chuckled tightly.

"Yes," he said without emotion. He stared straight ahead, looking at the road. "We must never do anything like that ever again." We sat silently for a while before the taxi pulled into the driveway.

* * * * *

Back at the hotel, we chugged bottle after bottle of water while waiting for an early dinner of fish tacos and nachos in the shade of the courtyard. After a too-short nap, a long shower, and a relaxing smoke on the rooftop, I headed into town to the Adoquin and the Internet café while Manfred arranged for the return of the catamaran. The sun hung low and red in the western sky, its power now mercifully diminished for the day. The café was empty and so was my inbox.

Undeterred, I wrote:

My Love,

Long ago, before the people settled here, the dread pirate Andrés Drake sailed the Pacific coast, trading for, or taking, the supplies he needed to continue his relentless search for Mexican silver and gold. At the village of Santa María Huatulco, he and his men captured a beautiful young Mixtec maiden after killing her father and five other village men in a dispute. She was so beautiful that Drake decided to keep her for himself, ordering her taken aboard ship.

The pirates continued up the coast and anchored in an uninhabited bay. The moon was new and the maiden knew her chance had come. There, in the dark of night, she left her cabin, crept quietly onto the unguarded deck, and made a brazen escape, jumping overboard and swimming to shore, swimming for her life in the moonless night. She crept up onto the beach and hid in the jungle. Drake sent his men to look for her, but they could not find her, combing the coastal woods in vain for several nights in succession. Soon the pirates began calling her *la escondida*, the hidden one.

Every time Drake returned to the bay, he ordered his men to search for her again. But they never found her. And the place became known as the bay of the hidden one, and later the hidden port. Puerto Escondido.

Come and meet me here, my love, and we can hide together.

Yours always,

David

Satisfied, I got up and walked back down the beach. I heard Mark's hyena cackle "Aha ha ha ha ha!" from the bar. He was sitting there across from a vacationing couple. He was tending to a large liter-sized Carta Blanca, and the ogre-ravaged remains of a piña colada sat before him as well. He took a long pull from his liter and slammed the bottle down on the bar. Reggae music played at a moderate volume from the speakers.

"Hey, hey Dimi! Hey! Can we, uh … you know … get rid of this nigger music? Aha ha ha ha ha! You know? Lets get some *speed metal* on there? Yeah!" He pounded his fists on the bar in rapid succession, flailed his head. "Duh duh duh duh, duh duh duh duh, duh duh duh duh! Aha ha ha ha ha ha! You know what I mean?"

Nonplussed, Dimitri said, "You don't like the music? Dimitri can fix it, sure he can! Let's just…" He pulled out a shoebox filled with old cassettes, placed it in front of Mark on the bar. "Just help yourself, man."

Mark rooted around in the box for a while, then pulled out a tape with glee. "Slayer! Yeah, Slayer!" Dimitri made a sour face, but took the cassette and popped it in the player. Harsh, grating electric guitar chords ripped into the lazy tropical air. The couple on holiday exchanged a furrowed glance, finished their drinks, and departed up the beach.

"He's driving away the business." I looked over at Manfred, who seemed refreshed and more-or-less back to normal.

"Dude, you know vat? He's already had four of those liter-sized Carta Blancas, and he is now working on his third piña colada!"

"How long have y'all been down here?"

Manfred looked at his watch. "Only about an hour and a *haf*."

"Jesus."

"Yes, I think ve haf a problem wit der Ogre."

Mark's stopped his head-banging momentarily and threw back the last of his liter. He yelled for another. Dimitri looked depressed.

Manfred shook his head. "I think I've had about all I can take of Mr. Hanson for one day. He was fine until we got here. I went up to Dimitri's cabin there to use the bathroom…"

"At his place there?" I pointed to the group of thatched cottages.

"*Ja*, that's it. He's got a little outhouse there. And when I returned the Ogre was all crazy and rednecked-out, yelling and drinking like a fish."

"Maybe he's thirsty from his swim," I said idly.

"No, it's something else. … I've seen him drunk before, but this is…"

Just then Mark spied us and came over, holding up his full liter of beer like a king's scepter. "Hey, hey David! Slayer! Aaarrrrgh! Aha ha ha ha ha!" He did a little ogre-jig head-bang in the sand, spilling some beer. "I tell you what, this is the place! You know?"

I suppressed a chuckle, shaking my head. "Don't you think this music is sort of out of place here?"

"*Heeeell* naw! This is *slow* music! You know? Just go on and listen to your Air Supply, Aha ha ha ha ha!" His face was beet red, his eyes bulging.

Manfred looked disgusted. I shook my head again. "What was wrong with that reggae? And how many of those liters have you had, man?"

"I don't know, *a few*. Who *fuckin' cares*?" He threw his arms in the air over his head. A stream of beer flew from the bottle and landed on the rump one of Dimitri's dogs, laying the sand. He promptly licked it off himself before getting up and moving to a safer distance from the Ogre. Mark sat down. "Dimitri gave us credit at the bar!"

I sighed. "I know."

A tall, well-muscled white man carrying a surfboard came walking up the beach, passing between us and the surf. Faded tattoos covered most of his tanned frame. Nappy dreadlocks hung limply across his shoulders. A petit, well-toned young woman followed along with him.

"Goddam race-traitor. He's worse than a nigger!" Mark bellowed none too softly. The man had to have heard, but he didn't even turn his head. The woman glanced over, but wasn't sure what to do, or even which of us had spoken, so she just kept on walking with her dreadlocked companion.

"Oh, for fuck sake! Will you shut up with that redneck bullshit already!" I said, standing up next to Mark. I leaned over him, spreading my arms out wide to my side. "Quit trying to start something! You don't even know that guy! What's your problem?"

"Fucking white nigger. I hate those goddam Rastafarians!"

"He's not even black!"

"I know! Wiggers are the worst kind!"

"What the fuck are you talking about?"

"Those goddam Rastafarians, they *hate* white people!"

"I think you got it the wrong way 'round, dufus." I said, looking down on him, literally.

"That guy was white," Manfred deadpanned.

"Yeah, and he's joined 'em! Goddam wigger, it makes me sick!"

I looked at the sand, trying to find some way to communicate to Mark the utter idiocy and self-indictment of his statement, as I had done several times before. Enraged, I stood over him, forgetting his size advantage. "So they hate whitey, and you just hate 'em right back … repeating the same pattern of hate since time immemorial … like some goddamn tribal monkey!" I was livid.

Manfred stood up, extended his hands toward me, palms forward in a calming gesture. Mark looked up at me, as if noticing my agitation for the first time. He looked away, muttering. "Hell, yeah. Fucking race-traitors. Goddam Rastafarians." He got up and walked back to the bar, ordering another piña colada.

Manfred said, "See what I mean? He's been like this since we got back."

"You left him alone with Dimitri?"

"Just when I went to the toilet."

"Oh. Oh shit." I held my head in my hands.

"What is it?"

"I think … I hope he didn't…"

"Vat are you talking about, David?"

"Well, Dimitri … I think he gave Mark some, uh, coke, maybe."

"You are not taking about de *Coca-Cola*."

"No. … Well, I'm not sure, but I do believe Dimitri has some. A fellow came by yesterday, while you were gone. It was that guy, Adolfo."

"What's he got to do with it?"

"He's the one who brought Dimitri the coke, I think."

"Oh, great. So, ve rented a sailboat from a cocaine dealer?"

"Well, I'm not sure about that, now, man. He's really just a respected local businessman. And about the coke, I could be wrong. I just know for sure he had some smoke. … We should have warned Dimitri."

"Warned him about vat?"

"*Warned him not to give cocaine to ogres.*"

"David." Manfred turned to look at me. "Are you sure?"

"No man! I *just said* I'm not sure. It's just ... it would explain a lot."

"*Und* did you do some?"

"Who, me? Well, we *are* on holiday." Manfred looked at me intently, eyes boring in. "No, no man, I didn't ... I don't do *that* stuff. It's shite. It'll rot your nose out." I unconsciously rubbed mine. I just hung out with the Scots at the pool all day."

"Mmm-Hmm."

Manfred seemed satisfied. "Alright, dude. But *ve haf got* to keep an eye on Mark."

"Yeah. I think he's starting on towards Minotaur-mode."

"Super."

Up at the bar, Mark drained the last of his ogre-sized beer and sucked down the remainder of his piña colada. Before he could order any more, we moved up and collected him.

"Let's go get some dinner!" Manfred said.

"Hell yeah! I'm gonna get me some chicken!"

"Vell, if that is what you want, Mr. Hanson, I'm sure we can find you some nice yard-bird somewhere."

We began walking toward town. Dimitri – much relieved – immediately changed the music back to something more palatable. Overhead, the sky darkened and rumbled ominously from time to time, but still would not yield up the precious rains held in the threatening clouds.

* * * * *

Dinner was horrible. Mark twice spilled his water glass, and twice he sent back his thin, rubbery steak for further scorching. The Perla Flameante served no *pollo*, and Mark would have none of the wonderfully prepared seafood there-featured. Manfred and I grimly endured his ogrish bellowing, belching, and fist-pounding. The wait staff began to seat the incoming patrons well away from us in the half-filled restaurant, and others finished their meals quickly, leaving without dessert or after-dinner drinks. A constant stream of whiskey flowed down Mark's gullet. As we left our stale, smoky corner, the wait-staff gratefully ushered us to the exit, and Manfred was forced to leave an over-large tip for honor's sake.

As we waited beachside for the maddened Minotaur to finish using the sacked establishment's john, Manfred said disgustedly, "That's it, dude, I've had it. I need a break from the goddam Ogre! You take him for a while."

"Oh, come on. Is he really that bad?"

"You saw him in there! Every person in that place could hear him! Now half the tourists in Puerto Escondido know all about Mark Hanson's opinions on race, religion, and wrestling."

"*Wraslin*," I said, quoting Mark's earlier speech with dialect intact.

"Whatever. I can't deal with it anymore. I'm going to take a walk, then perhaps go for a swim, upstairs." I was sure this was a day Manfred would never forget, one of very few days in his entire life in which he had almost died. I wished I could say the same.

"Okay, man. I'll tend to this one."

"Just see that he stays away from that coke dealer of yours!"

"Man, he's not my … he's not a … Okay then, we'll see y'all later." Mark burst through the restaurant's portal. The flimsy wooden-slat doors flipped back suddenly and smacked against the stucco wall, nearly clocking an incoming Mexican couple. They leaped out of the way as Mark staggered down the front steps, looking on his grotesque brown smile with horror.

"Hey guys! Let's go to a bar in town, you know! What d'ya think?"

Manfred simply turned around and started walking up the beach, away from the hotel. I said, "Yeah, Manfred's gotta go do a thing, man. Let's go get a beer."

"No! Whiskey!"

"Uh … why don't we just mellow out with some brews, you know? Just take it easy? The night's young. We don't want to peak too soon."

"Aww, hell man! You're as bad as Manfred! Goddam killjoy!" Mark's eyes darted about wildly, bulging, his face flushed. The veins on his crimson neck were frighteningly visible, like Frankenstein's monster.

"Hey, look … alright, just take it easy! We'll go get some fucking whiskey, okay?"

"I tell you what! You know?"

I sighed. "Do I know what, Mark?"

"Huh? David, what are you blathering about? Aha ha ha ha ha!"

"Jesus. Let's go, man."

We found a nearly deserted little bar, set between a closed bank and a refuse-filled alley. Street dogs skulked about the alley's entrance. A tired old Mexican man helped prop up the bar, and the bartender was himself half-asleep. I ordered a whiskey for Mark, a Modelo for myself. Mark and I sat at a table on the Adoquinado with our drinks.

"Hell, David, if'n I see me that goddam Rastafarian again, mmmmah tell you whut…"

"You're not gonna do a *goddam* thing, Mark, you hear me?"

"But I…"

"No! I don't want to hear any more of your barbaric redneck bullshit, okay? You're gonna end up in a goddamn Mexican prison, talking like that. … Is that what you want!? Now let's just enjoy our drinks. Enjoy our vacation!" I shook my head, disgusted, frustrated. I just couldn't bridge the gap, couldn't help my brother see the error of his ways.

Mark sat sullenly awhile, then tossed back his whiskey all at once. "You're as bad as Manfred," he muttered, getting up and lumbering over to the bar. The old Mexican man woke up, noticed the Ogre with a start, and began almost-imperceptibly moving down the bar away from him. As he poured the drinks, the bartender warily eyed the beast-man before him. Mark came back with two whiskeys.

"Yeah, you're as bad as that damn kraut, but it's all right, man. I still love ya. Aha ha ha ha ha!" He sat down heavily, placed a whiskey down in front of me.

"No thanks!"

"Yes. Drink it. Drink the whiskey!" He was leaning over close to my face, and I could smell the flammable breath.

"Oh, well..."

"Drink it! Aha ha ha!"

We clicked glasses and tossed back the off-brand whiskey. After a while we had a few more. It grew dark as we sat there drinking, watching the European tourists wandering by wearing their Umbro gear and football jerseys, strolling the cobble-stoned Adoquinado in the shadowy dusk, large styrofoam cups filled with frozen daiquiri or piña colada or margarita clutched loosely in their hands. *Los norteamericanos* strolled by wearing baseball caps and sneakers, some distinguished clearly by the white tube socks pulled halfway up their legs. Urchins ran about, begging change. A man down the way on the sidewalk began strumming a guitar, his case open before him for offerings. Three members of the dog pack began fighting over a gristly bone, scuffling and snarling before a scrawny pup swooped in and sprinted away with it. I cheered for him, but nobody else noticed. We finished our drinks and began walking down the busy street. The party in Puerto Escondido was just getting started.

So was Mark Hanson. "Aha ha ha ha ha! Yeah, *whhoooeee*! *YEEEEEEE – HHAAAWWWWWW!*"

He hollered the rebel yell into the night, the sound echoing off the buildings, through the town, and down the beach. The dogs startled and ran, passersby stopped and turned to stare at the Ogre-cum-Minotaur. Mark continued down the sidewalk, smacking a wooden sign with his hand. It swung wildly on its hooks. "Aha ha ha!" Hey, David, let's go to a club, what d'ya think? You know?"

"Sure man. You're definitely club material. Let's go to that discothèque up the way there, up past the money exchange. Some dancing will probably do you good."

"So, what do you think?"

"About what?"

"Going to the club?" His pale blue eyes were glazed, unfocused.

"Uh, sure man. Let's go."

"Where! Where is it?"

"Man, what the fuck is wrong with you? Jesus! Were you listening to anything I was saying? Goddam!"

"Hey, *sorry* David, damn!" We walked along for a few moments, then: "So where is the club again, David?"

"Oh, fuck it, just follow me man. It's up past the fucking money exchange, alright?"

"Okay, Jesus, you don't have to get so worked up about everything! Just calm down, alright?" He hiccupped once, and again.

I finally understood Manfred's acute disgust. I had now had an ample helping myself. We walked up the boulevard and found the discothèque. I paid the large, well-muscled doorman the cover charge and in we went.

Colored lights flashed, pulsing in synch with the groove emanating from gigantic speakers set in the corners of the large, dark chamber. The place was filled with dancing people. The music seemed to shimmy in and around my body, seeping in through my skin, my toes and fingers, spreading through my limbs, slithering up my spine, splashing out again through my fingers and toes, out the top of my head. I was a vessel. I settled in on the dance floor with multiple others, the mass of dancing people shifting and swirling like a sort of moving psychedelic collage. Someone handed me a hopeful pill. Mark settled in at the bar with some more whiskey, and I was well to be rid of him. He slumped over the bar, holding it up like the tired old Mexican man down the street.

I danced, working up a fine, sweaty lather. I was burning off the beer, burning off the whiskey, burning off all the damn toxins. The leg was quiet. It felt damn good. I danced, laughing with the ladies out there. We were all having the best time. But not Mark. I glanced over at him as I worked my way around, gyrating wildly. The Ogre stood by the bar, swaying ever-so-slightly. His lips moved, but no one was nearby to hear his demented rantings. He amused himself; I could just hear his hyena laugh even over the loud pulsing music. To hell with him, I thought. Let him hold up the bar. I'm here to have fun, right? Let him have his whiskey. Let him be an ogre! I danced and danced like that for a long time, my unwinding mind cycling around with my sweaty grooving body.

I paused as the music slowed, the DJ taking a break to swap records on his turntables. I breathed deeply, catching my breath. Across the room, through the mass of happy celebrants, I saw a large dreadlocked form. The goddam Rastafarian. I had to move quickly. I felt in my pocket for the pepper-spray. I went over to the bar to collect the Ogre before chaos ensued.

Mark was gone. I scanned the crowded room, desperate. Too many people ... where was he? There! I saw his large head well above the throng, moving quickly, shoving folks aside ... and I was too late.

He had found his chosen nemesis. I heard a mighty, inhuman roar, and then the sickening *smack* of flesh striking flesh with great force. The music stopped entirely as the Rasta-man careened backwards into the turntables, burying the poor DJ under the wooden table and thousands of dollars of sound equipment. Several other bystanders had already been knocked down by the battling duo, creating an impromptu battle-circle.

It was a clash of the titans, Minotaur Metalhead *versus* Goddam Rastafarian. The Rasta-man didn't stay down long; in fact he popped right back up with a speed which belied his mass. He was almost as large as the Minotaur, née Ogre. *Smack! Bash!* Around and around went the two giants, fists flying. The crowd had backed well off in an understandable attempt at self-preservation.

The doorman-bouncer came running up, pushing his way through the crowd in an urgent effort to separate and evict the two combatants. I followed along in his wake, hoping to extricate Mark before somebody died or ended up in a Mexican prison. The doorman emerged right between the fighters, and they both smacked him square in the face at the same time. He went down, lying motionless, face-down on the shiny dance floor.

I kept moving, keeping my distance, circling around. Rasta-man hit Mark with a solid *thwack!* A right-fist to the eye. Mark staggered, recovered, and swung a sloppy haymaker. Rasta-man ducked, but the sudden dodge upset his balance slightly. He tottered briefly, and I went in, thrusting my foot against the ankle holding his weight, just as I had trained. The ankle collapsed, and Rasta-man went down hard on his side, surprised, his wind gone. Then I gave him a good three-second shot of pepper-spray right in the face. He clutched his eyes and began thrashing around on the floor like a half-crushed insect, wailing. His dreads swung wildly around his head like Medusa's unruly snakes.

Before he could recover, I grabbed Mark and yelled in his ear, "Go! Go!" I sank my fingernails into the flesh of his mottled arm and purple neck, trying to keep hold of him. He shook himself like a wet dog, and his pale blue eyes seemed to re-focus, as if he were just waking up. All the while I was dragging him along, grabbing a huge chunk of flesh out of the back of his arm, pinching hard to keep his attention. He had gone completely quiescent now, allowing himself to be led along like a chastened housedog. The crowd parted before us. We left a numb silence in our wake, the only sounds the anguished moaning of the Rasta-man, still on the floor. I glanced at the bartender on the way out.

He had never even ventured forth from behind his well-stocked barricade. We stumbled through the exit, out into the town.

Day Eight

I came to, disoriented. I rubbed my eyes blearily. I was there on the roof of the Flor de Alejandra, swaying slightly in a hammock, the morning sun just beginning to arc across the tops of the hills down the coast. Mark Hanson was laid out across the tiles on his belly, surrounded by half-crushed Modelo cans and lime rinds. A slight line of drool ran from his purplish, bruised cheek to form a pool on the tile. I watched the slight rise-and-fall of his ogre-bulk as he breathed in, out.

In a flash, the entire horrific spectacle of the previous evening came to my mind: the copious whiskey, the dancing, the fighting, the pitiful Rastafarian wailing and thrashing around on the dance floor, our mad escape through the stunned crowd and down an alley, along the shadowy beach, ducking into the bushes and behind beached fishing boats whenever we heard the ATVs, finally, with Mark sweating and coughing, the night porter admitting us into the sanctuary of our hotel.

Manfred had already gone to bed, but the Scots had received us on the terrace, giving Mark a hero's welcome. We had drank and boasted the night away, yes we had, there by the pool. Or *they* had, Mike and Jill hanging on Mark's every bragging word. I had had little to add to the saga, having sunk into a deep funk, nursing Modelos and no small amount of tequila. Now I shook my head in shame, looked again at the slumbering Ogre, down from his minotaur-esque were-madness. I realized suddenly that I had used the pepper-spray on the wrong combatant.

There was still a cold Modelo in the cooler, but my stomach turned at the thought of *cerveza*. I craved solid foods that morning. I went downstairs to my room. Manfred was toweling off inside.

"Good morning, David."

"Yeah, mornin'," I croaked.

"Did you sleep on the roof?"

"Uh, yeah. In the hammock." My head ached. I found my Excedrin, took three as the first course of my morning meal.

"So! How was your evening with Mr. Hanson?"

I looked at him, shook my head. "Not so good, man, not so good."

"Oh? What happened?"

"Let me take a shower. I'll tell you all about it over breakfast."

* * * * *

Later, behind Carmen's La Patisserie, across the alley from our hotel, Manfred and I sat in a pleasant courtyard, fruit-laden trees and palms all around. A large white bowl sat on our table, filled with slices of mango, banana, and pineapple, along with freshly roasted *café con leche*. Manfred had just finished a TV-quality spit-take with his brew.

"You ... you *maced* the guy?" he sputtered.

"No, it wasn't Mace. Pepper-spray. Essence of cayenne pepper in the eyes, the nose, it really hurts. And yet it does no lasting damage."

"Oh Jesus, David!"

"I know. But what was I supposed to do? I mean, you *saw* the other guy ... he's almost as big as the damn Ogre!"

"Yes, but..."

"Hey man. I had to get Mark out of there! We were headed for a Mexican prison, for sure."

"Vell why didn't you mace him instead? That goddam Rastafarian didn't even *do* anything!"

"Yeah, I, uh, ... I did think of that too. A bit late, though. My only regret. But a big one." I said ruefully.

"Vell. Now what are we going to do, David?"

"I don't know. I think the police will be looking for Mark."

"Well, so will that goddam Rastafarian!"

"Yeah." I nodded my head solemnly. "Yeah, I guess he will."

"*Scheisse.* Ve can't afford any more episodes like this."

"No shit! Look, man, I tried to keep him out of trouble. But he's a grown man, er, ogre ... and he insisted on more whiskey. And then we let him get into the Peruvian marching powder."

"Yes, yes! David, ve need to tell Dimitri absolutely no cocaine *für* der Ogre!"

"I know."

"Under any circumstances!"

"*I know*, man. I'll tell him."

"*Gut. Und* ve must keep a close watch on him from now on. No telling vat kind of madness he will get into. Ve must keep him out of da Mexican prison!"

"You're right. He's very close to the edge."

"*Ja ja.*"

"He's completely out of control. There's no telling what he'll do now." I held my hands up in the air helplessly. "Just so you know, I did the best I could last night."

"Hmm. Ve are going to haf to keep him out of town as well. Water sports, da beach … but no more whiskey, no more bars, no more discothèques! I think he should haf only *das Bier*!"

"Yes, you're right, restriction to *cerveza* only.

We paid our bill, went down to the beach and the cabana-bar. Dimitri was there. "*Buenas días*, you two! There you are! What can Dimitri do, you know? Anything at all?"

Manfred waved at Dimitri, went over to a reclining beach chair in the shade. I came right up to the bar.

"Hey Dimi. Uh, can you make a Bloody Mary?"

"*Can* Dimitri do it? *!A Dios mío!* Just you wait! Here we go!" He began the whirlwind, the little tornado inside his cabana. I watched, ever bemused.

"Uh, hey Dimitri." He paused, came over closer. "Uh, you know … just so you know. Mark … you know, our other friend, Mark? The big one, uh, *el ogro*?"

"*Sí sí*, I know him, dude." He nodded, his eyes were bloodshot and wide over gaunt, grizzled cheeks.

"Well, just … he has health problems. He only has a few years to live."

"Oh no!"

"Oh yes. It's very sad. Anyway, we have to take care of him, you know?"

"Dimitri knows!"

"Uh, yes. So, we can't … I mean, we can't have any of the, ah … white stuff for the, ah … for Mark. *¿Comprende?*"

He looked up at me quizzically, shook his head. "*No se.*"

"Yeah, he can't have any *cocaine*, see? His health…"

"*Bueno. Claro que sí*, no problem at all, dude."

"Great. See, that what he did yesterday was almost the death of him."

"No? *I* didn't give him any yesterday."

"Uh … no? We thought…"

"No! Just you, *amigo*! I just gave you that … hey! You want, we can go up to the cabin! Or I'll just lay you out a line right here!"

"Oh, well … I could do with taking the edge off…" I looked back at Manfred. He was parked in the beach chair, staring out to see in the morning shade, reclining. No one else was nearby. I looked back at Dimitri's gaunt face, nodded. "Maybe just one. Thanks, man."

"Of course!" He began breaking it out, shaking some flaky, impromptu powder onto a plate, snaking it around a sliced lime. He found a straw, cut it in half, and, bending over the table within the cabana, snorted the powder up in one quick intake of breath. He handed me the straw, and I leaned over and did my best Dimitri impression. The powder tingled my nose, and then turned to a pervasive burn throughout my upper sinus. The rush hit me hard. I felt my heart booming and my pupils dilate. I steadied myself against the bar, sniffling. Dimitri swayed a bit, his eyes wide and unfocused, then he seemed to remember something. He looked around his bar, quite unsure. "Ah…"

"My drink. The Bloody Mary?" I said through my pounding heart.

"Oh! Oh yes, *bueno*, coming right up. Yes!" The drink was ready in no time at all.

After another stabilizing Bloody Mary, I went back up to the roof. Mark was awake, sitting tranquilly by the pool, drinking the last Modelo.

"Well, there's the champ his own self."

"Oh, hey David."

I sat down at the table next to Mark. Cans and lime rinds were strewn about everywhere, along with a dusting of pot remnants and stems on the table. The cap to the tequila bottle sat before me, but the bottle itself had vanished from view, nowhere to be seen. The table and surrounding pool grounds had become a sort of deranged montage, an artistic representation of our chaotic train-wreck-of-a-vacation, a reflection of my internal state. I wondered how the hotel's staff was beginning to perceive us, or if they even cared. In any case, I lacked the urge to clean just then despite my boundless energy.

I looked over at Mark, sitting there nursing his morning beer. He stared out to sea, his swollen, purplish face relaxed, at peace with the world. I was quite the contrast, as angry as I had ever been, jacked-up with white fury. It enraged me to watch him in his apparent but deceptive placidity. "So. Have you calmed down then, off your damn minotaur high?"

"Aww, hell, that goddam Rastafarian bastard had it coming, you know? Fuckin' wigger."

I sighed, pressure welling up within. "Mark, will you…" I breathed deeply a few times, slowly counting to ten. "Look … for the benefit of the group … will you please just – calm the fuck down!" I slapped a crushed Modelo can from the table, through the air and into the pool like a thrown pebble, skimming the water's surface. Mark looked over at me, still relaxed and tolerant.

"David, it was just a bar fight. What the hell do you care?"

"It was … Just a bar fight? For fuck sake, man, this is Mexico! You'll end up in a…"

"I know, I'll end up in-a Mes-kin pri-son," he chanted, waving his arm about like he was directing an orchestra with a baton, his beer sloshing onto the tiles. "Relax, David. You know? Just take it easy."

"Take it … what the fuck? You're the one throwing people around the damn bar!"

"David, just relax. I…"

"Yeah, I'll fucking relax, all right! While you're in fucking jail!"

"Hey, you're the one that maced him!"

"Aww … fuck it." I stalked away, leaving him there with the rest of the refuse.

* * * * *

Back on the already stifling beach, pulsing waves of heat came off the sand like a nuclear furnace, and Dimitri was poor company, but was nonetheless a welcome change from babysitting the Ogre. He offered me two different impromptu lines of cocaine, both of which I accepted, along with various beers and piña coladas on our tab.

After I had calmed down, I went back to collect Mark. There on the door of my room was a folded piece of paper. Within the paper was a five-pound note drawn on the Bank of Scotland. The paper contained Jill and Mike's goodbyes, their e-mail addresses, a statement that I was 'not like the others', and an invitation to look them up if I ever made it to Scotland. If I did, the five pounds was for my first in-country pint. I chuckled, thinking of the lashing rains and gray days of Glasgow, the brogue reverberating through a dimly-lit pub as I tipped back my golden pint.

The Ogre had to be rousted out of his room. I banged on the door.

"Mark!"

No answer.

"Mark!" I banged again. "Let's go snorkeling!"

I heard shower sounds, splashing and coughing. Eventually, the Ogre emerged. He appeared quite refreshed from his bathing. Aside from the swelling and discoloration, his face looked quite all right. We walked down to Dimitri's to find Manfred and Adolfo sitting at the bar. Manfred remained shirtless, his skin still too tender to accept one. But he seemed chipper enough.

"Well, howdy there Mr. Hanson! How vas your outing last night? I heard you had quite a time of it!"

"Uh, yeah. It was nothin'. Just a guy who got what was comin' to him!"

"Looks like you got some of it too."

"Aww, hell, that's nothin', just some scrapes. You sh…"

"I should see the other guy, right?" Manfred smirked. Mark said nothing further, concentrating instead on his beer.

As we all settled in at the bar, Adolfo looked over at Mark's puffy, discolored face. "So. That was you last night?"

Mark did not respond, only looked deep inside his beer.

"Wow!" Adolfo shook his head. "Hey, I wouldn't show my face in town for a while if I were you."

Manfred said, "Why not?"

"The police *and* that surfer guy are looking for him. He broke that guy's ankle, and destroyed ten thousand pesos-worth of the DJ's sound equipment."

Mark spoke up now. "That's bullshit! That goddam Rastafarian knocked down the DJ booth himself, and anyway I barely touched the guy! David here maced him!"

I stood up off of my stool, pointed my finger in Mark's face. "Oh, thanks a lot, ass! I was trying to bail your ogre-ass out of a jam!"

Adolfo was alarmed, watching us with wide eyes. "Hey man! I'm just tellin' you what I heard. Don't blame the messenger."

We sat for a while in sullen silence, nursing our beers. Even Dimitri was respectfully quiet. We were mourning the death of our fun, the death of our vacation. Our *holiday*, as the Scots had put it. I toyed with the corners of a newspaper on the bar in front of me. Its headline read: *!Es la Guerra!* It is war. I looked at it more closely. "Jesus." I handed it to Manfred. "Is that what I think it is?"

Manfred looked at it a minute, then began translating. "In rural Oaxaca, a truckload of villagers armed with machetes and AK-47s massacred ten miners from a neighboring village. The two villages have disputed the rights to the mine for centuries." He put down the paper.

"Do you think that could have been that truck we saw in the mountains, you know, the one filled with those angry, menacing-looking guys, in the back?"

"That, or they vere just going to work. With our luck though…"

"Yeah, our luck. Our trick-ass luck." I shook my head, thinking.

Manfred swiveled abruptly off his stool, said, "Dude, can I borrow your knife?"

"Uh…well, yeah." Suddenly and irrationally wary, I handed it to him. He walked over to a large dirty off-white house near the mouth of our alley. An old Mexican woman came out on the porch and looked down at Manfred standing next to a gigantic aloe plant in a big clay pot. After they had talked for a while, he came back with a few large stalks of aloe, oozing clear juice from the cut ends. He handed me back my sticky knife, which I wiped clean on some bar napkins. Manfred began smearing soothing aloe-pulp all over his reddened body.

"I guess this sun here is a little more intense than that pale German sun."

"*Ja ja*, or even the sun in Texas."

"That old lady just let you chop off her plants?"

"You know vat, David? I very respectfully asked her if it would be possible to go ahead *und* get a couple of stalks for my sunburn."

"Nice lady."

"*Ja*, very nice. *Sehr freundlich. Ja*, you would be surprised what a little civilized kindness can accomplish in this world."

I smiled. "*Ja*, as opposed to *ze* barbaric redneck bullshit."

"Aww hell! Y'all quit talkin' that kraut talk down there! Talk American!"

"But Mr. Hanson, ve are in Mexico."

Well goddam, then, talk Meskin! Jesus!"

* * * * *

After a relatively quiet lunch where our discovery of *pollo* fairly soothed the Ogre, we went snorkeling. We avoided the Adoquinado, sticking to the beach. The heart of the tourist season was fast approaching, the beach becoming steadily more crowded since we had arrived in a nearly empty Puerto Escondido days before. We walked around many groups on beach towels and blankets. Children ran about with balls and frisbees. Stoned surfers passed us toting their colorful boards, headed in the opposite direction, for Zicatela Beach. The beach was swarming with folks. Several times, ATV-mounted cops passed on patrol, but we were never stopped or scrutinized. No one in the world looks exactly like Mark Hanson, but at least now we had some coverage in numbers. We were hoping one ogrish gringo looked much like another.

Past town, the beach abruptly stopped, running up against a series of low hills. We mounted a well-worn trail, hiking up and over the rocky terrain. Waves crashed violently against the base of the scrubby hills below. Mark stopped several times to catch his breath, smoking most of the way. I joined him at the last stop, sharing another one of Manfred's well-rolled Js. The trail then descended rapidly, the steep incline affording a lovely view of Manzanillo Beach. Set in a small, well-protected, horseshoe-shaped bay, here the swimmers and snorkelers could enjoy a tranquil surface while viewing the ocean's treasures beneath. We rented our gear at the booth and swam out into the bay.

The water was pacific, warm and clear, the waves gentle and regular. Beneath the surface, tens and hundreds of brightly colored fish moved in unison, the blue and red and yellow schools swimming together with the precision of a drill team. Bulbous coral made snaking, irregular reefs below, sometimes mounting rocks to within a few feet of the gently undulating surface. Anemone swayed gently in the underwater current. The scene was stark and shockingly beautiful.

I moved out a little further and stopped swimming. I hung on the placid surface, breathing slowly through my snorkel, staring absently at the reef below me. About 30 or 40 feet down, at the entrance to a cavern, stood a fearsome-looking barracuda, motionless. I could clearly see his dagger-like teeth, several inches long, as his mouth opened and closed slowly, rhythmically. I felt suddenly out of my element and vowed to keep an eye on the large, ancient predator.

Escaping the interest of the knife-jawed sentinel lurking below, I continued floating, taking in the reef's activity silently from above, beginning to feel a part of the aquatic community. To my right, from the open sea, I saw something large moving, and I looked over to see a ray, a *huge* manta ray, heading straight for me, but at least 20 feet below. He was mostly black with two white triangles on either side of his head, two more on the tips of his wings, and one on his tail. At the front were two large horn-ish protrusions on either side of the head, pointing straight forward. He moved gracefully, effortlessly, his wings flapping slowly and gently as if flying through the sea. I was terrified and awed, paralyzed. Aware that the manta is a filter-feeder, harmless to humans and eating only tiny sea creatures, I forced the fascination to triumph over the fear. His speed remained constant as he passed directly below me, unaware of, or unconcerned with, my presence. I thought him nearly 20 feet across, wing tip to tip. No doubt he was used to seeing humans in this area by now, non-entities in his food chain. The encounter left me feeling satisfied and I slowly made my way back in, glancing back occasionally at the menacing dinosaur-fish further below.

Manfred was sitting there in some chairs next to two large-boned Dutch girls, now wearing a shirt, his exposed skin glistening with aloe. He introduced us, and we chatted with the husky pair for several minutes, but their conversation was lackluster and uninspired. Turning to me, Manfred said, "So, David. We've got two more nights down here. We must insure Mr. Hanson stays out of da town, out of da clubs. If he runs into the police, he'll end up in a Mexican prison. And if the goddam Rastafarian's friends catch up with him, vell … you may have to mace someone again."

"Yeah..."

"Vat is his damn problem, anyway?"

"The Minotaur becomes disoriented outside of his lair?"

"Yes, yes! He really would rather be back in San Antonio at the Dog House, drinking Lone Star, barbequing chicken on da grill."

"Yeah."

"Vell, this is my last long trip with that one."

"Oh? You're not going traveling with him again?"

"Can you blame me? He's alright on a two- or three-day road trip, but not ten!"

"Well, he means well."

"Hmm."

"He just has a lack of moral … decency … of basic respect for other people … sometimes." What was I saying?

"*Vell* … He is alright as long as he stays off da powder."

"Well, uh … Dimitri says he didn't give Mark any cocaine."

"You believe him?"

"Yeah. Actually, I do, man. Why would he lie?"

"Da da ding ding dang, da da ding da da dung." Manfred scanned the horizon, threw up his hands. "So, he's just that deranged, then."

"I guess, yeah."

The Dutch women had overheard the entire conversation, and were staring at us in shocked disbelief. It was no use trying to explain.

A few meters down the beach, a topless woman sunned her back. A Mexican man with his family walked by. As they passed, the man kept his head and eyes straight ahead, scrupulously avoiding seeing the sunbathing woman. The man's wife also stared ahead, watching her husband from the corner of her eye for errant glances. The happy little Mexican children trailing along were oblivious to the spectacle, as well as the parental tension it had caused.

Mark splashed up still wearing his face-mask and flippers, lurching out of the shallows like the Ogre from the Black Lagoon. He had difficulty walking over the sand in his flippers, which made him waddle comically. The little children suddenly took flight, squealing. Mark walked purposely close to the topless woman, then turning over, staring brazenly.

"Hey guys, what d'ya think?"

"About what," I deadpanned, "the titties or the fish?"

"Man, David, the fish! Weren't they awesome?"

"Yes they were. I think I'll have two for dinner."

"Uhhhggg!"

"Is that Ogre-speak? Can you translate that?"

"Huh? David, what in hell are you blathering about now?"

"No, I think that was Minotaurese," said Manfred.

"Was that Minotaurese for 'red snapper'?" I asked. "'Mahi-mahi'?"

"Aww, hell. What are y'all talkin' about this time, guys?"

Manfred put an end to this round. "Oh, nothing, Mr. Hanson. Let's head on back to da hotel."

We walked back up over the hills, down to the crowded beach. As we passed the town I claimed some errand and parted with my companions. Manfred gave me a knowing smile as I left. I ignored him, and walked into the crowded *el centro* and straight to the Internet café.

My e-mail in-box was empty. Well, well, well. I logged off and re-set the computer. As I walked down the beach to the hotel I kept my mind scrupulously focused on absolutely nothing at all. It was safer that way.

* * * * *

After the group was freshly showered, and Manfred had once more politely raided the old lady's aloe garden, we dressed for dinner and dined in the hotel's restaurant. Outside, the monsoon threatened noisily again, dark clouds billowing in from the sea, but the dry season still stubbornly refused to yield. Our good host Paul came to lispingly inquire about the quality of our stay. "Hello there. How ith everything going?" he said, calmly.

"Fine, just fine, thank you," Manfred said. "Ve are having a wonderful time."

"Good. That is very good." He cleared his throat, took in a deep breath. "I just wanted to remind you about the Masked Ball. While dress is casual, masks are mandatory, but don't put yourself out finding one in town. I doubt there are any left anyway, and we'll certainly have plenty of masks here for all the guests. It starts at nine tomorrow evening, and runs until a bit after midnight, when we unmask. The party will be on the terrace. It's quite the event around here. We are *so honored* to have been selected to host this year's annual Ball. It officially inaugurates the tourist season. We had hired a DJ, but just today he canceled unexpectedly. I am going to town now to try to secure another. So, will you be interested in making your reservations?"

Thank you," Manfred said. He looked around the table, eyes settling on Mark. "We will let you know early tomorrow."

"Very good." Paul cleared his throat again, exchanging a wilted look with his colorful shoulder-mounted avian companion. "Ah, there is just one more thing. There have been some, ah, complaints, ah, from the other guests." His eyes nervously scanned the ground, but the brightly colored bird stared at us.

"Complaints?" Manfred asked.

"Ah, yes. About the noise. The, uh, *loud laughing*, late at night. Other strange sounds … Most of the people of course sleep with their windows open, and the noise from the roof does carry…"

Mark raised his beer bottle to his mouth, took a long foamy swig, slapped the bottle loudly on the table, and belched. Conversation in the restaurant halted as diners started at the loud report. I put my head in my hands.

Manfred said, "Oh yes. Don't worry about a thing. Ve will most certainly pay attention to the noise levels."

Paul nodded, relieved, his bird bobbing its head in unison with its owner, or perch, anyway. "Thank you! Thank you so very much."

Mark turned his bleary red eyes upon the man. "Hey, yeah, don't mention it. Aha ha ha ha!"

Paul beat a hasty retreat as we, the unwitting Ugly Americans, dug into our succulent dishes.

* * * * *

Having left Manfred re-applying aloe to his scorched skin up on the roof, Mark and I took an after-dinner stroll to the icehouse up the alley to get some more supplies. Inside, my emotional dam was breaking, and I was in a black mood, in no way prepared to endure ogres or trick-ass cheating wives or any other bullshit. She had not written me, and my sorrow was projecting itself into an irritable anger, again. I felt betrayed and used, once again. I could not stop torturing myself with thoughts of the fun she must be having with her husband, while I had…

"Hey, hey David. Hey, why don't we go into town for a minute, get some whiskey, you know?"

"No. We've got plenty of tequila."

"Aww, that cactus juice!"

"And we're going to have all the beer you could drink." I looked over at him. "Even you."

"I don't know man, I can drink a lot! Aha ha ha ha! One time, I was with Timmy and Mabrito and the Hube at a bar, you know? We drank … oh, I don't know … I had…about, I guess, twenty beers, or so. You know what I mean?" He looked over at me for confirmation. I walked on without any acknowledgement. "So, I got up from the table, and … you know? I walked over to the bathroom, thinkin' about this chick, and … you know what I mean? I used the john, you know, walked out past the kitchens, and I, hey, you know?" He looked at me, begging my acquiescence.

"I fucking understand, man!" I was gritting my teeth so hard it was giving me a headache.

"And I was thinkin' about this chick, you know, and she'd screwed me over, like they all do, not worth a shit, aha ha ha ha ha! You know what I mean? Hey, David, white women aren't worth a shit, you know? They're nothin' but lesbians and nigger-lovers! Aha ha ha ha ha!"

"Jesus. Will you just get on with the story?"

"So, … um … What was I saying? Aha ha ha!"

I sighed. "You were about to punch the freezer."

"Yeah. That's right. So, I saw the door to the freezers, and it was this thick metal, this steel, and … you know? Hey, know what I mean?"

"Goddam! I fucking know!"

"And I just smashed it with my fist, yeah! Aaarrrghhh!" He smacked his huge fist heroically into his monstrous open palm. "And later, when I got back to the table, I sat there, but no one would believe my hand was broken, you know? It was all swolled up real big. Hey David, you know what I mean?"

"Holy shit, will you shut the fuck up! I know what you fucking mean, goddam, man! Why do you have to ask me that every time, you … you idiot! Fuck!"

Mark glared at me darkly. We had stopped, facing off in front of the icehouse. The old wrinkled Mexican men sitting there in wicker chairs on the porch all stared at us as I screamed at Mark Hanson.

"Oh, so I'm an idiot?" he said, quietly.

"Yeah! You know what I mean?" I turned and went into the store. Mark followed after a while.

* * * * *

Later on the roof, Manfred and I were deep in the Modelo-filled ice chest. Mark was deep in the tequila bottle. All caution long gone, Manfred was bent over the table rolling a joint.

"You know what, Mark," I began, "we've been friends a long time."

"Aw hell, here it comes." He pulled on the tequila bottle as he stared at me steadily. His eyes were cold lumps of onyx in the night.

"You're damn right! I'm about fucking tired of you fucking this up!"

"Hell, man, what the fuck are you talking about?"

I got up with my beer, began pacing. "Starting fights out there. Yelling your barbaric opinions to the world. Who wants to hear it? Who the fuck cares?" I paced back and forth. "I sure as shit *don't fucking care*!" I did not care about anything.

"What's your problem, David? We're on vacation! We're *supposed* to go nuts, you know what I mean?"

I wheeled around, stabbing my finger toward Mark. "I *don't* know! I don't know! I *never* know what you're talking about! *What the fuck* are you talking about!" I stood there for a moment. "Oh, fuck it." I lay down in the hammock, my heart beating like a ragged horn. I knew I needed to cool off.

Manfred sat up straight with the rolled joint in his hand. "Here you go, David, you want to light this up?"

I sat for a second, then pulled on my beer, "Naw, thanks. That'll just make me think about all this shit even more."

Manfred looked at me for a minute. "Alright, David." He was silent for a moment while he lit the spliff. "Are you doing alright? What's got you so upset, some woman problems again?"

I sat up in the hammock. "*Me*? Doing *alright*? I'm fine, it's this damn ogre fucking it up!"

Manfred and Mark and I sat there a while, saying nothing. There was nothing really to say. We drank in silence, the other two smoking on the doobie, Mark glaring at me intermittently.

He turned to me darkly. "Yeah, don't get too comfortable in that hammock, there." He lowered his head, dark eyes gleaming forth from beneath lowered lids. "You've got another thing coming."

I glanced at him, suddenly mindful of things like distances and angles and how fast I could spring up out of that goddam hammock, with or without a busted leg. I felt around in my pocket and grimly realized the pepper-spray was back down in the room. Manfred just sat there calmly, smoking away.

Mark said, "Yeah." He glared at me, hatred in his black ogre-heart. "Yeah. You fuckin' hippies. Fuckin' yuppies. You're all the same. Always talkin' shit, right. Always tryin' to start somethin' you can't finish." He took another long swig off the near-empty tequila bottle. "Pushin' your weight around. Rich fucks. Thinkin' y'all own the goddam world. Yeah."

At least he was finally showing some class consciousness, I thought, getting worried. He never took his black eyes off me. I didn't respond. There was nothing to say. Either we were on, or not. I was ready to move, though. My alcohol-sodden nerves were enlivening with a healthy shot of hormones from the adrenal gland.

Manfred said, "Mark, you want another hit?"

"Yeah, gimme som'o'dat ol' nigger-shit." He looked at me, took a deep drag, coughing it out. "David, all you yuppies are the same. Talkin' shit. I oughta fix you, though. You're not like the others. *You should know better*, you know? You're such an *asshole*, goddam!" He smacked down on the table. "But I'll fix you. Oh, I will." He glared menacingly. "I will. *You know what I mean?*"

I got up from the hammock, walked toward Mark and the ice-chest. I got a beer, then I stared down at him. I saw his cold, pale blue eyes, strangely rimmed in black. Face to face with the Ogre, feeling the look he had never aimed at me before, I forced down the fear for the second time this day. Holding his eyes, I said, "I don't give a good god damn about you and your little problems. And I'll tell you this: I saved *your ass* last night, and you fucking know it! My debt to you is now re-paid. I owe you nothing further."

I walked away from the pair, half-expecting Mark to erupt behind me. Nothing happened, but I did not care. I did not give a good god damn anymore.

* * * * *

I went down to my room, completely alone in the world, intending to take some of Manfred's papers and Adolfo's weed-gift down to the beach, drink a few piñas at the bar, and fade into the night, hopefully forever. The half-light shone on the mural, the smoke billowing from the temple, the priest's arms raised to the sky. Perhaps the sacrifice would yield some magic, that was the eternal hope. I needed some magic to escape the hole I found myself in. But I feared that, like the Cloud-People, I too was doomed. Gritting my teeth, I made my way down to Dimitri and tequila and snaky lines on a plate and ... oblivion. It was inevitable anyway.

Day Nine

My head was pounding. The damn camels and lightning bolts were back, and nothing, not even Excedrin, would help. One thing, maybe. I left Manfred in his slumber, stumbled down to the beach and Dimitri. I parked myself at his bar for the day. This foul day, our ninth day of holiday, the ninth day since I had heard Regina's musical laugh, this our group's last ridiculous day in Puerto Escondido. I would just sit here by the bar, just see just how many *cervezas* a grouchy, lovesick gringo's tired body would hold. That would help my head, but not my heart.

She hadn't e-mailed me. She would not make it down here. Our plans were foolish and futile. She was stuck back in Oaxaca City, six hours of northward-bound tortuous mountain driving … not far at all, really. Captive to her husband, captive to her marriage, unable to break away to the coast. And me unable to make it the short distance back to her. She might as well have been on the far side of the damn moon. So there was no going back. Not now there wasn't. I sat there at the bar in the mid-morning sun drinking *cerveza*, accepting my foul fate. Really I just didn't want to think about any of it anymore. Ever again.

The season was now full-on on down at the beach. Various and assorted tourists swarmed about. Large groups of *norteño* surfers walked down the beach with their boards and shrieking children splashed about the shallows. All the cabana-bars were open now and doing a brisk business, Dimitri's included. Our paradise, our beach … what mere days before had been our idyllic isolated haven, was now a Mecca for surfers and tourists. Mark's despised Hippies and Yuppies were everywhere, far too many for one ogre to fight alone.

No, there was no going back to simpler, more peaceful times now. The hidden bay was no longer hidden. Some things could never be captured. Or, even if captured, could not be held. They would inevitably disappear into the night. You just have to enjoy them while they last, enjoy them for what they are, the fleeting nature part of the bitter-sweet flavor of the thing. And perhaps that is the way it would be with Regina, a brief fling, the springtime getting the better of us.

But it was time for her to emerge from the shadows as well. I would have to wait for the moment of truth, yes, wait in painful purgatory for two more months, but I would force the choice if necessary. Not carelessly, not presented as an ultimatum, but lead her into revealing herself, her ultimate desire. Somehow lead her to see that this can't go on, that a decision must be made…

Manfred and Mark came down to the cabana. Uncharacteristically, Manfred right away ordered a liter of Carta Blanca, a hearty Mexican breakfast. Mark and I looked at him, then at each other. We shrugged, went back to our own beers.

Manfred said, "So, David. I just signed up for the Masked Ball with Paul. Are you going?"

I sighed, yawned. "I don't know. I doubt it. Is that *the plan*?" I said sarcastically, irritably.

"You know vat, David? Why don't you get ready and go ahead and fuck yourself."

Mark stood up, holding both hands up in the air in a gesture of benediction and peace. "Hey, hey! Let's not fight, guys, you know?"

"I was only asking, David. You don't have to be such an *Arschloch*."

"Bloody shite, man, I was just wondering if *both* of you were going, you know, the fucking plan, man? Jesus!"

Mark chimed in. "Yeah, dude, you have been an asshole lately. Last night…"

"Don't *you* start chiming in on me, dammit!"

"And I don't go in for that Mardi Graw bullshit anyway."

"Fastnacht," Manfred said.

"The thing's like Mardi Gras, or Carnival, or Fastnacht or whatever," I said. "They all come from the same Roman festival of Lupercal. Same as Fiesta, when you get right down to it."

"No," said Manfred, "I thought Fiesta was from the defeat of the Mexican Army under Santa Anna. At San Jacinto, Battle of the Flowers, *nicht*?"

Mark said, "Then why are all the Meskins going downtown to party?"

"*Ja*, it's like the Japanese celebrating the bombing of Nagasaki," said Manfred. He took a long pull on his liter.

"No, including Fiesta, all these Western spring festivals have their origin in the pagan Lupercalia. But you're right about the Mexicans and Fiesta. No one knows their own history," I said. "Unconscious peasants. ... Dimitri? *Una mas cerveza, por favór*?"

"Sure thing, dude."

I came back to the question at hand. "No, I think I'll pass on the local fiesta thing. I'm just going to sit here all day and drink Mexican beer."

Manfred stared at me. "That sounds exciting."

"And then, tonight, uh, at the end of the day or whatever, I won't be in the mood for any trick-ass parties, people shaking their shite in my face. So I'm just going to sit here and drink Mexican beer all night *as well*, until you come down tomorrow morning and drag my happy ass into the Buick and take me back to Texas."

"Are you not having a good trip, David?" asked Manfred.

"Fuckin' great," I said, slurping down some more beer. A little spilled out down my chin, into my beard. "A goddam riot."

"So vat are you going to do today, Mr. Hanson?"

"Aww hell, I don't know."

Manfred, clearly disgusted with the both of us, got up and walked up to the dirty off-white house with the aloe garden. The old woman came out and they began a long discussion about the beneficence and many uses of aloe, or so I assumed.

Adolfo came by the cabana. After he and Dimitri did their daily business, he said, "Alright! Who wants to go deep-sea fishing?"

Mark sat up straight. "Hell yeah! I'm for that!"

"I thought you didn't like fish."

Mark looked at me, unsmiling. "David, I don't like to eat 'em, I … aw, hell. Anything beats this scene. Same ol' thing, might as well be listenin' to Air Supply! When will something just *happen*!? This conversation's pointless!" He shook his head, went off with Adolfo for the marina.

Manfred came back toting aloe stalks again. He began smearing fresh pulp about his reddened flesh. "Ver is Mark?"

"He went deep-sea fishing with Adolfo."

Manfred looked at me, speechless. I just shrugged, shook my head. We drank a few more beers, then Manfred said, "I'm going to go hang out by the pool for the afternoon. Coming?"

"Naw man. I'm fine here." I turned my dead stare down at my half-empty beer.

"Suit yourself." He walked up to the alley.

I drank a few more beers with Dimitri, accepting his various impromptu powdery overtures all the while. The heat grew powerfully with the morning. I took my shirt off, and my floppy fishing hat, and put them on the bar. My topsiders were scattered in the sand by my feet. I was going to get drunk in the sun, and I did not give a good god damn. Some time later Tom of Vancouver shambled over, looking ever the dishevelled bum. I could tell he didn't give a damn either. I liked that about Tom of Vancouver. He drank a few cool ones, then asked no one in particular, "Wanna smoke a joint?"

I shrugged. "Sure."

"It's at my place. It's not far."

I followed him up the alley, past the Flor de Alejandra, across the access road and into a complex of half-finished, bunker-style concrete structures set in a mango orchard. Rotten mangoes lay all about in the shade like crushed dreams. Odd pieces of soggy clothing hung from lines strung about the area. Little children and mangy dogs, equally unattended, crawled and trotted around the rubbish-covered grounds. We went up some discolored concrete stairs, and into Tom's abode. It could not have been called a house. There were no windows, and the single entrance was merely a gaping hole in the rebar. I wondered in what kind of structure did he dwell in Vancouver. I envisioned him panhandling out of a wet cardboard box on some busy Vancouver street-side, tourists stepping over him, clucking. Then, somehow flying down here on a budget airline, perhaps with his trust-fund allowance, here where his hard-earned Canadian dollars would stretch quite a bit further. Why not? Some bums probably lived the good life, at least part of the time. Tom was just an off-duty bum.

He produced a doglegged spliff and lit it up. "This is the special stuff. All the way from the interior of BC, aye?

"Wow, you mean the mountains east of Vancouver?"

"North of Vancouver, actually."

"How do you … get it in, to Mexico?"

He pretended he hadn't heard me. "The mangoes are great, eh?"

"Huh?"

You can just get 'em, ya know? Just get 'em off the ground and eat 'em. They're great."

"Oh, uh, yeah, they're pretty good."

"They're free."

"Oh no?"

"Oh yah."

Tom's conversation didn't improve much with the application of high-grade BC bud, so after we'd smoked that J, I left as soon as I was politely able, plucking a mango on my way out, headed for town, buzzing gaily, obliviously.

* * * * *

My bare feet slapped on the cobble-stoned Adoquinado. *Plip! Plop!* Each step was soothingly hypnotic, mantra-like. My mind gratefully slipped into an active, focused trance, aware only of the necessary navigation, dodging tourists and surfers, little brown Mexican kids in bright yellow swim trunks, my feet slapping down *plip! plop!* I stopped in a cantina for a beer. Then I continued walking. I didn't have to think about anything. It was a good way to spend the day.

I drank eight or ten beers that way, gobbling a few fish tacos and a ceviche for alcohol absorption purposes. I walked a while, then sat and nursed a few more Sols and watched the people amble by. I didn't want any company. My beer was my best friend. And the sacrificial fish. Who would wish to befriend the philanderer? Only the beer and fish, trusted fish…

Everyone around me was an alien. Everyone went about their business, speaking strange tongues. I got up and continued my walking meditation. I was alienated from them and their Mexican world. The people walked around me, like water flowing around an island in a river, no one speaking to the strange drunken gringo philanderer. I stopped walking, looked up and saw the good old Internet café.

I paid the attendant his ten pesos, logged on. No messages. Not one. I sighed heavily, got up, walked out, *plip! plop!* through the tourist-clogged town, onto the simmering beach. Nada. *Todo para nada.* The hot sand burned my feet, but I didn't give a good god damn. Purposely avoiding shade, I fire-walked up the rest of the beach, the scorching pain in my feet matching that inside, the external pain bringing me some relief from my focus on that internal pain. It felt good now, like an old friend. I came to Dimitri's cabana.

"Hey dude. You left these here." He reached under the bar, came up with my hat, shirt, and deck shoes, and placed them on the bar in front of me. I accepted them wearily.

"Thanks Dimi. Piña colada?"

"Sure dude. Anything you want." He began his whirlwind.

The sun was hot on my sweaty skin, so I put on the shirt, leaving it unbuttoned against the sweltering humidity. Dimitri finished making my drink, realizing as he placed it in front of me that I was gripped by a mood, of no mind to talk. He busied himself with the other customers, leaving me to my sodden musings.

Alles für'n Arsch. Todo para nada. All for fucking nothing. It was truly hopeless. She couldn't even send a courtesy e-mail, telling me to not expect her. She probably had Javier looking over her shoulder at every computer terminal along their route. So what? She's married, I said to myself, slurping piña colada. Married, and not going to leave him. That's right. *And not going to leave him.* I let it sink in. So what if I love her? She's married. Just using me, she is. Manfred and Mark were right, damn them. She was only using me for her own emotional gratification. I was playing the chump for sure. I was the dancing bear, the star of the show as her emotional tampon. I spat into the sand, disgusted.

I have my pride. Sure I do! She won't leave him for me, and I have my pride. It's all pointless anyway. Yes, the conversation is pointless. *So quit looking for her e-mail like a dog begging scraps!* I slurped the piña again, shook the alcohol-laced cobwebs out of my foggy head. Finally, I sensed, a cold clarity was coming to my thinking. She obviously won't leave him, so where does that leave me? Up the river. Chump City. Out of the classroom without a hall-pass, and here comes the principal. I shook my head again, slurping away. Won't leave him. Using me. So have to leave her. I have my pride. End it cleanly. Sometimes a clean break is better. *Just stop the damn thing from killing me any further.* That's what it has to be. It is all about self-preservation. *Save my ass from this hell.*

Yes, and there was my decision. *Quod erat demonstrandum.* Suddenly I felt better. I put down the piña, turned around and leaned my back against the wooden bar. I took a deep breath. The beach was still swarming with folks. The late-afternoon tropical sun blazed away, but the thatched roof of the cabana threw beautiful shade on my burnt feet. I moved them around in the cool sand, feeling the weight of the decision – now made, tangible and real – lighten my heart. I breathed in deeply, feeling the pressure ease off of my entire body as the breeze blew across my skin. I looked up, up the beach. Javier's lanky form slowly strode across my field of view.

My mouth hung open like a wittol's slack-jawed gape. I was frozen. The only thought in my stunned mind was that if Regina's husband turned and saw me then, he would see my mouth hanging open like that. He would see me and just burst out laughing. Then the adrenalin hit. I turned around toward the bar. I saw the floppy fishing hat sitting there next to my leather topsiders. I grabbed the hat, pulled it down low over my head, dropped the shoes down and quickly donned them. Then, cautiously, I turned slowly but – I hoped – casually to my right, trying to keep my face covered with the brim of the hat. I felt like I was covered in bright neon signs. There he was, still loping up the beach toward the opening of the dirt alley, his long, drawn face wearing its habitual hangdog scowl. I still couldn't believe what I saw, and, like a cartoon character, I rubbed my eyes with both fists closed. Still the apparition remained. I looked at the empty piña colada with some suspicion.

My whole body felt charged with energy. I had an instinctually aggressive feeling, like I could chimp-charge the bastard and finish it all right there, take my prize. My hands shook, and my stomach tied itself in knots. I fought back the nausea, tried to focus on my breathing.

Javier walked on, his lanky form awkwardly unfolding itself as if he had just learned to walk. What was his problem? In San Antonio he had never stood his ground. He had caught me with Regina at Manfred's pig-roast … obviously … doing something, and he had just stared at us. Why wouldn't he stand up for himself? If only he had confronted me, early on, we could have avoided this whole thing. But he had had to stay aloof, creating a vacuum to be filled. He lurched on, up the beach, across the sand. I watched him go. What was his problem? He had a new problem now.

Javier entered the alley, headed, I assumed, for the toilets. Where was Regina? It took me a few moments to see them, sitting on a towel down by the water. Just directly between the ocean and Dimitri's cabana. There she was, *la escondido*, the maiden hiding in plain sight. I couldn't believe the luck. I didn't know whether to feel blessed or cursed. As I watched her from Dimitri's cabana-bar, my knuckles involuntarily rapped on the wooden bar once, twice, thrice.

Regina sat cross-legged on their beach-towel, half-turned away from me, the outline of her hourglass silhouetted against the beach. The sight of her literally took my breath away. She was a divine apparition of feminine beauty. I staggered over to Adolfo's catamaran. The other two fellows on the towel must be Cesar and Miguel. We had never met, so they wouldn't recognize me. I had to catch her eye before Javier returned.

I leaned up against the catamaran, holding onto the rigging with one hand. I felt drunk and detached, disconnected from what I was doing. Everything seemed surreal. I was conscious of posing. I laughed giddily to myself. I was modelling a new line of casual beach attire. Oh, man. Got to stay serious. Get a grip.

I looked over at her, waiting. Hurry Regina! Look here! I yelled the thoughts out of my frantic mind, willing her to see me. Here! Look here! She was chatting with the two fellows, their backs toward me, their black ponytails trailing down their bronze skin, glistening in the sun. Something about the scene unsettled me, some *déjà vu.* She paused in her conversation, turned her head slightly, and finally saw my gringo ass posing ridiculously on the catamaran. Her mouth dropped as mine had done, hanging open for a moment. Then she caught herself. I grinned, and just could not stop grinning. I could see she was struggling hard to act normal, to not smile. I laughed and laughed, knowing I would remember this moment for the rest of my life, whatever else happened.

That thought brought me back to reality. Got to focus. Got to get some sort of plan. But it was hard to think. Damn *cerveza.* How many had I had? I could not believe she was here, right down the alley from my hotel. I had walked right by the whole group of them, mere feet away.

I checked the alley. Still no Javier. I looked back down at Regina on her beach towel with her escorts. Looking at her made me feel strong. Looking at her made me feel like a force of nature. Nature abhors a vacuum. I breathed in deeply, enjoying the surge of energy.

I walked back over to the bar and Dimitri. Soon Javier loped back to his little beach party and sat down next to Regina. I knew what Regina would do, and sure enough, within a few moments she excused herself and headed up the alley. As she passed by, about ten meters away from me, she said out of the corner of her mouth, quietly, "Follow me!"

I waited a decent interval, looked down at Javier. He appeared to be in conversation with his two longhaired mates. I tried to walk casually up the alley, but I felt like lasers were lancing into my back. I dared not turn around to see if anyone had noticed the drunken gringo with the funny hat trying to saunter up the way. I walked up to the Flor de Alejandra. Regina's tall, slender form was leaning gracefully against our dusty Buick with the Texas plates. She was grinning widely, her eyes sparkled and shot through me, a lightning bolt thrown by the jaguar-god. Her dark-blonde hair was pulled back from her high forehead, which was now reddening in the sun.

I walked up to her. We looked at each other for a minute, just staring into each other's eyes. We were both grinning, and not a little bit in shock.

I took her hands. “I can’t believe we pulled it off.”

“No.”

“We make a great team.”

“Yes. That we do.” But then she began to cast nervous glances over my shoulder, down the alley.

“Come with me,” I said, pulling her into the hotel lobby. I took her on around to the dining area. We approached a table, and I motioned to a chair, took one myself.

She stood there looking at me. “What happened to your manners?”

“Huh?”

“Aren’t you going to pull it out for me?”

Smiling wryly, I got up somewhat sheepishly, quite aware of how awash in beer I was. But I managed to pull out her seat and return to mine without stumbling. I took my floppy hat off and laid it on the seat next to me. We stared at each other for a while.

“So,” she broke the silence.

“So.”

A boy came over from the bar. “Something to drink?” I asked her.

“*Yo quiero una agua con gas, por favór.*”

I ordered the same, wisely trying to dry out a bit. When the boy returned with the bottled water, my hands shook a bit as I picked it up, whether from alcohol or shot nerves I couldn’t say.

“So how’s your Spanish coming?” she asked.

“Pretty good. *Poco y poco.* I don’t really need it much down here on the coast.”

We sat a few moments more, just looking at each other, her eyes entrancing me again. I didn't know what to say, where to begin, or how I felt. "So, you're here," I started lamely.

"Yes. I can't believe it." She sipped delicately on her water.

"No. No, I can't either. I didn't think you would make it."

"I didn't either. It was like pulling teeth. They really think I'm a crazy woman, the way I insisted on leaving Oaxaca City and blazing down here today for no reason really. We just got here a few hours ago."

"How did you pull it off?"

She smiled. "I was such a bitch! I *insisted* that we come to the beach. And they didn't even want to come here! They wanted to go to Huatulco instead. But I got into a big fight with Javier. He's so mad at me!" Her smile widened, showing her perfect teeth.

"Well, I tried that act with my boys, but I guess I didn't have your feminine wiles. Anyway, only one of us needed to succeed."

"Yes." She set down her drink and looked at me.

We were quiet for a while after that. We just stared at each other over the table. I wanted to kiss her.

She said, "You're so red. And sweaty!" She laughed. "You smell like a brewery."

"I, uh, yeah. I've just been hanging out on the beach all day, drinking beer. We're leaving tomorrow. I really didn't think you would make it!"

"I know. I liked your e-mails, telling me you were here, and then the story of the Mixtec maiden. I like the way you wrote it."

"Well, I am a writer."

"Is the story true?"

"You mean was there really a maiden who escaped the dread pirate Drake and hid in the woods here?"

"Yes"

"Well, it's the legend of the founding of Puerto Escondido. What do you think?"

"I think so."

"Me too." I reached across the table, taking one of her hands in both of mine.

"Regina."

She looked at me, her wide eyes luminous. She sighed softly.

"I want to see you tonight."

"I don't know," she shook her head, "Javier is already suspicious, I think."

"He thinks ... what? That you wanted to come here to see me? What are the odds..."

"I don't know! I didn't *ask* him. He's just acting funny."

I took a deep breath. "I understand if you can't come. But I have to see you again. Just try. Meet me on the beach. At midnight."

She paused. "I'll ... try. I can't promise anything."

Of course she could not. She was married. But I just squeezed her hand, said, "I know. It's okay. I've missed you."

"I missed you too! So where are Manfred and Mark?"

"Manfred is upstairs in the pool. We have a pool on the terrace there. And Mark is, uh, deep-sea fishing."

"*Is* he?"

"Yes. He's quite the sportsman … apparently."

"Ah. I bet y'all have had a great time."

"Oh well. Yeah, but I think everyone is pretty much tired of each other. Mark has been a real ogre."

"Oh? He always seemed nice to me. A little rough around the edges maybe…"

"He just needs to get back to Texas. That's his home."

"Hmm. Yes, that's right, the Dog House. And what all have y'all done so far?"

"Oh, this and that, you know. Manfred always has everything planned out for us." I didn't want to talk about the damn group.

Paul walked up with his bird.

"Hello there! One other member of your party … Manfred? … has made a reservation for himself this evening. But not your, uh, *large* friend." He frowned, then asked me, "But he didn't know … will you be attending?" He looked over and smiled at Regina.

"Oh yeah, the thing. I, uh…"

Regina said, "What's this?"

I waved my hand around vaguely. "Oh, it's a, … fiesta deal…" I deferred to Paul.

"Puerto Escondido's annual Masked Ball," he said. "We're hosting it this year, on our terrace. The entire town will simply explode!" He waved his hands about, the bird flapping its wings in unison. "Dress is casual, and if you don't have a mask, we will provide one. Would you like to make reservations?"

Regina and I exchanged a pregnant glance. Her eyes gleamed. She moved her hand around, taking one of mine. "David, do you think we could…"

I grinned, catching on. "We could try. We sure could!"

Paul looked confused. I looked up at him. "Paul, I think I would like to reserve for two, please."

"Great. I'll put you down then, you and your, uh, guest." He smiled again at Regina, then looked back at me, gave me a little wink. "See you there!"

"Nice bird," she said as he walked away.

I looked at her for a minute. I noticed her shoulder, tropical sweat glistening along the curve of her collarbone. I could feel my pulse quicken. "Do you think you'll be able to slip away?"

She grinned, showing her beautiful smile again. When she smiled like that the entire room lit up. "Don't you see? I can bring the whole group, Javier and Cesar and Miguel. We'll be wearing masks! And so I can see you." *And continue to prolong the inevitable*, I thought. Continue your torture of me. Was it done wilfully or obliviously? I could hardly resist the urge to ask that question, but I had to suppress the urge to find the answer, for it mattered not, I told myself, over and over. It did not matter whether she was selfishly using me for some sick and twisted game with her husband or whether she was hopelessly in love with another man, as I was with her. All that mattered was that she choose now, come out of the forest and declare her love for me, or return to her life in the Mexican jungle. Or something like that. That was what *I* needed from her.

As it was, I half-expected Javier to come walking into the hotel lobby at any moment, looking for his errant wife, whom I so foolishly loved. "Don't you think this is kind of risky? Couldn't we just meet at the beach and, you know, hang out together ... by ourselves?"

"Oh now, this'll be fun! *Romantic,* even? Don't you think?"

I stood up, pulling her up by the hand. "This is what I think." I pulled her to me and kissed her hard. She was surprised at the sudden intimate contact with the sweaty beer-bear, but settled in nicely. When we finished we stood very close, in each other's arms. We were breathless. I was slightly dizzy. My entire body was purring. I couldn't speak, so I kissed her again. Afterward we just looked at each other, standing there in the dining room of the Flor de Alejandra. I could smell her, no perfume but something delicate and clean and feminine. I wanted to keep her with me always.

She sighed, said, "I want to stay, David. But I have to ... you know." She giggled. "How long can I be using the bathroom for?"

I chuckled. "Yeah." But instead of letting her go, I pulled her closer and kissed her neck, under her ear. I could taste the sea salt, feel her respond to my touch. Her hair was bound up for the beach, but a strand of it was loose, tickling my cheek. I took in her scent again. "I don't want you to go," I whispered.

"I know." We held each other for a time, then started for the door and the alley. Just before we went back out into the sun and public view, she pulled me into an alcove and kissed me properly again. I held onto her hands for a while longer. She looked behind her at the alley, then back at me. She ran her hand along my hairy chest. "My, you're sweaty." She licked her lips. I thought I was going to die right there. "And you smell like beer." She laughed. "But…I can't stay." She looked down at the ground. "What happened to your leg?"

"Oh, uh, that's nothing, it doesn't even hurt anymore…"

"Hmm." She smiled. "You're such a mess."

You have no idea, I thought. I placed two fingers under her chin, gently tilted her face up, level with mine. "Regina. We don't have to do it like this. It doesn't have to be this way. We need to be together." We held each other's eyes for a long moment. "Come back to San Antonio with me."

She looked back down at the white tiles between our feet.

"I … I just couldn't. I wouldn't have a husband when I got back there."

"Yes, you would." Her gray-blue eyes, inscrutable, came back up to meet mine. "Yes you would," I repeated. I let go her hands, gave her gracefully sloping shoulders a soft squeeze. "Just come with me. Leave him *now*. We can just be together."

She looked into my eyes, but could not hold my gaze. "It's … David, it's more complicated than that."

"I love you!"

"I love you too. But..."

"*That's as complicated as it needs to be.*" I stared at her.

She finally stared back at me. I could not tell what she was thinking. "I will try to come alone tonight. But I may have to bring all of them along, the bastards. I'm so sick of them!"

"You don't have to be with them."

"Oh, David." She hugged me close, and I could no longer see her expression. I felt her sigh against me.

"I'll try to see you tonight," she said softly into my shoulder. "When does it start?"

"Starts at nine. I'll be here. I don't know what mask Paul will have for me, though. Or what mask you'll be wearing."

"I can spot you anyway, by the way you move. I'll know," she said.

"*Du auch, mein Schatz. Ich liebe dich.*"

"*Ich dich auch.*" And she left, striding down the alley toward the beach, not looking back. I watched her walk away numbly, then turned, headed for the pool.

* * * * *

Manfred sat in the shade with two other people, a man and a woman. He was rolling a joint, saying, "...and wit da tobacco in it, you save your *marey-wan-a, und* get even more high."

"Do you get a better buzz from the added tobacco?" the man asked. "Kind of a synergistic effect?"

"*Ja genau*, that's it exactly. … Howdy David. Grab yourself a beer *dere*."

"I'm quite alright." I floated down into a chair, smiling. I really couldn't help it. Manfred noticed my change in general attitude, stopped and regarded me closely. "Alright dude. This here is Matthew, and his lovely girlfriend Jennifer."

"Matt," said the man, hand extended.

"David. How d'ya do."

"Hi," said Jennifer with an airy wave from her spot in the hammock.

Manfred continued the lesson. "And da filter means that ven you get down to the last part, da roach, you are only wasting a little tobacco, and not any marijuana. It is a much more efficient smoking system." He held up the finished product. "Ding, da da ding dang dong. David? Care to do the honors?"

I smiled at him. "No thanks. I'm quite alright."

Again he looked at me quizzically. "Okay, dude. Matt?" Matt lit the euro-joint, and they passed it around. I got up and wandered over to the edge of the terrace. I looked down at the beach, but a copse of trees blocked the view of our stretch of beach. No matter. I knew she was down there. I was euphoric. I could not stop grinning, a subtle, gentle smile. I ambled back over to the gang. I felt like I was floating across the terrace.

Matt was saying, "…much more high than from a regular joint!"

"*Ja, ja*."

"I mean, this is great!" It was great indeed.

Jennifer giggled in her hammock.

"*Ja, und* see how much pot ve haf only used?" Manfred pointed proudly at the sack. "It is *ze* proper method of marijuana utilization technology."

"I'm *much* higher than I get back in Arizona!"

Jennifer giggled again.

"You live in Arizona?" I asked.

Matt smiled back at me. "Well, we *used* to live in Tucson. But we're on our way to New York, via Oaxaca."

"David, are you sure you don't want a beer or something? There's the tequila." Manfred pointed at the bottle, since found. He had been drinking it all day, and now it was much depleted.

"No thanks, man. I'm fine." I got in the pool, swam around, happy as a trout in the cool water. Manfred stared at me, wondering. I knew he was curious as to what had smitten me. Let him wonder. Everything was mighty fine.

Matt rather stonily said, "Yeah, Jesse Jackson called it 'Hymie-town,' and that's fine with me. Be right at home in New York, the Jewish capital of the world."

"*Ach, ja*? Are you Jewish?"

"All my life. What, uh…" Matt paused as he hit the joint, "what, uh, part of Europe are you from?"

"Vell. I am from Germany."

Matt coughed. I smiled at the irony, the legacy of our granddads' victory over the Nazis – a German and a Jew smoking a joint together in Mexico. What a wonderful world.

I broke my fast, took the joint. We were all silent for an awkwardly long moment, broken finally when Jennifer giggled once again from the hammock. I liked Jennifer.

"*Ja ja*. So, are you going to the ball tonight?"

Jennifer said, "We'll be there!" Her sentence dissolved into laughter. I started laughing too. Everything was quite all right.

"Vell, I am going to shower before dinner. David, I know you don't want to go to the thing tonight, but ve are all planning to have dinner downstairs, our two new friends and myself. Care to join us?"

"Oh, no man, I'm *going* to the thing. I just made my reservations with Paul."

Manfred looked at me intently. "Really? I thought you were just going to sulk in your beer all night."

Even that didn't arouse my ire. I affected an upper class English accent, annunciating my words carefully, formally, mocking Manfred right back. "Nooo, I have changed my mind. Now I'm *not* going to sulk in my beer all night, but instead will come along to dinner with you all, and then join you at the ball." Jennifer burst out laughing again. Soon we were all laughing. Then, without warning, it began to rain on us, there on the terrace of the Flor de Alejandra, slowly at first, then with greater intensity, pelting us with big fat raindrops. The rainy season had come. Things were changing.

* * * * *

I kept checking my watch throughout dinner. Paul came over and played the host for a while, but – much to my relief – was for some reason discreet enough not to mention the sudden unexplained appearance and disappearance of my beautiful 'guest' in front of Manfred, who surely would have guessed my game. I can't remember what we ate that night. Nine o'clock could not come quickly enough. I tried to distract myself with the table's conversation.

Matt was saying, "I don't like how the administration is so belligerent. War is their first choice, not their last."

"*Ja*, vell, dey did knock down two of your buildings."

I interjected, "*They!?* Who, the Iraqis? Nope, not them." I shook my head. "The Saudis, maybe. But not the Iraqis."

Matt said, "Yes, and they've used it as an excuse to create a totally new geopolitical situation. Nine-Eleven changed everything. I had this strange feeling when I was there, in New York, a few months after the attack. There was still this terrible smell in that part of the city, by the Hole, and everyone was eerily quiet. Then a flat-bed truck came by, with a twisted steel … thing, on the back, almost the size of the truck. It was part of the wreckage, part of the buildings, and as it went by, everyone – workers, tourists, passersby, even the street bums – stopped what they were doing, stopped everything, and just watched it go by in silence. Weird."

Jennifer said, "And so now it's war without end!"

"*Ja ganau, und* I think that Iraq is next. Maybe Iran or North Korea after that."

Matt said, "You don't think so?"

"*Doch*! Vat is to stop them? Now's their chance to remake the world as they will, thanks to Nine-Eleven."

"I don't think they *meant* for that to happen," said Matt. "The prior-knowledge theory just doesn't hold water."

"Ahem!" I coughed. "Operation Northwoods." I coughed the words. "Ah-huh ah-huh!" No one paid me any mind.

"No," said Manfred, "but just because a disaster occurs, man-made or natural, does not mean people in power suddenly become saints, or stop maneuvering for more power. That's how *volk* always act when they haf power. Right, David?"

"Huh? What was the question?"

"Where were you?"

"Oh, just … thinking…"

"You looked far away there."

"I, uh … was just thinking about the Gulf of Tonkin Incident. Or what Mark would say if he were here."

"Mark's your other friend?" Jennifer asked.

"*Ja ja*, he's deep-sea fishing."

"Will he make it to the ball?" She asked.

"I rather doubt that," I said. "He doesn't enjoy the festive-event thing. But if he were here he would no doubt be defending the administration, saying we should rally around the President in this time of war."

"Well," said Jennifer as she sipped her Sol, "that certainly would liven the discussion up a little bit!"

"Too boring for you?" asked Matt.

She winked at him. "Not with you here." She leaned over and kissed him.

I looked at my watch. Not quite eight yet. Time seemed to be moving very slowly indeed.

* * * * *

After dinner, Manfred and I took a constitutional along the beach. It had stopped raining. After the bustle and crowds of the hot day, the evening, post-rain beach was deserted, as if the town's denizens were readying, holding their collective breath for the night's explosion of madness. The calm before the storm. I could not help scanning the beach for any sign of Regina and company, but no doubt they had retired to a café or restaurant or hotel along with most of the other tourists when the skies broke.

Manfred was walking along quietly beside me, barefoot in the cool sand. Dimitri's dogs accompanied us on our walk, trotting all around in a loose, shifting perimeter. We passed a beggar. I checked my empty pockets, then looked at Manfred. "Daily civic duty?"

He tossed his head. "To hell with de damn duty." We walked on a while more. "So David. How's it going with you these days?"

"Pretty good man, pretty good."

"Hmm." He eyed me curiously. He had deep circles under his eyes.

"What do you think Mark is doing?" I said.

"Fishing, I suppose."

"How long does it take, do you think? A deep-sea excursion like that?"

He shrugged tiredly. “I don’t know, David. I really don’t care anymore.”

“What about the plan?” I smiled at him.

“You know vat, David? Fuck da plan.”

I was agreeable. “Alright then.”

We neared the aloe garden. “Just a minute, dude. Your knife, *bitte*?” I gave him the blade. He walked up to the house, unfolded the blade and cut off a large stalk, returned already smearing the sticky gel over his grossly reddened shoulders.

“Why don’t you just use sunscreen?”

“Vell David, they put all kinds of unhealthy chemicals in da formula there. I do not vant to subject my body to such toxins. It is unhealthy.”

I looked at his lobster-skin, his blistered shoulders. “*That’s* healthy?”

“David, just … don’t worry about it, alright.” He shook his head, face hardening in annoyance. We walked up the alley to the Flor de Alejandra in silence.

* * * * *

Just after nine, Manfred and I left our room wearing our finest Hawaiian shirts. They were clean, if not freshly pressed. Paul had come through indeed with a choice selection of masks. The night porter fulfilled his new charge well, sitting by the hotel’s entrance with a big cardboard box full of all kinds of masks. No mask, no entrée. But no dress code, either. The concept of ‘masked ball’ brought to my mind images of a big band and sequined evening gowns, highballs and hair gel. But this was to be a beach-style ball. We had mashed up our tropical look with *carnival.*

Even at five minutes past nine, the first floor of the Flor de Alejandra was half-filled with masked celebrants on their way upstairs. I turned my bear mask over in my hands, admiring Paul's choice for me. I knew it would look good with my shaggy mop of long brown hippie-hair and my hairy chest showing from under my partially buttoned shirt. I would be a big, sweaty, hairy dancing bear tonight, as inevitably. I chuckled, donning my mask.

Manfred and I went up the stairs to the terrace, which had been transformed. Colored lights were strung everywhere. Behind the wet bar, a bartender was pulling heavy duty on a margarita machine, with beer, wine, and mixed drinks also available. The DJ – not the one from the club, thankfully – spun some hip jams in the sea-side corner. This was not your father's masked ball.

I looked over at Manfred and growled.

"*Ja*, dude, you're a scary dancing bear, alright."

"At least I don't look like a clown."

"Vell, David, that's because you're not wearing a clown mask, like me."

"Correct. ... I wish Mark were here. He could wear an ogre mask. Or one of the demon masks from the Dog House."

"*Ja ganau*, or just come as-is." I moved out amongst the folk, and Manfred went directly to the wet-bar.

The whole idea of such a party as this was to remain masked at all times in public. Straws were available for the facilitation of beverage consumption, or one could simply lift the bottom of the mask slightly above the mouth, then lower it again after the frontloading was completed. At no time was one to run about unmasked, not until the unmasking at midnight. This both served my ends, as I would not be spotted by Javier, but also hindered me, for I would be unable to tell if Regina was there yet. I moved over to the margaritas, grabbing another one for the thirsty Manfred as well.

It was one of those hellishly long hours of waiting, waiting with no end in sight. I was not even sure she would come. Probably she won't, I said to myself. All the same, I kept my margarita intake to a minimum. Matt and Jennifer arrived, and we all had a laugh over our wacky masks. The party had begun.

Paul came over, recognizable even in his colorful duck mask, as his now-other, ever-present bird-head bobbed about on his shoulder. I wondered why the bird didn't just take flight into the open night air. He lisped, "I would like to introduth you to the *Alcalde* of Puerto Escondido, Thseñor Filipe Cantú." We all shook hands. The town's mayor wore an elephant mask. Manfred and Señor Cantú began a rapid-fire conversation in Spanish. Paul leaned over and stage-whispered to me, "His cousin is the local judge. A good family to know, yes?"

"No doubt." I continued to scan the crowd impatiently. I wanted another margarita, but made myself wait. I needed to be clear-headed tonight. Or so I hoped. I was beginning to doubt my ability to recognize her body despite the mask when I saw her, moving through the crowd, coming from the stairs. She somehow looked elegant even in a well-traveled maroon sarong. She had let her honey-colored hair down, cascading all over her splendid shoulders. She was unmistakable, even with a plumed peacock mask, purple, gold, and green, covering the upper half of her face, giant peacock feathers streaming gracefully up and off to the sides. Seeing her, I felt that wrenching flutter grip my heart, washing over me, like something merely physical turned into pure energy and injected directly into my soul, up my spine. She appeared to be unattended.

"Can I get the lady a drink?"

She turned around smoothly, as if dancing. "Why, yes. That would be lovely." We laughed at each other, her voice like a gently flowing musical stream.

"Are you alone?"

"Yes. I told him about it, but he has family around here that he doesn't really get along with, so he didn't want to come. He didn't want me to come, either. We got into a big fight, yelling at each other. Cesar and Miguel were so embarrassed, but they were stuck there with us in the room. Finally I just stormed out." She smiled bravely, but I could see she was shaken, nervous.

"It's alright now."

"Then he yelled after me, 'Go on then and meet your lover!'"

I looked at Regina there on the balcony of the Flor de Alejandra in Puerto Escondido, one thousand miles from home. "Come on and let's get that drink."

"Will you get me a beer? I'm going to find the bathroom."

I pointed to it. "See you in a minute."

I walked over to the wet-bar, collecting myself, as well as a beer and a margarita. How could Javier have known? I tried to breathe slowly and deeply. Manfred came over, grabbed my arm.

"There you are, David. Two drinks now?"

"Uh, yeah. It's, uh, a chaser."

"Hmm. Okay, vell, you'll never guess who I ran into."

"What? I mean, who?"

"Javier's uncle."

"*What*!?"

"You just shook his hand, dude. The mayor? *El Alcalde de* Puerto Escondido?"

I stood there, glad my bear mask covered my second gaping wittol-face in the same day.

"*Ja*, I forgot all about it. Javier told me he had family here."

"In Oaxaca?" I said. "I thought he was from Monterrey!"

"*Ja ganau*, but he's got a couple of uncles down here."

"Yeah. Well, that's fucking interesting, man. Good for him."

Manfred looked at me in that unnerving way that he had, as if he could see into you. "Well David, I thought so too. Just thought you'd like to know."

"Sure but … what would I care about his ass, anyway."

"Okay then, just don't get so verked up!"

"I've got to go." I stared off, away from him.

"David, I vas just…"

"Not now, man!" I walked away.

"Go on then, *Arschloch*," he said to my retreating backside.

I found Regina in one of the sea-side corners of the terrace. She was looking out at the ocean, the wind pushing her golden tresses back from her head. I handed her the beer. "Did you know Javier's uncle is here?" I could see her grey-blue eyes through the holes in her mask.

"What?"

"He's the mayor. That's him … over there, in the elephant mask."

"I *know* he's the mayor, and the other uncle's a judge. That's why Javier didn't come. I told you he has family here. He doesn't talk to this branch much, and wanted to avoid the big Mexican family reunion." She rolled her eyes behind her mask.

"Hmm. Just as well."

"Remember, he didn't even want to come to Puerto Escondido. That's why. Plus he knew Manfred had planned to bring y'all here. He says this place is a big tourist spot anyway." She sniffed.

"Manfred told him at the pig-roast we were coming here, huh?"

"I believe it was Javier's idea, his suggestion to Manfred to come down to Puerto Escondido. He thought y'all would have fun here. That was before he saw us together."

"Oh." Or was it? Oh shit. Was I being set up? Was this a ruse on Javier's part, this recommendation to come visit the town controlled by his relatives? All strategically hidden by his feigned reluctance to come here? Done to lure me into a trap, where Javier and his relatives would throw me into a Mexican prison to rot? All that bastard needed was the legislative branch of the local government and he'd have the whole damn thing sewn up. But I suppose the mayor and the judge would be sufficient to take care of a meddlesome, philandering gringo. Or just another tourist gone "missing" perhaps, probably to do with drugs, the body never found. It would happen before I even saw it coming, like a lightning bolt thrown by the jaguar-god. They know how to deal with law-breakers in Mexico. That kicked up the adrenaline to a new level, and I looked around me, suddenly paranoid at all the anonymous people surrounding me.

The party on the roof began to swell, both in numbers and in an ever-mounting sense of urgency. The fiesta was on in town too. Looking out over the rooftops, one could see the people, swarming about, snaking down the alleys and streets of the town like drunken centipedes, cheering the party on. Fireworks went off over the town, and from the fishing boats in the shallow bay came fiery missiles, arcing over the darkened sky, reflecting off the water in bright red, white, and green. Children and adults screamed and yelled down below on the beach. The night was blossoming with the cacophony of fiesta, of the universal spring celebration.

Like the planets in their celestial cycles, always the same, yet always changing, people rotate in their rhythmic cycles as well, ever the same, ever changing. However far you go, you always end up at the same place. No matter how fast you run, you cannot escape yourself, or what awaits you, whatever it may be. Perhaps it was inevitable that I was doomed, having angered the gods so.

I went back up to the bar to grab another round of drinks. Manfred was there, holding up the bar. He didn't look so good, his full day of drinking taking its toll. A few empty margarita cups sat on the bar in front of him, and some more lay crushed about his feet. He clutched a full one tightly, swaying, grinning a rather deranged grin under his clown mask. I wondered if all the empties were his.

As I walked back to Regina I saw a man in a black jaguar mask standing next to her. Some unconscious recognition of body posture and such provided an instant identification: Javier. I kept walking on past them, a disquieting sensation disrupting my fiesta cheer. This was getting a little too literal for my taste. I could tell Regina had noticed me, but there was no help for it, no help at all. I just had to wait my turn, as always. As I stood brooding over the jaguar mask from a safe distance away, Jennifer and Matt came over again.

"Great party, isn't it?"

I nodded to her. "Sure is." I saw her beer was almost empty. "You look like you could use a cool one." I handed her Regina's beer. Javier could service his wife now. It was his turn now. I remembered how they had taught us in grade school how much fun it is to take turns, and even to share. I gritted my teeth, wondering if I was already in the trap, wondering if it would be sprung any second.

"Thanks! Got one too many?"

I shook my head. "No, sometimes I just overreach a little.

Matt nodded garrulously. "Yeah, I know how ya mean."

But he didn't, not really.

Then it was the pig-roast all over again. Regina kept running alcohol to Javier, and as soon as he was drunk enough, she and I would sneak off for a few hasty, passionate moments in some shady corner. I wondered if we were addicted to the thrill of the illicit rendezvous as much as we were to each other. After a tantalizingly infinitesimal period of liaison, we departed our kissing-corner separately and at staggered intervals, hearts beating wildly. There is no better high than kissing a beautiful woman with abandon, especially when mixed with a shot of adrenalin as a danger-chaser. My nerves were those of a man balanced precariously on the razor's-edge.

The party's frenetic pace wound up, up. The DJ, picking up the vibe from the crowd, changed rhythms, spiking the tempo. The dancers by the pool moshed on, fully engrossed in the music now. A woman squealed wildly in delight, and someone was pushed fully clothed into the pool, splashing folks nearby. It seemed as if everyone was talking at once, all jabbering incoherently.

Manfred wobbled over, very drunk now. He mumbled something about aloe and shambled downstairs. I shook my head, wandered over to the wet-bar. Javier was there, drinking a margarita. Our eyes met through our masks, and

I nodded sagely in greeting, suddenly glad for the calming alcohol. The black jaguar nodded back to the shaggy bear before him. I ordered from the barkeep, consciously changing my voice a bit so as to disguise it. I made it gruffer, more bear-like, of course. Regina came over, keeping her back to me, and talked with her husband. I got my drink and got out of there, still gritting my teeth with the tension. I walked over toward the edge of the terrace and leaned against the rail.

I looked at Regina and her husband. Such a strange couple. Never did they smile at each other. The only time they touched was when Javier felt it necessary to publicly mark his territory, and on those relatively rare occasions he would merely smooch her in what I considered to be a disgustingly affected manner. But then, I was admittedly biased. They rarely held hands, or exchanged the casual physical affection which is the norm for couples to occasionally display in full view of others. Whatever love and affection they may have once shared seemed to have long since evaporated. I could not understand what inertia still held them together, for it seemed that was all that actually kept her from me. I became bitterly impatient standing there surreptitiously watching their stiff interactions.

Javier was getting steadily drunker, thanks to Regina's liberal ministrations, now her signature move. He slowly and carefully made his way to the jakes, making the journey the precise evolution that only a man who is very drunk can properly perform. I watched him deliberately place first one foot forward, then the other. After he passed from view,

I immediately strode up to Regina and grabbing her hand, hauling her along despite her feeble protests, pulling her with me to our darkened corner spot under the thatched awning. I thrust her down into a chair, placing her just on the edge of it. "Hey!" she said. I pulled up my bear-mask and knelt down before her, drowning out her words with a savage kiss. Her comment died on her lips, smothered in a wave of passion. Our bodies ground together fiercely. I did not give a good god damn if Javier came up right then. He could watch for all I cared. I loved this woman, and that justified everything.

Something was wrong. I felt Regina's body stiffen, saw her eyes widen in surprise. I backed up, stood up, reset my mask and moved away from her to the edge of the terrace. My heart thumped wildly and I leaned casually on the rail, looking out at the beach, wondering what may be approaching from behind. It was dark on that part of the terrace, dark and secluded. I heard Regina shift around in her seat behind me.

"There you are," she said, as if Javier had been lost.

"Here I am," he slurred the English words in his Spanish accent. English was the odd couple's *lingua franca*, their common fluent tongue, which they used to talk efficiently if not intimately. I heard him walk up to her. Had he seen us? There was a silence that stretched out, and I knew they were kissing. I gripped the rail, squeezing it hard. I could hear rustling sounds as they touched one another. *Is that your choice then?* I grit my teeth hard, the muscles in my cheeks bulging, tears of rage welling up in my eyes. *Then why did you come here?* I knew they kissed and fucked and did all the things a cohabitating couple does, but I could not bear this. Could not bear it. I thought of my bear mask and bit my lip to keep from laughing maniacally.

He having marked his territory, they began talking inconsequentially. I turned around slowly. He had seated himself next to her in another chair. Neither of them could see me behind them in the night. We were all facing the fiesta on the terrace. He reached over and touched her hand, which she immediately removed to her lap. He looked at her in the darkness.

"You would hold it if it was your *lover's*." Drunken, he loaded the word with scorn, making it a dirty thing. I suppose to him it was.

"Oh, don't start. I'm so sick of your damn *suffering*!"

"My suffering? How can you..."

Her voice sharpened. "You know, I could just get a flight back to Texas."

"*¿Cómo?*"

"There's an airstrip here, just outside of town. I could get a flight to Mexico City, and then back to Texas. I don't think I want to be on this trip with you anymore."

"*Es loco*. Just calm down, you are not rational." Hoo boy, that was sure to be a winner.

She glared at him. "You're the one who gets upset every time I try to use the damn Internet!"

"That is because you want to talk to *your lover* so badly."

"Leave me alone!" She slapped him suddenly, got up and stormed off. I couldn't believe my eyes. Javier sighed like it happened every day, got up with much drunken care and followed behind, feebly pursuing her. I didn't understand why he put up with that. Despite my philanderer's guilt, I respected him even less than ever. Really, I just hated him. Goddamnit. I sat down in the chair and put my head in my hands. Things were happening too fast. I didn't like it a bit. But I could not let go. I could only bite deeper. I gnashed my tortured teeth behind my bear mask.

Manfred came over, clown mask on, shirt off, aloe smeared all over his torso and his lobster-limbs. I suppressed a chuckle, looked around to see if anyone else saw the funny German clown-lobster.

"*Ja*, howdy there David, da da ding dang ding."

"Hey Manfred. You look well." I snickered, barely suppressed a guffaw.

"And how's the dancing bear?"

"Fuckin' great, man." I smiled wanly.

He paused for a moment. "You look a little down, dude."

"Yeah man."

"Smile! *Ja ja*, it's fiesta! Fiesta again! And you're da dancing bear!" He reached out and slugged me on the shoulder weakly. He wobbled unsteadily. He was as drunk as I had ever seen him.

"Yeah, it is. I am. I am a dancing bear, here for your amusement." I danced a little jig for *Herr* lobster-clown.

It was Fiesta all over again, a fiesta to remember, a fiesta to forget. And I was a dancing bear, as-always. I took a long drink from my margarita. I left Manfred sitting there, absorbed in his medicinal aloe treatment. I found Regina by herself near the bathrooms. Heedless of the danger now, I approached her openly.

"Are you alright?"

"I'm fine." She wiped away a tear.

"Where'd he go?"

"I told him to go away. He's such a bastard."

You know who's not a bastard? "Ah, he left?"

"I think so. I don't know."

I held her for a few minutes. "Let's go get a drink."

"Good idea."

We relaxed a bit by the bar, trying to just enjoy the time together. For a while there was no sign of Javier. Manfred was too drunk to recognize anybody with their masks on, but he still seemed to be having a good time. So was I, until the jaguar-faced Javier appeared again. He trudged up the stairs and slowly walked out onto the terrace. He did not even look at Regina, but avoided her, looking out at the sea. Why wouldn't he just leave us alone? But he let Regina be for now, giving in and casually talking to his uncle instead, and to other folk who wandered by. His uncle seemed glad enough to see him, kissing his cheeks and embracing him. Regina and I stayed within a small circle of celebrants, drinking and laughing as if all were well, and I was careful not to be too close to her, or to be seen by him to be touching her. It seemed to work marvellously, until Paul came up by the pool with his bird. I knew something was wrong. There was something I had forgotten.

The music suddenly stopped. Into the silence, Paul came up with a microphone in one hand, margarita in the other, swaying dangerously, his bird flapping its wings quickly to maintain its balance. He looked up, embarrassed, then stepped up in front of the DJ's tables.

"It's time! It's time! *!Es tiempo! !Es tiempo!*" The bird flapped its wings madly. "It's midnight! Unmask!" He stripped off his duck-face. "Unmask!" He threw his mask into the air. I had forgotten about the unmasking at midnight. "*!Desenmascárate!*"

I grabbed Regina's hand. "Let's go." We moved through the throng toward the stairs. People were packed tightly, yelling and whooping, throwing their masks up, along with some quantity of beverage, and we became sodden with booze while navigating our way off the terrace. As we made it to the stairs, I turned around and gave one last look to the terrace-side fiesta. I could see Javier and Manfred clearly. Both had doffed their masks, and both were standing face to face staring at each other, Manfred in the drunken shock of pleasant recognition, and Javier in the darkly-green-burning jealousy of a cuckold who has just put it all together. I hastened Regina down the stairs, out of the Flor de Alejandra, onto the night time beach.

* * * * *

We huddled together in a dark alcove, tight and close between thatch-roofed buildings, halfway down a secluded alley off the beach. Dimitri's dogs panted nearby, lying there on the cool sand. Through the sea breeze we could still hear the fiesta continuously erupting in the town.

"I'm sorry this evening didn't turn out to be more romantic," I said.

"You don't think this is romantic?"

"Well, uh … of course it is."

She was trembling in my arms. I took hold of her, lifted her. I perched her on a low wall and kissed her. I pushed her knees apart with mine, and moved her dress aside. Before she could protest, I entered her, and she gasped. Then she grabbed and pulled me closer. I made love to her like it was the last time, the only time. I managed to make her cum before I did. She kissed me deeply as I finished.

I looked into her eyes, her face flushed. We re-set ourselves, glancing around self-consciously. We were, and had been, unseen. Alone.

"He's going to come looking for me."

"You think so?"

"Oh yes. He will for sure now that he knows you're here."

"Regina, just … just stay with me. Or go back to your hotel room tonight, if you have to, say your goodbyes or whatever. Just leave him! You don't need to be with him. Come with me. I mean it." We stared at each other. "I love you." That was my pitch.

"I love you too…" She was trembling again. "Oh, David, you're just … in love with my shell."

"No. Don't say that. Just come! Tonight, or tomorrow morning. We're leaving then, and you can come with me."

"I don't know…" She was staring at the ground, frowning, thinking hard. "I could meet you here, maybe. … I need to talk to him. I can't just disappear."

Was this breaking my way? "I agree." I thought she was making sense. "Just tell him you're going back with us. There's no point in arguing with him about it."

She looked at me, still frowning. "I have to go."

"Now?"

"I don't want him to catch us here."

"I don't care if he does." And I didn't, not anymore.

"*I* care! I am so sick of this double life!"

"That's why we need to end this now. Just come with me."

"Yes, end it now..." she said slowly, thoughtfully. She was looking at the ground again.

"So, I'll be out here, right *there*," I pointed toward the hotel, "at seven AM." She looked at me, her eyes opaque, inscrutable. "So, just bring your things, and we'll leave straight away. Okay?"

"I'll do my best. You know I can't promise anything."

"Damnit, Regina ... what do you mean, you can't promise anything?" I said in frustration. I was so sick of hearing that. But no, I wouldn't force it. This was her choice, and she would make it tomorrow morning by seven at the latest. I could let her sleep on it, if necessary.

Dimitri's dogs became aroused with a canine start. Low, ominous growls now emanated from their throats. Collectively, they all rose and trotted in the direction of the water. I saw Javier's lanky form loping along near the low surf. He did not see us.

Her expression unreadable still, Regina watched him walk away, up the beach, the dogs trotting alertly behind him. Regina's face was tightly controlled. We held each other for a few more minutes, and then she said, "Goodbye, David." Was that goodbye for good?

I gave her my room number at the Flor de Alejandra. "If anything happens tonight, just come and the night porter will let you in. I'll leave your name with him."

She hugged me once, tightly. We kissed briefly, and she walked away, looking nervously over her shoulder. I watched her walking, then I stood in the entrance of the alley for a time, savoring the memory of the encounter, satisfied in the knowledge that I had done my best to lead her to her choice. Was it goodbye for good?

* * * * *

I walked down to the beach, to the edge of the water. I looked out at the black Pacific, lit now only by a few remaining fishing boats and yachts. The party was raging up on the terrace and down the beach in town. Except for Dimitri's returning dogs, I was alone. I walked around in the surf, letting the lukewarm water lap up around my ankles. I kept thinking of the jaguar mask. Was there another lightning bolt coming? I left word with the night porter. Then I went up to my room, avoiding the party upstairs, still going strong. Long hours passed before I found sleep.

Day Ten

Manfred was snoring loudly in his bed when I awoke. It was only five-thirty, but I was wide awake. I got up quietly, showered and dressed quickly, and went down to the beach. On the way out I nodded to the night porter, still on duty.

"*Señor*, your *chica* no coming here."

"Thanks, Manny." I tipped him twenty pesos. "Have a beer for breakfast."

He smiled. "*Gracias, amigo. ¿Y tu?* "

"*No este día,* Manny. Not today." He shrugged. I went down to the beach, finding the catamaran. I lay on its tattered canvas, damp with the early morning dew, cooling my fevered head. The grey dawn was approaching slowly, too slowly. I could still see the stars faintly above.

I heard a loud noise from the direction of the alley. Manfred, clad only in shorts, was lurching around on the old woman's patio. His blisters had broken and peeled, and his general redness had faded somewhat. He came up to one of the aloe plants, grabbed hold of a stalk, and tugged it free. He put too much drunken strength into the pull, stumbling backwards and knocking over another potted plant. Pottery crashed noisily, breaking apart, dirt spilling onto the tiles. Manfred hastily retreated back up the alley with his gooey stalk. Just as he passed out of view, out of the house came a portly middle-aged man wearing a wife-beater. He looked at the mess and scowled, then immediately stomped up the alley. I could see the night porter and him talking. Then the man stormed angrily back down the alley and entered his house. I shook my head. What's that damn kraut getting himself into now?

Speaking of krauts … I looked at my watch. Just after seven. The sun was almost showing, its rays barely peeping over the ridge of mountains behind the sleepy beach town of Puerto Escondido, and still no sign of the hidden one. Where was she? Would she come? I got up out of the catamaran and walked aimlessly up the beach. I kicked an empty beer bottle, watching it skip across the dew-covered sand. Where was she? I looked at my watch. After seven-thirty now. She knows we're leaving. My leaden heart dropped into my belly with the realization. She's not coming. For whatever reason, she would not be joining me. That was it. If she would not come now, after last night, she would not come ever. *That was her choice then.*

Someone was coming though, I noticed. It was three men moving quickly down the beach toward me, running. I squinted, trying to see … it was Javier, plus his two mates, Cesar and Miguel, both of whom had their long black hair bound behind them for combat, the Aztec Triple Alliance, heading straight for me. My mind flashed to the jaguar, my dark dream materializing before my eyes. My luck had run out. The lightning was building in the sky. In Mexico they know how to deal with law-breakers, with bride-thieves.

I turned and hastened up the alley to the Flor de Alejandra. I noticed a little group gathered outside the entrance, clustered next to the dusty, pearl-white Buick with Texas plates. Parked behind the Buick were two police ATVs. I was cut off.

Two black-clad *policia* stood there by the entrance with the man in the wife-beater from the aloe-garden house down the alley. Manfred came to the entrance of the hotel and stepped out. Behind him stood Manny the night porter. Javier and his Aztec warriors were advancing up the alley behind me. I moved closer to the group, wondering if the police were friend or foe but preferring them regardless to the obsidian blades that awaited in the other direction.

Manfred looked quite hung-over, but spoke his usual quick Spanish to the police. "Yes?"

The older cop spoke up, also in rapid Spanish. I could barely follow. The cop spoke to Manny. "Is this the man who came in with the plants?"

"Yes, this is the man. He came in with the plants." Manny must have been promised more than twenty pesos from someone to rat on Manfred. To the man in the wife-beater the older cop said, "Is this the man who you saw take the plants from your grandmother's house?" The man nodded vigorously. "*Si Señor, si Señor*, this is the man who took the plants from my poor grandmother's house. He was seen coming there many times last night. He..."

The older cop nodded to the younger cop, who stepped up to Manfred. The older cop said, "*Señor*, we are now arresting you for the thieving of the plants." Manfred began to protest. "Please do not speak now. It is the law. You may speak to the judge." The younger cop took hold of Manfred firmly and placed handcuffs on him. I could hardly believe my eyes. Manfred was going to a Mexican prison. Or jail, at least.

Meanwhile, Javier and his Aztec warriors had circled around me, cutting off all retreat. I saw them, but I couldn't just leave Manfred. As Manfred was about to be led away, Javier came up to the police and said, "*Señor*, I am Javier Cantú. The *Alcalde* of Puerto Escondido is my uncle. I was here last night at the fiesta, and I saw this man also involved in the thieving of plants." He levelled a steady finger at me.

The older cop stood forward. "You are the *alcalde's* nephew, *Señor*? You can prove this?"

Javier produced his Mexican identification, passed it over with some other folded papers. "Our family is from Monterrey, you will see. My uncle is Filipe Cantú, son of my grandfather Raul Cantú. Ask my uncle and he will confirm all that I have said."

The cop passed back the ID, minus a certain sum. He looked at Javier. "Everything is as you say, *Señor. Señor* Cantú is at the harbour now, but ... so this man also was involved in the thieving of plants from the old woman's house?"

The man in the wife-beater groaned, "My poor grandmother!"

Javier nodded gravely. "It is as I have said."

"You son-of-a-bitch, you're settin' me up!" I snarled. Blinding pain bloomed from my left kidney as one of the Aztec warriors struck me from behind. I went to my knees, nauseous. The younger cop came and roughly pushed me all the way down on my belly, my face ground into the dirt and sand of the alley. I felt his bony knee as he knelt on my back. Everything was a scramble after that. I was handcuffed, roughly hauled to my feet, and frogmarched up the beach, already teeming with hung-over life. I had sand and grit in my eyes and could not focus, could not see. Halfway down the beach I heaved, vomiting on the younger cop's shoes. He just laughed, said to the older cop, "We shall have to get him some tea!"

Through the town they marched us, past gawking tourists and locals, up to a white building. Puerto Escondido's civic building did triple duty as the city hall, police station, and post office. A jail was in the back of the building. It was filled with drunken *norteamericanos* and besotted *eurotrash*. We had found our new home.

The cops uncuffed us and shoved us into the drunk cell. I received no tea. As the door slammed behind me, I hollered, "I want to see the consul, the US consul, man! Get the ambassador! I'm a US citizen, I got rights!"

Manfred said in Spanish, "*Señor*, I am a German citizen, please contact the German consulate." The cops were all ignoring us anyway.

I looked at Manfred. "I thought you were a US citizen?"

He smiled wanly. "Vell David. I actually haf both passports."

The jail smelled of vomit and urine. Rats and roaches scurried about the dark, dirty corners of the jail. I said, "Well, here we are in the damn Mexican prison, just as the prophecy foretold."

"David, this is a jail, not a prison."

"Oh Jesus."

Javier came up to the bars, completely ignoring Manfred and glaring at me with a maligned husband's hatred. I walked right up toward the bars, angrily, and he backed away, out of reach.

"I saw your Texas plates, you fucking gringo!" He spat. "I knew you were here the entire time!" I just stared at him, contemplated giving him my middle finger, that international salute of derision. He was silent for a moment, his brow furrowed. "I do not approve of what you two have been doing. In any case, *my wife will remain with me!*" So, he was finally furious. "When I return with my uncle, you will see what happens to you!" He turned on his heel and stalked out of the building. This was *no bueno.* I suppose this was the moment he had been waiting for to express himself, his plan progressing nicely now.

"*Vat* was that about, David? He could haf got us off, his uncle is da mayor!"

"Well, I … you know man." I turned toward Manfred. "I guess I fucked it up."

"Mmm." He shook his head.

"Well, what about you, ass, getting busted pinching bloody aloe plants? What the hell is that about?"

"*Halt die Klappe*!"A drunken man lying in the corner yelled at us in German to shut up. Manfred soothed him with a stream of calming, gutteral German, and the man lay quiet once more. To me Manfred said, "*Ja ja*, I just didn't think it would be *us* in da prison."

"Yeah. Javier and his uncle – or uncles – can keep us here for how long, do you think?"

He looked at me. "Vell David. I don't really know. I suppose that depends on the judge, Javier's *other* uncle." My stomach was a knotted pit of cold anxiety. My mouth tasted of acidic bile, my head throbbed, and my hands shook. I sighed, began pacing. Javier had departed, gone to the harbour to fetch uncle *alcalde*. The cops were laughing at us. "You have very big trouble now, gringo," one taunted. Manfred sat there quietly, and I paced back and forth. "*Señor*, please just calm yourself. You will see the judge today, or maybe tomorrow, and he will give you the good justice. Maybe Ixcotel Prison!" I continued my angry pacing vigil.

Out the open door at the front of the building, which faced the tourist district and the beach, a strange procession appeared. A group of Mexican kids came up the street in pairs, one after the next, five pairs in all. They were looking around, calling to people, shouting, but I could not hear what. Finally the last set of brown urchins passed by. I rubbed my eyes, scratching the sand and grit into them further. The Mexican children weren't the spectacle; like a troupe of miniature pall-bearers, they were toting a giant fish, a blue marlin, apparently, holding it up off the ground on their shoulders.

"H E E E E – H A W ! ! ! Aha ha ha ha ha!" came the braying call from outside. So they had found Mark too, the bastards. Then came Javier's uncle. I groaned in despair. We were doomed, well and truly fucked now. There was Adolfo. So they had him too, probably as a witness. Soon would come Dimitri, no doubt. It was a complete roundup; they had the entire gang. Here came Mark. Next, strangely, came a man with a large, archaic, professional-grade camera. I supposed it was for the mug shots. I waited, but Javier did not enter the civil building. The *alcalde* said, "One moment please, *Señor*, while I gather a proper escort." Then he noticed that Mark was not listening.

Mark's mouth was hanging open as he stared at his two friends behind bars. His mouth opened and closed like the mouth of a giant, misshapen fish. "David? Manfred!? Ohh nooo! What the hell did y'all do!? Aha ha ha ha!" He laughed, but I could see he was worried. I could also see he was tremendously drunk. I immediately feared for the safety of all the police personnel in the building. Then I feared for Mark, for I knew there was only one brutal and final way to put down an enraged minotaur.

"I, uh … we…"

"I vas borrowing an aloe stalk *und*…"

"How do you *borrow* a stalk, Manfred?" Mark asked.

"Mark, da nice old woman said that…"

The *alcalde* stepped up, surveyed us through the bars. "Mr. Hanson, these are your friends? Ah, Mr. Winkler. We met last evening, on the terrace, I believe. ... You boys have an enjoyable fiesta?" He smiled at us without any hint of irony. We looked at each other.

"*Señor* Cantú, this vas all a big misunderstanding. I had permission from the old voman to use her aloe plants, but den her grandson, I guess..."

Mark, sounding for all the world like any small-town Southern politician, said, "Aww, hell, mayor, these two're with me."

The *alcalde* recognized the tone and didn't hesitate one instant. He turned and clapped Mark on the back, said, "Well, Mr. Hanson, that is all you have to say. If these two are friends of yours, and, ah ... as long as it is simply a misdemeanor such as the thieving of plants, then..." He questioned the police, who corroborated Manfred's statement that we were indeed thieves of aloe. The police looked glum, denied any further gringo booty. The *alcalde* said, "Let them go!"

I looked at Manfred, puzzled. "I don't get it."

"I don't either."

The senior cop said in Spanish, "But *Señor*, your nephew said that he saw these criminals inv..."

"My nephew!" spat the *alcalde*. "If he would spend more time home with his family, and not running around in the North with..." he sighed tragically, "...he marries a blonde woman and thinks he is king! So, let them out!" The cop came over with a key, and with the lack of paperwork characterizing jails throughout the country, we were freed. The other prisoners behind us grumbled in envy. The *alcalde* rubbed his hands together, saying, "And now for the photo." Mark just grinned like a kid at Christmas. Mark and the photographer followed the *alcalde* out into the street.

I looked at Manfred. "What the hell, man? What about Javier?"

"*Ja*, dude, ve need to get outta here."

I nodded. "No doubt." We followed along outside, into total pandemonium. It was as though the fiesta had never ended. There was a huge crowd, everyone was cheering. A woman came up and kissed Mark, right on the lips. She was very drunk, everyone was drunk; the entire group had been partying all night. There were the ten barefoot Mexican kids again, still holding up the biggest damn fish I had ever seen, a giant gleaming silver and blue fish, the size of a small boat, with a sword for a nose. I could smell its strong fish-smell from where I stood, and there was the photographer, pushing Mark over with the fish and the Mexican kids and the *alcalde*, and *click* went the camera, *click, click, click*. Someone actually handed me a beer. The fiesta was still going strong.

I took a big slug from my fortuitous *cerveza* and made my way over to Mark, who was vigorously pumping the *alcalde's* hand. "What the fuck is this, man? What's this all about?" He continued shaking hands with others in the crowd. I tapped him on the shoulder forcefully. "What is up with the fucking fish, man?" I was losing my cool, becoming excited and irritable from the fatigue and stress.

"David, I caught the fish! Took all night!"

"What?"

"The fish!" He pointed his sausage-finger and strode over to his catch.

"I see the fish, man, what the fuck?" I said to his back.

The *alcalde* turned to me and said, "Your friend has caught the biggest fish in the history of Puerto Escondido! We measured it at the harbour, just over *five meters*!" He smiled smugly, a politician's smile. "It is a good omen for the coming year, catching such a fish during the town's fiesta, and at the beginning of the rainy season. It means good luck for all. And it was during my term in office! Never before have we seen such a fish. Your friend, *Meester Hanson*, has done a great thing." He smiled again for the crowd and the cameras, which I now noticed were clicking constantly, capturing my third wittol-gape of the last 24-hours for posterity.

Mark came over with Manfred. "Hey, hey! Manfred said y'all need to get out of here, got some trouble with, ah … with that girlfriend a' yore's husband. *Man*, David." He shook his head. "What did you fuck up this time?"

I looked at the *alcalde*, busy shaking hands, now accepting *una cerveza* himself. "Yeah, we gotta go, man. Javier'll be back here any minute, and then I think we'll all end up in that Mexican prison. And Javier's other uncle is the judge, so ..." I looked at him significantly, trying to convey the gravity of the situation.

Mark was laughing so hard he could not speak. His shoulders shook. Finally he said, "Good for you! Alright,

alright, let me get this donkey show on the road. H E E – H A W ! ! ! Aha ha ha ha ha!" He went over to the *alcalde*, said a few words. The *alcalde* spoke to the police escort, and soon the entire entourage was moving down the beach in the direction of our hotel. The crowd of thirty-odd soon grew, swelling as we picked up more folks along the way. We were a regular fiesta fish-parade. Mark stayed up in front with the monstrous marlin, the ogre-fish, *el salvador*. The *alcalde* marched along beside Mark, waving. The police rode along, flanking the crowd on their ATVs. I couldn't believe our luck.

Manfred found me in the throng. "Dude, ve *haf* to scramble. No telling ven Javier vill turn up."

"Yeah, I know. Uh, okay, I'll pack up our stuff. Get Mark's key and get his shit together, alright?"

"*Ja ganau*, that sounds *gut*. Get the key to the Buick from our room *und* load her up, and I'll settle da money with Paul."

"Okay!" We were at the hotel now. All was chaos, unbelievable madness. Word of the monstrous fish must have traveled ahead. There were at least a hundred people there by this time, yelling and whooping. Mark mounted our Buick and stood on the hood, spraying champagne over the mad crowd. They cheered and yelled for more.

I ran up the stairs, taking them two at a time. No time to properly pack, grab the bags out of the closet, open drawers, no matter what's Manfred's and what's mine, sort it out later, gotta go, gotta go, gotta scram, don't forget the toiletries, ah fuck, the shampoo, all wet anyway, get more later, whose shirt is that, fuck it, it goes in there, zip it up, done! I came up on Mark's room, yelled to Manfred, "Don't forget to settle up with Dimitri!" and he yelled back at me, "Go! Go!" and off I was, toting three heavy bags, taking the stairs three at a time, whoops, missed one and slam I go, on my ass, right down to the bottom of the landing. The bags saved me from a hard fall, and I was gathering them all together again when Paul came up, bird on shoulder. He said, "You're leaving so soon? The fiesta's still going on, there's a party outside, and the biggest fish..."

"Yeah, Mr. Paul, it's been *real*, uh, nice and all ... but, ah, Manfred'll settle up with you, he's coming down now..." and I was out. The entire alley had turned into an impromptu block party. It took me a minute to make my way to the Buick through the throng. I looked up and the ten little Mexican urchins were swarming over our filthy, slime-covered Buick ... our lovely Buick, now with a fifteen-foot fish draped over the top lengthwise, its' tail dangled halfway down the windshield.

There was Mark, holding a liter of Carta Blanca aloft. "Hey, hey David! *Whoooayee*! Aha ha ha!" I was never so glad to hear that ogre-roar. He grabbed the back of my head and pulled me toward him in a gesture of brotherhood and celebration. Our foreheads smacked together. "Aha ha ha ha ha ha!" I felt the world grow dim. I staggered, stunned, then stood dizzily, looking dumbly at the fish laid atop the Buick.

"Mark ... Man, we can't take that thing. We have to go, I'm fucking serious! We..."

"No! I caught that fish, all by myself David. It took me *all fucking night!* Ten hours *of war*, David, and not you, n'nobody else is gonna take it away!" Mark's black-rimmed blue eyes bulged in his large skull. The tough, leathery skin on his face was an intense shade of purple-red, part sunburn and part exhilaration.

"Well ... uh..." I simply didn't have time to argue about it. But I couldn't get the trunk open with the fish head atop it. "Here, help me with this..." With Mark's ogre-strength we got the trunk open and the bags in. I opened the driver's side door and cranked up the engine. "Jesus, Mark! That smell! You can smell that fish in here!"

Mark stood outside my open door. "Aww hell, you'll get used to it dude."

"I thought you didn't like fish!"

"Man, I don't like to *eat* 'em, I..."

"Then why do we have to take this damn thing?"

"No!" He smashed his ham-fist down on the Buick's hood, leaving a noticeable dent. He pointed at me. "I'm takin' that fish to Texas, and that's all there is to it! My cousin's a taxidermist."

"Oh Jesus."

I looked around for Manfred. There was no sign, and Javier had to have figured out by now that we weren't in jail anymore. Our time was running out. The kids began lashing the stinking fish down with fraying nylon ropes.

"David, hey! Roll the windows down. So we can tie 'er down!" Rolling down the windows only made the smell worse. The children ran the ropes through the open windows, firmly securing the giant fish to the roof of the Buick.

Manfred was still missing. We had to go. The party was still growing around us. Someone pressed a large tequila jug into my hand. I looked, and it was the goddam Rasta-man, balancing precariously on crutches. I swigged the tequila and passed it back. Mark's evil twin was now our buddy at the crazy fish-fiesta. I took a large gulp from the jug, steeled myself before taking another, then handed it back to the Rasta-man with a nod of thanks. He was either unaware of, or unconcerned with, my role in his battle with the Ogre.

We were almost out of time. I saw the *alcalde* talking to someone, arguing, his hands jerking up and down vehemently with Latino emphasis. He pointed toward our Buick. Then I saw that it was Javier that he was arguing with. Both of them were looking our way, arguing about us, their arms gesticulating, waving up and down with great feeling. I was glad Javier didn't get along with his politician uncle.

Manfred appeared at last. He shoved Mark's large duffel into the passenger side. "Mark…here!" I helped, passing it back to him. Then Manfred got in, sat down. A large potted aloe plant sat on his lap. Soil spilled out onto his shorts and the seat around his ass. "What … what *the fuck*, Manfred!?"

"Vell if dat *Arschloch* vants to get me locked up, he can get ready and go fuck himself!"

Mark belched loudly. "Hell yeah! If yer gonna get arrested, at least get the plants for it!"

I put the Buick in drive and began slowly, very slowly, easing my way up the alley, through the drunken throng.

The Rasta-man banged on our hood, leaving another dent. He and Mark exchanged bellowed roars of farewell.

"What the hell is going on with that, Mark?"

"Yeah, he was out on that fishin' boat with me, we just sorta had to be friendly out there, law of the sea, you know, aha ha ha! That's when everything started to get weird. He's an alright guy, you know?"

"Wha…?" I was speechless. I turned to Manfred. "Did you settle up with Dimitri?"

Eyes red, he replied, "Yes David, I had to roust him out of his bed, that is vat took me so long. And then we, uh…" he sniffed. "*Und* den I saw *diese hier* plant…"

"Come on, let's go!" Mark roared. "This conversation's pointless, I'm tired of these damn Injuns, aha ha ha ha ha!"

We were getting nowhere through the fiesta crowd with half the town packed into the alley. The Buick simply could not make any headway through the mass of humanity. A cop rapped his knuckles on my door. It was the same one whose shoes I had puked on earlier that morning. Here we go, I thought. He said, "*Buenas días, Señor*. The *alcalde* said he wishes you, our honored guests, a safe journey home, and he thinks it would in fact be wise for you to leave at this very moment."

I tried to speak, but the cop held his hand up, open palm toward me. "*Vaya con Dios*, he said to tell you. *Ahora, Señor*." He stood back, began clearing the crowd away from our path. I pulled up the alley, driving the not-so-pearly white Buick with Texas plates and giant stinking fish out onto the service road, the fiesta still roaring wildly behind me. I left Javier and his *alcalde* uncle arguing there in Puerto Escondido, there with the hidden one. I was leaving paradise behind too, and I could scarcely believe it. As I drove out of town and up the coast, I realized that I was leaving it all behind me.

* * * * *

In my haste, I had given little thought to our direction or destination. For now, we were headed west, through the coastal jungle. Manfred was full of energy, busily consulting the Hippie Book. "If we continue this way, we will eventually reach Acapulco, and then we can take a *cuota* a good deal of the way to Taxco."

"Yeah, that sounds good."

"... *und* there is no faster way to reach Taxco anyway, so..."

The Buick was struggling now, having real trouble. Pulling out of Puerto Escondido, when we hit about 30 miles per hour, it had revved violently, then suddenly lurched forward, and then the engine had quickly gone back to normal. Now we were up to cruising speed, but the dummy light had come on, a faint amber glow in the afternoon sun urging me to "CHECK ENGINE." I imagined myself pulling over, getting out, lifting the hood, and, seeing the engine, saying, *Yep, still there*, and getting back in and driving away.

"I wonder what I'm supposed to check the engine *for*."

Manfred leaned over, "Dat could be a lot of things."

Now I noticed that the "TEMP" gauge was far over to the left, well beyond the mid-point, and nearing the red. *Bong, bong.* A warning tone sounded, and the temperature gauge ticked into the red.

Mark said, "Aww, Jesus, man, we're fucked! We're not gonna make it!"

"We're overheating." I said.

"Turn off there!" Manfred was pointing to a dirt road on the left. I turned and rumbled down the road slowly for a moment before stopping and turning off the car. We got out and lifted the hood. Wisps of steam came off the top of the radiator cap as the release valve whistled. Mark was panicked. "What the fuck are we going to do now?!" He lit a cigarette.

"*Vell*, we haf to let the engine cool off for a while. After that, we can open the radiator and assess the situation, maybe add some water … if we can find some."

"We have a few bottles in the car," Mark said.

"Yeah, but let's not go dumping them into the radiator just yet. Manfred's right, we need to let it cool off for a bit. … And it might not be such a bad idea if we weren't visible from the highway. There may be people looking for us, and they'll definitely know us when they see us. … Or smell us." I looked at Mark significantly. He refused to take the bait.

"I think we are okay there." Manfred was pacing around. He stopped and pointed down the road. "Is that a lake?"

"Yeah, I think I saw a sign for a *laguna* just before we stopped." We walked a few hundred yards down the road in the mid-day shade before coming upon a shallow coastal lake. A dozen or so ducks flew overhead and landed *en mass* on the lake surface, entering the water gracefully and gliding to a stop with admirable efficiency. On the far side appeared to be wetlands, perhaps brackish or tidal. A primitive fisherman's trail went off in either direction along the lakeshore. The scene was peaceful and quiet, a welcome relief from the madness of the day so far.

We walked down the trail a short ways and found a small beach. We shared a joint, and after an hour or so somebody mentioned that we should probably check on the car. "The engine should be cool by now," Manfred said. But cool or not, the engine would not start. I waited a few minutes and tried again, but the engine would not catch. We all got out of the car again and stood there, not quite knowing what to do. Mark lit another cigarette. Manfred re-applied his aloe. We soon moved away from the derelict Buick due to the stench, re-congregating several yards further down the road. Flies were beginning to gather around the fish, creating a gray-ish cloud above the Buick.

Manfred looked at Mark and me with his usual calm gaze, but through clenched teeth this time. "*Ve* are going to have to flag someone down. I propose that I go back into town while you two stay here with the stuff. The rental company will pay for someone to come and pick us up and fix the car."

Mark and I looked at each other. "Uh, okay, I guess." We discussed the matter a little further and confirmed that this was apparently the best course of action. We certainly didn't want me on the road, either alone or with Manfred, and there was no chance of Mark leaving his prize. Plus, Manfred still seemed energized from his recent rendezvous with Dimitri. And perhaps a tad guilty for the sailing fiasco.

"I haven't noticed many cars on the road, so I will start walking and hopefully someone will come along before I reach da town." We further decided that it was best for him to walk back the way we came, because we knew that there was a town ... at least a few miles back, but seemingly not too far, and there appeared to be nothing ahead on the map.

Manfred walked up to the road and remained there for a moment before walking off in silence. Mark and I looked at each other again. "Man, this thing fucking reeks."

"Hey, David. Let's push the car down to the lake so we can watch it from the little beach there, on the shore."

"Great idea," I said. I got behind the wheel and put the Buick in neutral. Mark got behind, and we pushed, me from the driver's doorway. Once we got her moving, I was able to do the necessary rudimentary steering with my right hand while I pushed with my left. At the end of the road, I hopped back in and pressed the brakes lightly, bringing the Buick to a halt with a *screeeek*. I retrieved some provisions from the car and then we made a second trip back for the cooler before settling in for the duration on the soft sand.

Gusts blew across the *laguna* and small waves lapped at the foot of the modest beach. I was laying with my head on my bag and staring up at the trees, lazily watching birds fly past overhead and listening to froggies croaking in the marsh, when my hand came across the brown paper bag I had acquired in Oaxaca. I thought for a moment: Not a good idea to be traveling with these again, and not a lot more opportunity take them on this trip. In fact, come to think of it, the conditions were almost ideal. Now was the time.

~ Teonanácatl: Food of the Gods ~

The dried fungi were chewy, with a palpable taste of earthy mold, chalky and slightly bitter at the finish. We washed them down with a couple of Modelos, sitting there on the secluded lakeshore, the sense of anticipation building. I wondered how many people before me had sat here on the shore of this small coastal lake, or on the beach beyond, taking mushrooms. They grew like weeds in the highlands. How long had it taken some hungry soul to try one, to discover the unseen properties? And what was it like to be the first one, wondering perhaps if this was it, you were going crazy now, or dying? We had been doing it since time immemorial, as best the anthropologists could tell. As with the language of the Cloud-People, we would probably never truly know.

The sun was now past it's prime for the day. A fish jumped, flopping down again with a splash, breaking the silence. Grasshoppers buzzed from the weeds, their noise seemingly growing louder. I looked around, wondering what lurked in the dense coastal forest. Mark took notice.

"You still worried about that whole Regina business, about Javier?"

"Well, he did come after me this morning, along with his two buddies. If the police hadn't been there … well, I probably would have made it back to the safety of the hotel, but … it was three against one … again." I looked at Mark, the irony not lost on me.

"You think he'll be lookin' for ya?"

"Well, not out here, that's for sure." I chuckled.

"You know, for what it's worth, you got a lot of balls, David."

I laughed, clapped Mark on the back. "Thanks man. For all the good they do me, hey?"

"Aha ha ha! No, really David." He looked over at me. "I really actually respect what you did."

I stopped, looked up at him. "Mark, you know … I didn't expect that out of you. That support. Thanks, man."

"Yeah. I mean … you know? … That woman is *German*! You know? And *hot!* She shouldn't be with a *Meskin* guy. … You know what I mean?"

"Oh Jesus. *Oh, lawd Jesus.*" I clasped at my heart and affected staggering backward, channelling Fred Sanford. *"Oh, lawd hep meh! I'm comin' 'Liz-bet! Ahm, a-comin'!"*

"Ahahahahaha!" We dissolved in to giggles. I was euphoric. I noticed the sand against my skin, yet I seemed to float. Was I touching the ground? No, there was a thin layer of softly bubbling air between me and everything else. Or my skin was electric. Something was building inside. I was smiling broadly and could not stop. Happiness moved over me like a wave, engulfing me. I could not remember ever having been so happy. Everything in the world seemed right. "Ahhhhh..." I said to no one in particular, the sound humming out of me. "Oh, wow." My entire body was vibrating. Ecstasy.

Motion drew my eye, and I saw Mark waiving his hands in front of his face. "Woooo ... oh. Man. David. Ohhhhh ...." he moaned, turning glittering eyes on me. "Holy shit. How long does this shit last?"

"Ha ha ha ha ha ha!" He was feeling it, and it was suddenly comical to me. "Six to eight hours. Uh, five or seven, I mean. I don't know. We ate a lot." I giggled again.

We were jawing away with enlarging pupils, chewing like cows, bovine and Buddhist in our expectant silence. I burped and almost hurled, tasting the fungi again, the foul mouth-odor of rotting dirt. Cannot lose the sacred medicine now.

Much difficulty speaking. How to converse? My mouth was still there, I felt it, fleshy in my hands. But it was not connected, somehow. Language ... what is it? Speech. I have to ... make strange sounds with my mouth? Alternating sounds. And he will understand somehow, decoding the sound-meanings? I found it mostly beyond me, or at least too much effort. The feelings came in ever-strengthening waves, and I wanted to cry, with sadness and beauty. Everything was so beautiful. Undulating colorful waves of time and matter and energy, finally beheld all at once. Time is a wave. The pattern was right before my eyes, obscuring everything else.

The foundations of reality were eroding, gone, washing away with the successive bounding waves of energy, in full color … the water a solid body as a liquid, the trees reaching, thrusting up from the Earth like feelers, nerve endings. I was laughing and sobbing at the same time, a well of emotions rising within me, emerging on the surface now. I felt the pain, and it was real. Out in the open now for everyone to see. But small. Everything was one, so that was just a little part of it, tiny in comparison. But why hide it? Everyone could see it now. *You're a sick bear. But it's ok*. It was just what happens to the apes on planet Earth, near the lake. I ran my hand up and down over my hairy bear-chest. Ape-chest.

"Hey, I'm Ape Lincoln!"

"We're apes who learned to play music." Mark lit up a cigarette, grinning.

"Yeah, and tie our shoes and *hwwwhatnot*. Yeah. And not poop in the house."

"Ahahahahaha!" We lost it completely, again, laughing like loons, rolling about uncontrollably, our sides splitting, aching. I writhed like a snake in joy, tears running down my face. Oh, it hurt, my sides. And my cheeks. I poked at the sore muscles in my face. If only I could stop smiling.

"Hey, David. What are you going to do when we get back? No summer school, right?"

I stood up, and put on my TV announcer voice. "My new soon-to-be released book: Losing 20 Pounds and Half your Liver in Just 28 Days ~ The Cocaine and Ceviche Diet MADE EASY" ... dissolving into fits .... then, "with a new ... chapter ... on margaritas and the multiple ... USES of green LIMES!"

"Ahahaha!" Mark was laughing giddily, sounding like a demented schoolgirl. He was happier than I had ever seen him. As we sputtered down, we found ourselves unable to make the speech-sounds again, found them unnecessary and completely irrelevant in fact, some greater understanding replacing it.

A billion stars projected their light onto my face, their photons gently bouncing off me, kissing my cheeks, sending me their message of soft light. The Milky Way was twisting and writhing like a giant mythological dragon somewhere far away. The Cosmos embraced me. Everything was here. *Everything will be okay.*

* * * * *

The Ogre appeared above me in the darkness, blotting out the stars, monsterish and misshapen, yet fundamentally benign. Slowly and gently, he moved a surprisingly cold beer into my numb hands, along with an uncut lime. "Here David, this will help keep you centered." It felt peculiar, hard and bumpy, as I rolled the small fruit in my fingers. He looked down at me. A large tear rolled from his giant black eye, making a gleaming trail of diamonds down his mottled Shrek-visage. "You know I love you bro. You fucking know I do. You goddam crazy bear."

A surge of emotion welled up within, and I realized that I couldn't hide it. My mask was coming off, my masks, all of them, "Man I ..." I choked, unable to continue. Somehow I had risen from the sand, and I found myself embracing my brother, no space between us now, again. "I'm sorry I'm such an asshole."

"AHAHAHAHA! I wouldn't have you any other way! Ah, hey ... you mind ... ah, could you ... uh, cut me off a little of that lime?"

"Sure man." I fumbled in my pocket for my knife and doctored the lime. We sat and drank, cocoons long gone, our wings spreading now like the rainbow trail of a butterfly. "You know man, by all rights, I should be rotting in the depths of Ixcotel Prison right now. And I would be, if not for you, man. You saved me again."

"Yeah, but you saved me too."

"Yeah, we saved each other. … Goddamn, I don't know what I'd do without you, man."

* * * * *

"Hey, man. David." He cleared his throat. "You know ... I'm just kiddin' about that n… about black people, and being racist, and all. … I don't really hate anyone, man. You know?"

"Yeah."

"I'm serious. I been thinkin' about it. That's just the way I was raised, you know, the way my family talks. And my father, he dudn't even hate 'em either, you know, he's just old school, I guess."

"Yeah, that's what I … I just want it to change so bad, man." I put my head in my hands and began to sob.

"How do you mean?"

"Well, man, it's just so pointless, you know? So much of our lives consumed with thinking about it, worrying about the color of skin. So many people hurt and so much lost because one person doesn't like someone else because of the way they look. It doesn't matter, none of it. People are so stupid...." I choked again, tears streaming down my face, I was crying openly right in front of my brother. I could feel the water running through my beard, taste the salt in my mouth.

"You ... you seem angry, man?"

"Yeah man, I've been angry for a long time. But it's time to let all that go. Now I just feel sadness ... Sad for all the people who have been hurt and killed in all the violence, and sad for all their families. All the people who coulda been something but weren't because somebody held 'em down 'cause they were different. I just don't see the point of any of it." I blew my snotty nose out onto the sand, Ogre-style.

"I didn't know you felt so, so ... deeply about it."

"It's just that when you talk like that, you know, it just hurts people, man. Hurts their feelings, makes them feel different than you, or less. But it doesn't change anything. Just makes them feel bad is all..." I trailed off, shaking my head. "There's just no *call* for it."

"I know. You're right, man. I just ... aww hell, I don't know. I'm just sorry is all."

"I know man. It's alright."

"Hell man, I aint better than anyone."

"Yeah." I could feel that he truly was sorry. And that he didn't really hate. I had never actually felt any real hatred in his heart, not like I had seen in many others. You behold that burning chancre once and you will forevermore know the difference. Of course he had fought the Goddam Rastafarian, but then, I figure some men just like a good beer brawl. I was the one who went and spoiled the fun with mace in the eyes and broken ankles.

No, it was just a mask for Mark, one he wore to be a good son, or one of the boys, or a good Southerner, one that had been passed down from generation to generation, another way to be masculine, a big man. No doubt there were many others for whom this was true as well, anti-racists hidden in plain sight, the silent majority allowing a fucked-up minority to drag down our society, drag it down to ape-hate. I would rip their masks off, all of them, with this love. One at a time.

* * * * *

"Hey, David, look at that!" Mark pointed to our right. We were standing facing the sea, the surf crashing before us a few feet away in a near-deafening crash and spray. Only, the surf was ... glowing blue!?

"What the....?" The glow was spreading all along the near-shore now. "Oh, my god! It's ... lit up. ... Like ..." For perhaps a hundred yards along the deserted beach, the surf rose up and crashed down in a bright, electric blue color, lighting up the night.

We were sitting now, mouths open, staring at the endlessly surging and receding blue, the most beautiful bright blue, glowing in the dark, moving in fantastic, endless patterns, flashing in the crashing surf. It was beyond words. I was entranced.

Day Eleven

I awoke to find myself lying on the beach, twisted in an awkward position, facing the ocean. The sun had not quite reached the horizon behind me. The surf was quiet, the tide low. I was covered in dew, my clothes damp, the sand sticking to my hands and face. In the half-light, I could see Mark a few yards away. I couldn't remember how we had gotten here. But I could remember the glowing waves, the intensely beautiful blue color, the patterns of light and texture pulsing with the luminous waves. Was that real?

"Mark." I croaked. "Mark!" He stirred, turning toward me sleepily. "The car, man. We should get back."

"Oh. Yeah." We got to our feet, looking around, dusting the sand from ourselves. We soon found a trail at the top of the beach using some dim, unconscious memory and followed it back, past the lakeshore and our little camp, toward the car. The Buick was gone.

"Oh, shit."

"Some damn Meskin stole the car *and* my fish! … My beautiful fish." Mark was distraught at the loss of his prize.

"Uh, well, I'm not so sure about that, man. Remember, it wouldn't start." I fumbled around in my bag, damp and still laying on the lake-beach, for the keys. They were gone. I looked up, sheepishly, suddenly afraid of the wrath of the Ogre. "The keys are gone," I said sheepishly.

Marked looked at me, a sense of betrayal crossing his tired visage. "You left the keys here…?"

"Man, I don't even remember how we got down to the beach, I mean the seashore, or whatever."

"Yeah, I don't either…"

"And, hey! What the hell happened to Manfred, man! He never came back … I guess?"

"I hope he's ok."

"Yeah, me too."

Mark looked dejected. "Yeah, but the fish is still gone," he mumbled. He lit a cigarette, and I bummed one as well. We sat at the end of the dirt road smoking, enjoying our nicotine breakfast. The sun was peeking over the horizon now.

"So, I think either Manfred was kidnapped, or killed, or whatever. *Or*, maybe he came and got the car last night while we were away from it, down at the seashore. That could have happened, right?"

Mark thought about it for a while. "I guess so."

"Well, that's the best-case scenario. And, think about it. Someone robbing us probably would have taken our bags too, and the cooler. You know, just put them in the car and drive away. Why leave the beers, the clothes, and just take the car? Maybe he's ok after all."

"Yeah, maybe. Seems kinda like wishful thinking, though." Mark rubbed his cigarette out underfoot.

"Well, we can't stay here all day. We should make a plan." I got to my feet. Just then a car turned onto the road. "This could be our ticket back to civilization." As the car approached, I could see the lights on top, *la policia.* Back to jail in Puerto Escondido, then on to Ixcotel Prison, perhaps? Well, there was no sense in running from it any more. Time to face the music.

The car stopped a few feet from us, and Manfred popped out of the back seat. "*Vere da hell have you guys been?!*" Two state police officers got out of either side, looking ready for a hike.

"Uh, we, uh..."

"I came back here for you guys about eight thirty, but there was no sign of you. I yelled and yelled, but there was no one here! I left your stuff in case you were nearby somewhere, but I had the car towed. Then I went back and reported you missing, *und* dey confirmed you weren't back at the jail in Puerto Escondido. If we hadn't found you this morning, they were going to start a manhunt. So where the hell were you?"

"Down at the beach." Mark said. "So, my fish is ok?"

"*Ja, ja*, just fine Mr. Hanson. And how are you? You look a little tired."

Mark looked relieved. "Aww, hell, we're fine. Just fell asleep on the beach is all."

"He means *another* beach, the ocean beach, down the trail there a little ways." I pointed behind me.

"Oh, *so dat's* why you didn't hear me." One of the policemen nodded, clearly following along with the conversation. He spoke to Manfred in Spanish. "He says to start loading your stuff. Let's go."

Soon we were on our way, the three of us crammed into the backseat of the late-1980s vintage Crown Victoria, bounding along the coast road westward, as we should have done yesterday. I got stuck in the middle, on the hump. "So, you have the car keys, then?"

"*Ja*. I found dem in your bag. ... You just left the car and the keys while you went to the beach?"

"Oh, well, uh." I nudged Manfred. "Yeah, we shouldn't have done that. ... I mean, *I* shouldn't have done that. Sorry, man." I looked at Mark.

Manfred nodded. "They gave me the choice of towing the car to Puerto Escondido or Pinotepa Nacional, so I told the guy Pinotepa."

"Ah, good," I said, relieved.

"They will be looking at it this morning. Ve should at least have a diagnosis by the time we arrive."

* * * * *

After a stern warning from the police officers about not wandering off into the Mexican wilderness, a routine I was getting used to by now, they dropped us off at the auto shop, apparently requiring no further paperwork or information from us. Manfred went into the garage while Mark and I went across the street to a *comida* for a quick bite. Mark was delighted with the availability of spicy chicken-kebabs, and he put away several. I couldn't quite overcome the lingering memory of my Revenge. We walked back across the street to the garage, and soon Manfred emerged.

"Water pump," he said. "We have a new one now, so we should be good to go." We followed him around the back of the garage to a large parking lot that was home to all types of motor vehicles in various states of repair, or disrepair. Toward the back stood the Buick, ogre-fish still intact. Cats were crawling all over it, swarming like rats, doing grievous damage to Mark's tuna.

"Hey, hey! Get outta there!" he roared, charging the car, terrified *gatos* scrambling in all directions, fleeing from the looming ogre's wrath. The cats had rent large, open gashes in the fish's formerly shiny surface, the pink meat visible at the bottom of the several holes. Loose scales lay about the fish and on the roof and flies buzzed around. After a brief inspection of the damage, we were back on the road, headed for Taxco.

* * * * *

I was making good time through the rolling green hills, heading inland now, trying not to push the Buick too hard. Mark was quiet in the back, but Manfred was his usual inquisitive self. "So David, I still don't know why you would just walk away and leave the car on the side of the road," he said thoughtfully.

"Well man, we took those mushrooms. I was tripping so hard, I don't even remember walking away from the car, honestly. Neither of us do."

Manfred whistled. "So, y'all were pretty fucked up, huh?"

I nodded. "Yeah. Yeah, that's safe to say. But it wasn't really like being drunk, or stoned even. … Actually, it was pretty incredible. Pretty powerful."

"Oh, *ja*?"

"Yeah. We just woke up on the beach, after …."

"After what?"

"It was the most incredible thing I've ever seen, man. We were hanging out on the beach in the dark, talking, and suddenly the surf just turned this bright, azure blue. It was moving everywhere, these giant blue waves, glowing, crashing. It was amazing. I couldn't believe my eyes."

"Were you hallucinating?"

"Well, yes. For hours, I was seeing these constantly shifting patterns and colors. And the sky… But, the blue glowing waves, I think that was real. I've heard about these phosphorescent tides, where the chemistry of the water makes it glow. I think that's what it was. … See if there's anything about it in the Hippie Book, will you?"

Manfred consulted the table of contents, then flipped to one place, then another. "Uh huh. It says they happen sometimes near these coastal lagoons, but they are pretty rare. Do you really think you saw one?"

"Yeah. … And that wasn't even the most unbelievable part." I glanced in the rearview mirror. Mark was staring vacantly out the window. "Mark swore off racism."

"*He did*?!"

I nodded. "And we talked about a lot of stuff. It was a good evening."

Manfred nodded as well, impressed. "Yes, it sounds absolutely groundbreaking."

Mark groaned in the seat behind me. He hadn't smoked a cigarette for hours.

"What's wrong with you, Mark?"

"Uhhahh … aww shit. Can you stop the car, David?"

I looked back in the rear-view mirror. He was sweating profusely, his face as pale as the belly of the fish lashed to the roof. "It's probably that big-ass tuna you're smelling that's making you sick."

Manfred, shirtless again, was smearing aloe pulp over his arms. He said, "*Ja ja*, we should really go ahead and dump that smelly fish."

"Hell no! And it's not a tuna. I…" Mark smacked the back of my seat, knocking me forward. The car swerved violently as I fought to regain control. "Stop the car!"

I pulled off onto the gravel shoulder of the curvy hillside highway. Mark lurched out the left door and immediately unloaded his five chicken kebabs into the middle of the road. A comida was there to the side; the old men sitting in front of it just sat there watching, clutching their orange Fantas, apparently unfazed by yet another gringo sick in the road.

Once we were underway again, Manfred and I looked at each other. "The Revenge," we said in unison. Mark groaned again. He did not smoke the entire way to Taxco.

* * * * *

Taxco was beautiful, a quaint, old-world city of terracotta roofs and narrow, twisting roads. In the center sits the monsterous Santa Prisca Church, an ornate baroque building built with the wealth taken from the surrounding mountains. We made it to the city in good time, late that afternoon, despite the frequent stops mandated by Mark's stomach. Everyone stared as we drove through the quiet, narrow streets. Children laughed and pointed at our giant fish. I just kept driving, eyes forward, hands at ten and two. We stopped and asked directions to a decent hotel, and the old man wanted to know how much we wanted for *el pescado grande*. Mark would have none of it.

We found a hotel. The valets shook their heads as we pulled up. But we didn't offer any explanation as to why we were toting a huge fish around the Mexican countryside, and they didn't ask. The hotel's courtyard was pleasant, spacious, and grassy, with three little stone monkey statues, their hands covering ears, eyes, and mouth, respectively – hear no evil, see no evil, speak no evil. The hotel only had a three-man room available, so we took it. The car and fish safely stowed, we hit the town for supper and shopping.

Taxco truly is the silver capital of the world. Silver mines, built by the Spanish, surround the mountain town. Silver shops abound on every little tortuously twisted street, and even little kiosks specializing in cold drinks and knickknacks also feature intricately wrought little silver clasps and earrings. We browsed a while, window-shopping. Mark, recovering from his Revenge, bought three red-and-black screaming Mixtec demon masks for the Dog House. An excellent choice.

Manfred purchased a lovely pendant for his girlfriend back in San Antonio. As I looked at the jewelry, I thought about what would look good on Regina. But what was the use? You cannot buy jewelry for another man's wife. You may buy her dinner, drinks, kiss her, make love to her, but you cannot buy her clothes or fine jewelry or diamonds or anything like that. Nothing enduring. Only insubstantial, transient items may be given, and these aptly characterize the entire empty affair. All things that you must enjoy while they last. Anyway, that ship had sailed. I bought my mother some earrings instead.

We had a fine dinner in one of the many rustic taverns. As we ate, a folk festival with clowns and jugglers and many children passed by outside. Afterward, a mostly-recovered Mark and I opted for a few drinks about town, but Manfred was feeling the toxic weight of the trip, and sought the rack. He walked alone to the hotel.

"Just a minute, Mark," I said as we passed an Internet café. I looked back at him, standing there holding his bag of silver items and demon masks. He said, "You go on, David. Do what you gotta do. I'll be right here."

"Thanks, man." I went in the café. There was no message from Regina in my in-box. I sighed. What was I doing? What was the point? I was still stunned, emotionally disoriented after the surreal events of the last several days. I put on a good face, went back out to Mark.

"Any word?"

"No man."

We walked on a while. "That place look good, up there?" he asked, pointing to a terrace-bar overlooking the city.

"Yeah man."

Day Twelve

I awoke overcome by a horrible smell; a foul, organic, death-stench. I gagged, then looked around the three-man room. Manfred slumbered on, and Mark was snoring loudly. That smell … I couldn't place it. That early in the morning, one doesn't … ah, yeah. Of course. The damn giant marlin, the ogre-fish. We all, all three of us, smelled like the damn thing. Mephitis by association. I took a shower, hoping to reduce the smell by one-third.

I left them in there with the stench and went out on the balcony for a toke. Mark was the first to join me. We sat out there enjoying our J and a lovely view of the city, slowly coming awake that Wednesday morning. Manfred stuck his dishevelled, sleepy-head out the door, a towel around his waist. "Dude? Do you know vere is my shampoo?"

* * * * *

Later, we were headed north on the *cuota*. I recalled the cloudy fish-eye staring at me balefully as I packed the trunk.

The hotel staff had been grateful to see us leave, waiving the parking fee, just happy to have the slimy Buick and its rotting ogre-tuna go away. We kept our faces straight all the while, paying our bill, loading the trunk of the Buick, one man holding open the lid of the trunk with the heavy fish-head, the others packing in the luggage. Not a hint of the insanity, of the stench, made its way into our visage. Deadpan, we went about our business, as the Mexican staff gawked, covered their mouths with their hands, ran to the bathroom to retch. We acted as if it was the most common thing in the world to drive around Mexico with a giant stinking fish mounted on your Buick. *Cra-zy fuck-ing grin-gos!* they thought as they smiled nervously. Hear no evil, see no evil, speak no evil.

Northeast of Taxco we approached Mexico City again. We found an off-*cuota* roadway in the Hippie Book well to the west of the DF, a route which skirted the western suburbs of the overcrowded megalopolis. As we drove into the heavily industrialized region of central Mexico, the air again became thick, hazy, smelly, a now-familiar yellow-ish color. Even our fish smelled wholesome and natural by comparison. The purple snow-tipped volcanoes rose vaguely, thousands of meters into the murky sky on either side of us, dwarfing the tiny Buick, with its miniscule fish and our little problems.

The road was poorly marked on the map. Mark was in the back, feebly attempting to navigate with the Hippie Book. "Here! Take this exit!" There was no exit, really, just a side entrance to the service road running parallel to our road, and there was no good reason whatsoever to deviate from our path. But Mark had convinced himself.

"Right here?" said Manfred. He looked at me. I shrugged.

"Yeah! This is our exit. Here!"

"Are you sure?"

"Go! Here!" At the last moment possible, Manfred jerked the wheel hard to the right, entering the service road. We were going quite fast, something over a eighty kilometers-per-hour. *Topes* crashed into our undercarriage, one after another. We were all jogged and tossed around in the interior of the Buick as the *topes*, like thick concrete baseball bats, smashed at our wheels and suspension. Manfred brought the car to a slower speed, but said, "Oh shit. *Sheisse*."

"What's wrong?"

"Look." The Buick still moving slowly, Manfred took his hands off the wheel. The old boat floated gently but hard to the left of its own accord. A muffled clanging noise could be heard, apparently coming from the rear axle. We had damaged the suspension, and the steering was halfway shot. Fortunately the Buick was yet somewhat drivable. We got back onto the proper road and began to come into the higher hills northwest of the DF, thankfully leaving the smoggy air below and behind.

A little after noon we clanged into a medium-sized mountain town a few hundred kilometers south of Querétaro. "Hey hey! Let's stop here, get some lunch, give the car a break. You know? Maybe have a look at it. You know what I mean?"

"Vell, Mark, I think the car's driving okay, but I am getting hungry."

"Fish, anyone?" I asked. We walked around the town's *el centro* until we found a chicken place. Whole birds turned on spits inside the open-faced *comida*. We bought Mark his very own chicken, smothered in spicy red *achiote* paste. He dug into his feast with gusto, not at all chastened by his most recent experience, smearing the reddened flesh all over his ogre-maw like a barbarian. Manfred and I ordered a bag of drumsticks. After munching down half the bag, we were stuffed to the gills. In the town's plaza, we came across a prunish old woman huddled in a wheelchair. A colorful Mexican blanket was wrapped around her, though the day was warm.

"Daily civic duty?" I asked.

"*Ja ja*, I think this will cover all of our missed lazy days there in Puerto Escondido." We gave the woman the remainder of the chicken bag, then went back to the Buick. We got back on the road, windows down to fight the entrenched stench and rid the interior of the accumulated flies.

* * * * *

It was my turn at the wheel. We were in the mountains near Querétaro, making good time. After a while of glancing at the gas gauge, I said, "Manfred. Hey man. When's the last time we filled up?"

He looked over. "Oh, I don't know. A few hours ago. We look full, though."

"That's just the problem. We've been driving for a few hours and our gauge still reads full. I think it's stuck; we *can't* still be full."

Manfred thought for a minute, doing some quick mental calculations. "So. I estimate we have about one hundred thirty-five kilometers to go before ve are sucking air."

"Hell no! Stop the car! Let's get some gas now, what d'ya think, guys?"

So we stopped at the next Pemex and got some gas. Mark thereafter mandated hourly stops for gas, which of course were unnecessary, but Manfred and I were too weary of it all to complain.

We were still not on a *cuota*, but were rather taking that back-road shortcut through the mountains west of Querétaro, trying to avoid Mexico City and link up with the *cuota* to the north. It was working fine, until the paved road, winding higher into the rugged mountains, ran out, becoming gravel. The narrow road hugging the mountainside still looked well used, however.

Like a stubborn old mule, Mark balked. "Well, I guess we'd better head on back. Have to go through Mexico City, I guess."

"Mate, what? Have you lost your marbles or whatever?"

"David, we can't go there! It's the mountains!"

"For fuck sake, man, it's just a little ways more to the damn *cuota*!"

"We'll run out of gas in the mountains!'

"We just fucking filled up with gas, ass!"

"You know vat? Why don't we go ahead and let me drive through these hills. *Ja*, I am a Bavarian, and these little hills are for me no problem." So we let Manfred drive us on the dirt road further into the jagged, hulking mountains. The road wound up and around the ridges, becoming quite steep. Mark chain-smoked in the back, unsmiling with knuckles white. Manfred was really showing off, I thought, but it was fun, sliding speedily around in the boat on the gravel roads, a wall of granite to the left, and out my window a sheer precipice tapering down into some stark, rocky gorge. The fish was sloshing around up top all the while, straining against its bonds. I made sure Mark kept a constant stream of calming *cerveza* coming my way. It was difficult to slice up the limes without cutting open my fingers as we careened madly around the curves, but somehow I managed.

"David, I am mighty impressed with your bartending skills, there, *ja ja*."

"Thanks, man, and I with your mountain-driving skills."

Mark was ever silent in the back, smoking like a chimney again.

In a little over an hour the road came away from the higher peaks, down to the *cuota* north of Querétaro. At Mark's loud insistence, we stopped at another Pemex for gas. Manfred got out and looked at the tires. They were shredded, worn down to bald spots in some places, looking like the surface of the moon in others, all irregular and badly torn. I expressed surprise that they were all still holding air. "Vell, *gut* ve are almost home, no?" Manfred kicked a tire. "*Ja*, these here tires will make it. Don't you think?" He blinked as he looked at me. Mark was listening intently.

"Well, I don't know. We could sure give it a try, though." Mark groaned. "Mark, you want to give it a try? Put in a few hours behind the wheel?"

"Hell no! You hippie bastards are crazy! I'm not drivin' that thing!" We got back in the battered Buick, back on the road.

* * * * *

When we arrived in the clean, tree-lined city of Saltillo late that afternoon, we had long since come out of the mountains of central Mexico, down into the sweltering northern deserts. The fish had lain atop the Buick the entire time, soaking up the sun's rays. As we drove, we had baked the fish, sort of an automotive culinary exercise, Julia Childs-on-Wheels. Soon, I supposed, it would be ready to eat. Certainly the flies thought so, swarming madly at every Pemex. Once, a mere hundred kilometers shy of Saltillo, we had all made a trip to *los baños*, locking the car up and leaving it unattended there by the pumps. As we came back we saw the cats had returned, enjoying a fortuitous feast on the Buick. Mark again drove them away, the sated cats escaping his ogre-charge with bulging bellies and mouths full of fish-flesh. The fish was a shredded mess by then, ripped open and well gnawed-on. We drove away from the Pemex in a crowd of flies. We tried once again to convince him to dump the damn fish, but again Mark would have none of it.

In Saltillo, we checked into a surprisingly luxurious but inexpensive hotel. The hotel management, however, took one look at our ogre-tuna and refused us the normally complimentary use of their parking garage. So we had to round the corner and pay to use another lot, a low-class lot, where fish-clad cars were allowed, if not as the usual customers.

Manfred knew of a five-star restaurant a few blocks away. He wanted to take us there, but said directly to Mark, "Now, ve must behave ourselves in this place. We are only five hours from San Antonio. I like to come down here some times on da weekends, and I don't vant to fuck this up."

Mark nodded solemnly. "I promise, Manfred. I won't fuck it up."

"*Gut.*" The dinner was excellent. We were in northern Mexico once again – steak country – so at Mark's urging I broke down and ordered one. It was thick and juicy. We all shared some Spanish red wine, with even Mark sipping politely on his glass. He ordered no whiskey, and kept his voice down during the entire meal.

"Yeah," he rumbled softly, "I sure had a good time down here with y'all."

"*Vell*, I'm sure ve all enjoyed it, *ja, ja*." Manfred and Mark both looked at me.

"It, uh … yeah. It went alright, I guess. Considering…."

Manfred turned his gaze to me. "So. Javier and his friends were out for blood the other day, aye David? Coming to get you, no?"

"Yeah, man. They sure were." I recalled the painting of the Aztec warrior, and the image of the three men closing in on me in the alley. And then I pushed the images from my mind.

"*Und* with Mark here gone fishing, you were in a tough spot. One might even say that, if I hadn't been there, things could have gone very badly for you, indeed."

"Aha ha ha ha ha!"

I was laughing too. "You mean you *and the cops*, man? Besides, I probably could have made it into the hotel before they got me. You know, if those police officers who came to see you hadn't been blocking my way."

His eyes were twinkling. "On that bad leg, you mean?"

"Aha ha ha ha ha!"

I smiled. "Oh well, the leg is much better now. Much better."

Manfred looked at Mark with a grin. "So, did she send them after you, or did Javier finally have enough of the meddling gringo?"

We had thus far not mentioned Regina or her husband Javier during the entire trip up from Puerto Escondido. I had not told my companions that she had agreed to meet me – or, to *try to* meet me, as she put it – the morning of our departure. And then had failed to appear.

"Well, man, she was the whole reason they came to Puerto Escondido. She brought the whole group down there, practically against its will, just to meet me. So I figured I had a shot, you know, for real. But she couldn't seem to bring herself to leave him, and I couldn't take the drama any more. So I decided to just lay it out for her. I told her to meet me that morning and come back to San Antonio with me – to leave him. She said she would *try* to come, but obviously that doesn't make any sense. If she wanted to leave him, she could just come. But she must have told him all about my proposal, and then I guess he finally decided to come after me."

Mark was shaking his head, apparently in awe rather than disgust. "You sure got a lotta balls, dude," he reiterated.

"That's … thanks, Mark. I think."

"*Ja*, dude, you sure do. On that we can agree. I only hope she was worth all da trouble …"

"No, of course she wasn't!"

"Aha ha ha ha ha!" We all had a good laugh at that.

"No, it's over now man. … I was just seeing the shell, wanting something to be that wasn't. And then she unmasked. Mark was right, she was just using me … for what, I don't really know. But it doesn't matter."

"I'm sorry, David. I won't say I told you so."

"Yeah, well. … I'm sorry that I put us in a bad spot. … But we probably would have been just fine if it weren't for your reckless breaking and entering of that poor old lady's home! Not to mention the theft."

"Aha ha ha ha ha!"

"Well, David, if you like her, you should go to Germany. *Ja ja*, many girls like her there. Single ones, too!"

"Aha ha ha ha ha!"

"Pass!"

"Aha ha ha ha ha!"

Back at the hotel desk, Manfred asked the staff where a whorehouse was for Mark, who happily took a taxi straight away. I walked around *el centro de* Saltillo for a while, enjoying the spacious, leafy plazas and bold statues. The dusky air was warm and mild. Kids on skateboards swarmed around, shouting happily in Spanish. One of them told me where an Internet café was. I had a nauseating knot in my stomach as I sat down at the terminal.

Her e-mail read:

Hello there!

Well, that sure was a close call. I had a lot of explaining to do that night. He wanted a divorce and everything, but I was able to calm him down. I can't believe I risked everything for that.

We went to some islands that were down the coast, and met some cool people. It was so much nicer than Puerto Escondido, not a tourist trap like that. So now we are in Guatemala, we took a chicken-bus here. This place is really different from southern Mexico, like night and day, the people here are so poor, there are filthy children crawling around on piles of trash, and the dogs are so skinny. It really is awful the way these people live, it makes you feel guilty how good we have it in the developed world.

Damn it, its always so hard trying to write you with that trick-ass bastard Javier always looking over my shoulder, he just now came in and caught me writing you and freaked out, now I have to go calm him down again, please just don't write me anymore, that will be easier for us both.

Regina

Please don't .... ? I stared at the screen for a while. It took a while for it all to sink in. My heart was beating fast, my adrenalin pumping ... I tried to rally, bravely but foolishly. I wrote:

You almost got me killed ...

But I erased that. Then:

Sometimes a woman's soul is like a candle
Burnt, recessed around the edges
Dipped down inside, melted
But with a wick, still there
Waiting to be lit
Alight!

I stared at the curser blinking steadily on the screen. It blinked and blinked. There I sat, in the hard plastic chair in the Internet café in Saltillo, watching the cursor blink on the screen. I knew then, beyond a doubt, that wick would not light. I knew that a dark, grasping shadow lay underneath the mask. I grit my teeth for a moment, then moved the cursor over and erased all I had written again.

The conversation was pointless. It was over. I logged off, paid the attendant, and walked out into the street. The evening air was fresh and pleasantly cool. I had come so close to disaster. I had enraged the jaguar-god. Yet I had made it out, nimbly dodging the lightning bolts, so many of them. And thanks to Mark, again. But I had come for the hidden-one, and I would leave empty-handed, lucky instead to simply have my life. And I was lucky to have learned the truth, without making the ultimate sacrifice. Yes, I was *lucky.* Cannot change what lies beneath…

Back to Texas

We could hardly approach the fish-covered Buick. The stench was truly toxic now, full-on rot, a step beyond the normal, nearly-unbearable death-stench. The damn cats had again found the carcass, glutting themselves on Mark's stinking catch, their fat bellies swinging below them as they waddled away. He cursed, examining the deepened gashes and tunnels penetrating the fish carcass. He swept some of the disemboweled intestines off of the roof with a stick. Still, we could not convince him to part with his decomposing prize.

"Look at it!" Manfred said. "It's ripped apart, *und* da ropes here have cut into the meat … it's no good even as a trophy anymore!"

"No! I'm not … my cousin, he can make any animal come to life, and you're not … No! I tell you what, this here fish is comin' back to Texas with me! And that's all there is to it! Y'hear!?"

That was all there was to it. I turned my head, nausea welling in my gut as I held up the heavy, fish head-laden trunk while Manfred loaded in the luggage. It was too much. As soon as Manfred shoved in the last bag, I let the trunk slam noisily, the fish-head smacking down on the trunk with a sickening *thwack!* Before I could catch myself, a great frothy white spume rose forth from my gut and through my face, splattering on the Buick and the ground up by the right front tire, freeing me of my entire breakfast.

"Yeah, that's what I said, David. It's how you began this trip, and it's how you'll end it. Aha ha ha ha ha!"

"*Ja ja*, he is consistent, no?"

"I'm driving," I spat, and we took our places in the boat.

The Buick was struggling again. It took until the fifth try to get it started. The gas gauge was stuck on full, leaving us with only educated guesses as to how much gas was really in there. The suspension was shot, the alignment off, the tires shredded, the brakes worn from many hard downhill mountain miles, and who knew just why the engine didn't feel like starting? At least the water pump was unlikely to fail! The damn dummy light came on again as we clanged out of Saltillo, headed north on the *cuota* trailed by a cloud of flies and fish-stench, the Buick making ominously strange noises as we warily crept our way over the last few hundred kilometers to the border. And I had forgotten: Mark had broken the seat. "Bullshit! I didn't do jack-shit to that damn seat, David!" The seat was all ogre-twisted out of alignment, but I didn't press the point, savoring the signature Ogre moment instead.

But then he gave me another such moment, one I had dreamed of for years, piping up from the back seat excitedly,

"Hey, Manfred. What do you call a honkey from Plano, Texas?"

Manfred turned around, smiling. "Plano honkey?"

"Das' right! Plano honkey!" He was grinning broadly, no longer afraid to be himself.

* * * * *

In between Saltillo and the border at Nuevo Laredo, we kept encountering checkpoints along the *cuota* run by the Mexican army. As we neared each checkpoint, signs warned us to slow our speed. A mechanism using an iron contraption and spikes was laid flat across the road, and could be used to instantly flatten all four of our tires if we did not obey. We slowed, pulling into line with the other vehicles. The soldiers were all small and very dark.

"These Mexicans look more like the ones down in Oaxaca," I said.

"*Ja ja*, it is the policy of the army here to station the troops recruited in da north down in the southern regions, and then send the southern Indian recruits up here. Most of these guys are probably from Oaxaca or Chiapas. Different tribes."

And that made it easier to smash the heads of protesters getting out of hand, I mused in the back of our Buick, easier if they are from different tribes. Here in Mexico, they know how to enforce respect for power. One of the soldiers motioned with his rifle for us to stop. In Spanish, the soldier said, "*Buenas tardes, Señor*. We are going to now search your car for illegal explosives." We all got out agreeably, and the rifle-toting soldiers came over with their bomb-sniffing dogs. The search was polite and professional, and was over inside of two minutes. As was stated, they were only interested in illegal explosives, and there were no power-trips or bad attitudes. Not a word was spoken, not a smirk given, about the fishy mess on top of the Buick, which now looked like a giant's – or an ogre's –week-old leftovers. We re-filled the trunk with our gear and were back on the road. At the other checkpoints they just asked us our business – we told them fishing – but did not search us.

After a couple of hours we were back in gritty, grimy Nuevo Laredo. After we had concluded our visa and automobile paperwork and were headed toward the international bridge, Mark looked wistfully over at the exits for Boy's Town, but Manfred said, "Mark! *Dass ist Scheisse*! That is why ve got you to da whorehouse in Saltillo last night!"

"Yeah, but the ones in Boy's Town are the best, you know?" Manfred just drove on toward the bridge. We had blazed across it on our way down, but the lines are usually longer to pass into the States than to get out, and so it was that day. We were in a line now, slowly working our way across the bridge, little urchins approaching us with shite trinkets for sale, one-legged beggars coming for alms. We were not in the interior anymore. We did our daily civic duty. But after they smelled the fish, they mostly stayed away.

Finally, almost two hours later, we arrived at the US side. The guards stopped us immediately. "No! You can't bring that thing into the United States!"

"Aww, it's alright, I'm declarin' it. Gonna have it mounted, you know? My cousin..."

"No! As I said, *sir*, you cannot bring the fish, ah ... remains, into the United States of America. It's a federal law, sir." We looked at Mark, but he just waved his hand, stared out the window. We had no choice but to succumb to the inevitable. We turned around. As we went back across the bridge, he said, "Maybe we can box it up, ship it over the border, you know? What d'ya think, guys?" But when we got back to the Mexican side, the border guards in their rumpled beige uniforms shook their heads. "*No, Señor*, you can no come here with de fish, *lo siento. Es la ley.*"

We had no choice. We were contraband-fish-laden international refugees, trapped between two countries, stuck in no-man's land. So we went back toward the US side, and halfway across the international bridge, we stopped. We all got out, untied the giant reeking carcass, and hastily shoved it off the top of the Buick, over the guardrail, and into the Rio Grande. I puked again after the putrid fish, my morning meal exiting forcefully through my mouth, burning as it went. It splashed into the river below, after the fish. I think Mark really did have the gleam of a tear in his eye. How he loved that fish. I could understand how he felt. And with that, we were rid of our giant piscine albatross. It was good to finally be done with it, our last baggage gone.

The Border Patrol at the bridge fined us nine-hundred and something dollars for polluting the waters of the United States with the fish carcass of a species not native to that ecosphere, or something of that nature. Thirty miles up I-35, at a Border Patrol checkpoint, we were hassled for two hours. A squat, masculine female agent pulled us into a small concrete interrogation bunker beside the inspection station. She had the classic militant lesbian look, with buzz-cut hair and a manly, muscular ass. She wanted to know where we had been, did we have any illegal drugs, did we associate with any drug dealers in Mexico, had we transported any illegal aliens, did we have *any* illegal drugs, and just what did we think we had been doing down there anyway? I struggled not to laugh in her miserable face, the modern American fascist.

It was only an impromptu, computer-generated, random stop. All of our names and social security numbers were run through the computer several times. As she interrogated us in the small room, a squad of jack-booted troopers swarmed over the Buick with their vicious, snarling dogs, scattering the luggage onto the pavement. The black-shirted agents spent a long time ripping the Buick apart, but of course there were no spoils of war for them in the Buick. In the end they fined us another fifty dollars US for the open bottle of rum I had forgotten to declare. I protested that it was more than half-empty, and for personal use only, but they just said that it was the law. When I agreed with them, they told me to watch that attitude, boy. It was good to be home. A normal day at the border. I thought again that the border is not the interior.

After we had all been patted down, they let us hastily re-pack the violated Buick, and we were on our way. Ten miles later, Mark, whom we had finally let drive now that we were on friendly turf, got pulled over by the Texas State Patrol and courteously handed a speeding ticket for being nine miles per hour over the limit. Back in the U – S – S – A. As Mark pulled away from the cop, he said, "Welcome back to Wally World! Aha ha ha ha ha!"

Two tiring, dusty hours later, we were in San Antonio. We dropped Mark off at the Big House. He ran around and got his old truck, then followed us to the auto rental place. The rental employee came out to inspect the Buick LeSabre, walking tightly around the battered sedan with a clipboard. We had just taken it through a car wash, but it still smelled strongly of fish.

"At the coast, were you?" asked the rent-a-car man, his logoed golf shirt uniform buttoned all the way up and tucked into his khaki pants.

"*Ja ja*, that's right."

I squinted at him. "The great outdoors." I intoned. Manfred glared at me.

Except for a thin strip of paint that the fish had taken off the top of the car, the Buick *looked* alright. On the outside, there was no sign of engine trouble, wrecked suspension, shot steering, worn brakes, and the gas tank even appeared to be full. Manfred said, "Yes, you know vat, I would like to go ahead and bring to your attention a minor problem.

We vere driving in Mexico, *und* ve noticed a slight problem ven we got ready to fill up these here tires." He pointed to one of the shredded Firestones. "See? It could be dangerous driving with these things. Perhaps they ought to be changed immediately."

I said, "Yeah, I guess we were just really lucky."

The employee frowned. "That's … these are horrible! I'll take care of that. You should get a free up-grade on your next rental. I'll make a note of it." He smiled as he marked the clipboard. "I think the next vehicle up is a Chevy Tahoe."

"That is very kind," said Manfred. "We vill take advantage of that." Manfred signed the forms, paid the amount due, and we piled into Mark's truck. Manfred told us how much Mark and I owed him for the Buick rental, and for all the hotels he had put on his credit card for convenience's sake. Mark handed over the cash for his debt. I said, "Uh, man, uh … I don't have…" my hands waved about vaguely, "…right now, you know, uh…"

"That's alright, dude. I understand. Just pay me ven you can."

As we pulled up to Manfred's house there in the loopland, I said, "Sure was fun, man."

"*Ja, ja*. I had a good time, fellas."

"Hey, yeah, me too, Manfred. It was real fun." Mark slapped Manfred on his sunburned shoulder. Manfred winced.

"Vell, okay. You guys take it easy, no?"

"See ya, Manfred."

"Yeah, hey, take it easy, man."

"Ciao."

As we pulled out of Manfred's driveway, the sight of Manfred's old catamaran gave me renewed bruxism and a dull, sickening pain in my chest. Mark said, "Home, dude?" I thought for a second. I had no desire to sit alone in my single-wide, thinking – worse yet, feeling – and tomorrow I would have to begin the careful process of liver regeneration, painfully home-bound with soaking salts, grapefruits, and ginger tea. The liver was capable of rapid healing, but not so the heart…"No. No, let's get some Lone Star and go to the Dog House. End this thing right."

Mark grinned. "Hey, alright!" We drove back to Alamo Heights, the Metroneck's old stomping grounds. We stopped at an icehouse and picked up a case of Lone Star. Lone Star cannot really even be called beer. Brewed from rice, corn, a little malt, and very little hops, the stuff was mostly water, but at least had some alcohol in it. It was sour shite, but at the end of the day we always drank it. Ten bucks a case. When we pulled up, Mark's maid took his bags into the Big House, and we took the Lone Star into the Dog House.

Mark put some soothing Pink Floyd on the CD player. He was busy nailing up one of his new screaming demon masks from Taxco on the tar-covered wall, when in walked Mr. Hanson.

"Well, hellooo theah, boys, y'all have an enjoyable trip?"

"Oh, hey there, dad!"

"Ah, Mr. Hanson!" We all shook hands. "Ah, yes. It was, ah…"

"Did y'all stay out of trouble? Out of all those Meskin prisons?" He grinned at us.

"Well, you know." I looked away. "Yessir. For the most part."

"We did have to bail this one out a coupla times. You know? Aha ha ha ha!"

"Mark here caught a fish!" I changed the subject.

"Oh? What kind of fish was it?"

"Uh, it was a…" Mark shrugged helplessly.

"Marlin. It was a blue marlin." I was smiling.

"And how big was this marlin?"

Mark said, "Well, it was…" He looked at me. "It wasn't so big. A few feet, I guess, maybe a little bigger."

I nodded in agreement. "Uh-huh."

"Mighty fine, mighty fine," Mr. Hanson said. "Well now, you boys enjoy your beer." He went back up to the Big House, back to his martinis and the BBC on the Box. Mark and I did enjoy our beer. Like battered, bloody warriors drinking in the mead-hall after the great battle, we retold tall tales of strenuous valor, our heroic exploits growing ever more exaggerated, the foes more formidable, with each retelling of the tale. The fish, however, never grew any larger. It was the end of the day.

Around midnight the door was kicked open suddenly. "Get your diapers on, boys!" came the call. It was Timmy. He eyes were red and wild, and he was jacked up. "Hey. You guys are back! How was the trip?" Timmy's tall, lanky form lurched unsteadily into the smoke-filled Dog House. Mark immediately changed the music to Slayer.

Timmy waited a moment and then went over to the CD player, taking off the offending Slayer and replacing it with some more ecumenical Santana. Mark scowled in his seat.

I handed Timmy a Lone Star out of the miniature fridge in the corner of the room. "Pull up a chair, man, and I'll tell you. Mark here caught a fish..."

From the walls, all the demon masks screamed down at us with their twisted smiles, and I could truly see what lay beneath. I smiled back at them. Timmy took a drink on his Lone Star, made a sour face, swallowed. He looked at both of us in turn. "So, how big a fish was it?"